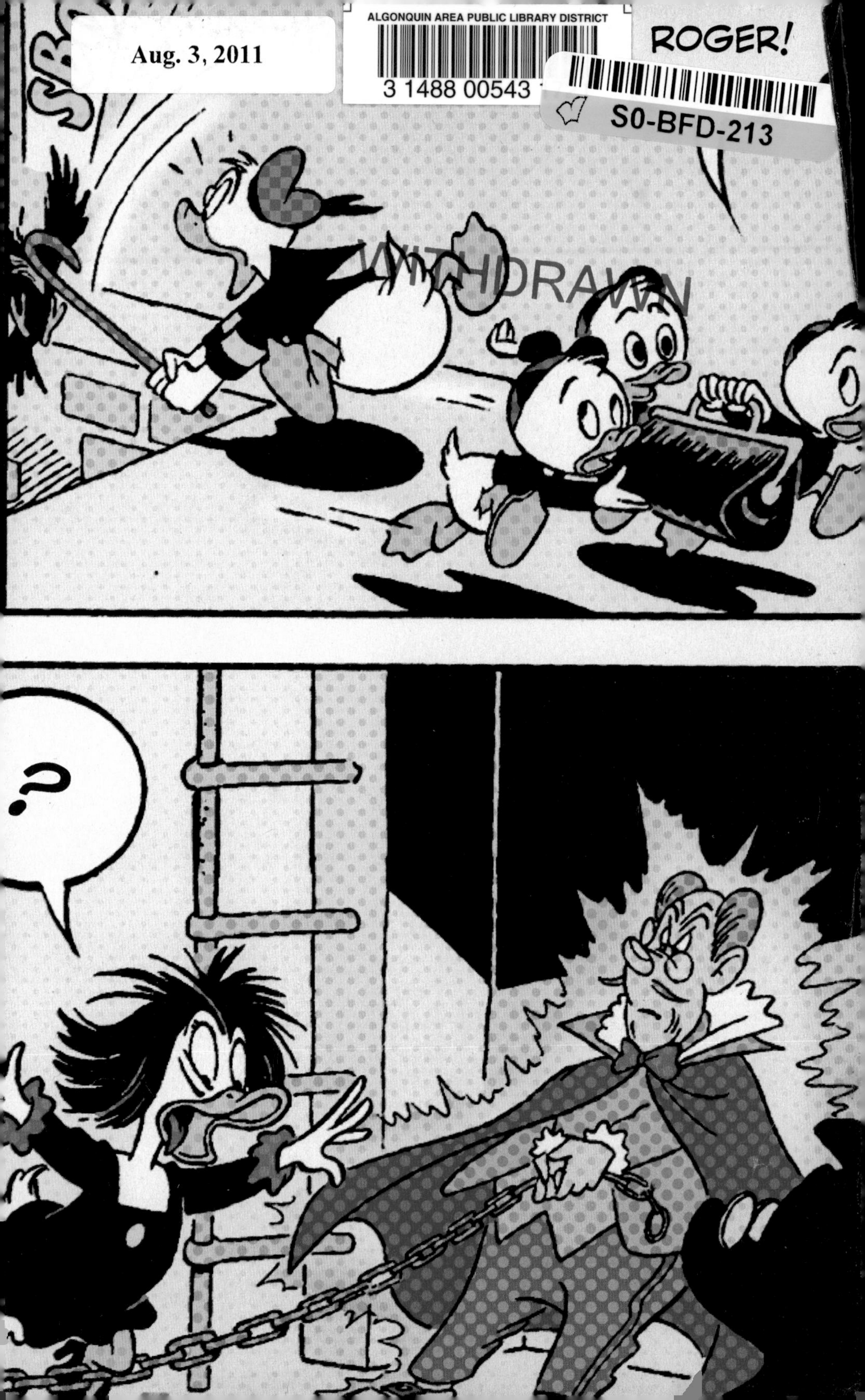
ROGER!
?

ROSS RICHIE
chief executive officer

MARK WAID
editor-in-chief

ADAM FORTIER
vice president,
publishing

CHIP MOSHER
marketing director

MATT GAGNON
managing editor

JENNY CHRISTOPHER
sales director

FIRST EDITION: FEBRUARY 2010

10 9 8 7 6 5 4 3 2 1
PRINTED BY WORLD COLOR PRESS, INC.
ST ROMUALD, QC. CANADA.

Office of publication: 6310 San Vicente Blvd Ste 404, Los Angeles, CA 90048-5457.

A catalog record for this book is available from OCLC and on our website www.boom-kids.com on the Librarians page.

WRITER:
PER-ERIK HEDMAN

ARTISTS:
WANDA GATTINO
& CARLOS MOTA

TRANSLATOR:
STEFANIA BRONZONI

LETTERER:
JOSE MACASOCOL, JR.

ASSISTANT EDITOR:
CHRISTOPHER BURNS

EDITOR:
AARON SPARROW

DESIGNER:
ERIKA TERRIQUEZ

COVER:
SCOTT GROSS

HARDCOVER CASE WRAP:
CARLOS MOTA

SPECIAL THANKS:
JESSE POST, LAUREN KRESSEL
AND ELENA GARBO

THE HUNT FOR THE OLD NUMBER ONE

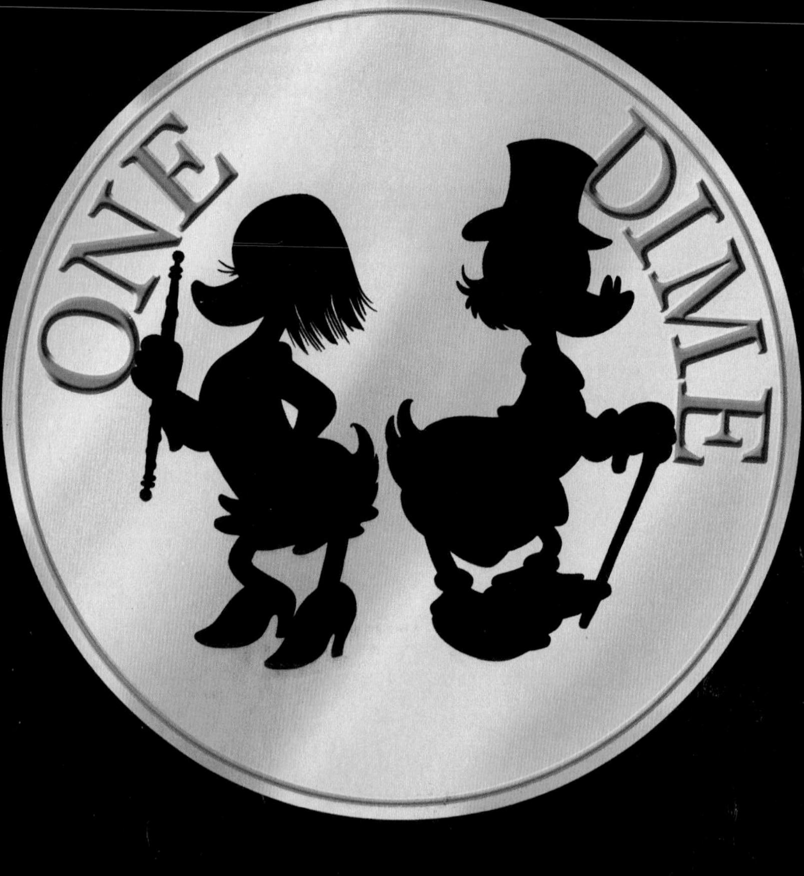
ONE DIME

CHAPTER ONE

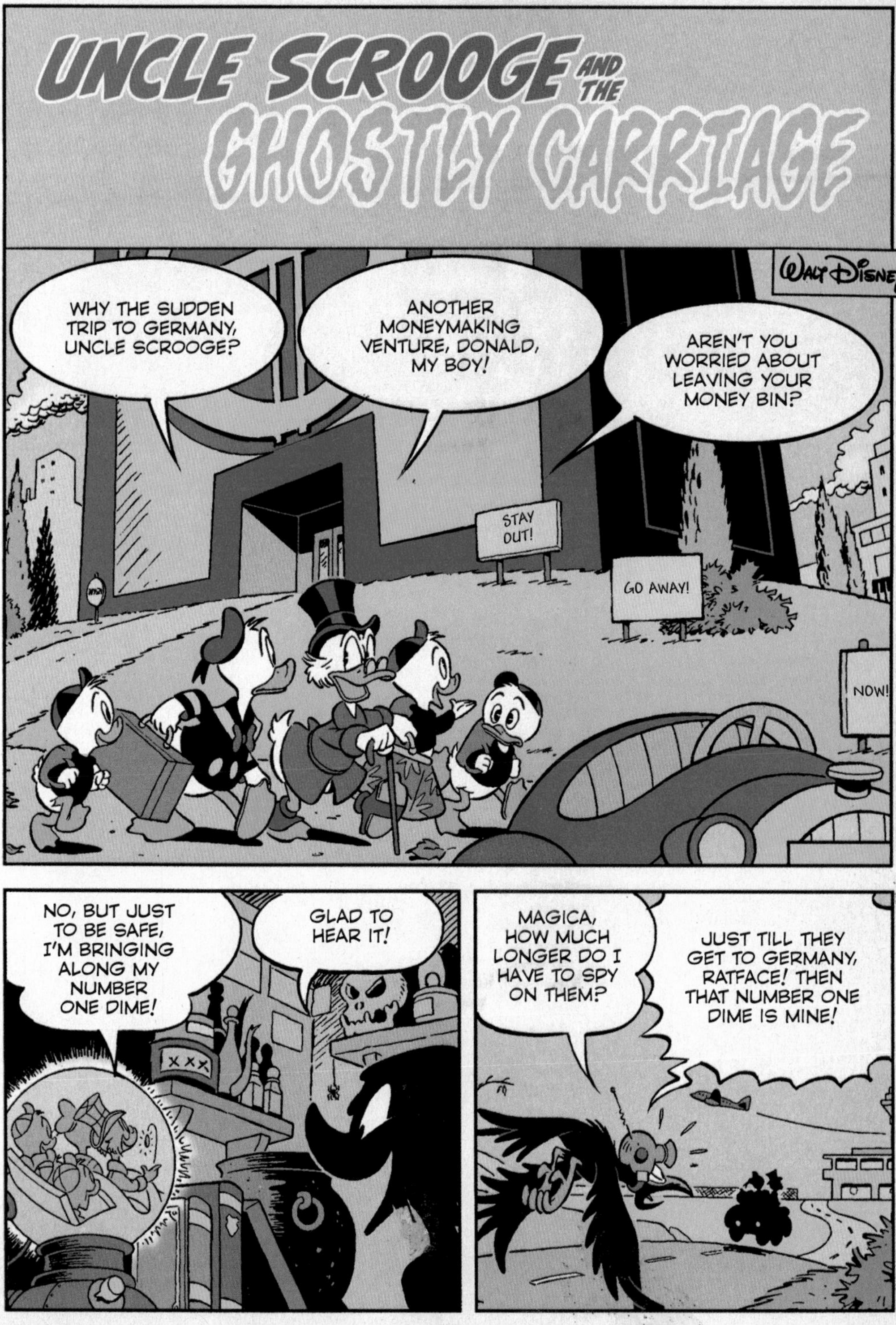
UNCLE SCROOGE AND THE GHOSTLY CARRIAGE
WALT DISNEY
WHY THE SUDDEN TRIP TO GERMANY, UNCLE SCROOGE?
ANOTHER MONEYMAKING VENTURE, DONALD, MY BOY!
AREN'T YOU WORRIED ABOUT LEAVING YOUR MONEY BIN?
STAY OUT!
GO AWAY!
NOW!
NO, BUT JUST TO BE SAFE, I'M BRINGING ALONG MY NUMBER ONE DIME!
GLAD TO HEAR IT!
XXX
MAGICA, HOW MUCH LONGER DO I HAVE TO SPY ON THEM?
JUST TILL THEY GET TO GERMANY, RATFACE! THEN THAT NUMBER ONE DIME IS MINE!

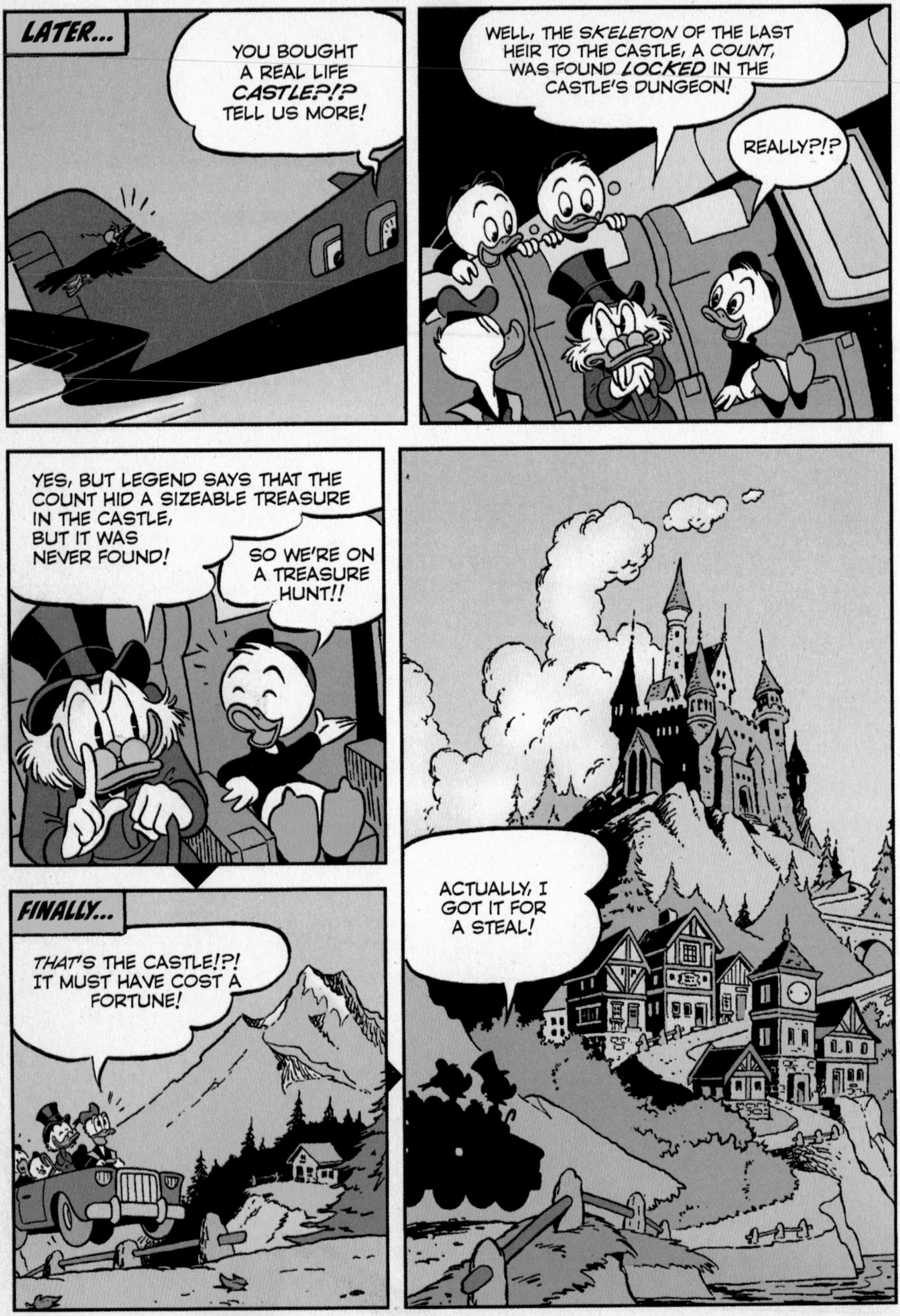
LATER...
YOU BOUGHT A REAL LIFE CASTLE?!? TELL US MORE!
WELL, THE SKELETON OF THE LAST HEIR TO THE CASTLE, A COUNT, WAS FOUND LOCKED IN THE CASTLE'S DUNGEON!
REALLY?!?
YES, BUT LEGEND SAYS THAT THE COUNT HID A SIZEABLE TREASURE IN THE CASTLE, BUT IT WAS NEVER FOUND!
SO WE'RE ON A TREASURE HUNT!!
FINALLY...
THAT'S THE CASTLE!?! IT MUST HAVE COST A FORTUNE!
ACTUALLY, I GOT IT FOR A STEAL!

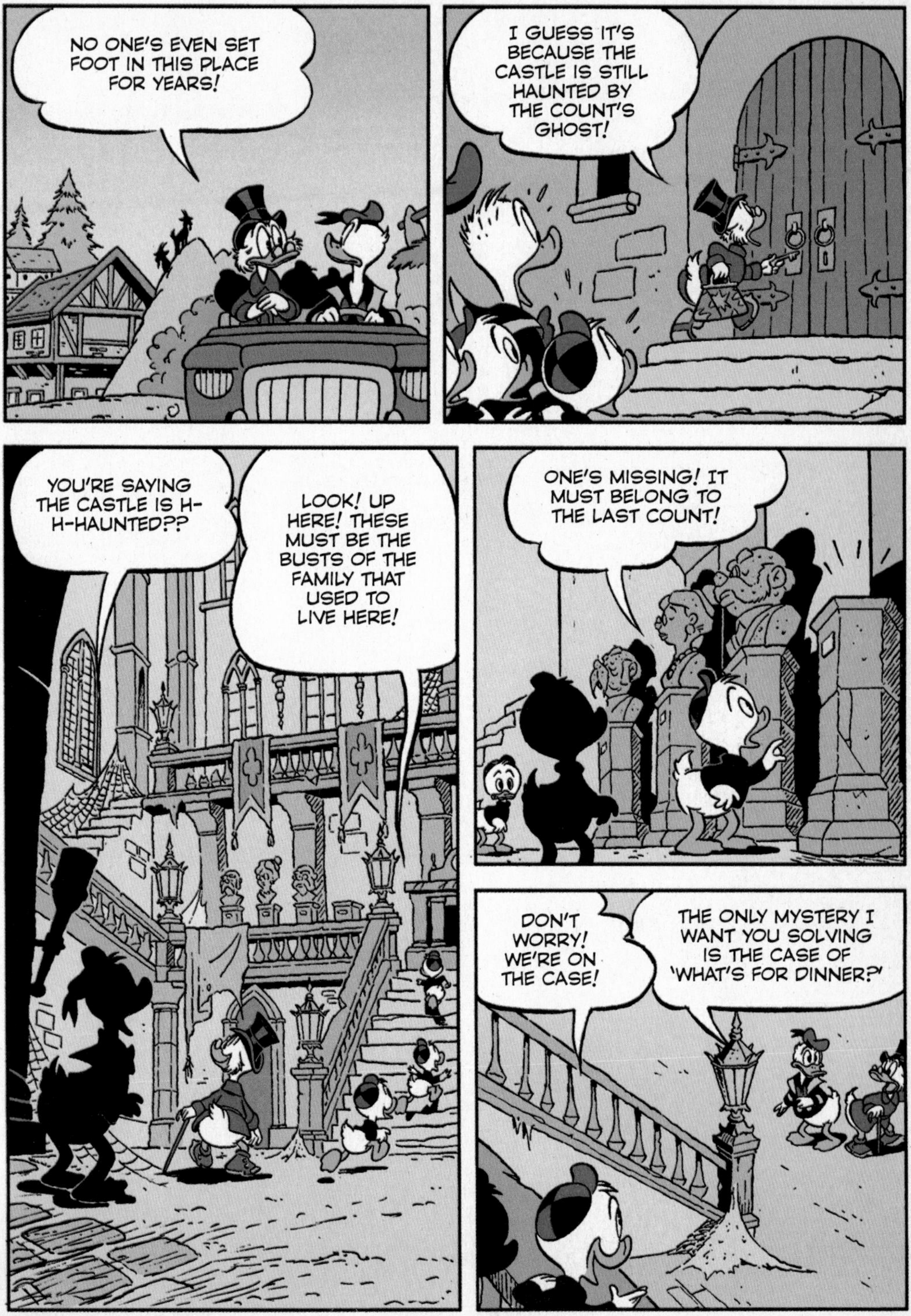
NO ONE'S EVEN SET FOOT IN THIS PLACE FOR YEARS!
I GUESS IT'S BECAUSE THE CASTLE IS STILL HAUNTED BY THE COUNT'S GHOST!
YOU'RE SAYING THE CASTLE IS H-H-HAUNTED??
LOOK! UP HERE! THESE MUST BE THE BUSTS OF THE FAMILY THAT USED TO LIVE HERE!
ONE'S MISSING! IT MUST BELONG TO THE LAST COUNT!
DON'T WORRY! WE'RE ON THE CASE!
THE ONLY MYSTERY I WANT YOU SOLVING IS THE CASE OF 'WHAT'S FOR DINNER?'

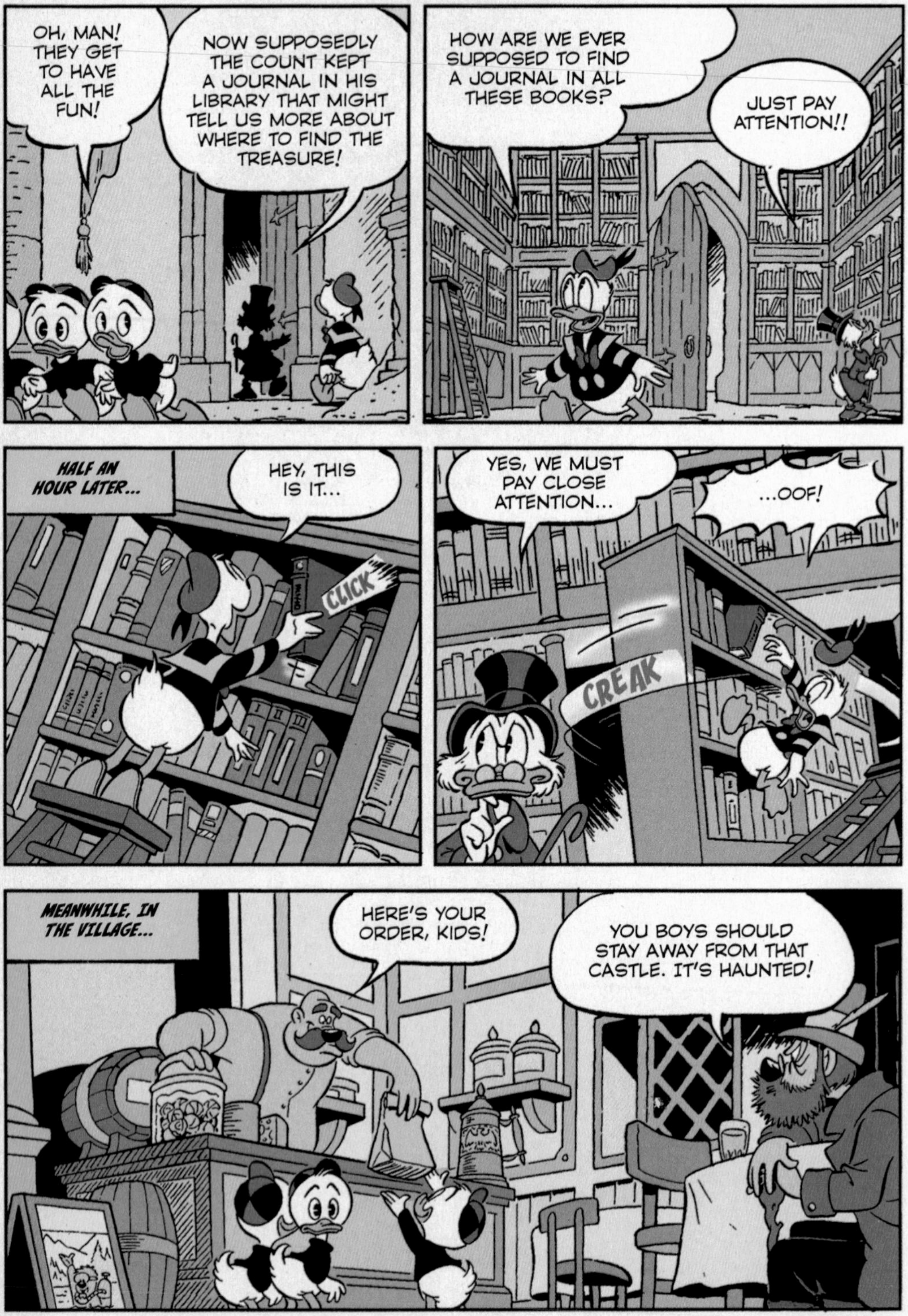
OH, MAN! THEY GET TO HAVE ALL THE FUN!
NOW SUPPOSEDLY THE COUNT KEPT A JOURNAL IN HIS LIBRARY THAT MIGHT TELL US MORE ABOUT WHERE TO FIND THE TREASURE!
HOW ARE WE EVER SUPPOSED TO FIND A JOURNAL IN ALL THESE BOOKS?
JUST PAY ATTENTION!!
HALF AN HOUR LATER...
HEY, THIS IS IT...
CLICK
YES, WE MUST PAY CLOSE ATTENTION...
...OOF!
CREAK
MEANWHILE, IN THE VILLAGE...
HERE'S YOUR ORDER, KIDS!
YOU BOYS SHOULD STAY AWAY FROM THAT CASTLE. IT'S HAUNTED!

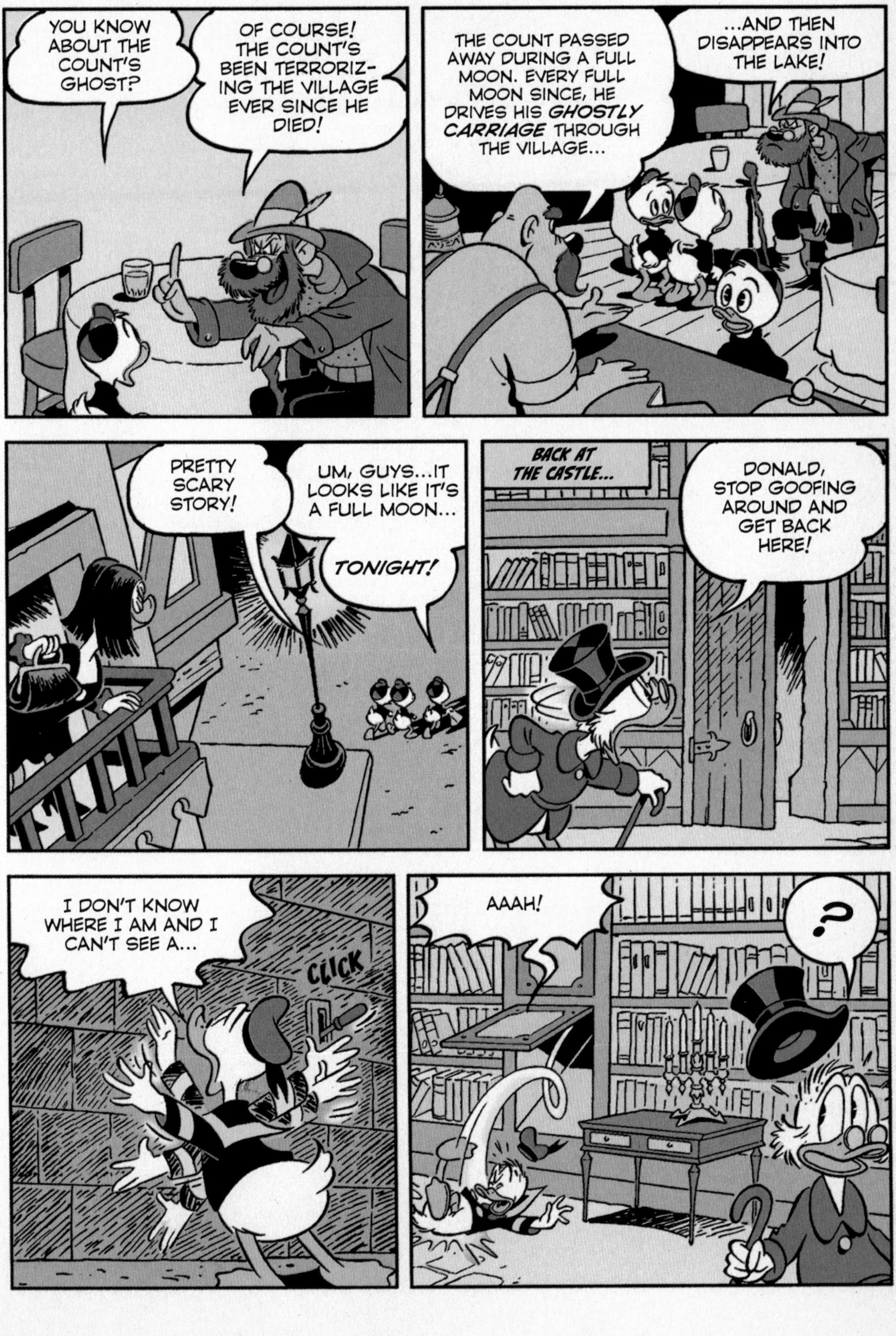
YOU KNOW ABOUT THE COUNT'S GHOST?
OF COURSE! THE COUNT'S BEEN TERRORIZ-ING THE VILLAGE EVER SINCE HE DIED!
THE COUNT PASSED AWAY DURING A FULL MOON. EVERY FULL MOON SINCE, HE DRIVES HIS GHOSTLY CARRIAGE THROUGH THE VILLAGE...
...AND THEN DISAPPEARS INTO THE LAKE!
PRETTY SCARY STORY!
UM, GUYS...IT LOOKS LIKE IT'S A FULL MOON...
TONIGHT!
BACK AT THE CASTLE...
DONALD, STOP GOOFING AROUND AND GET BACK HERE!
I DON'T KNOW WHERE I AM AND I CAN'T SEE A...
CLICK
AAAH!
?

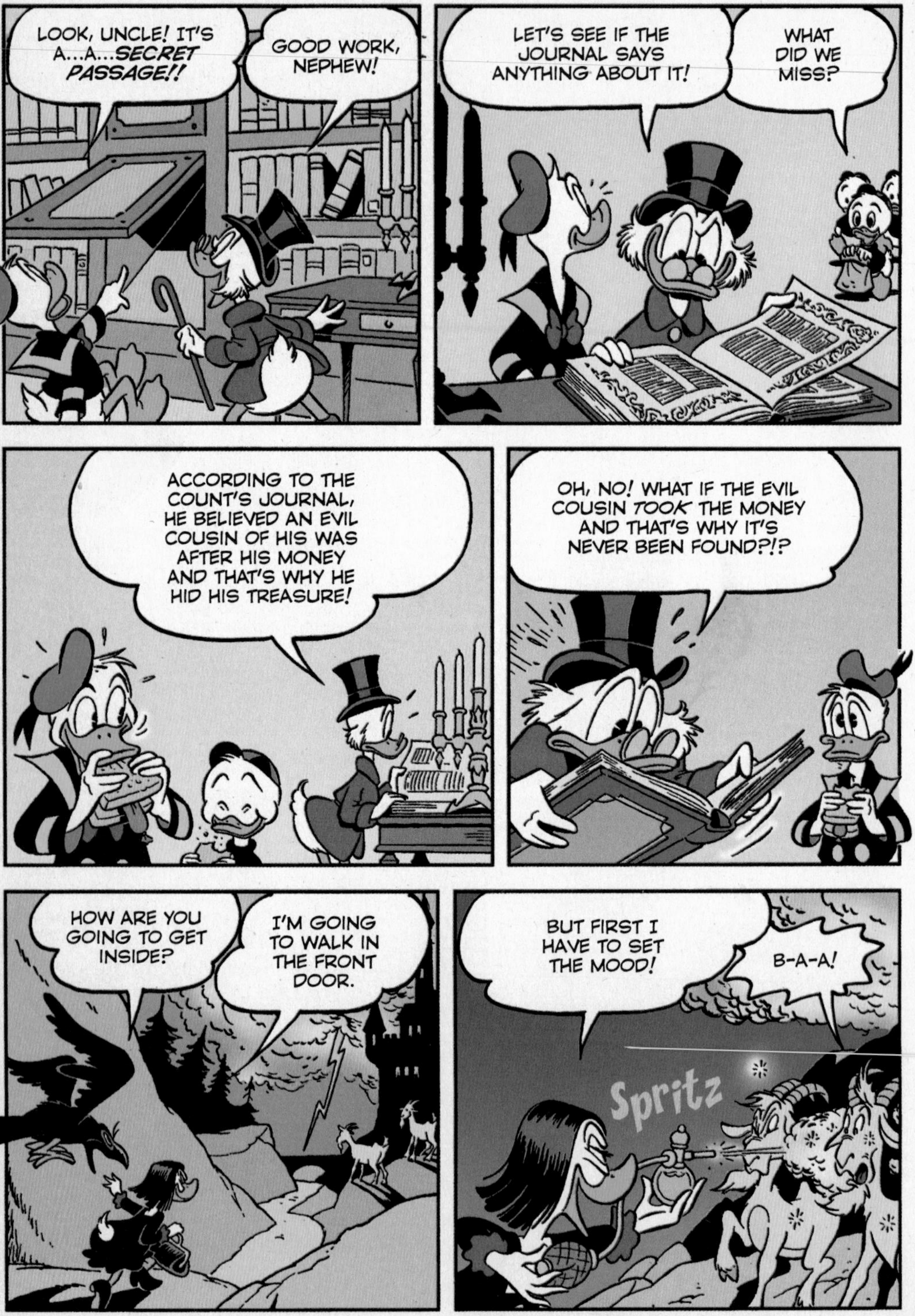
LOOK, UNCLE! IT'S A...A...SECRET PASSAGE!!
GOOD WORK, NEPHEW!
LET'S SEE IF THE JOURNAL SAYS ANYTHING ABOUT IT!
WHAT DID WE MISS?
ACCORDING TO THE COUNT'S JOURNAL, HE BELIEVED AN EVIL COUSIN OF HIS WAS AFTER HIS MONEY AND THAT'S WHY HE HID HIS TREASURE!
OH, NO! WHAT IF THE EVIL COUSIN TOOK THE MONEY AND THAT'S WHY IT'S NEVER BEEN FOUND?!?
HOW ARE YOU GOING TO GET INSIDE?
I'M GOING TO WALK IN THE FRONT DOOR.
BUT FIRST I HAVE TO SET THE MOOD!
B-A-A!
Spritz

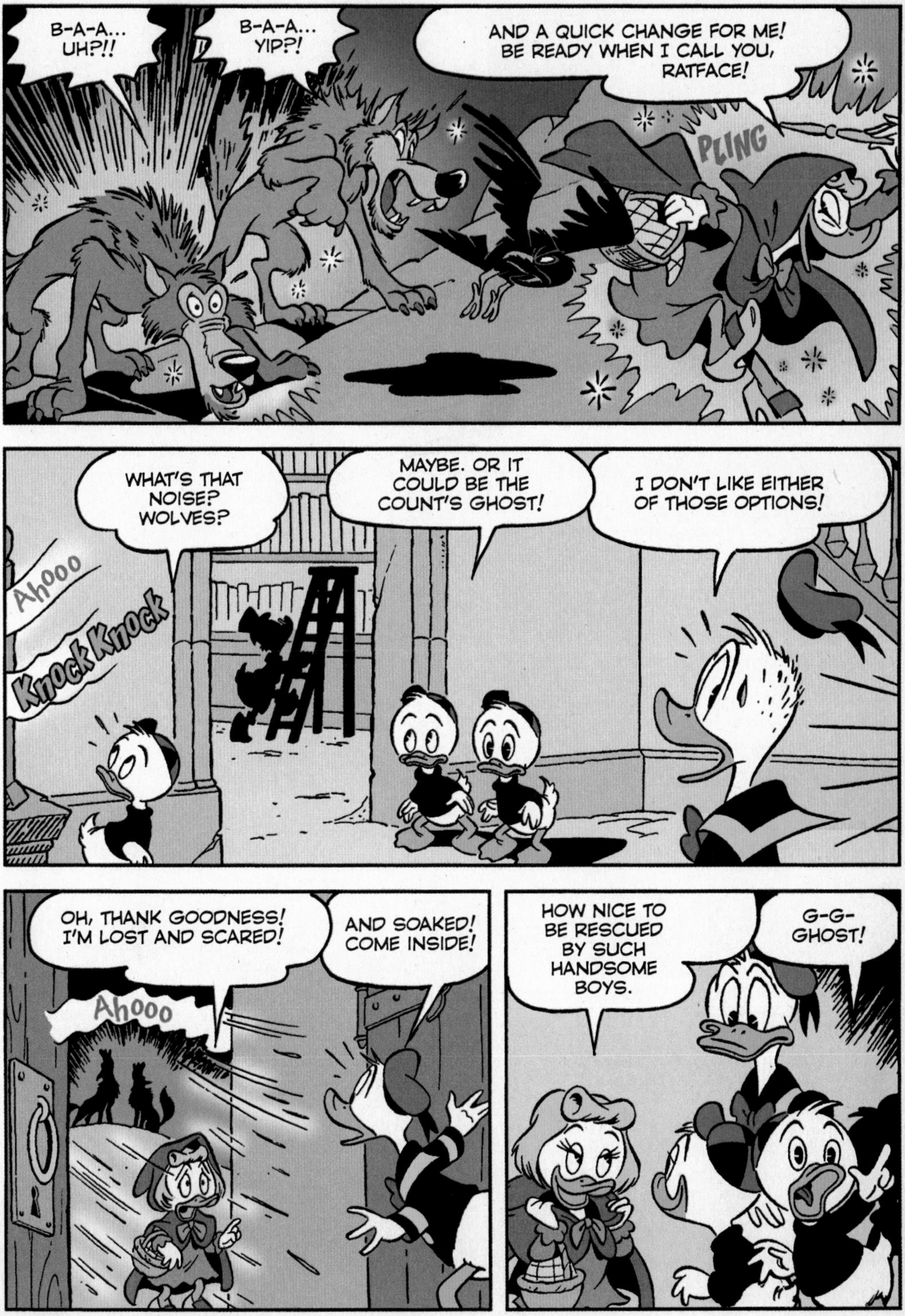
B-A-A... UH?!!
B-A-A... YIP?!
AND A QUICK CHANGE FOR ME! BE READY WHEN I CALL YOU, RATFACE!
PLING
WHAT'S THAT NOISE? WOLVES?
MAYBE. OR IT COULD BE THE COUNT'S GHOST!
I DON'T LIKE EITHER OF THOSE OPTIONS!
Ahooo
Knock Knock
OH, THANK GOODNESS! I'M LOST AND SCARED!
AND SOAKED! COME INSIDE!
Ahooo
HOW NICE TO BE RESCUED BY SUCH HANDSOME BOYS.
G-G- GHOST!

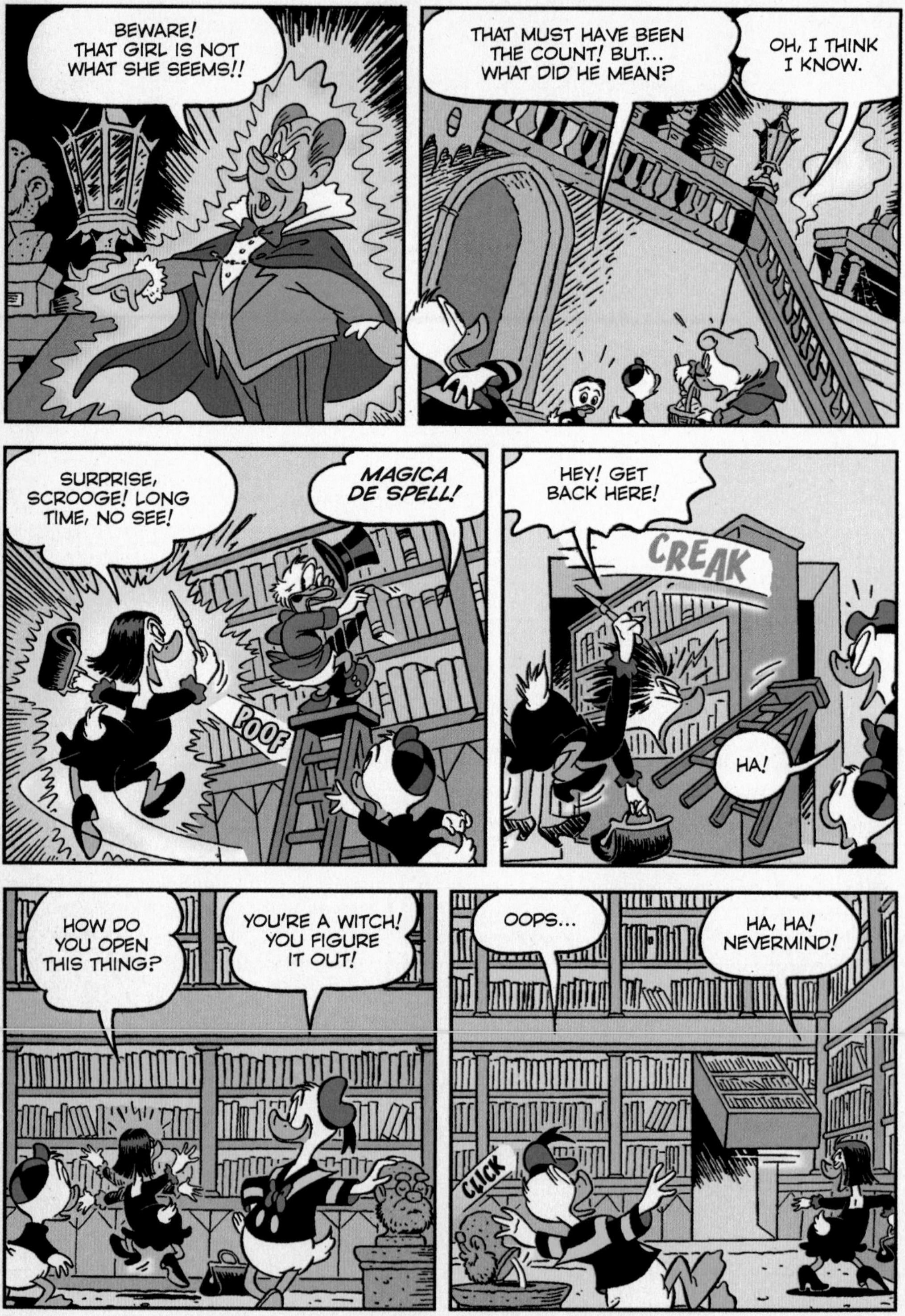
BEWARE! THAT GIRL IS NOT WHAT SHE SEEMS!!
THAT MUST HAVE BEEN THE COUNT! BUT... WHAT DID HE MEAN?
OH, I THINK I KNOW.
SURPRISE, SCROOGE! LONG TIME, NO SEE!
MAGICA DE SPELL!
POOF
HEY! GET BACK HERE!
CREAK
HA!
HOW DO YOU OPEN THIS THING?
YOU'RE A WITCH! YOU FIGURE IT OUT!
OOPS...
HA, HA! NEVERMIND!
CLICK

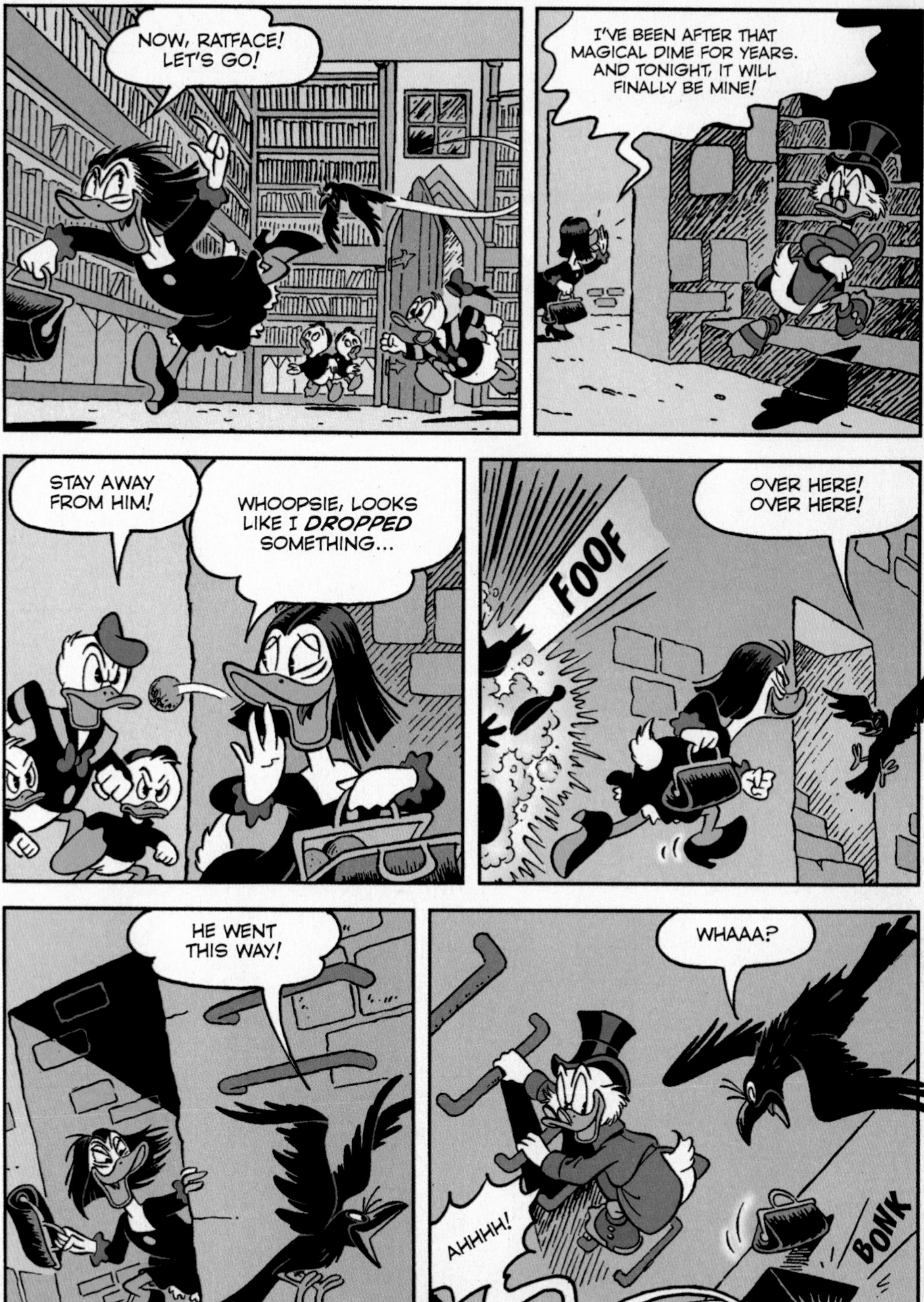
NOW, RATFACE! LET'S GO!
I'VE BEEN AFTER THAT MAGICAL DIME FOR YEARS. AND TONIGHT, IT WILL FINALLY BE MINE!
STAY AWAY FROM HIM!
WHOOPSIE, LOOKS LIKE I DROPPED SOMETHING...
FOOF
OVER HERE! OVER HERE!
HE WENT THIS WAY!
WHAAA?
AHHHH!
BONK

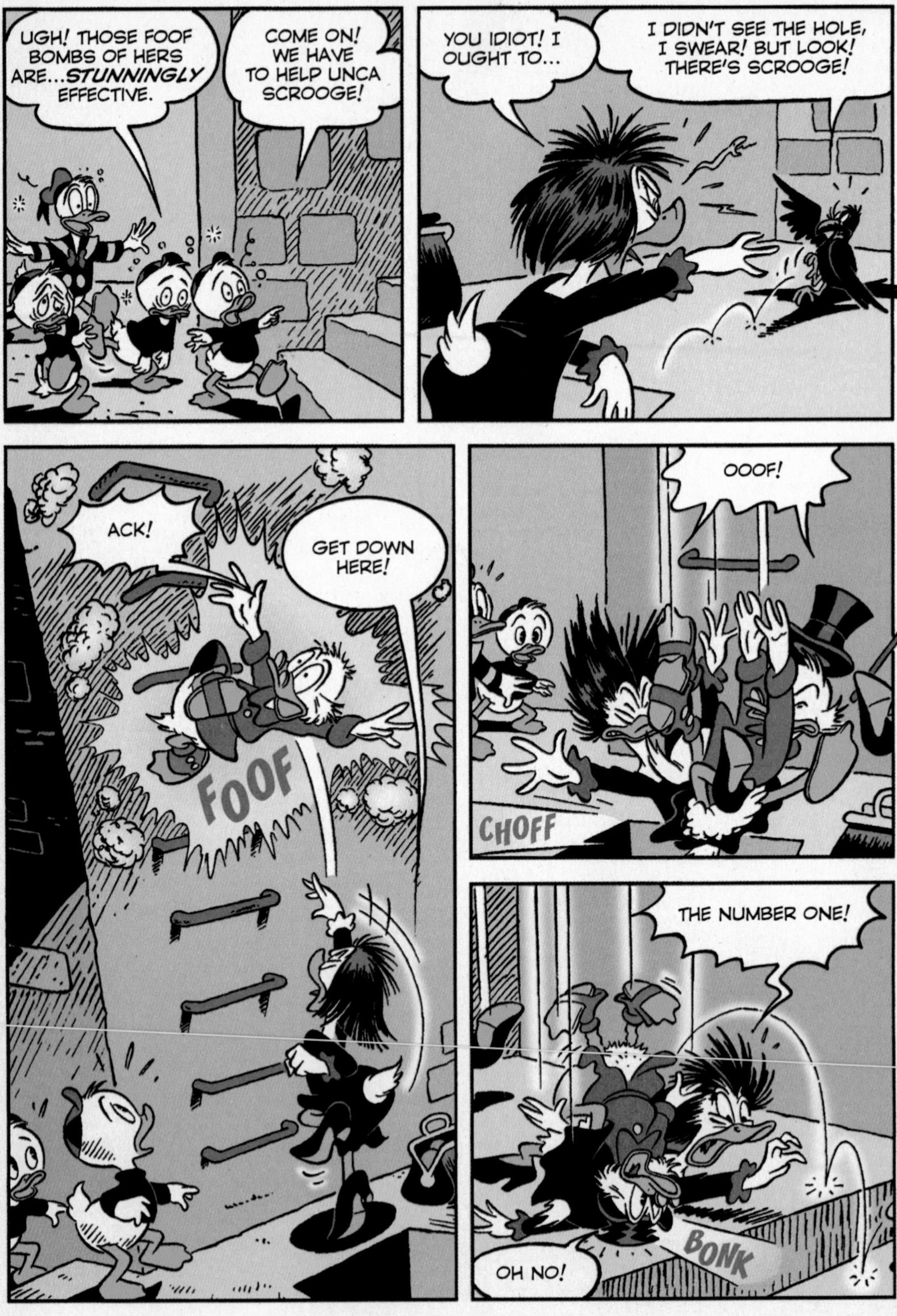
UGH! THOSE FOOF BOMBS OF HERS ARE...STUNNINGLY EFFECTIVE.
COME ON! WE HAVE TO HELP UNCA SCROOGE!
YOU IDIOT! I OUGHT TO...
I DIDN'T SEE THE HOLE, I SWEAR! BUT LOOK! THERE'S SCROOGE!
ACK!
GET DOWN HERE!
FOOF
OOOF!
CHOFF
THE NUMBER ONE!
BONK
OH NO!

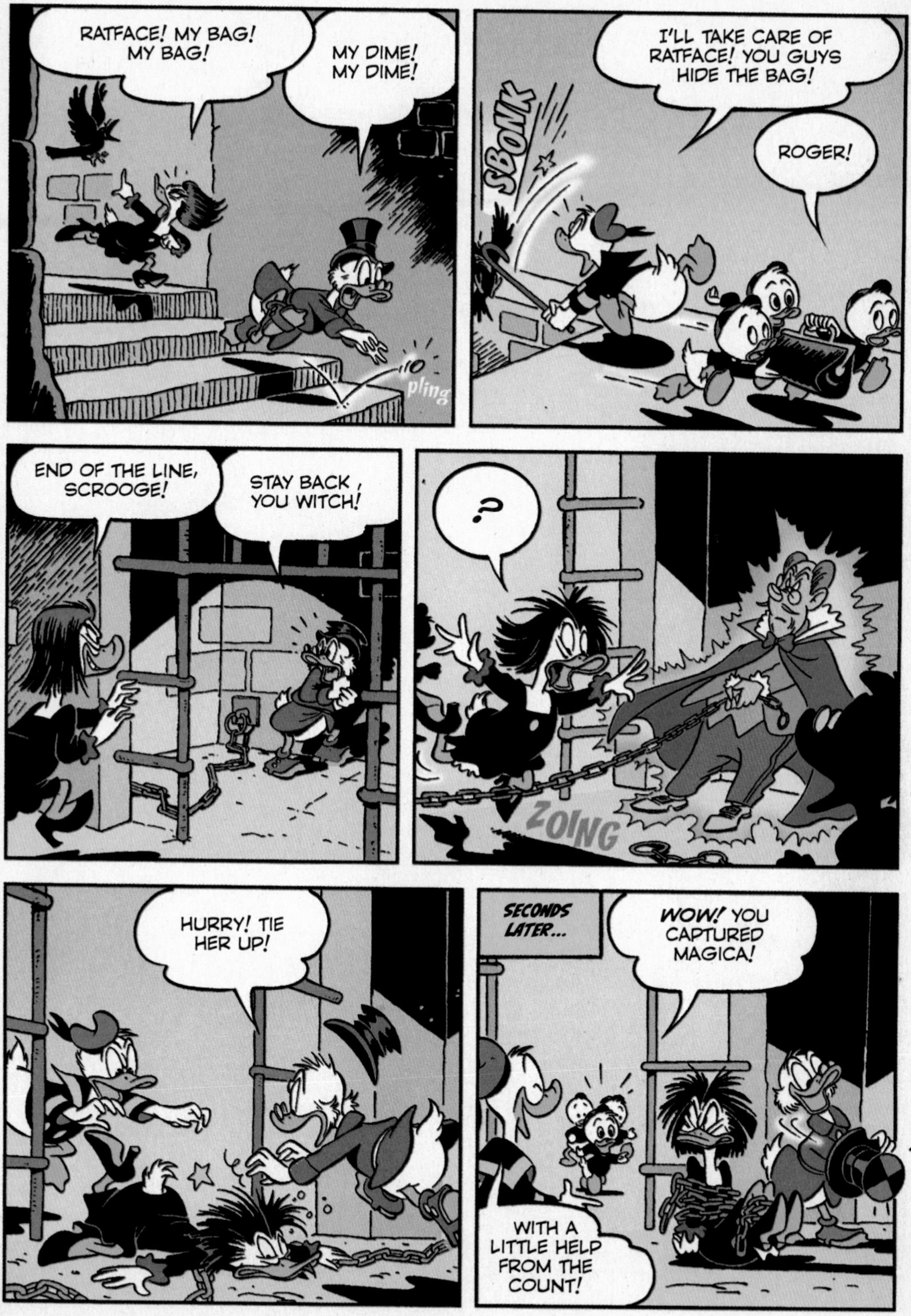
RATFACE! MY BAG! MY BAG!
MY DIME! MY DIME!
pling
I'LL TAKE CARE OF RATFACE! YOU GUYS HIDE THE BAG!
SBONK
ROGER!
END OF THE LINE, SCROOGE!
STAY BACK, YOU WITCH!
?
ZOING
HURRY! TIE HER UP!
SECONDS LATER...
WOW! YOU CAPTURED MAGICA!
WITH A LITTLE HELP FROM THE COUNT!

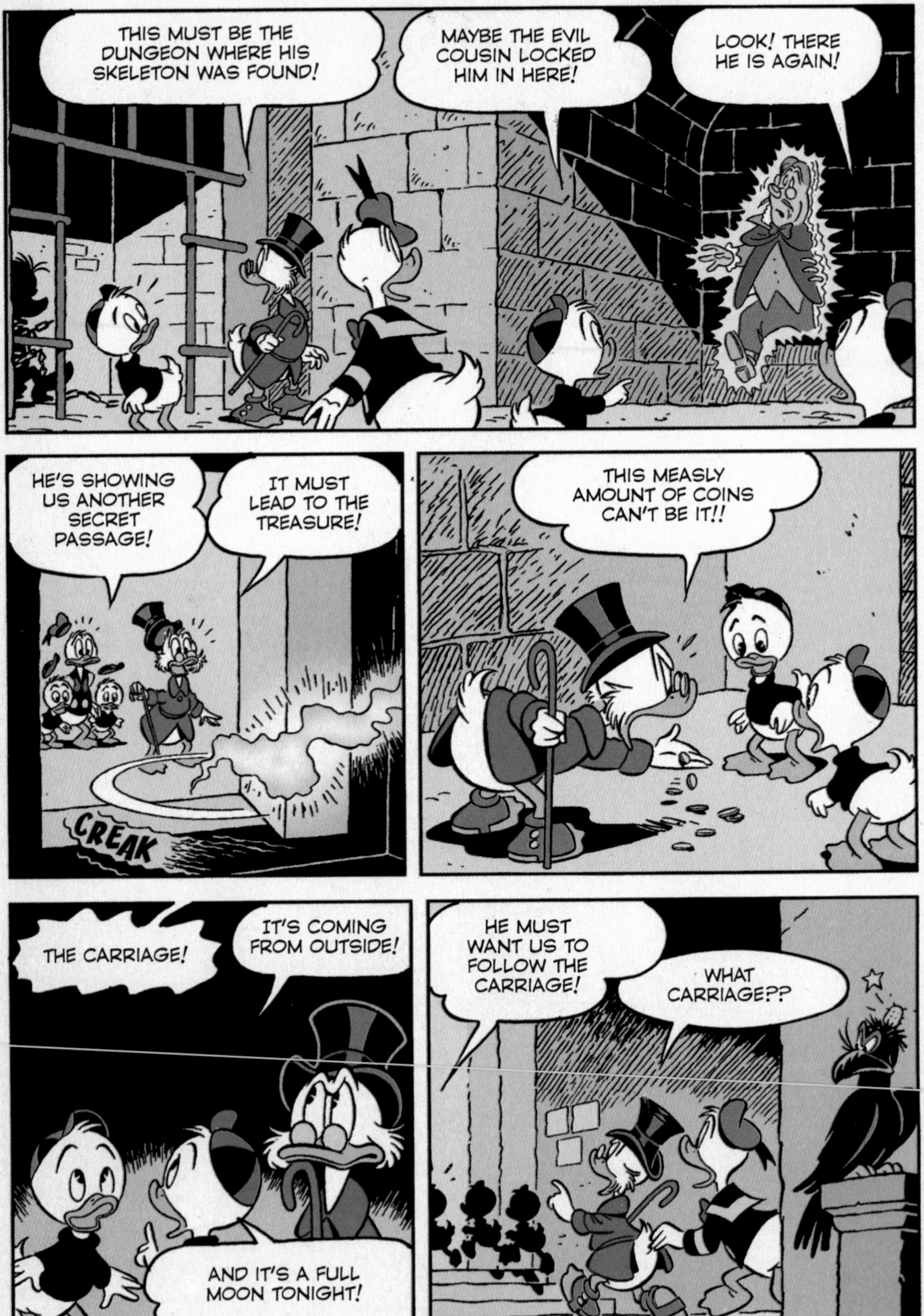
THIS MUST BE THE DUNGEON WHERE HIS SKELETON WAS FOUND!
MAYBE THE EVIL COUSIN LOCKED HIM IN HERE!
LOOK! THERE HE IS AGAIN!
HE'S SHOWING US ANOTHER SECRET PASSAGE!
IT MUST LEAD TO THE TREASURE!
CREAK
THIS MEASLY AMOUNT OF COINS CAN'T BE IT!!
THE CARRIAGE!
IT'S COMING FROM OUTSIDE!
AND IT'S A FULL MOON TONIGHT!
HE MUST WANT US TO FOLLOW THE CARRIAGE!
WHAT CARRIAGE??

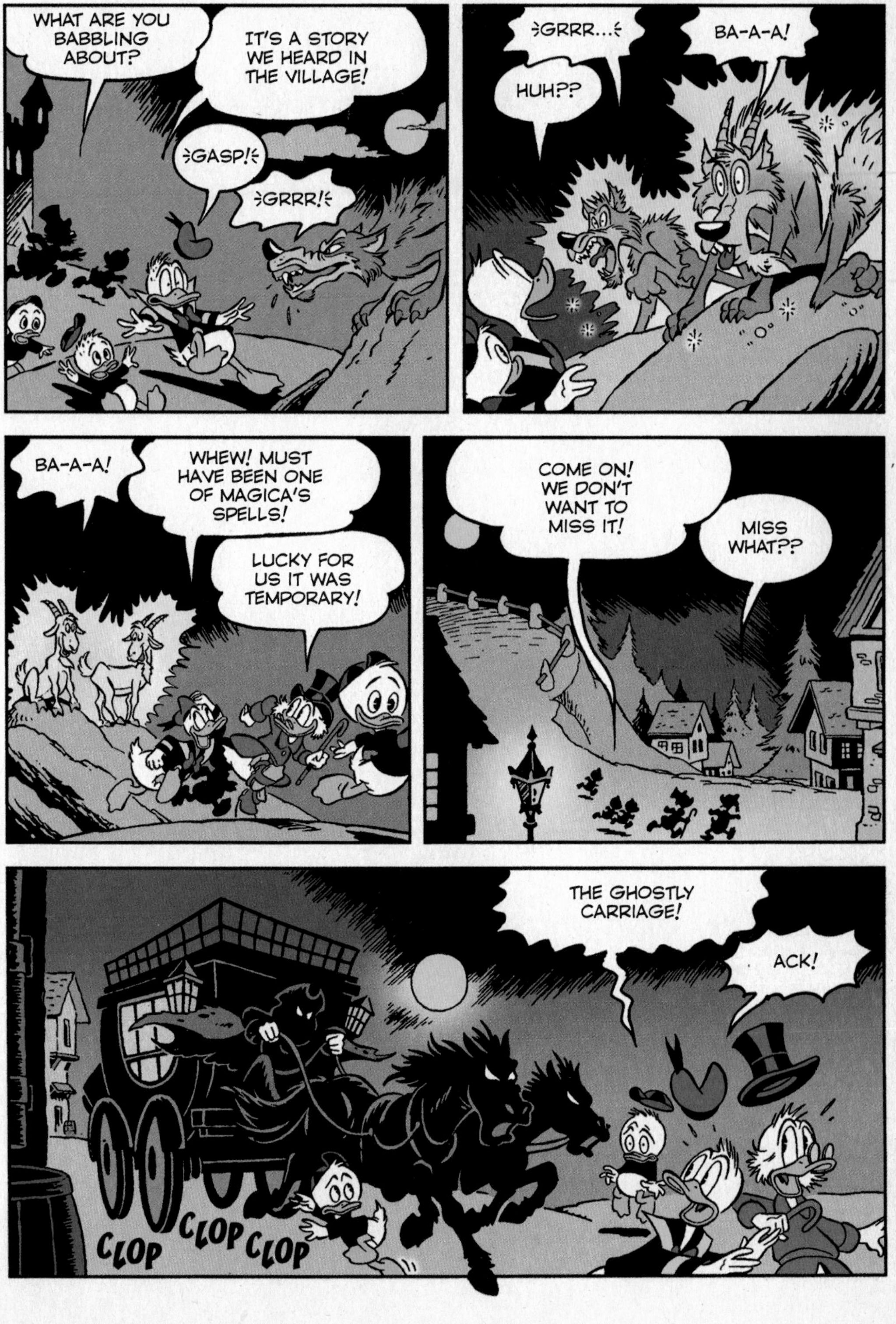
WHAT ARE YOU BABBLING ABOUT?
IT'S A STORY WE HEARD IN THE VILLAGE!
GASP!
GRRR!
GRRR...
BA-A-A!
HUH??
BA-A-A!
WHEW! MUST HAVE BEEN ONE OF MAGICA'S SPELLS!
LUCKY FOR US IT WAS TEMPORARY!
COME ON! WE DON'T WANT TO MISS IT!
MISS WHAT??
THE GHOSTLY CARRIAGE!
ACK!
CLOP CLOP CLOP

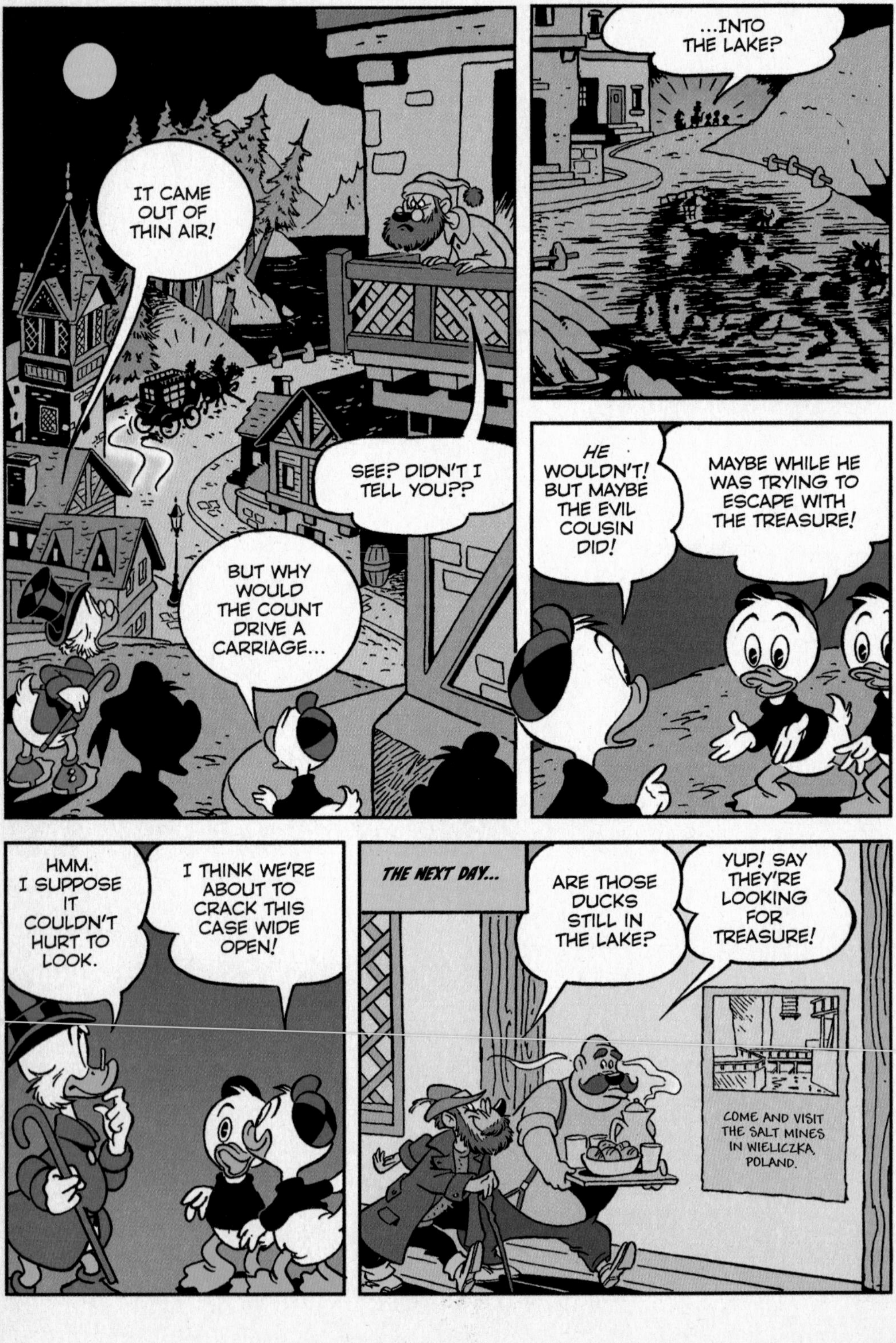
IT CAME OUT OF THIN AIR!
SEE? DIDN'T I TELL YOU??
BUT WHY WOULD THE COUNT DRIVE A CARRIAGE...
...INTO THE LAKE?
HE WOULDN'T! BUT MAYBE THE EVIL COUSIN DID!
MAYBE WHILE HE WAS TRYING TO ESCAPE WITH THE TREASURE!
HMM. I SUPPOSE IT COULDN'T HURT TO LOOK.
I THINK WE'RE ABOUT TO CRACK THIS CASE WIDE OPEN!
THE NEXT DAY...
ARE THOSE DUCKS STILL IN THE LAKE?
YUP! SAY THEY'RE LOOKING FOR TREASURE!
COME AND VISIT THE SALT MINES IN WIELICZKA, POLAND.

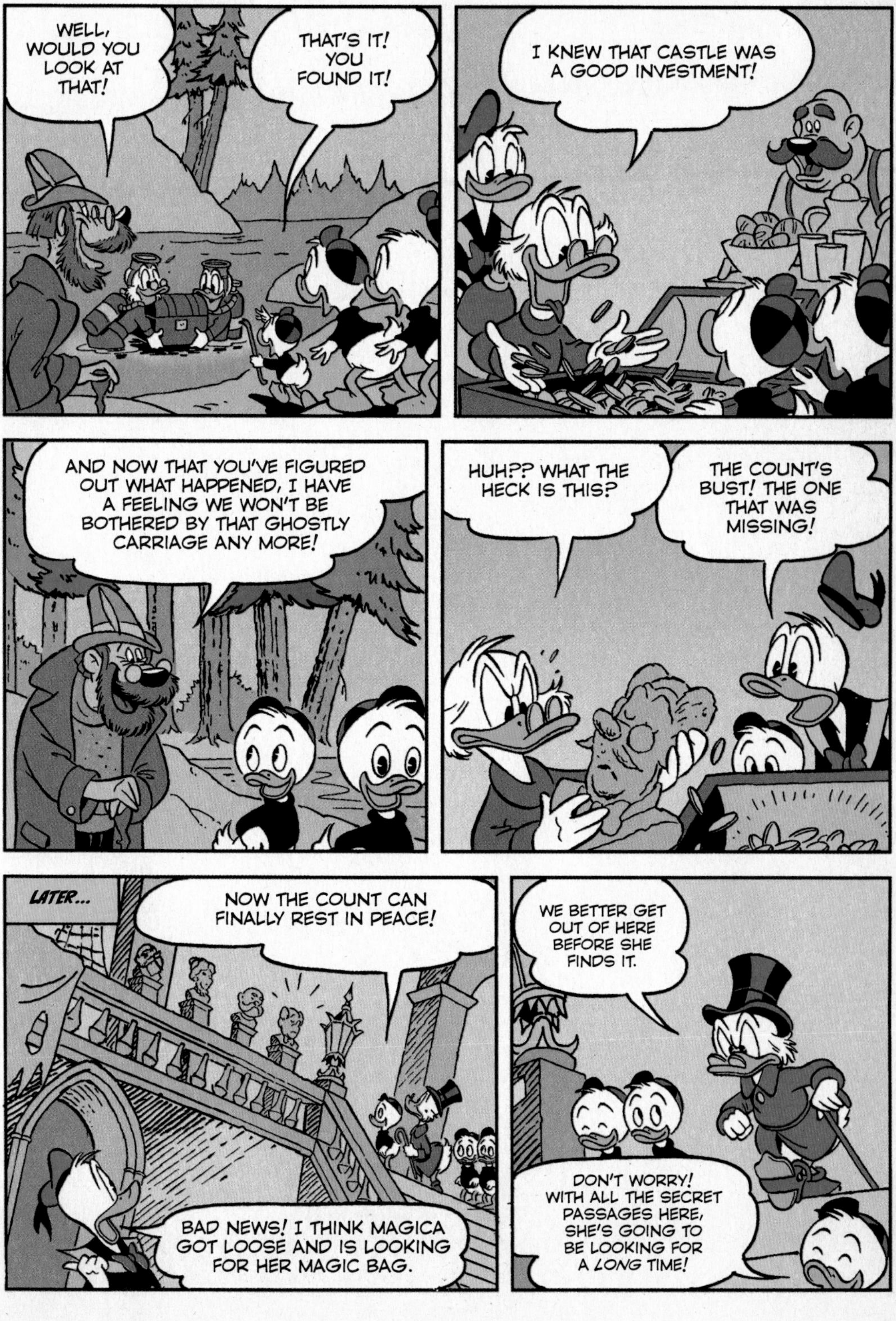
WELL, WOULD YOU LOOK AT THAT!
THAT'S IT! YOU FOUND IT!
I KNEW THAT CASTLE WAS A GOOD INVESTMENT!
AND NOW THAT YOU'VE FIGURED OUT WHAT HAPPENED, I HAVE A FEELING WE WON'T BE BOTHERED BY THAT GHOSTLY CARRIAGE ANY MORE!
HUH?? WHAT THE HECK IS THIS?
THE COUNT'S BUST! THE ONE THAT WAS MISSING!
LATER...
NOW THE COUNT CAN FINALLY REST IN PEACE!
BAD NEWS! I THINK MAGICA GOT LOOSE AND IS LOOKING FOR HER MAGIC BAG.
WE BETTER GET OUT OF HERE BEFORE SHE FINDS IT.
DON'T WORRY! WITH ALL THE SECRET PASSAGES HERE, SHE'S GOING TO BE LOOKING FOR A LONG TIME!

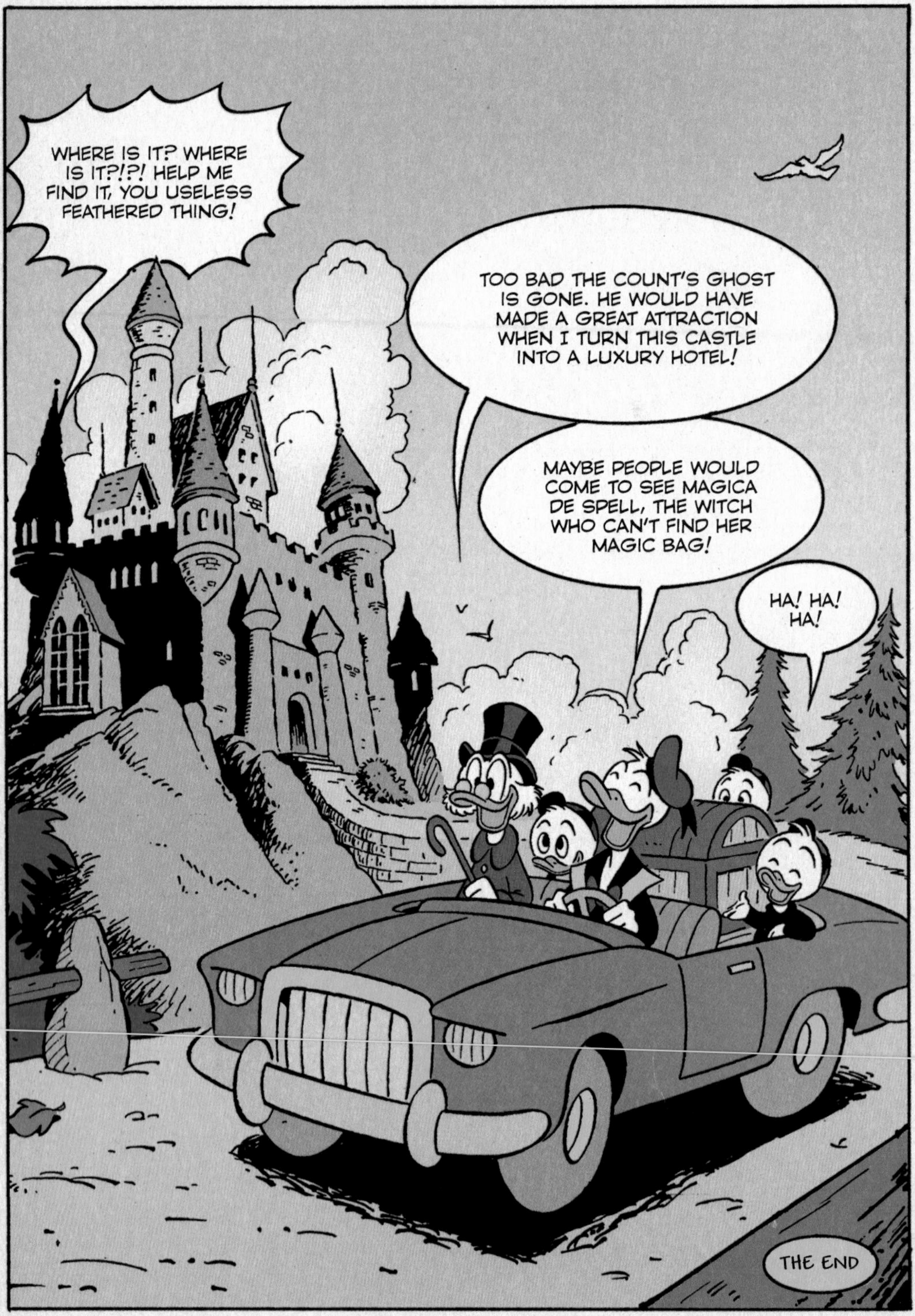
WHERE IS IT? WHERE IS IT?!?! HELP ME FIND IT, YOU USELESS FEATHERED THING!
TOO BAD THE COUNT'S GHOST IS GONE. HE WOULD HAVE MADE A GREAT ATTRACTION WHEN I TURN THIS CASTLE INTO A LUXURY HOTEL!
MAYBE PEOPLE WOULD COME TO SEE MAGICA DE SPELL, THE WITCH WHO CAN'T FIND HER MAGIC BAG!
HA! HA! HA!
THE END

THE HUNT FOR THE OLD NUMBER ONE

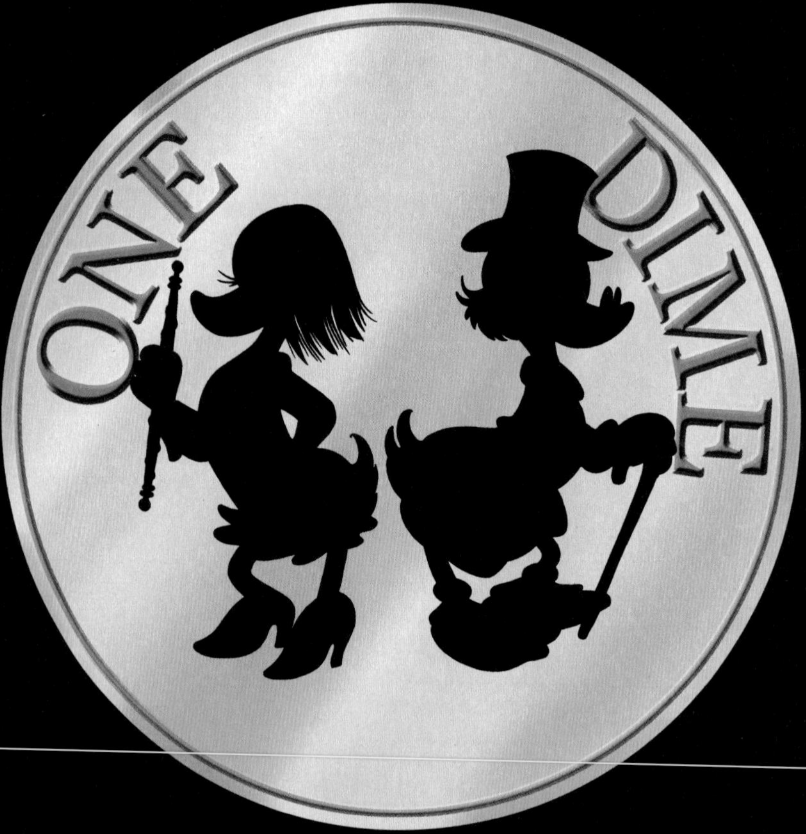
ONE
DIME

CHAPTER TWO

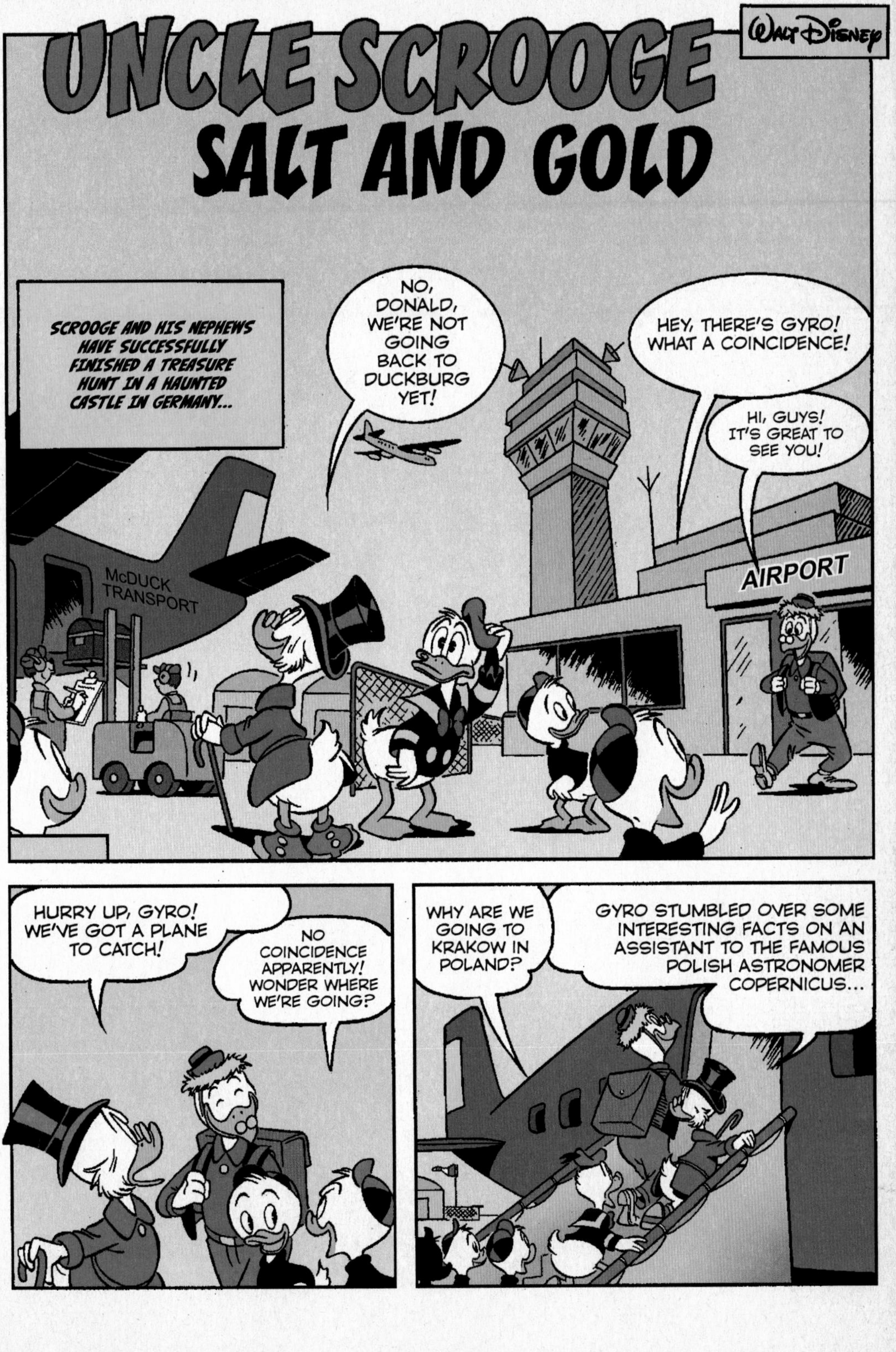
UNCLE SCROOGE
WALT DISNEY
SALT AND GOLD
SCROOGE AND HIS NEPHEWS HAVE SUCCESSFULLY FINISHED A TREASURE HUNT IN A HAUNTED CASTLE IN GERMANY...
NO, DONALD, WE'RE NOT GOING BACK TO DUCKBURG YET!
HEY, THERE'S GYRO! WHAT A COINCIDENCE!
HI, GUYS! IT'S GREAT TO SEE YOU!
McDUCK TRANSPORT
AIRPORT
HURRY UP, GYRO! WE'VE GOT A PLANE TO CATCH!
NO COINCIDENCE APPARENTLY! WONDER WHERE WE'RE GOING?
WHY ARE WE GOING TO KRAKOW IN POLAND?
GYRO STUMBLED OVER SOME INTERESTING FACTS ON AN ASSISTANT TO THE FAMOUS POLISH ASTRONOMER COPERNICUS...

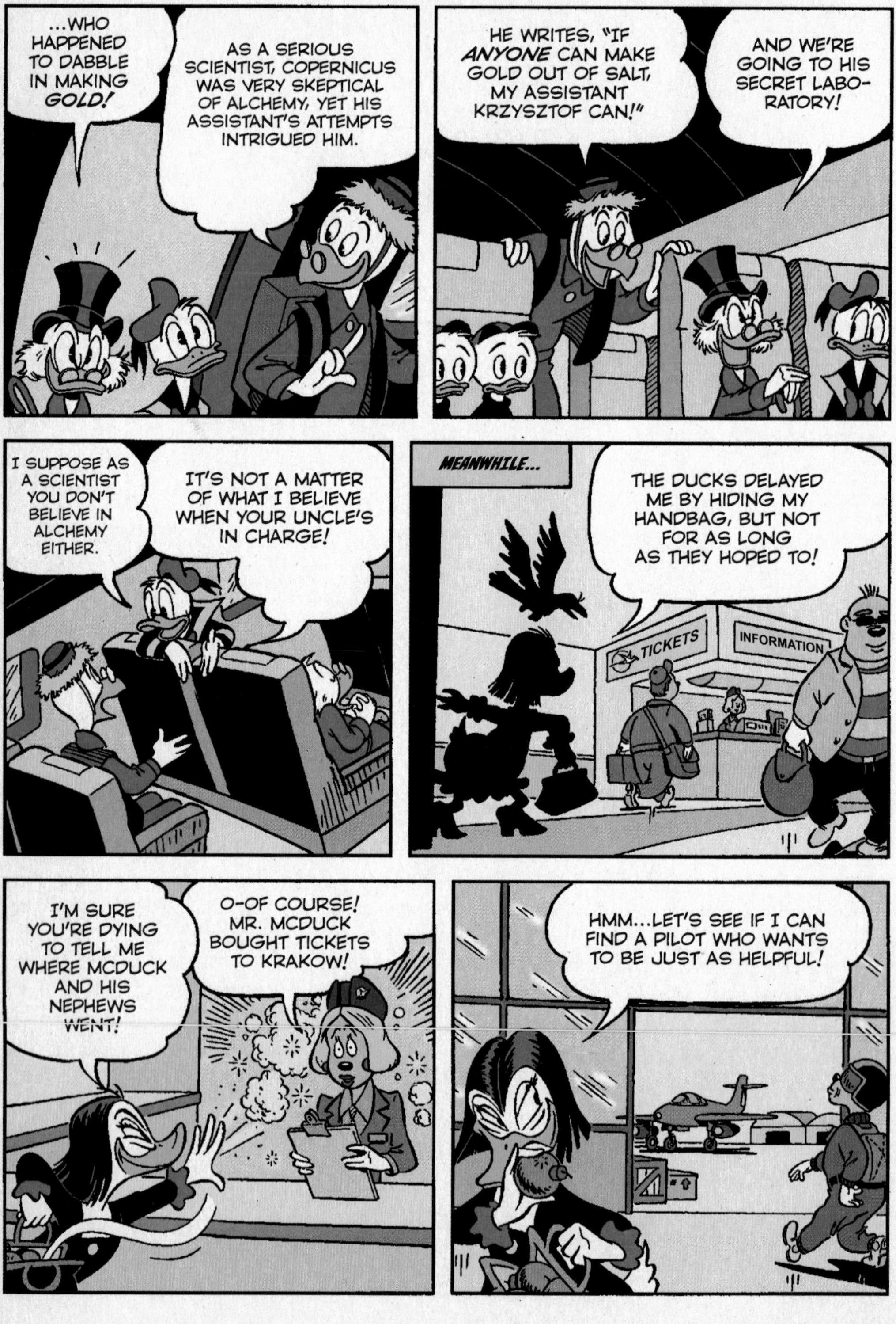
...WHO HAPPENED TO DABBLE IN MAKING *GOLD!*
AS A SERIOUS SCIENTIST, COPERNICUS WAS VERY SKEPTICAL OF ALCHEMY, YET HIS ASSISTANT'S ATTEMPTS INTRIGUED HIM.
HE WRITES, "IF *ANYONE* CAN MAKE GOLD OUT OF SALT, MY ASSISTANT KRZYSZTOF CAN!"
AND WE'RE GOING TO HIS SECRET LABO-RATORY!
I SUPPOSE AS A SCIENTIST YOU DON'T BELIEVE IN ALCHEMY EITHER.
IT'S NOT A MATTER OF WHAT I BELIEVE WHEN YOUR UNCLE'S IN CHARGE!
MEANWHILE...
THE DUCKS DELAYED ME BY HIDING MY HANDBAG, BUT NOT FOR AS LONG AS THEY HOPED TO!
TICKETS
INFORMATION
I'M SURE YOU'RE DYING TO TELL ME WHERE MCDUCK AND HIS NEPHEWS WENT!
O-OF COURSE! MR. MCDUCK BOUGHT TICKETS TO KRAKOW!
HMM...LET'S SEE IF I CAN FIND A PILOT WHO WANTS TO BE JUST AS HELPFUL!

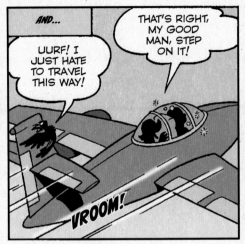

AND...

UURF! I JUST HATE TO TRAVEL THIS WAY!

THAT'S RIGHT, MY GOOD MAN, STEP ON IT!

VROOM!

THERE THEY ARE! EXCELLENT! NOW, BRING HER DOWN, CHUM!

SHORTLY...

THIS IS "COLLEGIUM MAIUS," A PART OF THE OLD UNIVERSITY WHERE COPERNICUS STUDIED AT THE BEGINNING OF THE 16TH CENTURY!

LOTS OF HIS INSTRUMENTS AND MANUSCRIPTS ARE KEPT HERE!

IN THE COPERNICUS MUSEUM...

WELL, YOU SEE, THE ARCHIVES ARE REALLY NOT OPEN TO THE PUBLIC...

...BUT BECAUSE MR. GEARLOOSE HAS SUCH A REPUTATION IN SCIENTIFIC CIRCLES, I'LL MAKE AN EXCEPTION!

THANK YOU, SIR!

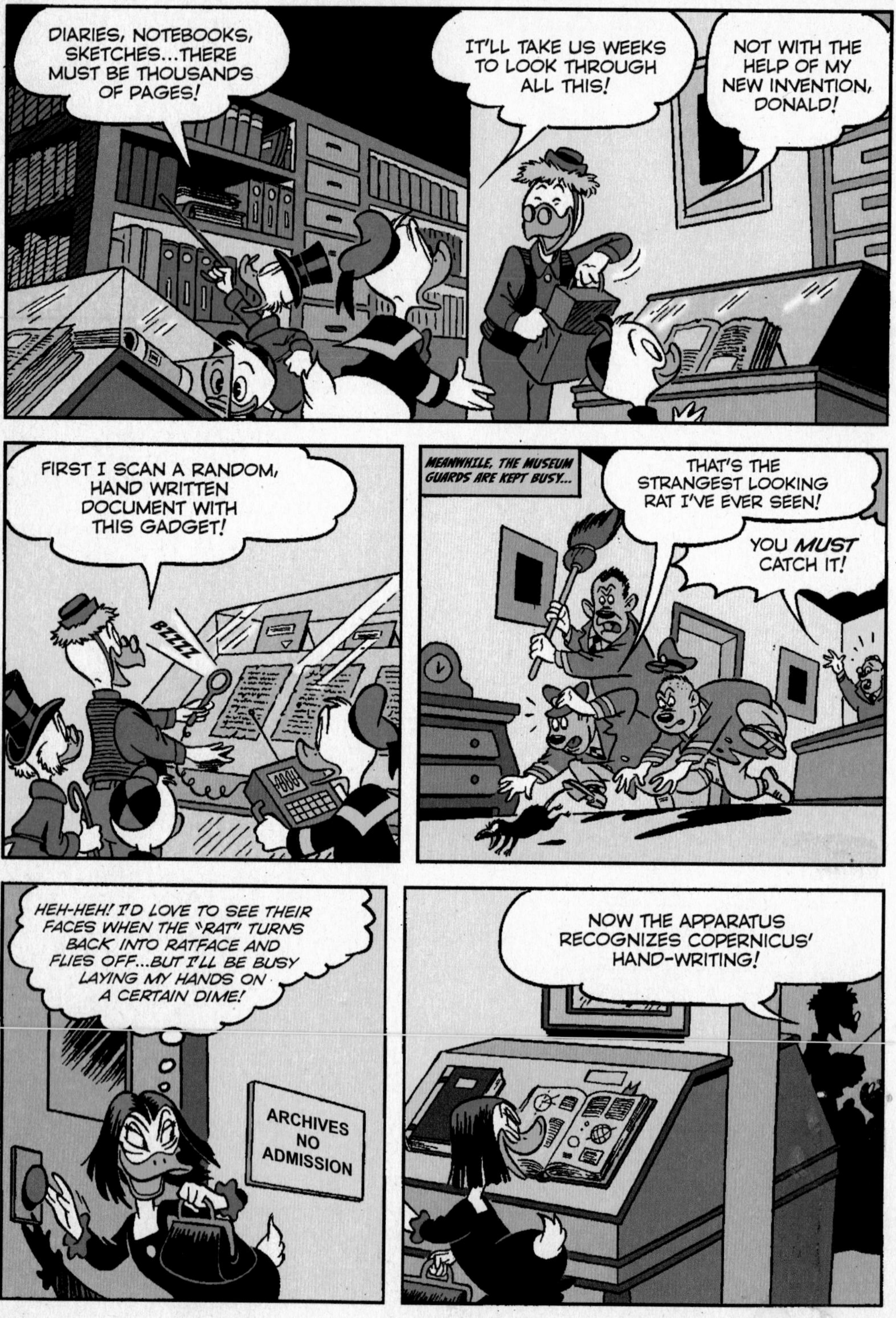
DIARIES, NOTEBOOKS, SKETCHES...THERE MUST BE THOUSANDS OF PAGES!
IT'LL TAKE US WEEKS TO LOOK THROUGH ALL THIS!
NOT WITH THE HELP OF MY NEW INVENTION, DONALD!
FIRST I SCAN A RANDOM, HAND WRITTEN DOCUMENT WITH THIS GADGET!
BZZZZ
MEANWHILE, THE MUSEUM GUARDS ARE KEPT BUSY...
THAT'S THE STRANGEST LOOKING RAT I'VE EVER SEEN!
YOU MUST CATCH IT!
HEH-HEH! I'D LOVE TO SEE THEIR FACES WHEN THE "RAT" TURNS BACK INTO RATFACE AND FLIES OFF...BUT I'LL BE BUSY LAYING MY HANDS ON A CERTAIN DIME!
ARCHIVES NO ADMISSION
NOW THE APPARATUS RECOGNIZES COPERNICUS' HAND-WRITING!

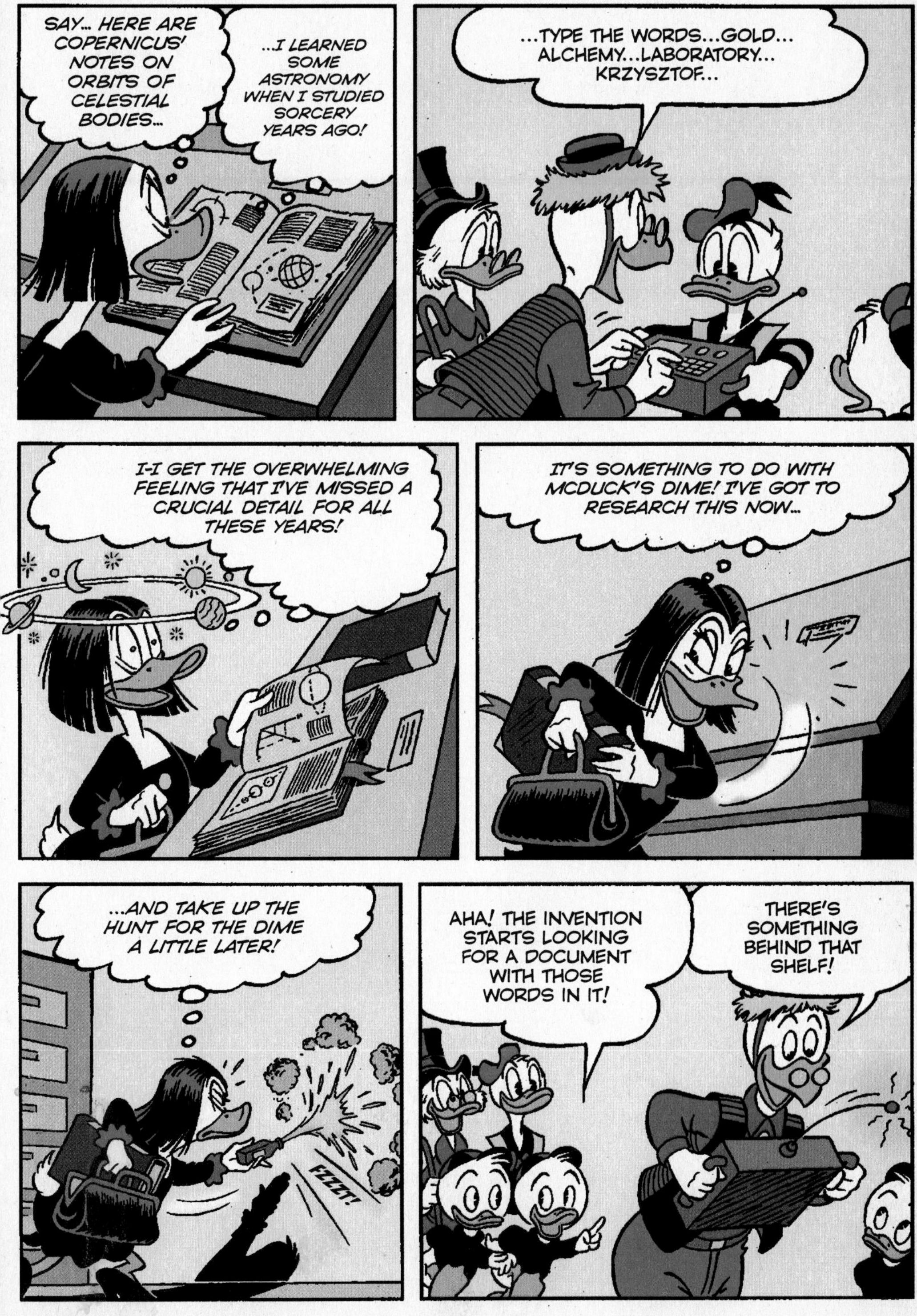
SAY... HERE ARE COPERNICUS' NOTES ON ORBITS OF CELESTIAL BODIES...
...I LEARNED SOME ASTRONOMY WHEN I STUDIED SORCERY YEARS AGO!
...TYPE THE WORDS...GOLD... ALCHEMY...LABORATORY... KRZYSZTOF...
I-I GET THE OVERWHELMING FEELING THAT I'VE MISSED A CRUCIAL DETAIL FOR ALL THESE YEARS!
IT'S SOMETHING TO DO WITH MCDUCK'S DIME! I'VE GOT TO RESEARCH THIS NOW...
...AND TAKE UP THE HUNT FOR THE DIME A LITTLE LATER!
FZZZT!
AHA! THE INVENTION STARTS LOOKING FOR A DOCUMENT WITH THOSE WORDS IN IT!
THERE'S SOMETHING BEHIND THAT SHELF!

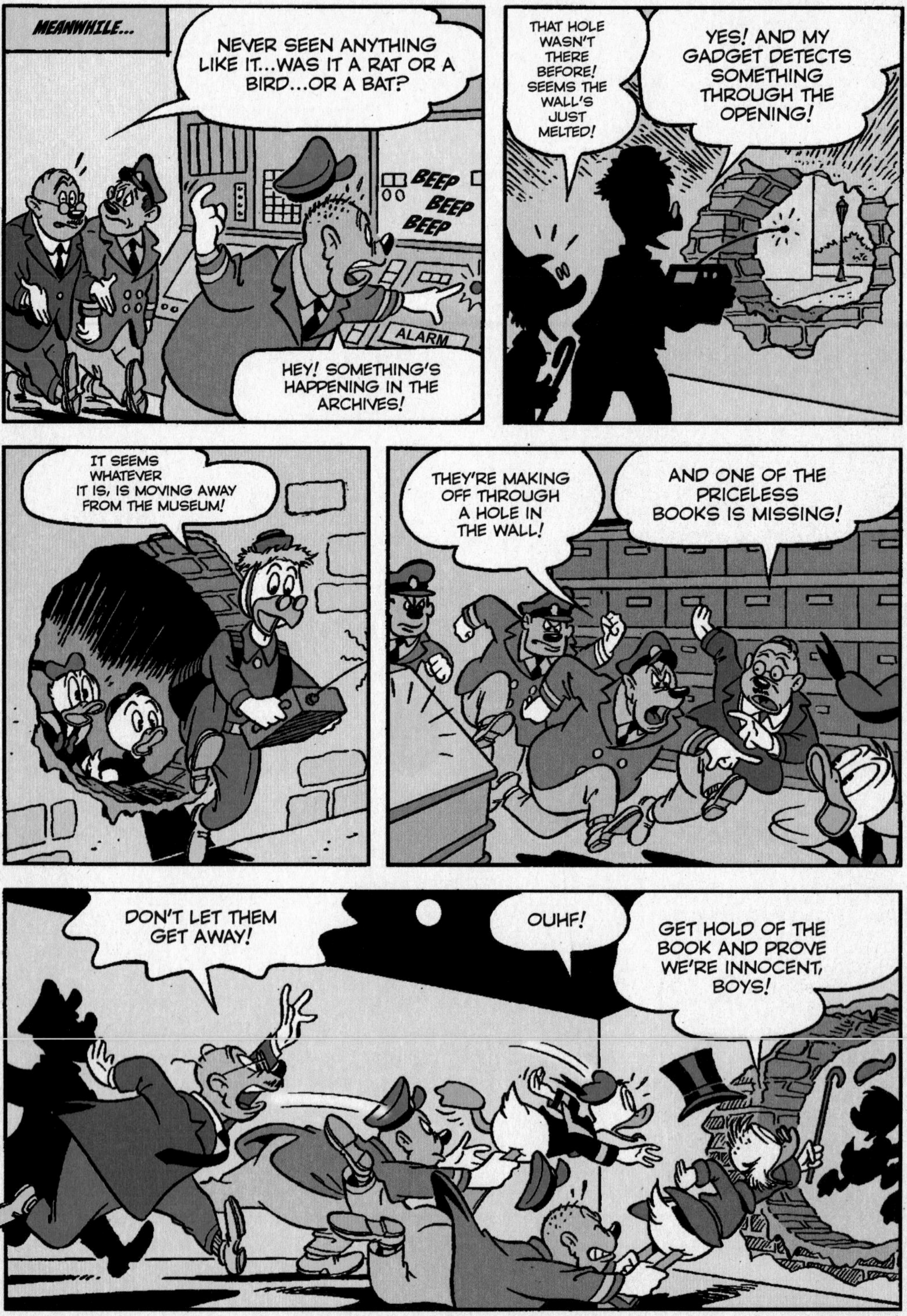
MEANWHILE...
NEVER SEEN ANYTHING LIKE IT...WAS IT A RAT OR A BIRD...OR A BAT?
BEEP BEEP BEEP
ALARM
HEY! SOMETHING'S HAPPENING IN THE ARCHIVES!
THAT HOLE WASN'T THERE BEFORE! SEEMS THE WALL'S JUST MELTED!
YES! AND MY GADGET DETECTS SOMETHING THROUGH THE OPENING!
IT SEEMS WHATEVER IT IS, IS MOVING AWAY FROM THE MUSEUM!
THEY'RE MAKING OFF THROUGH A HOLE IN THE WALL!
AND ONE OF THE PRICELESS BOOKS IS MISSING!
DON'T LET THEM GET AWAY!
OUHF!
GET HOLD OF THE BOOK AND PROVE WE'RE INNOCENT, BOYS!

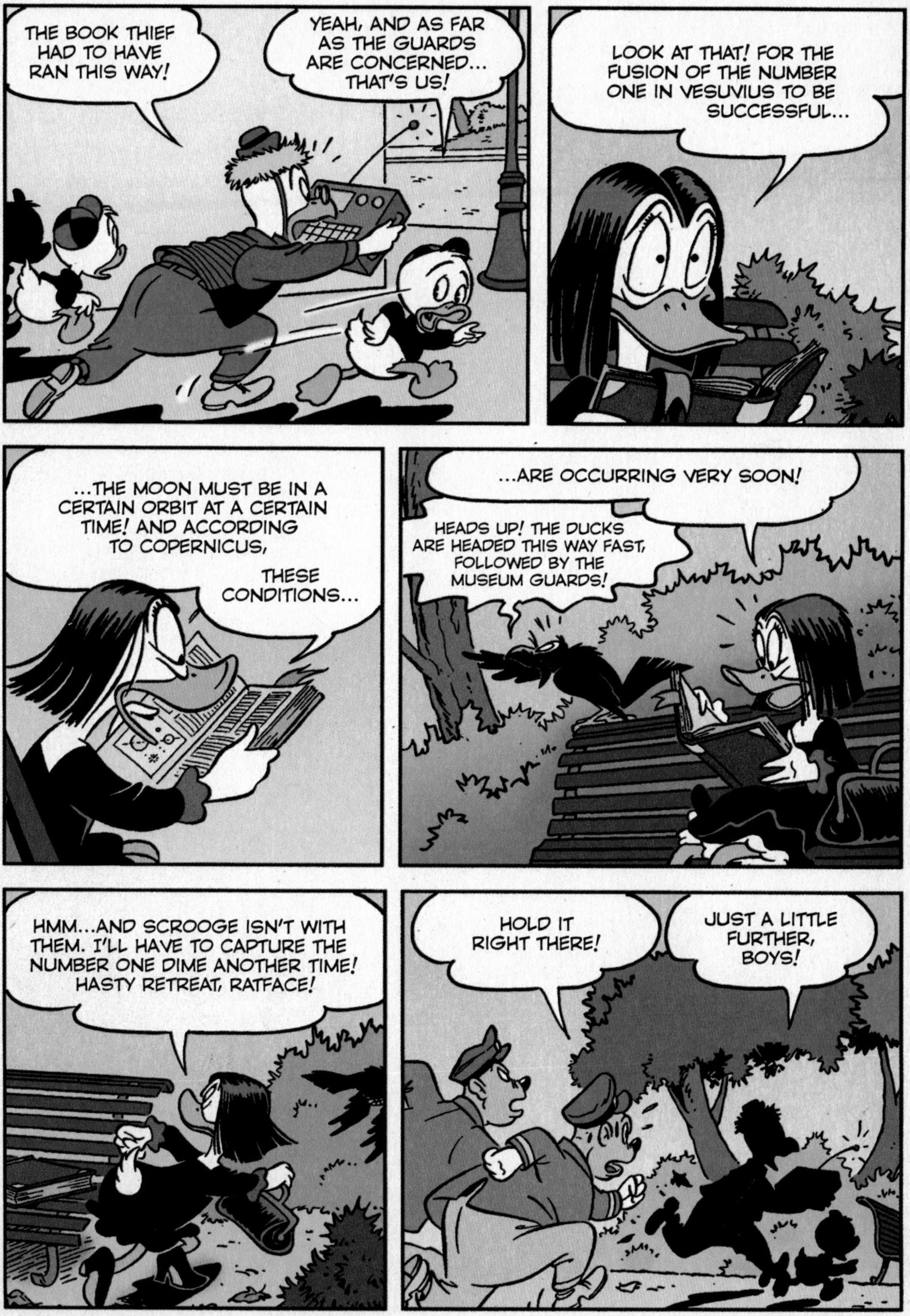
THE BOOK THIEF HAD TO HAVE RAN THIS WAY!
YEAH, AND AS FAR AS THE GUARDS ARE CONCERNED... THAT'S US!
LOOK AT THAT! FOR THE FUSION OF THE NUMBER ONE IN VESUVIUS TO BE SUCCESSFUL...
...THE MOON MUST BE IN A CERTAIN ORBIT AT A CERTAIN TIME! AND ACCORDING TO COPERNICUS,
THESE CONDITIONS...
...ARE OCCURRING VERY SOON!
HEADS UP! THE DUCKS ARE HEADED THIS WAY FAST, FOLLOWED BY THE MUSEUM GUARDS!
HMM...AND SCROOGE ISN'T WITH THEM. I'LL HAVE TO CAPTURE THE NUMBER ONE DIME ANOTHER TIME! HASTY RETREAT, RATFACE!
HOLD IT RIGHT THERE!
JUST A LITTLE FURTHER, BOYS!

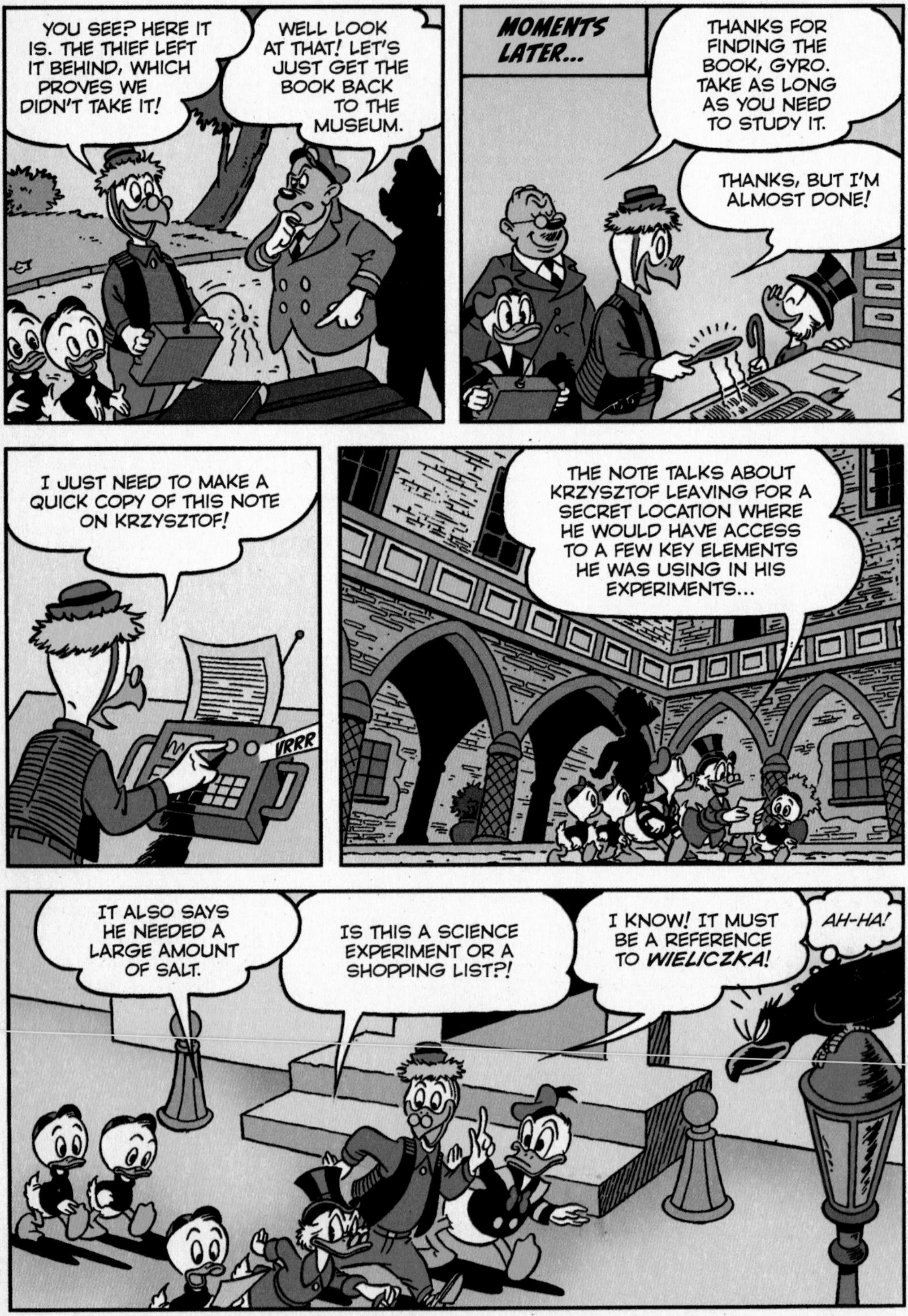
YOU SEE? HERE IT IS. THE THIEF LEFT IT BEHIND, WHICH PROVES WE DIDN'T TAKE IT!
WELL LOOK AT THAT! LET'S JUST GET THE BOOK BACK TO THE MUSEUM.
MOMENTS LATER...
THANKS FOR FINDING THE BOOK, GYRO. TAKE AS LONG AS YOU NEED TO STUDY IT.
THANKS, BUT I'M ALMOST DONE!
I JUST NEED TO MAKE A QUICK COPY OF THIS NOTE ON KRZYSZTOF!
VRRR
THE NOTE TALKS ABOUT KRZYSZTOF LEAVING FOR A SECRET LOCATION WHERE HE WOULD HAVE ACCESS TO A FEW KEY ELEMENTS HE WAS USING IN HIS EXPERIMENTS...
IT ALSO SAYS HE NEEDED A LARGE AMOUNT OF SALT.
IS THIS A SCIENCE EXPERIMENT OR A SHOPPING LIST?!
I KNOW! IT MUST BE A REFERENCE TO WIELICZKA!
AH-HA!

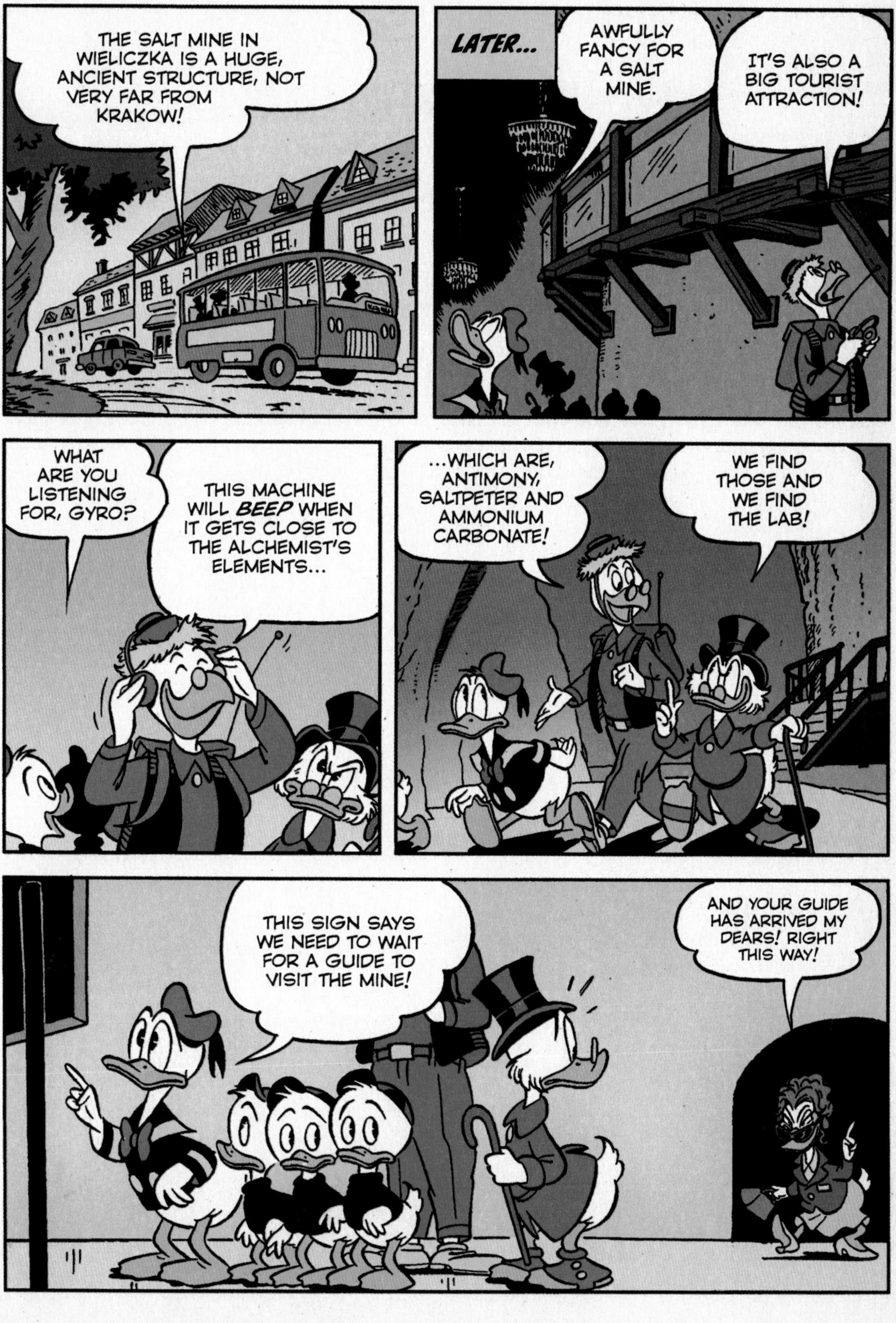
THE SALT MINE IN WIELICZKA IS A HUGE, ANCIENT STRUCTURE, NOT VERY FAR FROM KRAKOW!
LATER...
AWFULLY FANCY FOR A SALT MINE.
IT'S ALSO A BIG TOURIST ATTRACTION!
WHAT ARE YOU LISTENING FOR, GYRO?
THIS MACHINE WILL BEEP WHEN IT GETS CLOSE TO THE ALCHEMIST'S ELEMENTS...
...WHICH ARE, ANTIMONY, SALTPETER AND AMMONIUM CARBONATE!
WE FIND THOSE AND WE FIND THE LAB!
THIS SIGN SAYS WE NEED TO WAIT FOR A GUIDE TO VISIT THE MINE!
AND YOUR GUIDE HAS ARRIVED MY DEARS! RIGHT THIS WAY!

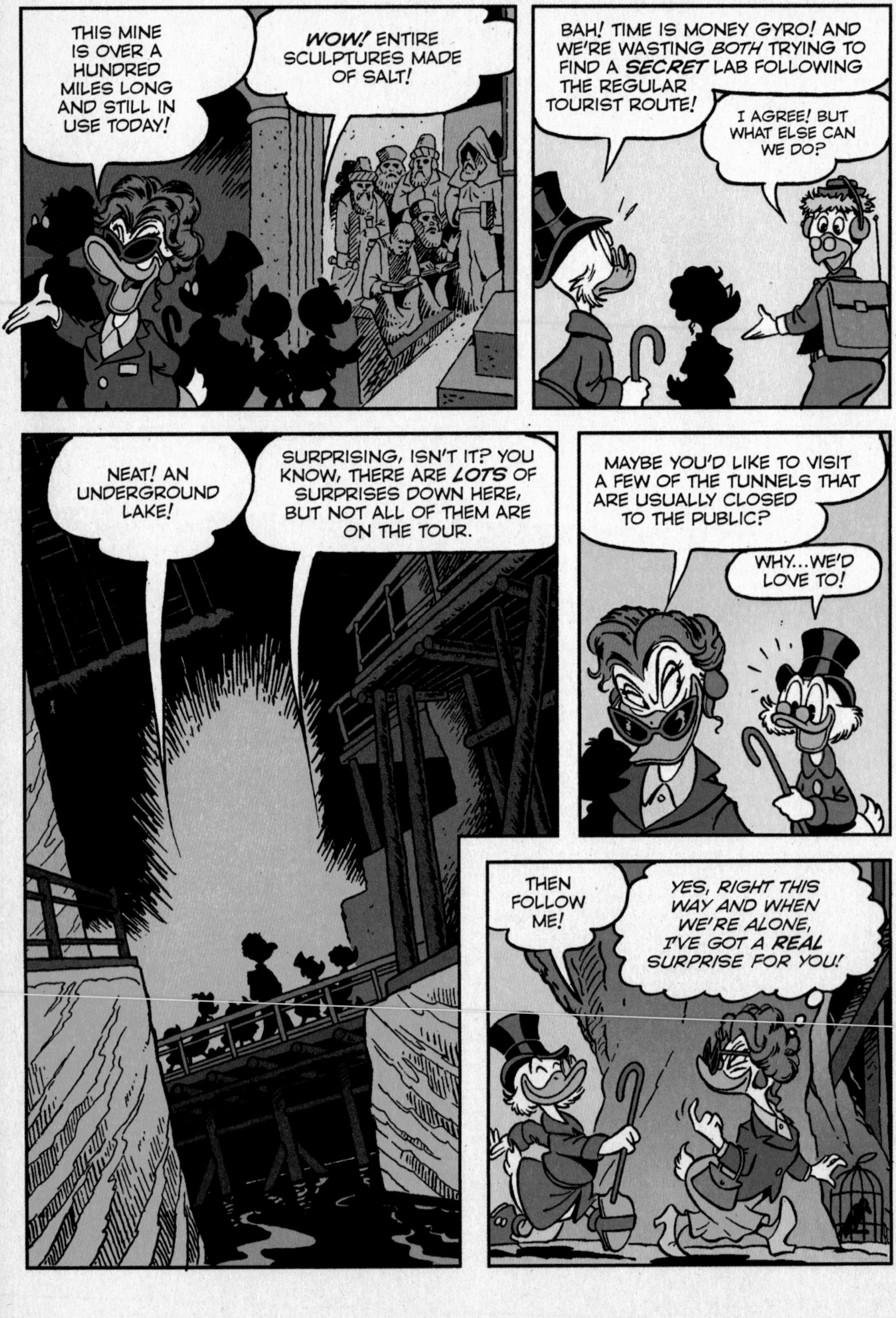
THIS MINE IS OVER A HUNDRED MILES LONG AND STILL IN USE TODAY!
WOW! ENTIRE SCULPTURES MADE OF SALT!
BAH! TIME IS MONEY GYRO! AND WE'RE WASTING BOTH TRYING TO FIND A SECRET LAB FOLLOWING THE REGULAR TOURIST ROUTE!
I AGREE! BUT WHAT ELSE CAN WE DO?
NEAT! AN UNDERGROUND LAKE!
SURPRISING, ISN'T IT? YOU KNOW, THERE ARE LOTS OF SURPRISES DOWN HERE, BUT NOT ALL OF THEM ARE ON THE TOUR.
MAYBE YOU'D LIKE TO VISIT A FEW OF THE TUNNELS THAT ARE USUALLY CLOSED TO THE PUBLIC?
WHY...WE'D LOVE TO!
THEN FOLLOW ME!
YES, RIGHT THIS WAY AND WHEN WE'RE ALONE, I'VE GOT A REAL SURPRISE FOR YOU!

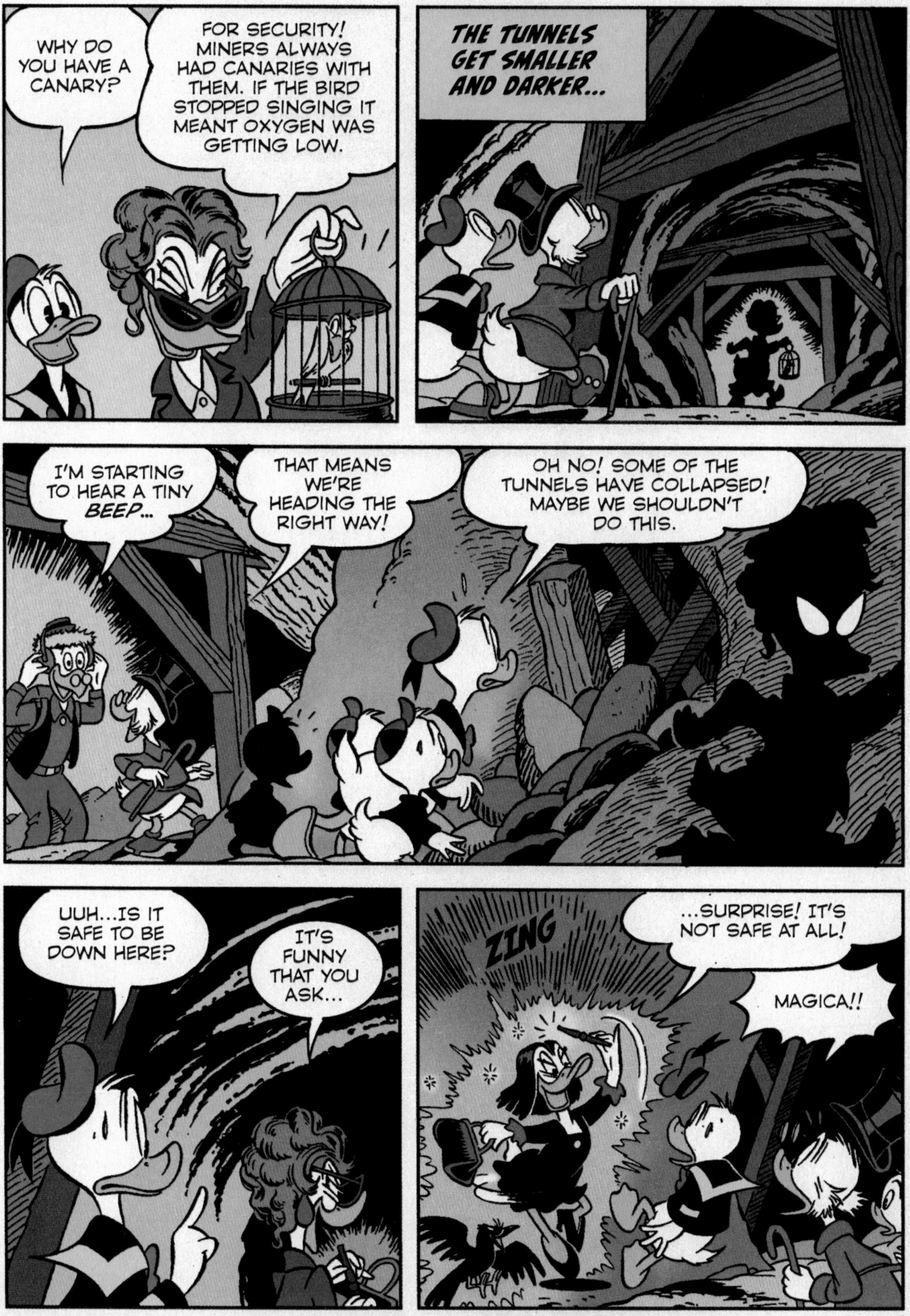
WHY DO YOU HAVE A CANARY?
FOR SECURITY! MINERS ALWAYS HAD CANARIES WITH THEM. IF THE BIRD STOPPED SINGING IT MEANT OXYGEN WAS GETTING LOW.
THE TUNNELS GET SMALLER AND DARKER...
I'M STARTING TO HEAR A TINY BEEP...
THAT MEANS WE'RE HEADING THE RIGHT WAY!
OH NO! SOME OF THE TUNNELS HAVE COLLAPSED! MAYBE WE SHOULDN'T DO THIS.
UUH...IS IT SAFE TO BE DOWN HERE?
IT'S FUNNY THAT YOU ASK...
ZING
...SURPRISE! IT'S NOT SAFE AT ALL!
MAGICA!!

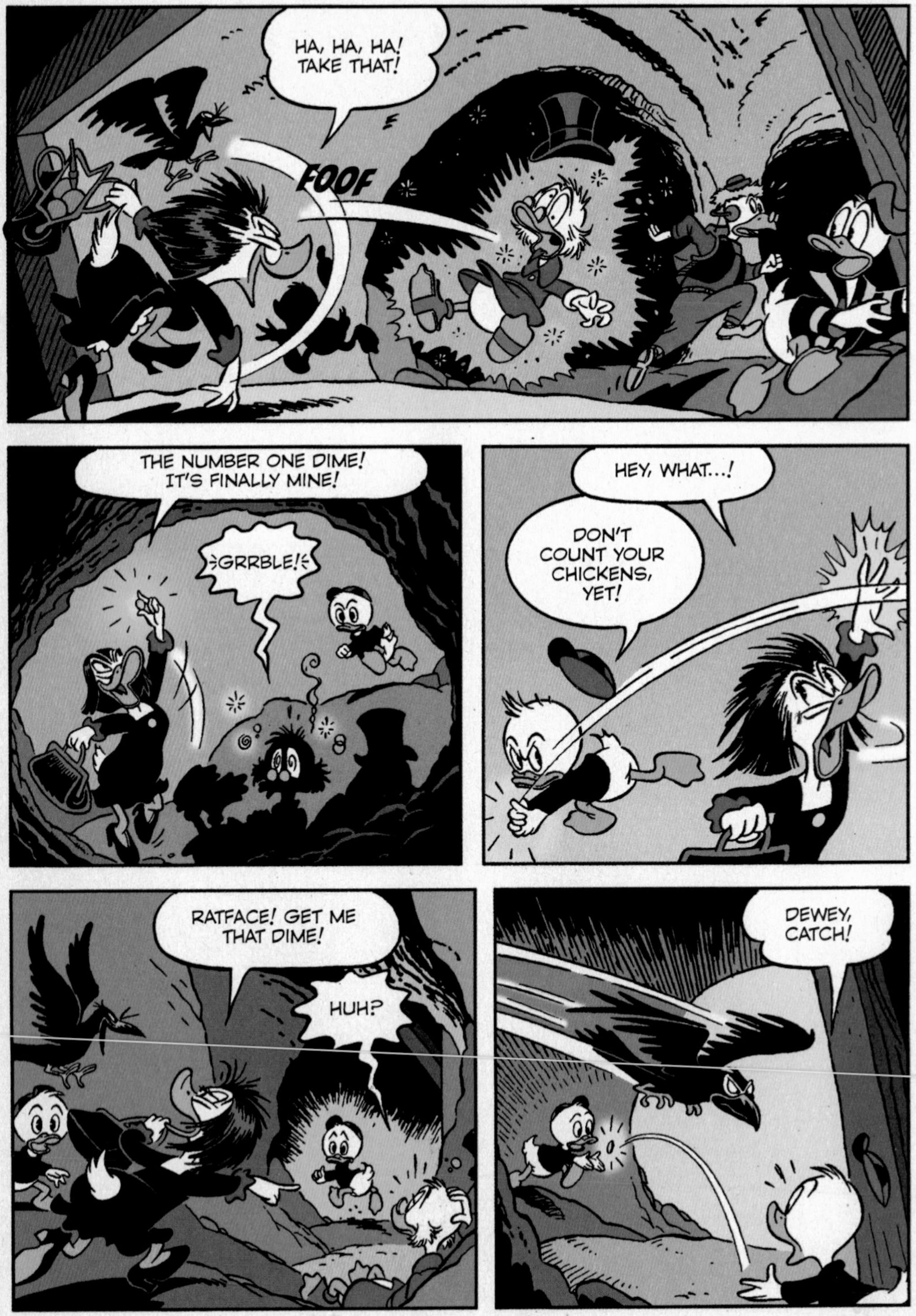
HA, HA, HA! TAKE THAT!
FOOF
THE NUMBER ONE DIME! IT'S FINALLY MINE!
GRRBLE!
HEY, WHAT...!
DON'T COUNT YOUR CHICKENS, YET!
RATFACE! GET ME THAT DIME!
HUH?
DEWEY, CATCH!

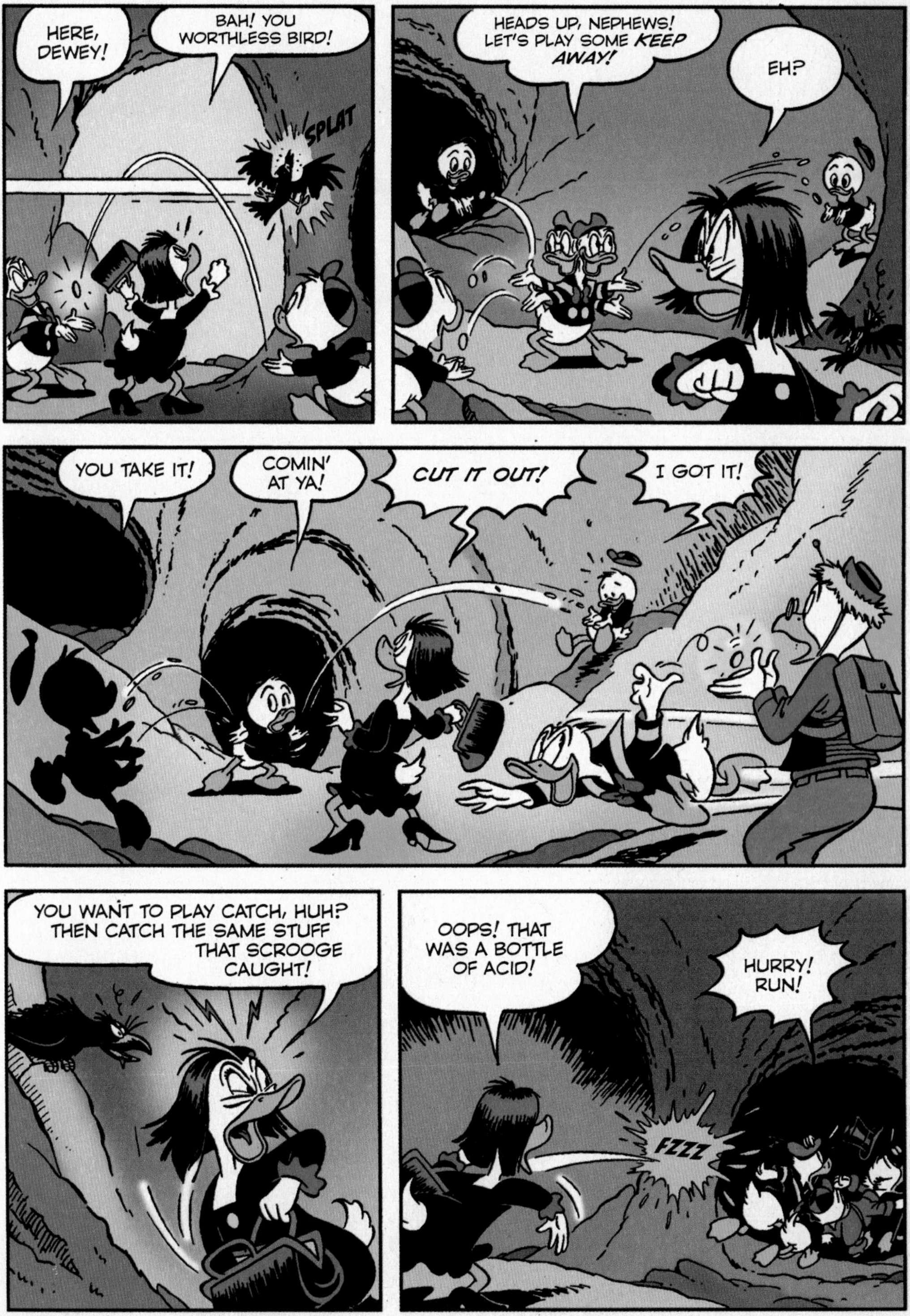
HERE, DEWEY!
BAH! YOU WORTHLESS BIRD!
SPLAT
HEADS UP, NEPHEWS! LET'S PLAY SOME KEEP AWAY!
EH?
YOU TAKE IT!
COMIN' AT YA!
CUT IT OUT!
I GOT IT!
YOU WANT TO PLAY CATCH, HUH? THEN CATCH THE SAME STUFF THAT SCROOGE CAUGHT!
OOPS! THAT WAS A BOTTLE OF ACID!
HURRY! RUN!
FZZZ

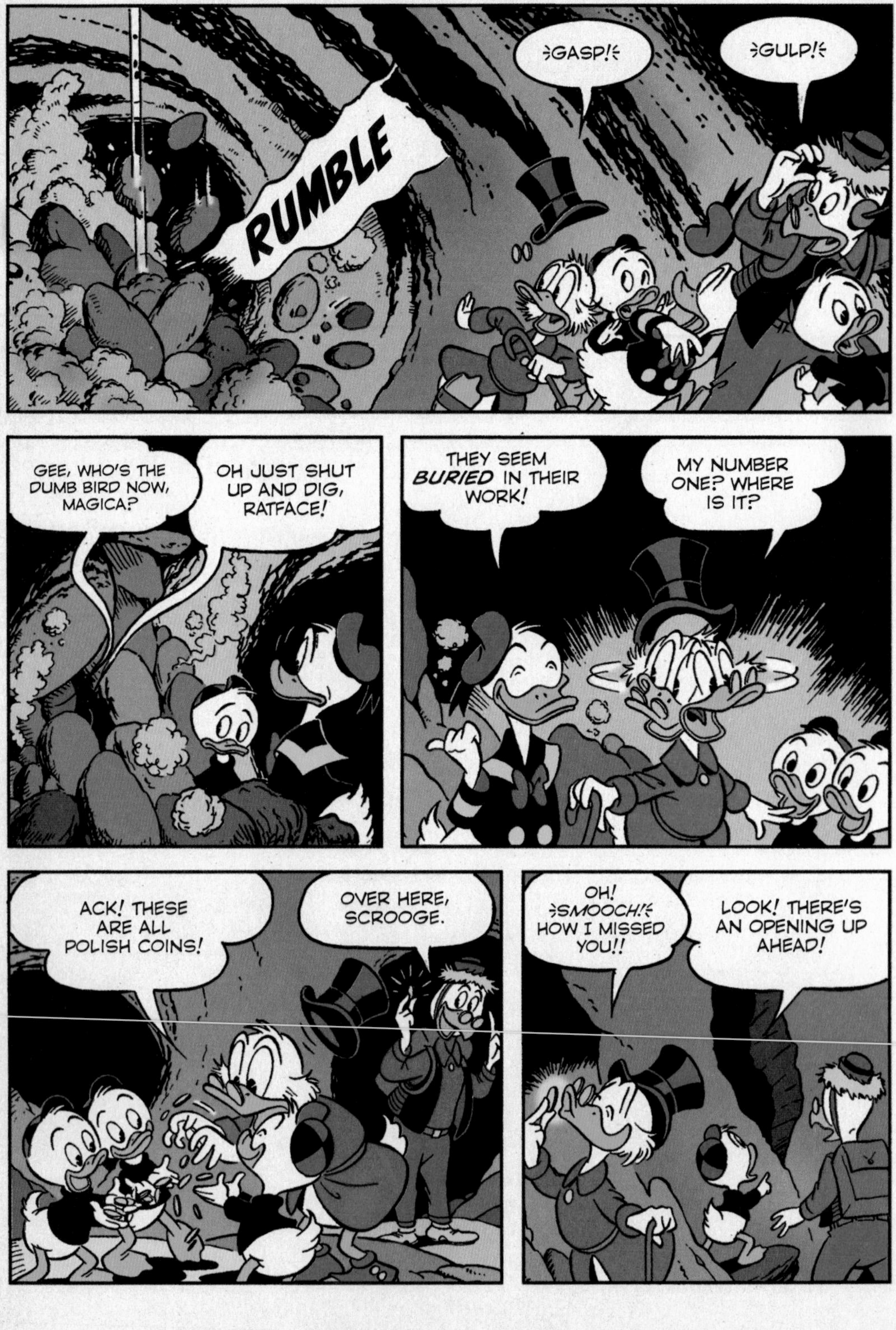
RUMBLE
GASP!
GULP!
GEE, WHO'S THE DUMB BIRD NOW, MAGICA?
OH JUST SHUT UP AND DIG, RATFACE!
THEY SEEM *BURIED* IN THEIR WORK!
MY NUMBER ONE? WHERE IS IT?
ACK! THESE ARE ALL POLISH COINS!
OVER HERE, SCROOGE.
OH! SMOOCH! HOW I MISSED YOU!!
LOOK! THERE'S AN OPENING UP AHEAD!

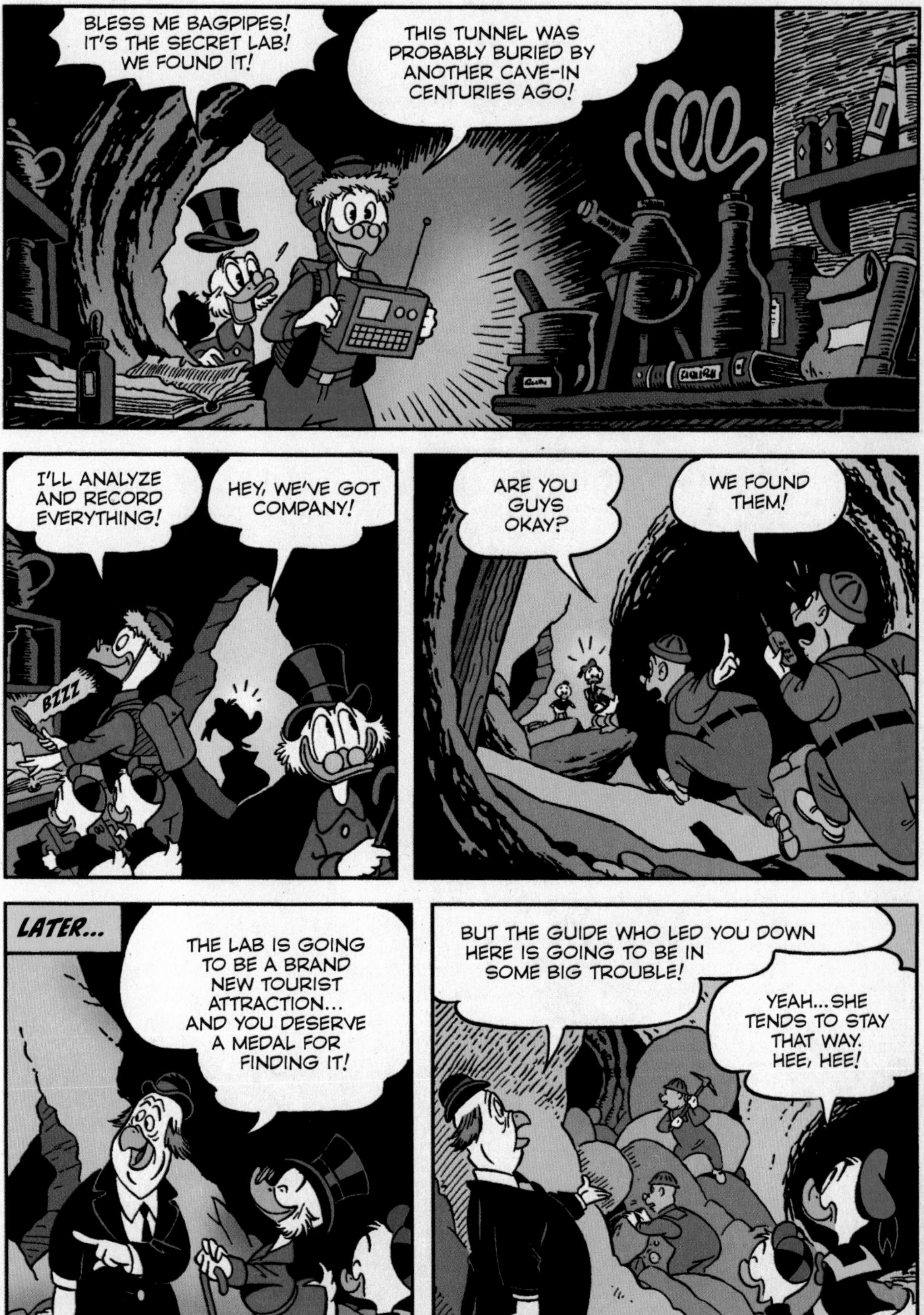
BLESS ME BAGPIPES! IT'S THE SECRET LAB! WE FOUND IT!
THIS TUNNEL WAS PROBABLY BURIED BY ANOTHER CAVE-IN CENTURIES AGO!
I'LL ANALYZE AND RECORD EVERYTHING!
HEY, WE'VE GOT COMPANY!
BZZZ
ARE YOU GUYS OKAY?
WE FOUND THEM!
LATER...
THE LAB IS GOING TO BE A BRAND NEW TOURIST ATTRACTION... AND YOU DESERVE A MEDAL FOR FINDING IT!
BUT THE GUIDE WHO LED YOU DOWN HERE IS GOING TO BE IN SOME BIG TROUBLE!
YEAH...SHE TENDS TO STAY THAT WAY. HEE, HEE!

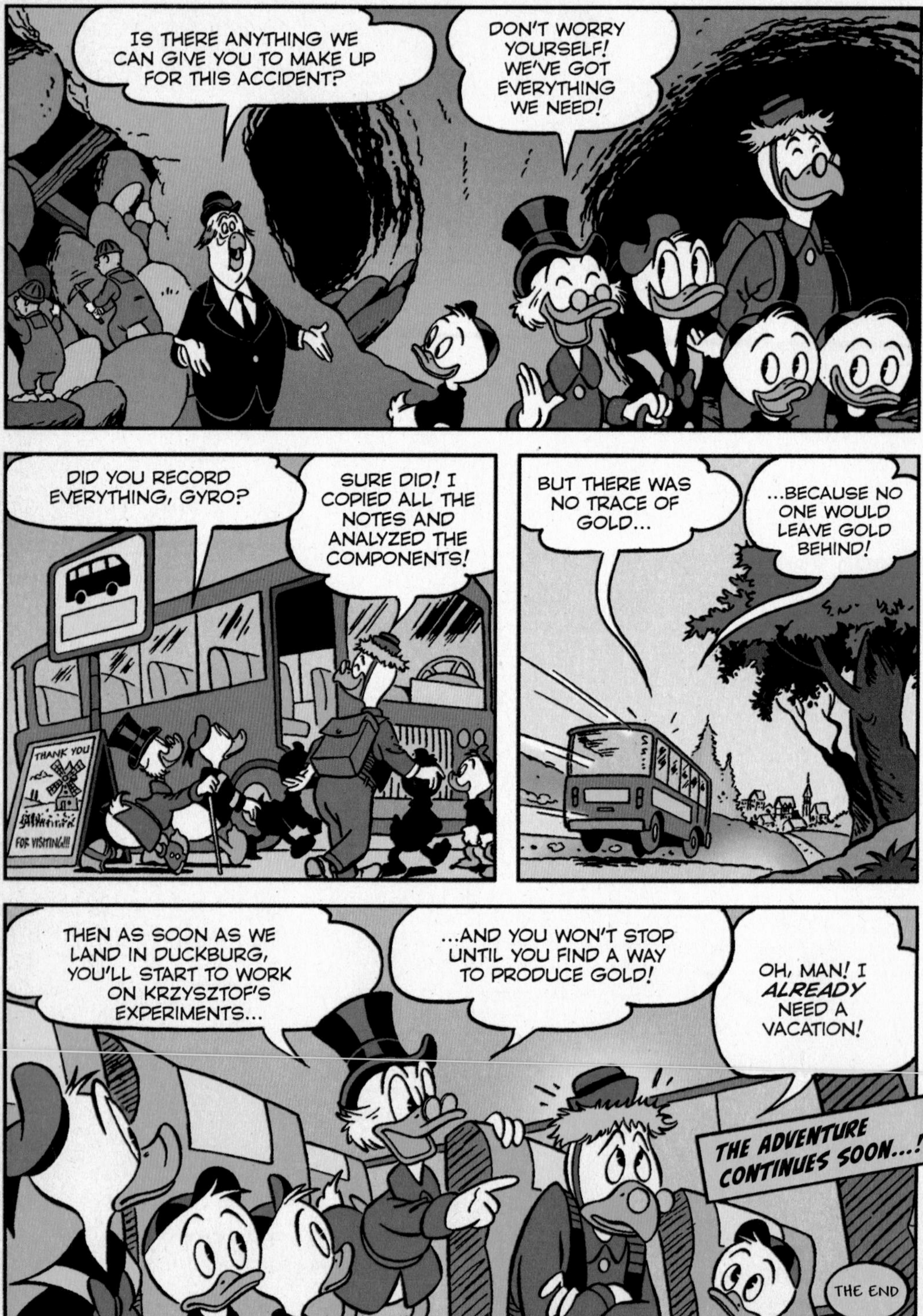
IS THERE ANYTHING WE CAN GIVE YOU TO MAKE UP FOR THIS ACCIDENT?
DON'T WORRY YOURSELF! WE'VE GOT EVERYTHING WE NEED!
DID YOU RECORD EVERYTHING, GYRO?
SURE DID! I COPIED ALL THE NOTES AND ANALYZED THE COMPONENTS!
THANK YOU FOR VISITING!!!
BUT THERE WAS NO TRACE OF GOLD...
...BECAUSE NO ONE WOULD LEAVE GOLD BEHIND!
THEN AS SOON AS WE LAND IN DUCKBURG, YOU'LL START TO WORK ON KRZYSZTOF'S EXPERIMENTS...
...AND YOU WON'T STOP UNTIL YOU FIND A WAY TO PRODUCE GOLD!
OH, MAN! I *ALREADY* NEED A VACATION!
THE ADVENTURE CONTINUES SOON...!
THE END

THE HUNT FOR THE OLD NUMBER ONE

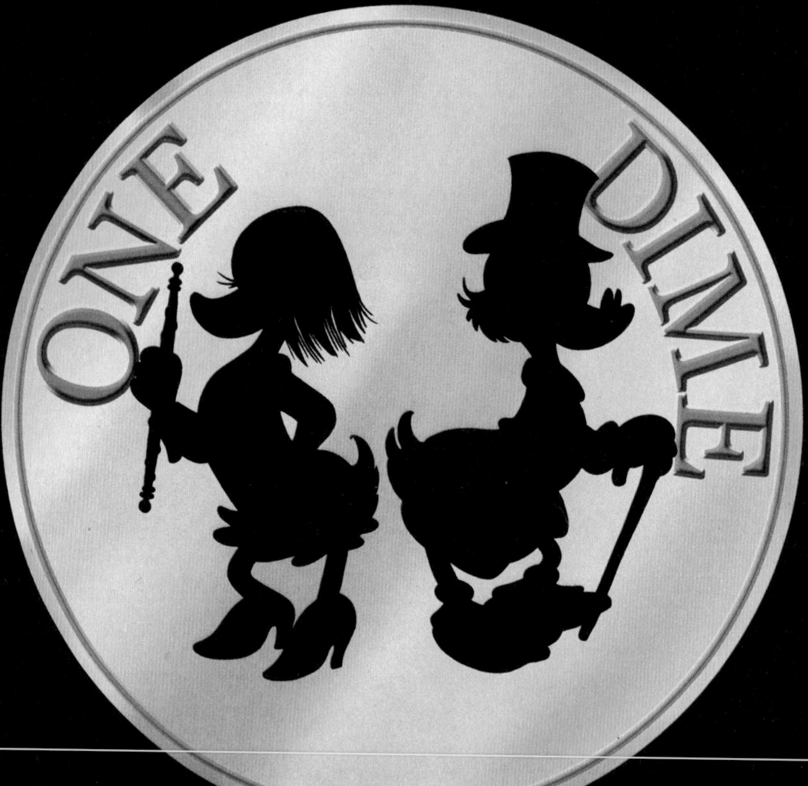
ONE
DIME

CHAPTER THREE

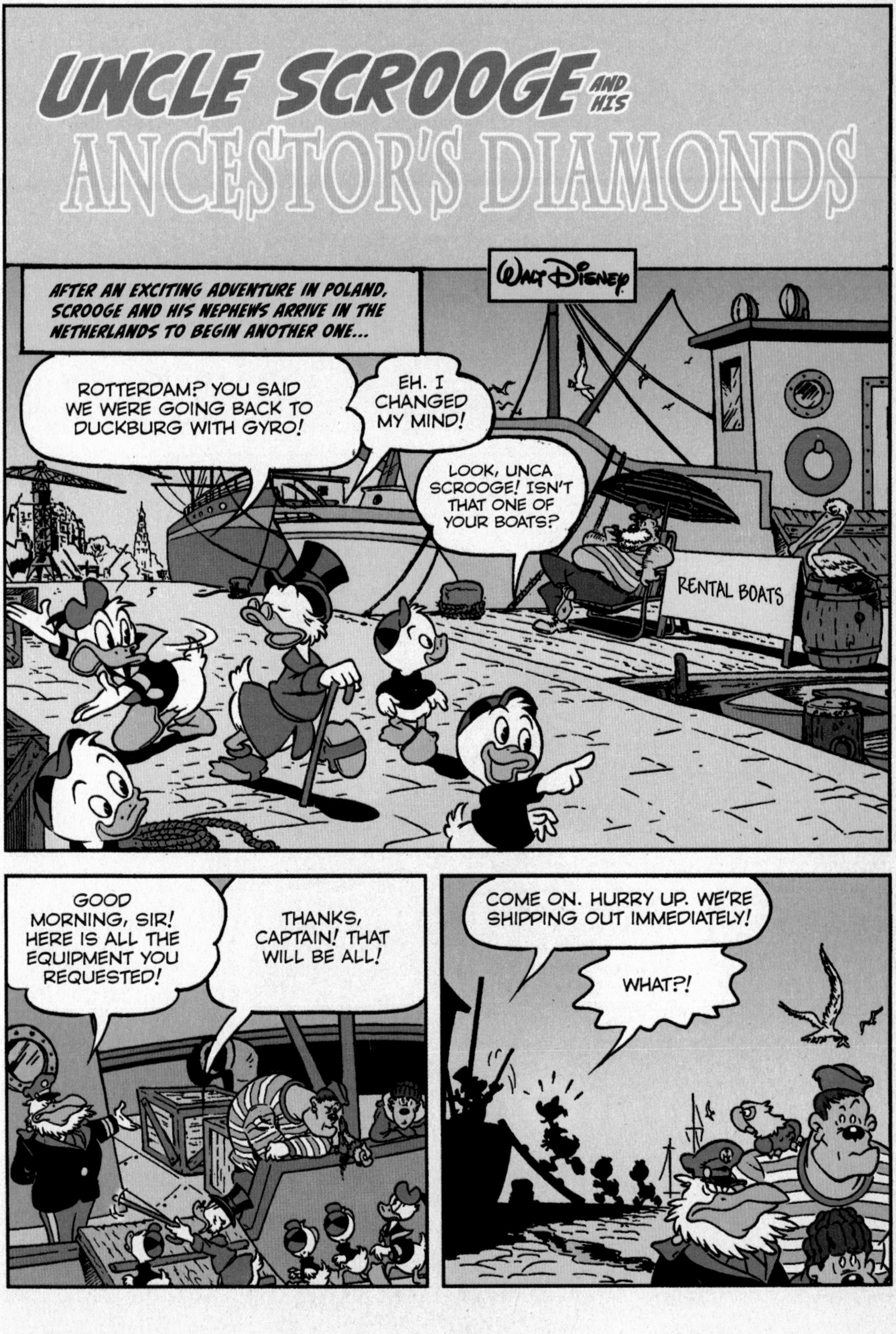
UNCLE SCROOGE AND HIS
ANCESTOR'S DIAMONDS
WALT DISNEY
AFTER AN EXCITING ADVENTURE IN POLAND, SCROOGE AND HIS NEPHEWS ARRIVE IN THE NETHERLANDS TO BEGIN ANOTHER ONE...
ROTTERDAM? YOU SAID WE WERE GOING BACK TO DUCKBURG WITH GYRO!
EH. I CHANGED MY MIND!
LOOK, UNCA SCROOGE! ISN'T THAT ONE OF YOUR BOATS?
RENTAL BOATS
GOOD MORNING, SIR! HERE IS ALL THE EQUIPMENT YOU REQUESTED!
THANKS, CAPTAIN! THAT WILL BE ALL!
COME ON. HURRY UP. WE'RE SHIPPING OUT IMMEDIATELY!
WHAT?!

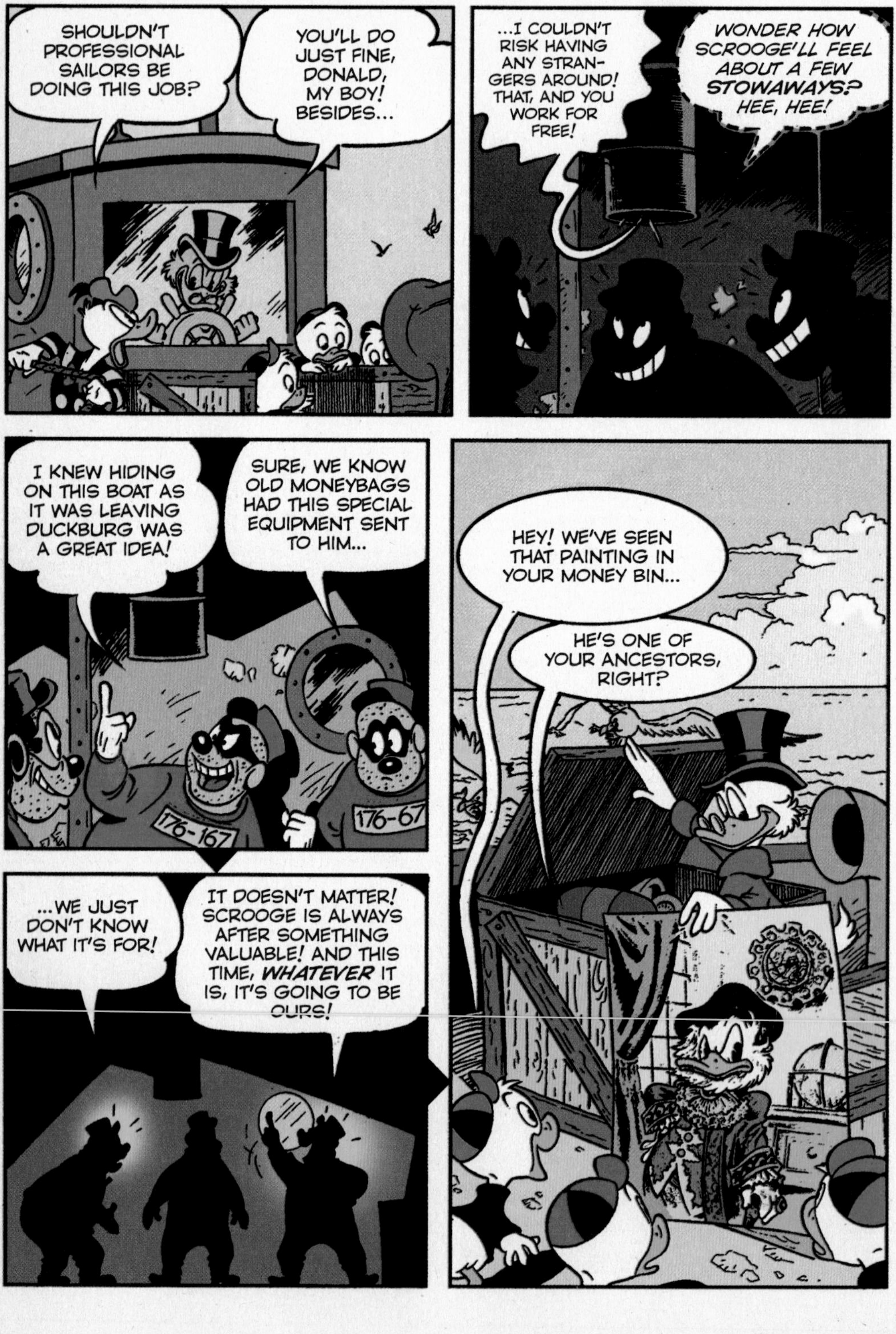
SHOULDN'T PROFESSIONAL SAILORS BE DOING THIS JOB?
YOU'LL DO JUST FINE, DONALD, MY BOY! BESIDES...
...I COULDN'T RISK HAVING ANY STRANGERS AROUND! THAT, AND YOU WORK FOR FREE!
WONDER HOW SCROOGE'LL FEEL ABOUT A FEW STOWAWAYS? HEE, HEE!
I KNEW HIDING ON THIS BOAT AS IT WAS LEAVING DUCKBURG WAS A GREAT IDEA!
SURE, WE KNOW OLD MONEYBAGS HAD THIS SPECIAL EQUIPMENT SENT TO HIM...
176-167
176-67
...WE JUST DON'T KNOW WHAT IT'S FOR!
IT DOESN'T MATTER! SCROOGE IS ALWAYS AFTER SOMETHING VALUABLE! AND THIS TIME, WHATEVER IT IS, IT'S GOING TO BE OURS!
HEY! WE'VE SEEN THAT PAINTING IN YOUR MONEY BIN...
HE'S ONE OF YOUR ANCESTORS, RIGHT?

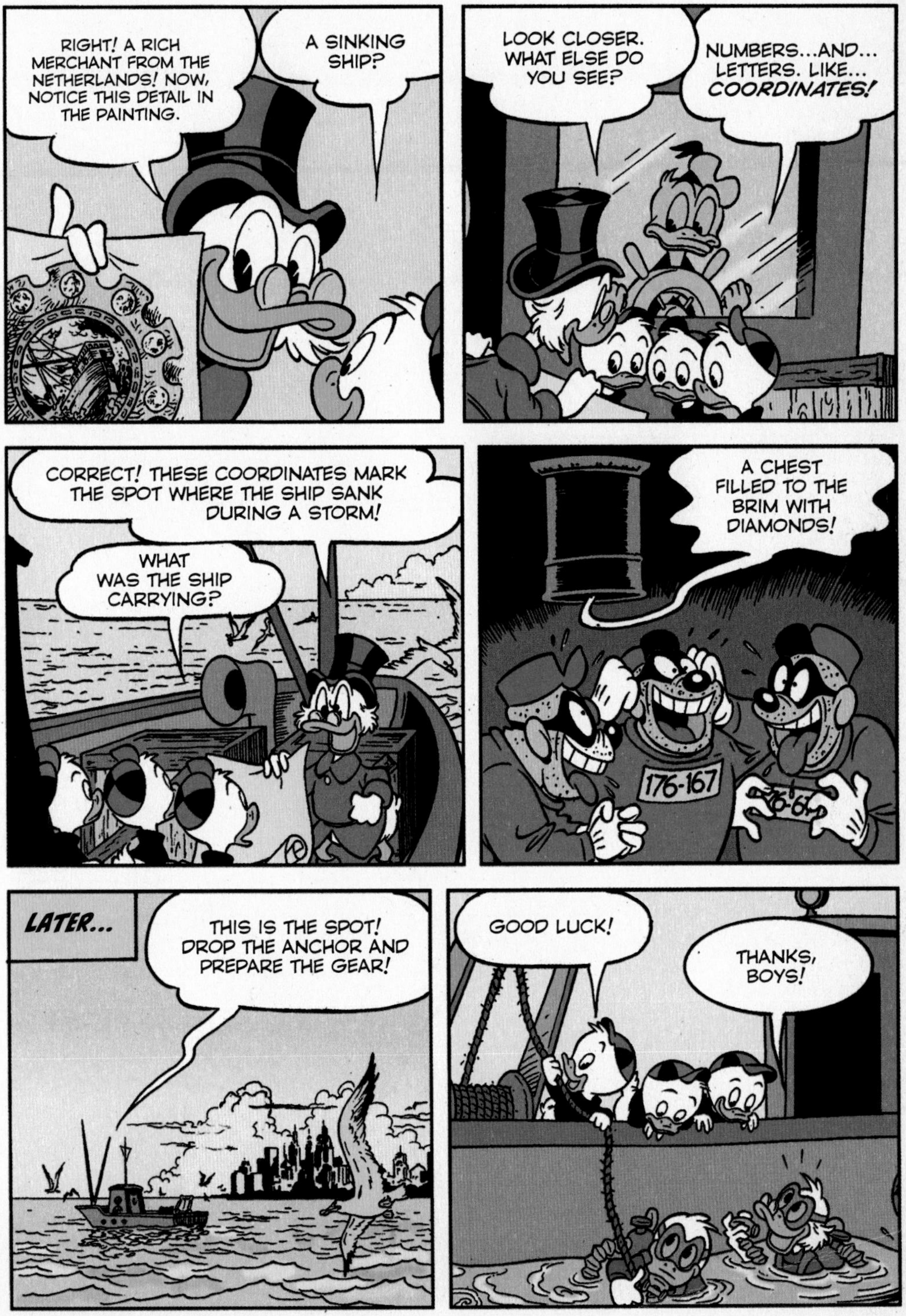
RIGHT! A RICH MERCHANT FROM THE NETHERLANDS! NOW, NOTICE THIS DETAIL IN THE PAINTING.
A SINKING SHIP?
LOOK CLOSER. WHAT ELSE DO YOU SEE?
NUMBERS...AND... LETTERS. LIKE... COORDINATES!
CORRECT! THESE COORDINATES MARK THE SPOT WHERE THE SHIP SANK DURING A STORM!
WHAT WAS THE SHIP CARRYING?
A CHEST FILLED TO THE BRIM WITH DIAMONDS!
176-167
LATER...
THIS IS THE SPOT! DROP THE ANCHOR AND PREPARE THE GEAR!
GOOD LUCK!
THANKS, BOYS!

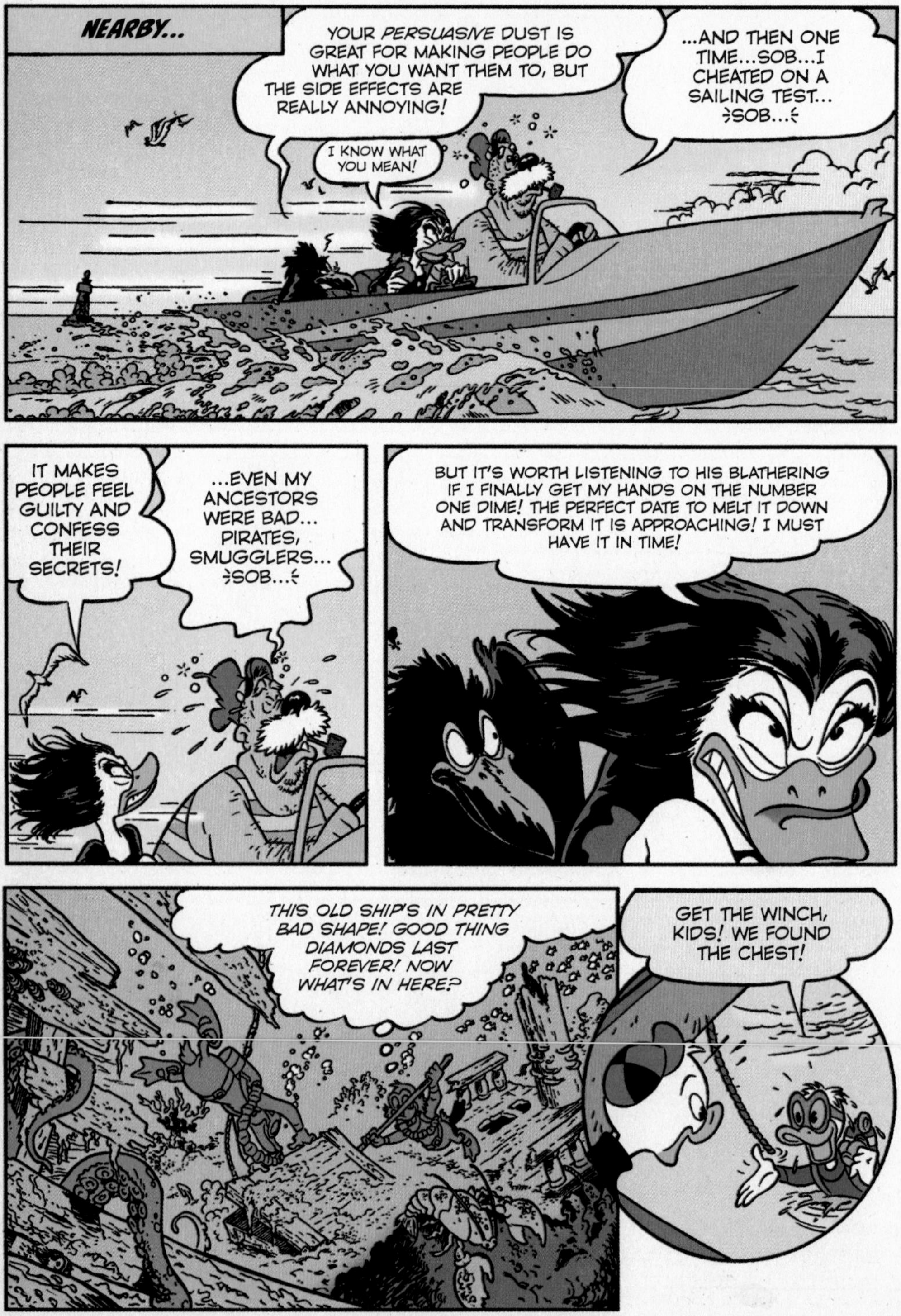
NEARBY...
YOUR *PERSUASIVE* DUST IS GREAT FOR MAKING PEOPLE DO WHAT YOU WANT THEM TO, BUT THE SIDE EFFECTS ARE REALLY ANNOYING!
I KNOW WHAT YOU MEAN!
...AND THEN ONE TIME...SOB...I CHEATED ON A SAILING TEST... SOB...
IT MAKES PEOPLE FEEL GUILTY AND CONFESS THEIR SECRETS!
...EVEN MY ANCESTORS WERE BAD... PIRATES, SMUGGLERS... SOB...
BUT IT'S WORTH LISTENING TO HIS BLATHERING IF I FINALLY GET MY HANDS ON THE NUMBER ONE DIME! THE PERFECT DATE TO MELT IT DOWN AND TRANSFORM IT IS APPROACHING! I MUST HAVE IT IN TIME!
THIS OLD SHIP'S IN PRETTY BAD SHAPE! GOOD THING DIAMONDS LAST FOREVER! NOW WHAT'S IN HERE?
GET THE WINCH, KIDS! WE FOUND THE CHEST!

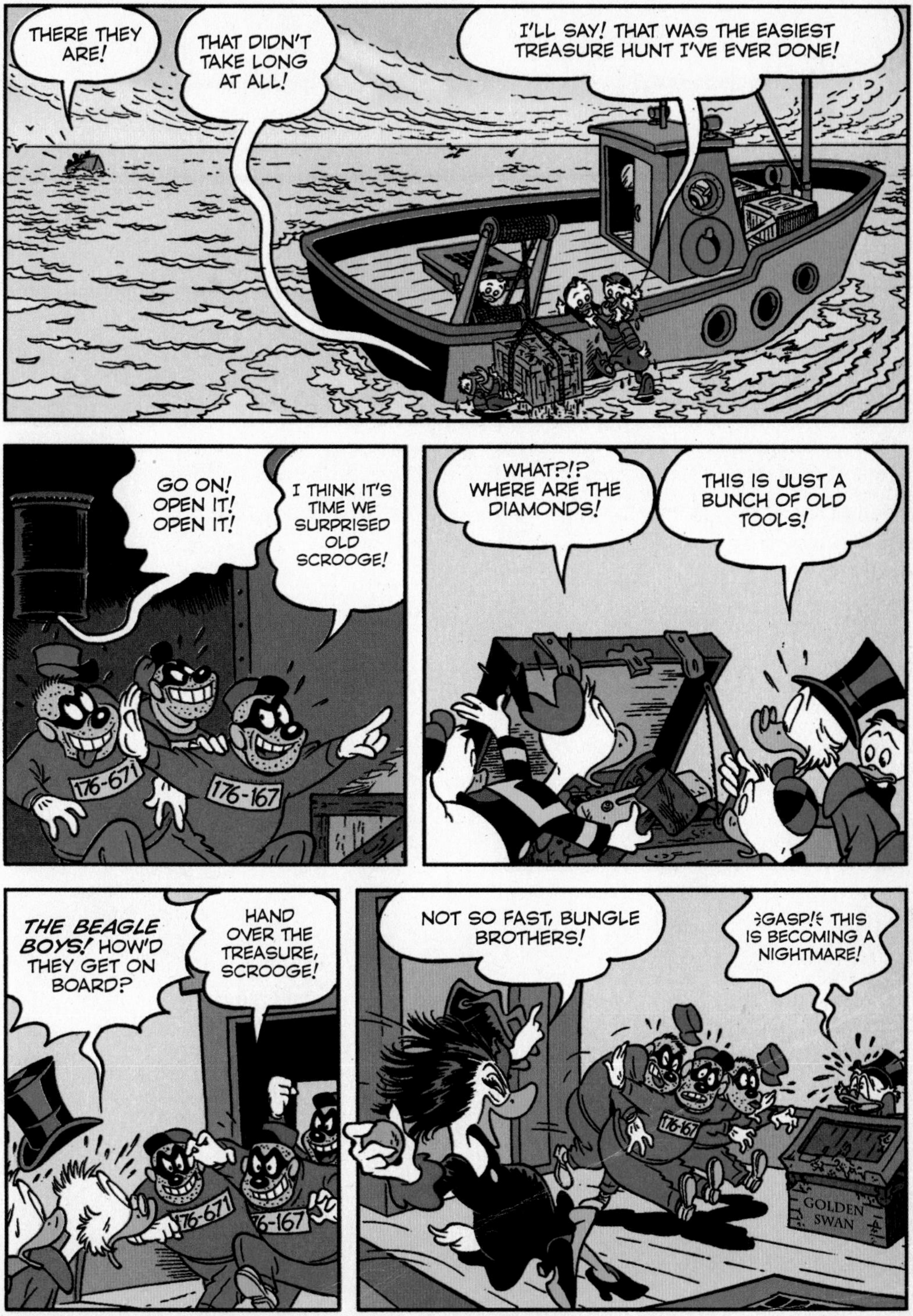
THERE THEY ARE!
THAT DIDN'T TAKE LONG AT ALL!
I'LL SAY! THAT WAS THE EASIEST TREASURE HUNT I'VE EVER DONE!
GO ON! OPEN IT! OPEN IT!
I THINK IT'S TIME WE SURPRISED OLD SCROOGE!
176-671
176-167
WHAT?!? WHERE ARE THE DIAMONDS!
THIS IS JUST A BUNCH OF OLD TOOLS!
THE BEAGLE BOYS! HOW'D THEY GET ON BOARD?
HAND OVER THE TREASURE, SCROOGE!
176-671
176-167
NOT SO FAST, BUNGLE BROTHERS!
GASP! THIS IS BECOMING A NIGHTMARE!
176-167
GOLDEN SWAN

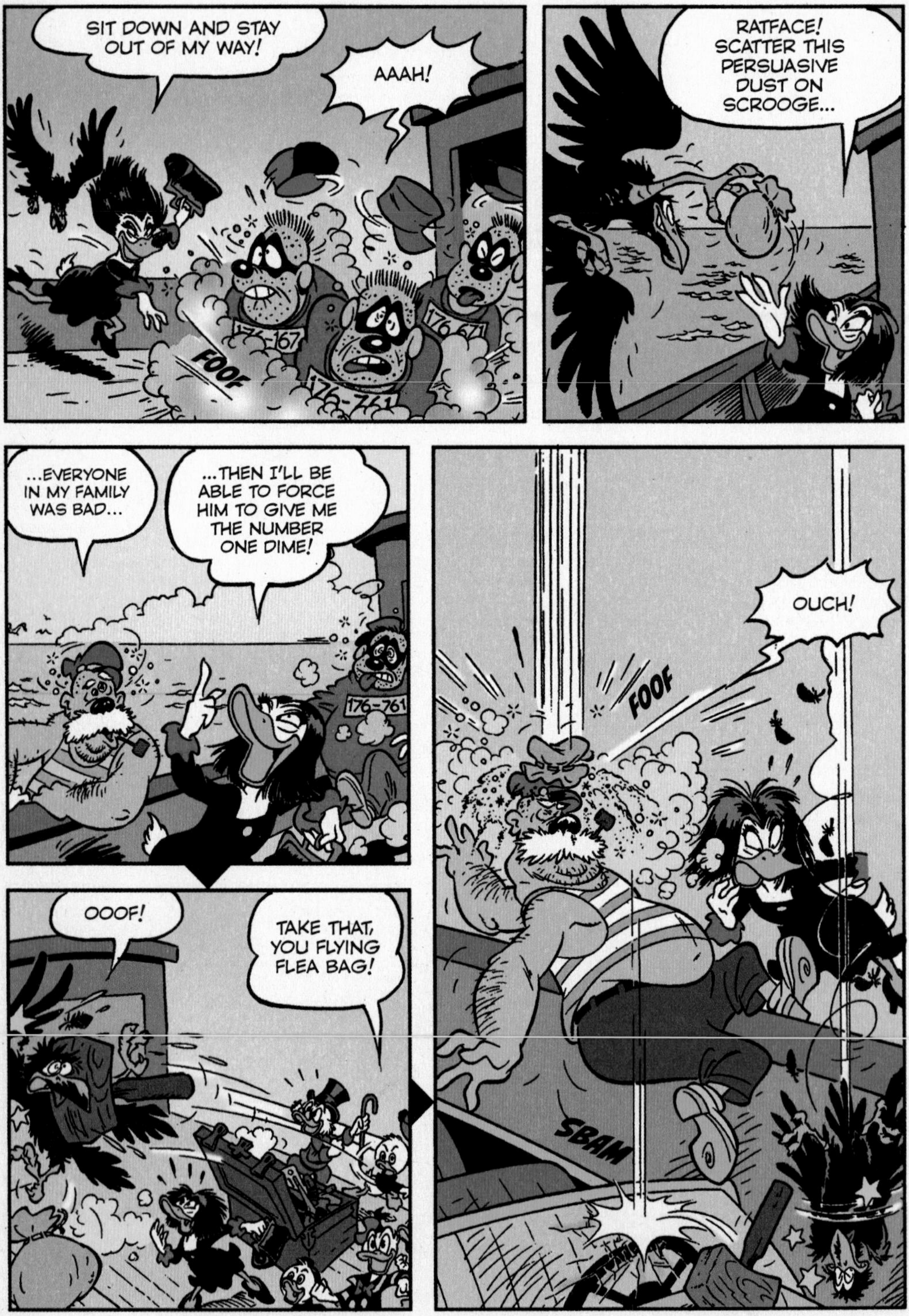
SIT DOWN AND STAY OUT OF MY WAY!
AAAH!
176-167
176-671
176-761
FOOF
RATFACE! SCATTER THIS PERSUASIVE DUST ON SCROOGE...
...EVERYONE IN MY FAMILY WAS BAD...
...THEN I'LL BE ABLE TO FORCE HIM TO GIVE ME THE NUMBER ONE DIME!
176-761
OOOF!
TAKE THAT, YOU FLYING FLEA BAG!
OUCH!
FOOF
SBAM

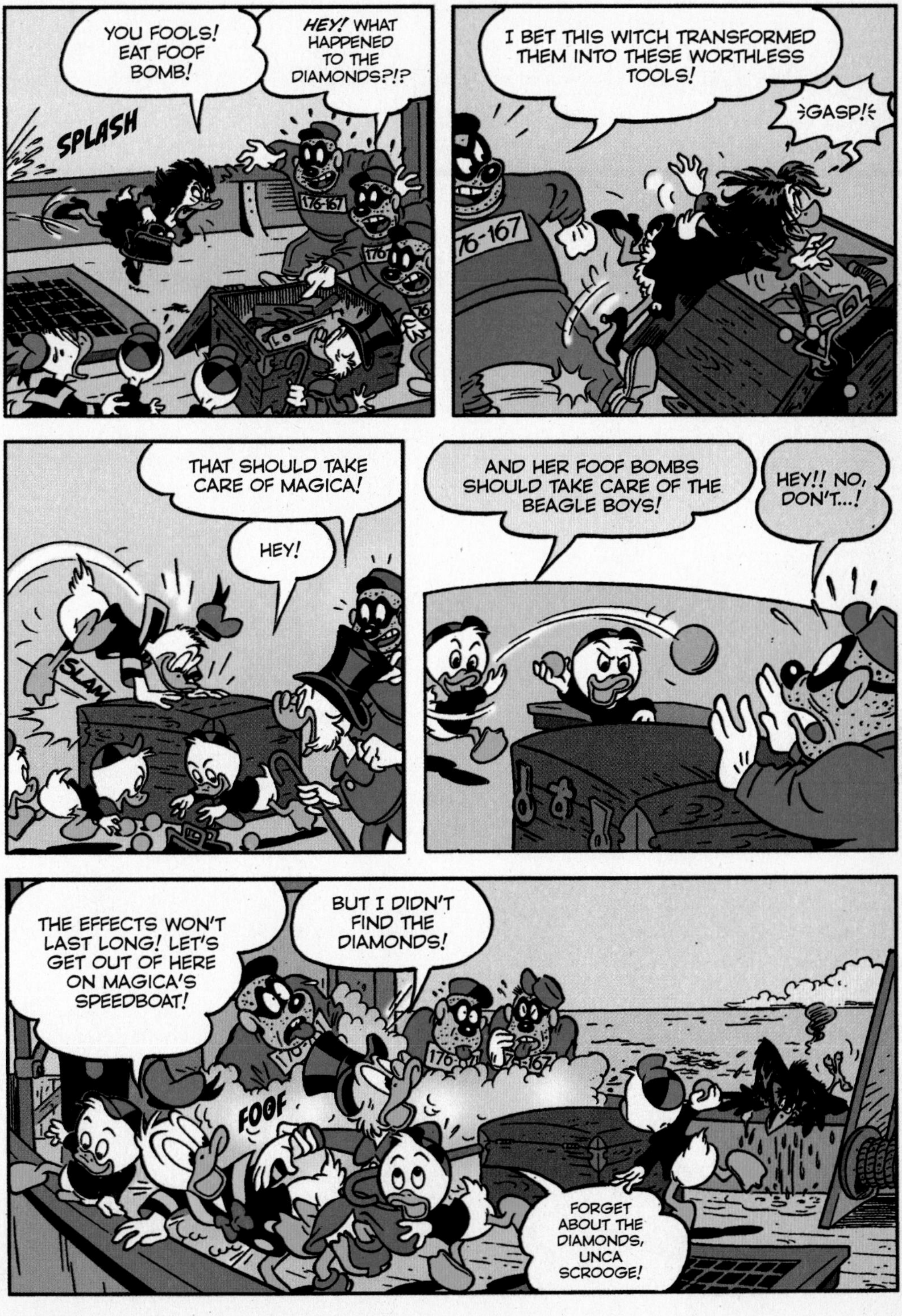
YOU FOOLS! EAT FOOF BOMB!
HEY! WHAT HAPPENED TO THE DIAMONDS?!?
SPLASH
I BET THIS WITCH TRANSFORMED THEM INTO THESE WORTHLESS TOOLS!
GASP!
THAT SHOULD TAKE CARE OF MAGICA!
HEY!
SLAM
AND HER FOOF BOMBS SHOULD TAKE CARE OF THE BEAGLE BOYS!
HEY!! NO, DON'T...!
THE EFFECTS WON'T LAST LONG! LET'S GET OUT OF HERE ON MAGICA'S SPEEDBOAT!
BUT I DIDN'T FIND THE DIAMONDS!
FOOF
FORGET ABOUT THE DIAMONDS, UNCA SCROOGE!

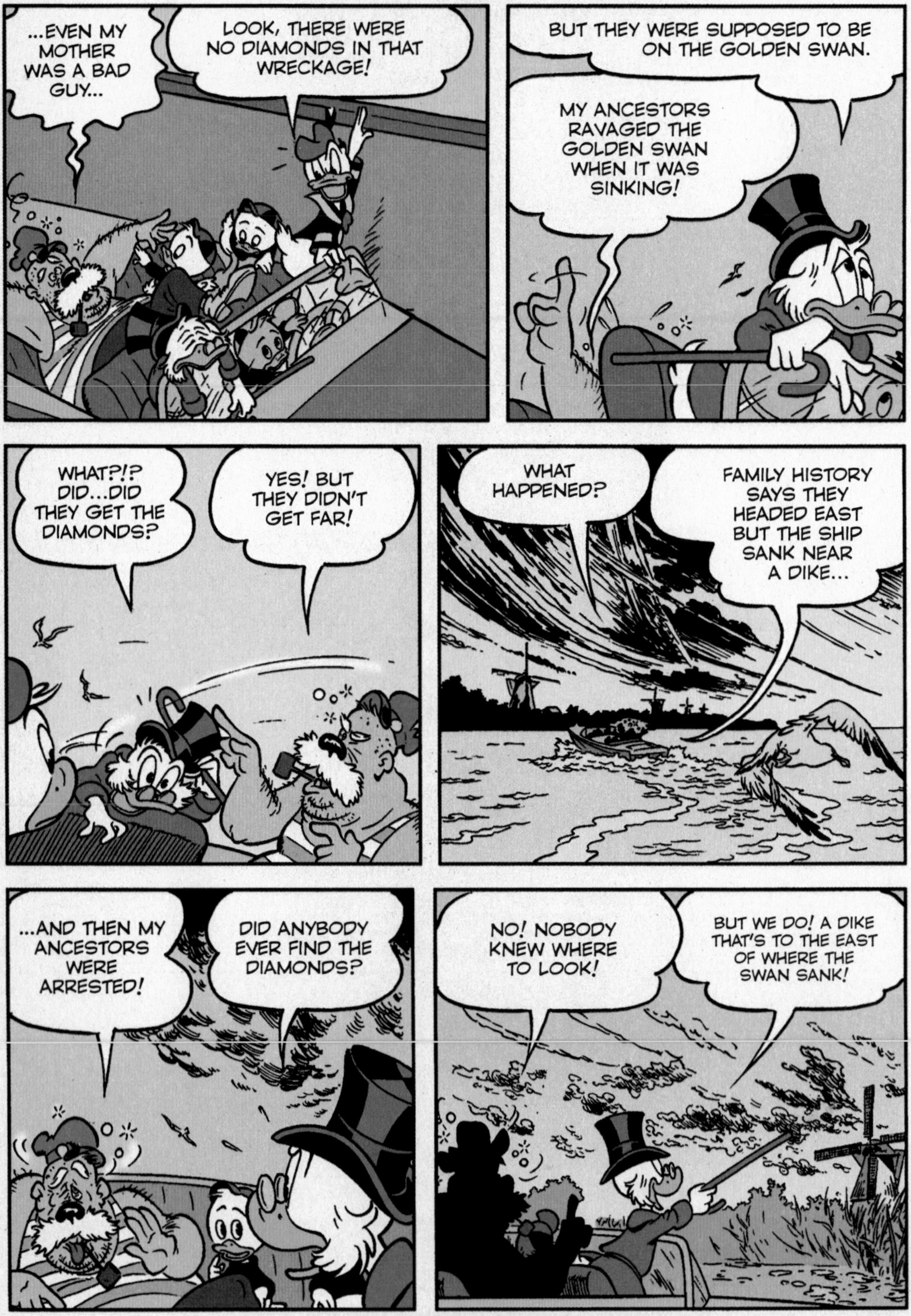
...EVEN MY MOTHER WAS A BAD GUY...
LOOK, THERE WERE NO DIAMONDS IN THAT WRECKAGE!
BUT THEY WERE SUPPOSED TO BE ON THE GOLDEN SWAN.
MY ANCESTORS RAVAGED THE GOLDEN SWAN WHEN IT WAS SINKING!
WHAT?!? DID...DID THEY GET THE DIAMONDS?
YES! BUT THEY DIDN'T GET FAR!
WHAT HAPPENED?
FAMILY HISTORY SAYS THEY HEADED EAST BUT THE SHIP SANK NEAR A DIKE...
...AND THEN MY ANCESTORS WERE ARRESTED!
DID ANYBODY EVER FIND THE DIAMONDS?
NO! NOBODY KNEW WHERE TO LOOK!
BUT WE DO! A DIKE THAT'S TO THE EAST OF WHERE THE SWAN SANK!

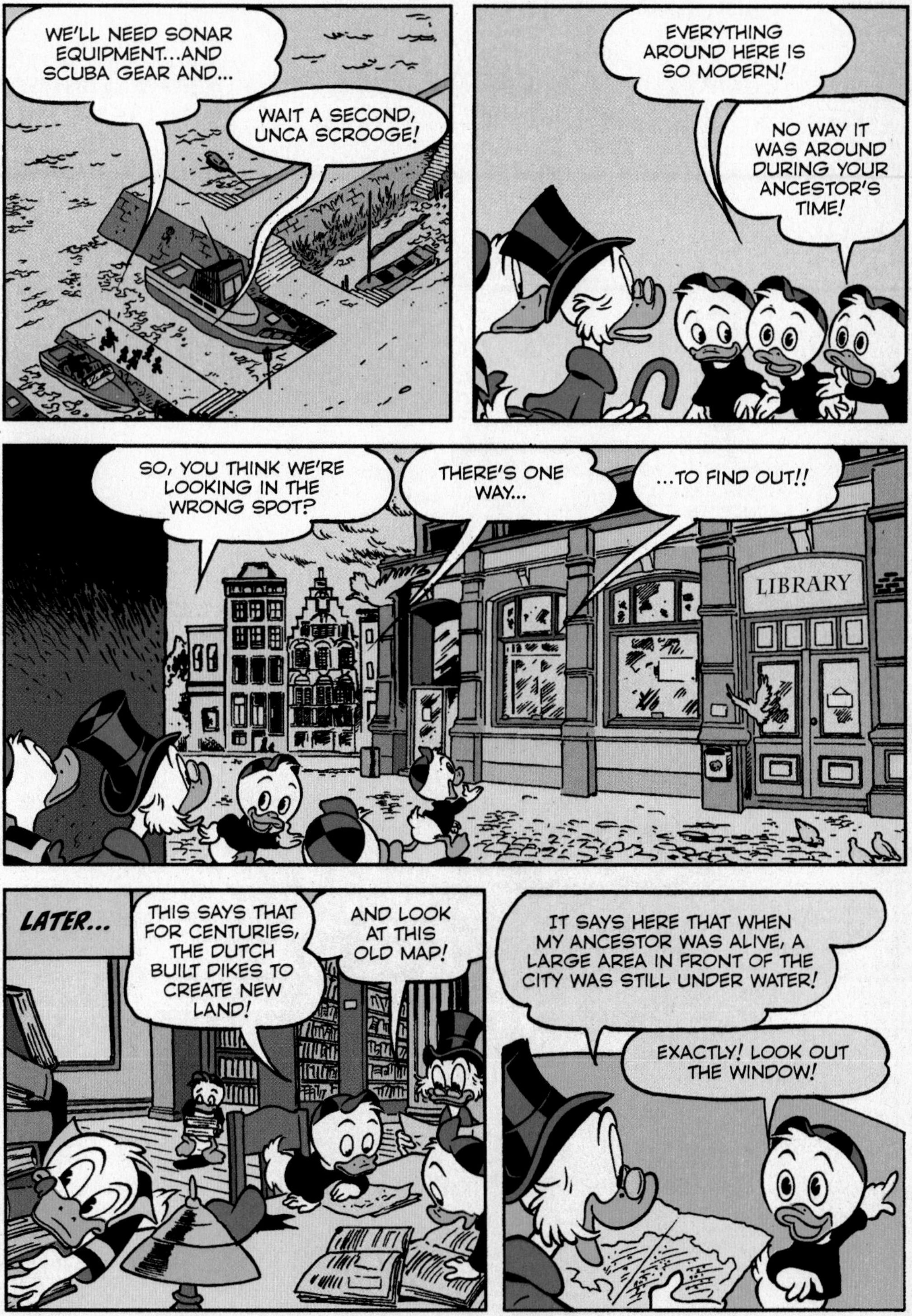
WE'LL NEED SONAR EQUIPMENT...AND SCUBA GEAR AND...
WAIT A SECOND, UNCA SCROOGE!
EVERYTHING AROUND HERE IS SO MODERN!
NO WAY IT WAS AROUND DURING YOUR ANCESTOR'S TIME!
SO, YOU THINK WE'RE LOOKING IN THE WRONG SPOT?
THERE'S ONE WAY...
...TO FIND OUT!!
LIBRARY
LATER...
THIS SAYS THAT FOR CENTURIES, THE DUTCH BUILT DIKES TO CREATE NEW LAND!
AND LOOK AT THIS OLD MAP!
IT SAYS HERE THAT WHEN MY ANCESTOR WAS ALIVE, A LARGE AREA IN FRONT OF THE CITY WAS STILL UNDER WATER!
EXACTLY! LOOK OUT THE WINDOW!

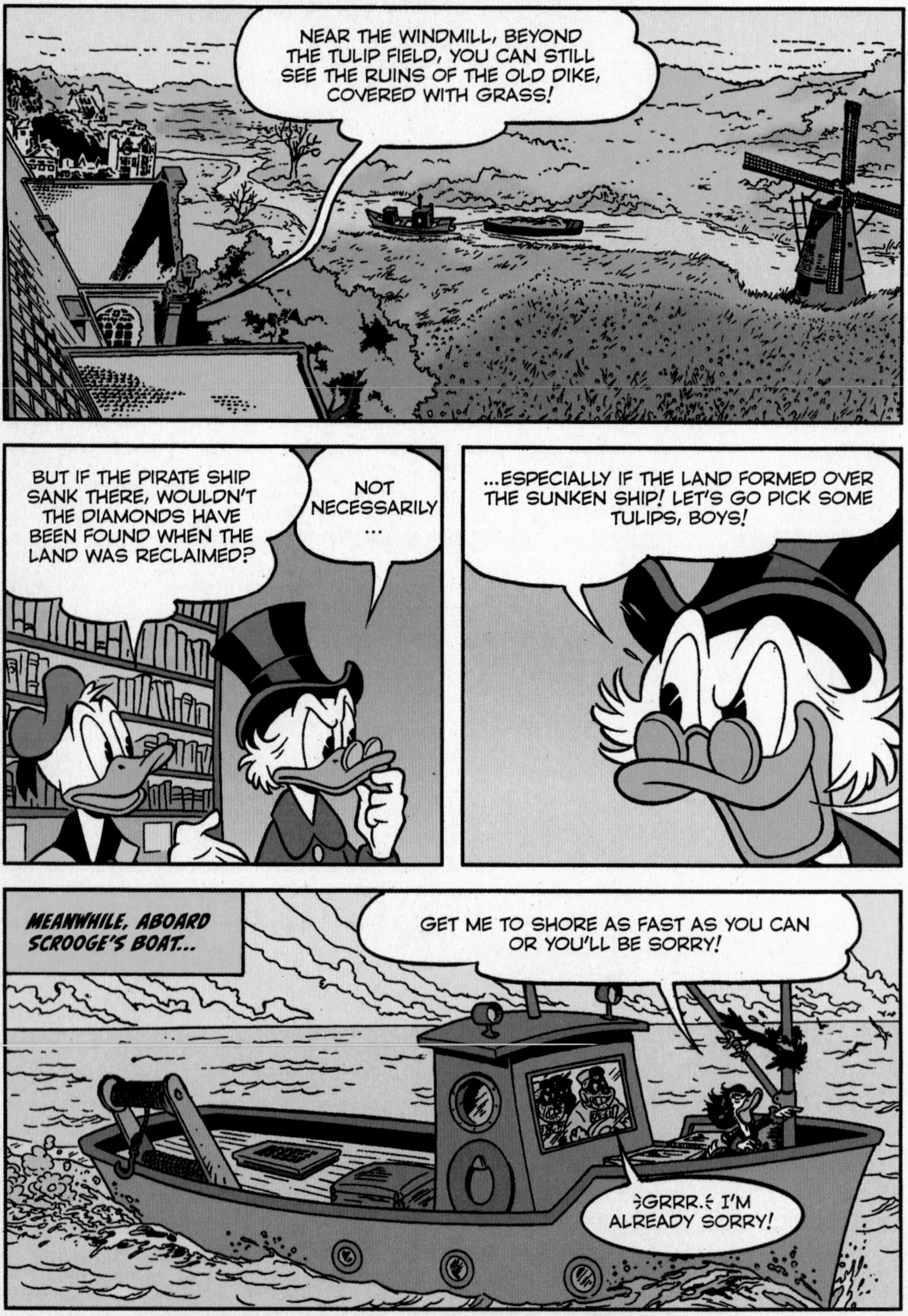
NEAR THE WINDMILL, BEYOND THE TULIP FIELD, YOU CAN STILL SEE THE RUINS OF THE OLD DIKE, COVERED WITH GRASS!
BUT IF THE PIRATE SHIP SANK THERE, WOULDN'T THE DIAMONDS HAVE BEEN FOUND WHEN THE LAND WAS RECLAIMED?
NOT NECESSARILY ...
...ESPECIALLY IF THE LAND FORMED OVER THE SUNKEN SHIP! LET'S GO PICK SOME TULIPS, BOYS!
MEANWHILE, ABOARD SCROOGE'S BOAT...
GET ME TO SHORE AS FAST AS YOU CAN OR YOU'LL BE SORRY!
GRRR. I'M ALREADY SORRY!

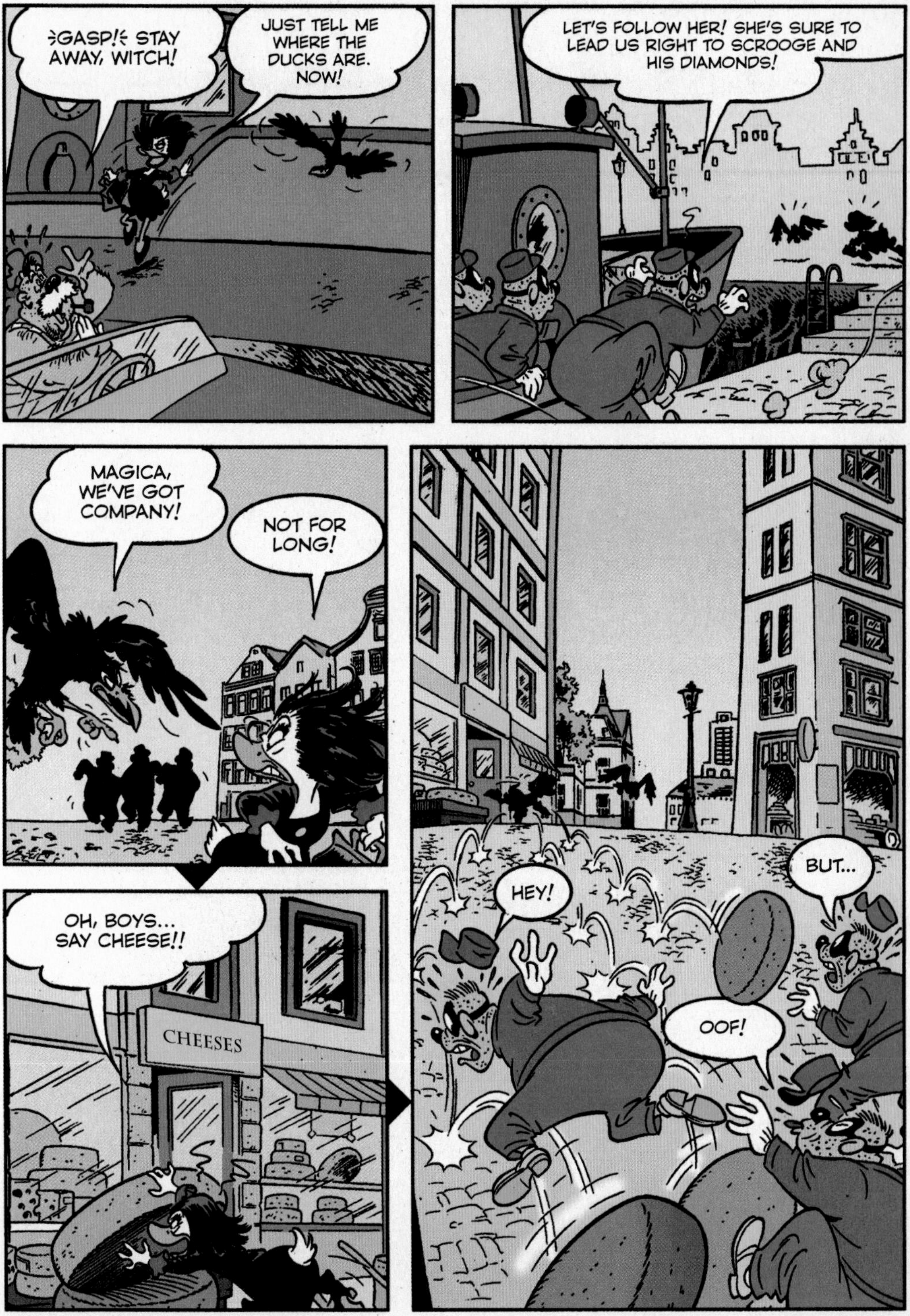

⋟GASP!⋞ STAY AWAY, WITCH!
JUST TELL ME WHERE THE DUCKS ARE. NOW!
LET'S FOLLOW HER! SHE'S SURE TO LEAD US RIGHT TO SCROOGE AND HIS DIAMONDS!
MAGICA, WE'VE GOT COMPANY!
NOT FOR LONG!
OH, BOYS... SAY CHEESE!!
CHEESES
HEY!
BUT...
OOF!

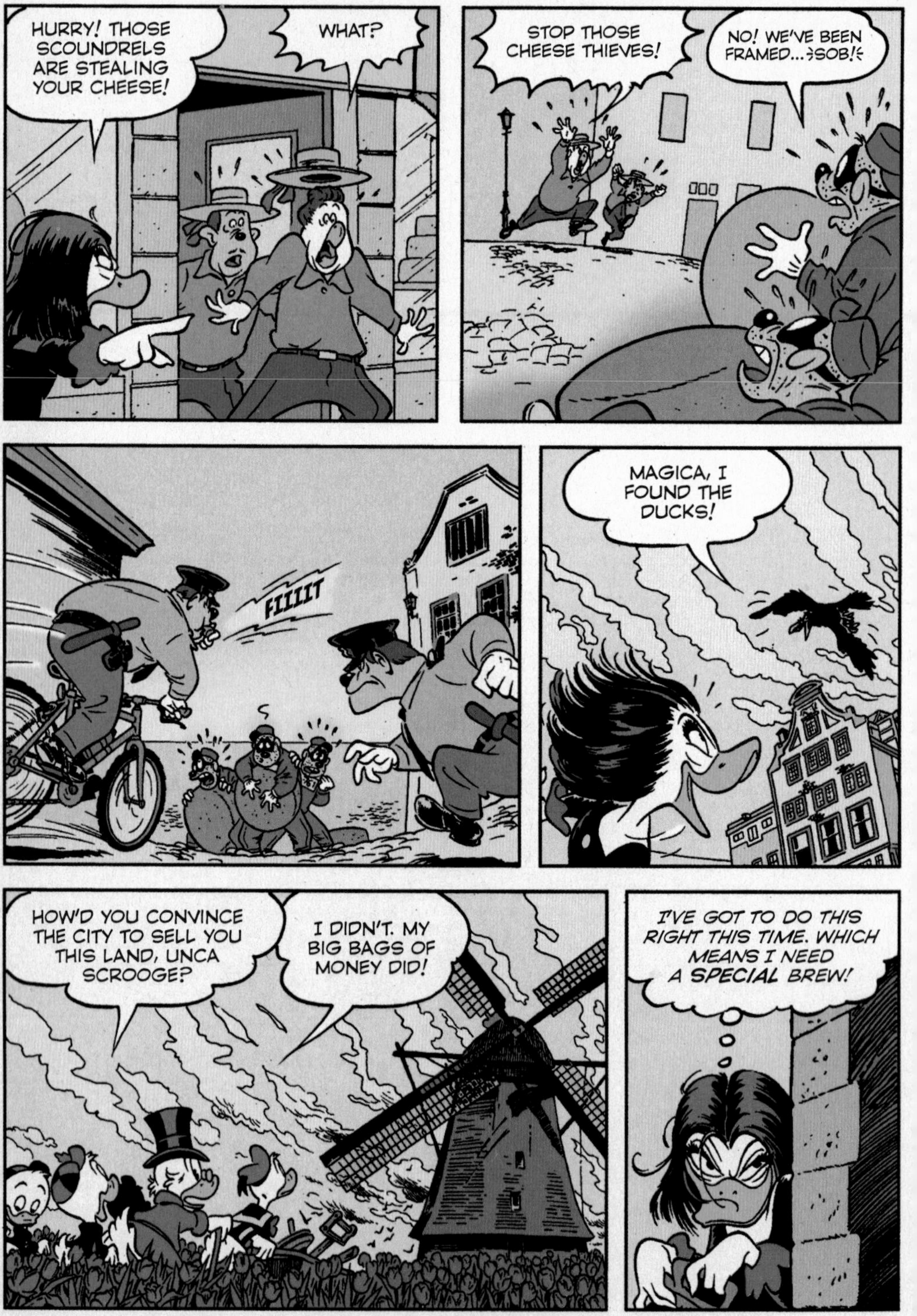
HURRY! THOSE SCOUNDRELS ARE STEALING YOUR CHEESE!
WHAT?
STOP THOSE CHEESE THIEVES!
NO! WE'VE BEEN FRAMED... SOB!
FIIIT
MAGICA, I FOUND THE DUCKS!
HOW'D YOU CONVINCE THE CITY TO SELL YOU THIS LAND, UNCA SCROOGE?
I DIDN'T. MY BIG BAGS OF MONEY DID!
I'VE GOT TO DO THIS RIGHT THIS TIME. WHICH MEANS I NEED A SPECIAL BREW!

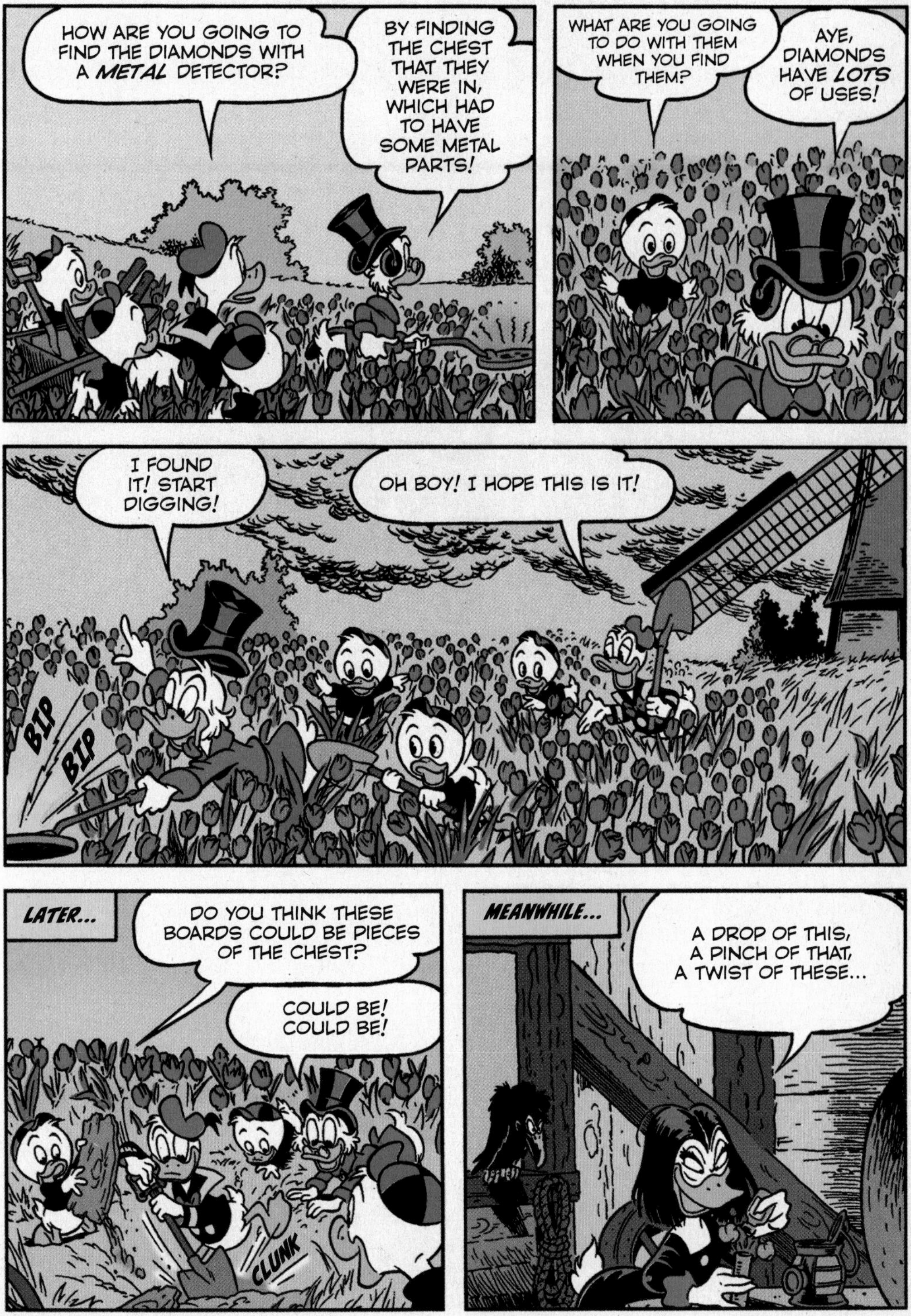
HOW ARE YOU GOING TO FIND THE DIAMONDS WITH A METAL DETECTOR?
BY FINDING THE CHEST THAT THEY WERE IN, WHICH HAD TO HAVE SOME METAL PARTS!
WHAT ARE YOU GOING TO DO WITH THEM WHEN YOU FIND THEM?
AYE, DIAMONDS HAVE LOTS OF USES!
I FOUND IT! START DIGGING!
OH BOY! I HOPE THIS IS IT!
BIP
BIP
LATER...
DO YOU THINK THESE BOARDS COULD BE PIECES OF THE CHEST?
COULD BE! COULD BE!
CLUNK
MEANWHILE...
A DROP OF THIS, A PINCH OF THAT, A TWIST OF THESE...

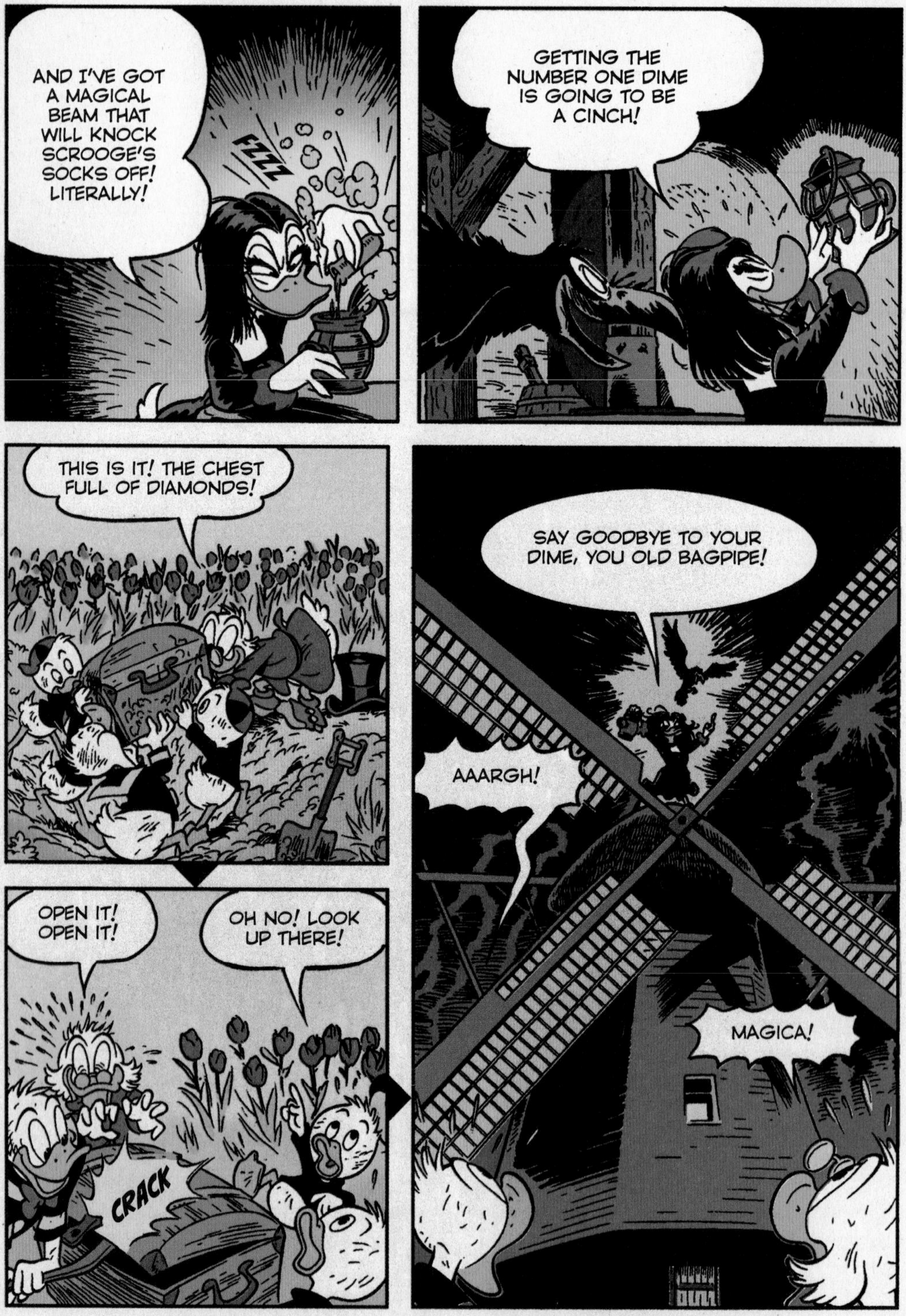
AND I'VE GOT A MAGICAL BEAM THAT WILL KNOCK SCROOGE'S SOCKS OFF! LITERALLY!
FZZZ
GETTING THE NUMBER ONE DIME IS GOING TO BE A CINCH!
THIS IS IT! THE CHEST FULL OF DIAMONDS!
SAY GOODBYE TO YOUR DIME, YOU OLD BAGPIPE!
AAARGH!
OPEN IT! OPEN IT!
OH NO! LOOK UP THERE!
CRACK
MAGICA!

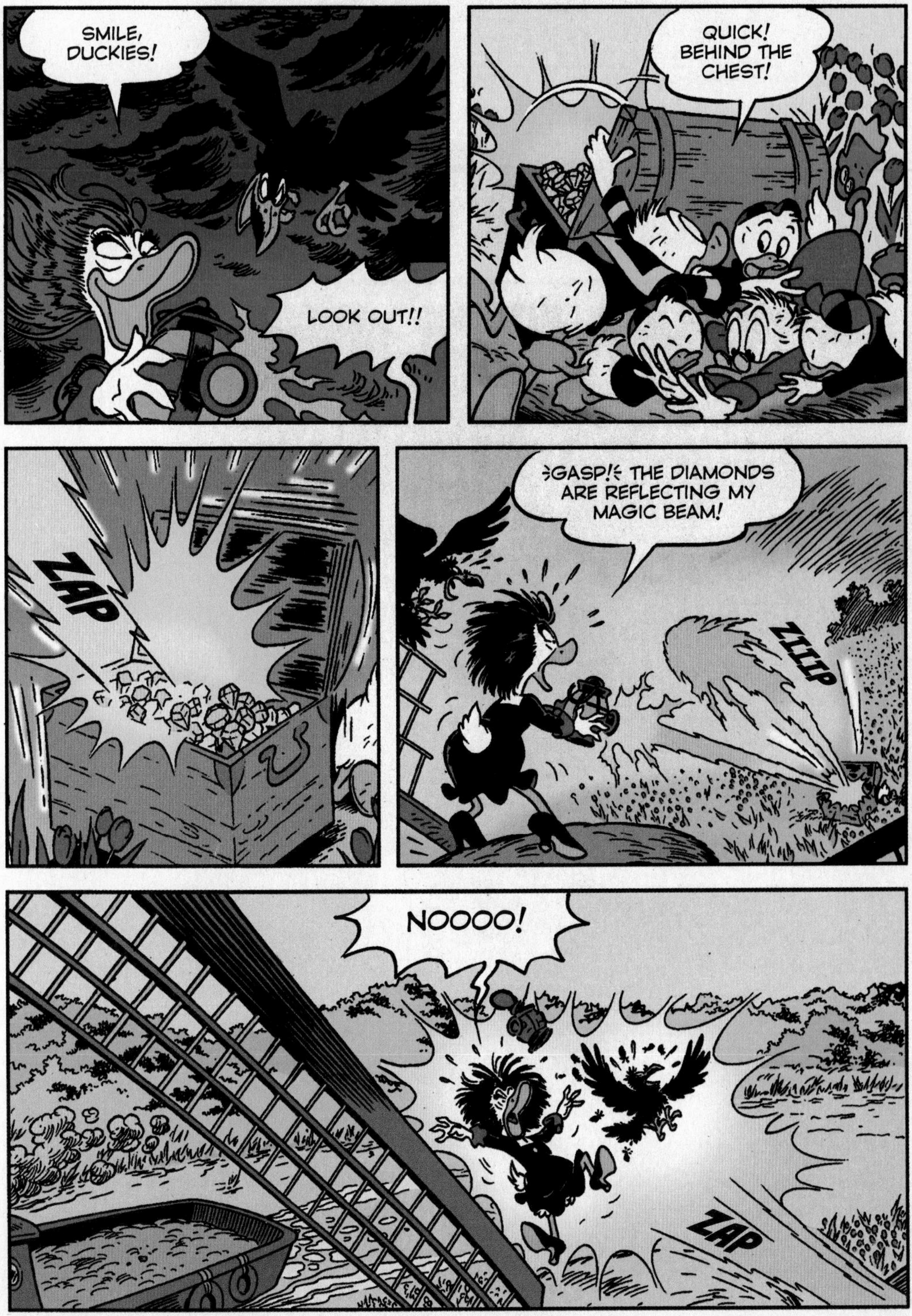
SMILE, DUCKIES!
LOOK OUT!!
QUICK! BEHIND THE CHEST!
ZAP
GASP! THE DIAMONDS ARE REFLECTING MY MAGIC BEAM!
ZIIIP
NOOOO!
ZAP

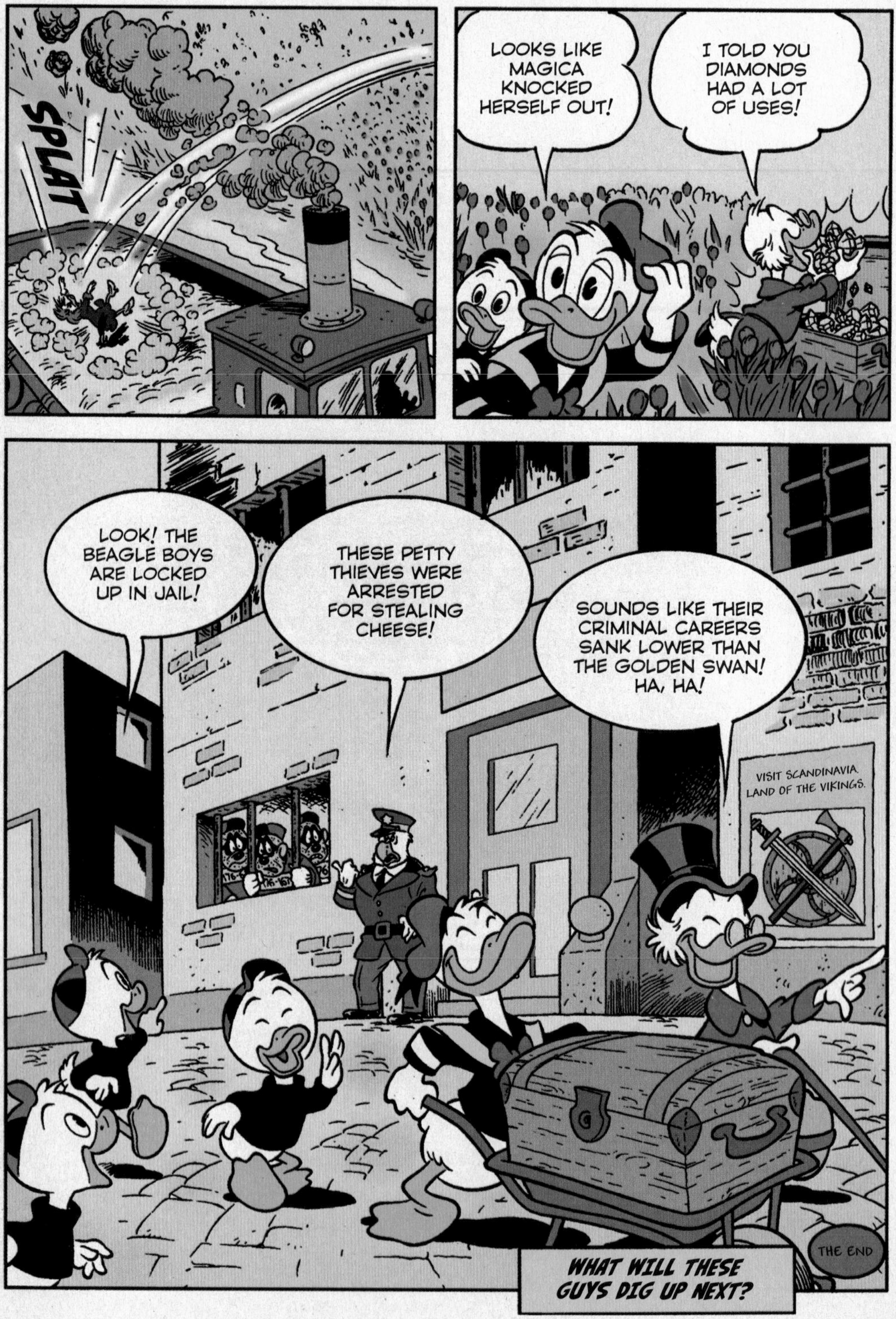
SPLAT
LOOKS LIKE MAGICA KNOCKED HERSELF OUT!
I TOLD YOU DIAMONDS HAD A LOT OF USES!
LOOK! THE BEAGLE BOYS ARE LOCKED UP IN JAIL!
THESE PETTY THIEVES WERE ARRESTED FOR STEALING CHEESE!
SOUNDS LIKE THEIR CRIMINAL CAREERS SANK LOWER THAN THE GOLDEN SWAN! HA, HA!
VISIT SCANDINAVIA. LAND OF THE VIKINGS.
THE END
WHAT WILL THESE GUYS DIG UP NEXT?

THE HUNT FOR THE OLD NUMBER ONE

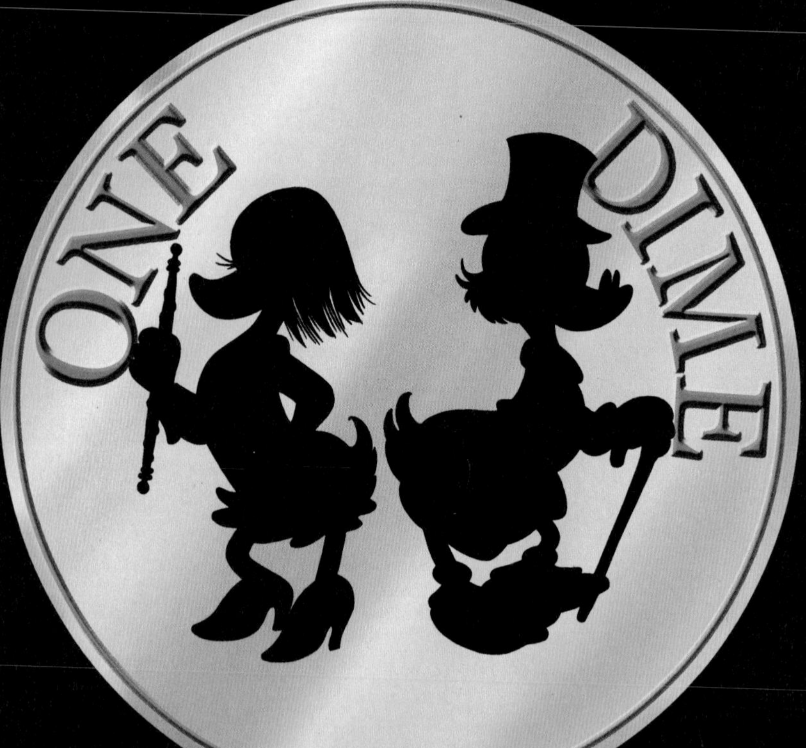
ONE DIME

CHAPTER FOUR

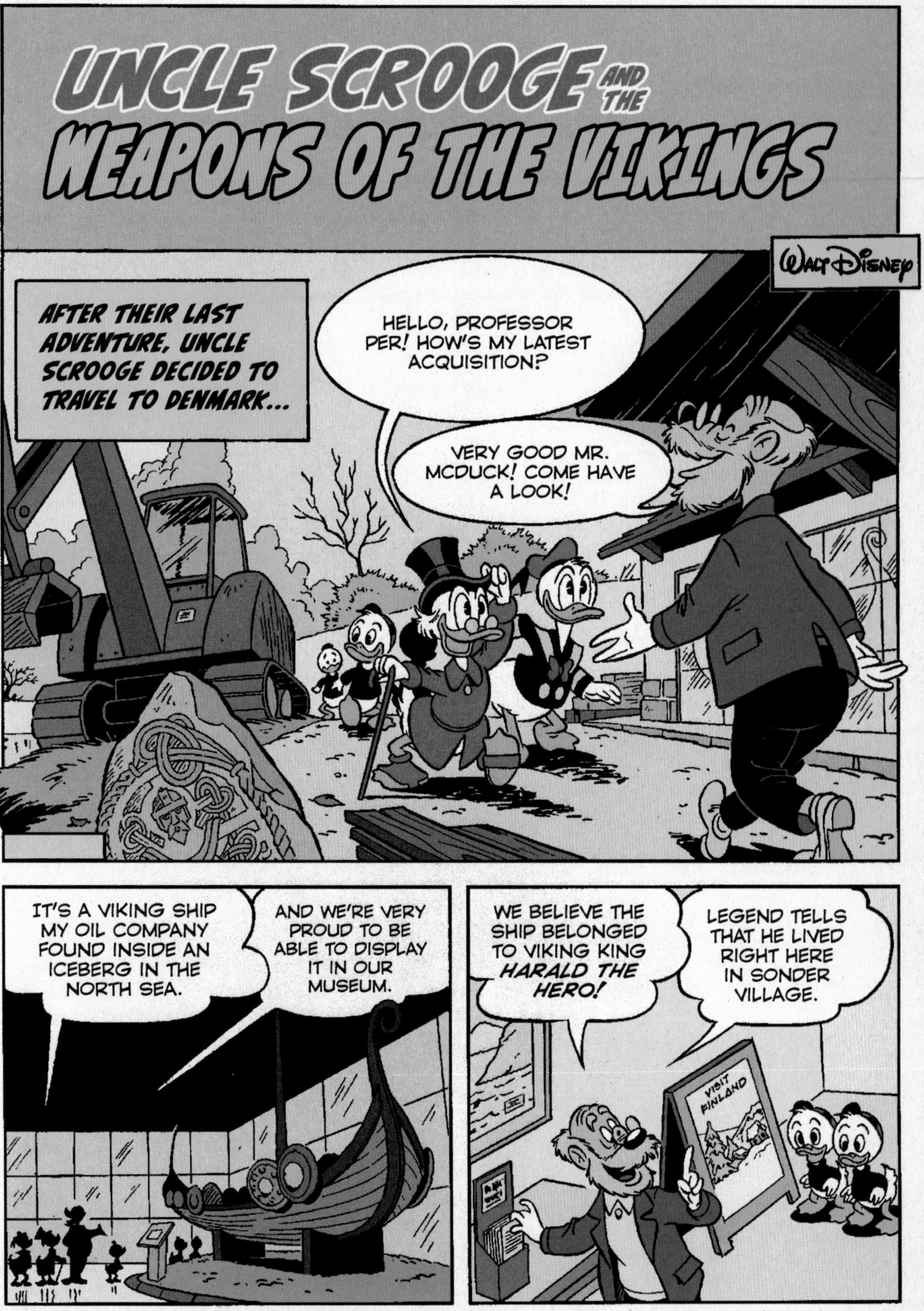
UNCLE SCROOGE AND THE WEAPONS OF THE VIKINGS
WALT DISNEY
AFTER THEIR LAST ADVENTURE, UNCLE SCROOGE DECIDED TO TRAVEL TO DENMARK...
HELLO, PROFESSOR PER! HOW'S MY LATEST ACQUISITION?
VERY GOOD MR. MCDUCK! COME HAVE A LOOK!
IT'S A VIKING SHIP MY OIL COMPANY FOUND INSIDE AN ICEBERG IN THE NORTH SEA.
AND WE'RE VERY PROUD TO BE ABLE TO DISPLAY IT IN OUR MUSEUM.
WE BELIEVE THE SHIP BELONGED TO VIKING KING HARALD THE HERO!
LEGEND TELLS THAT HE LIVED RIGHT HERE IN SONDER VILLAGE.
VISIT FINLAND

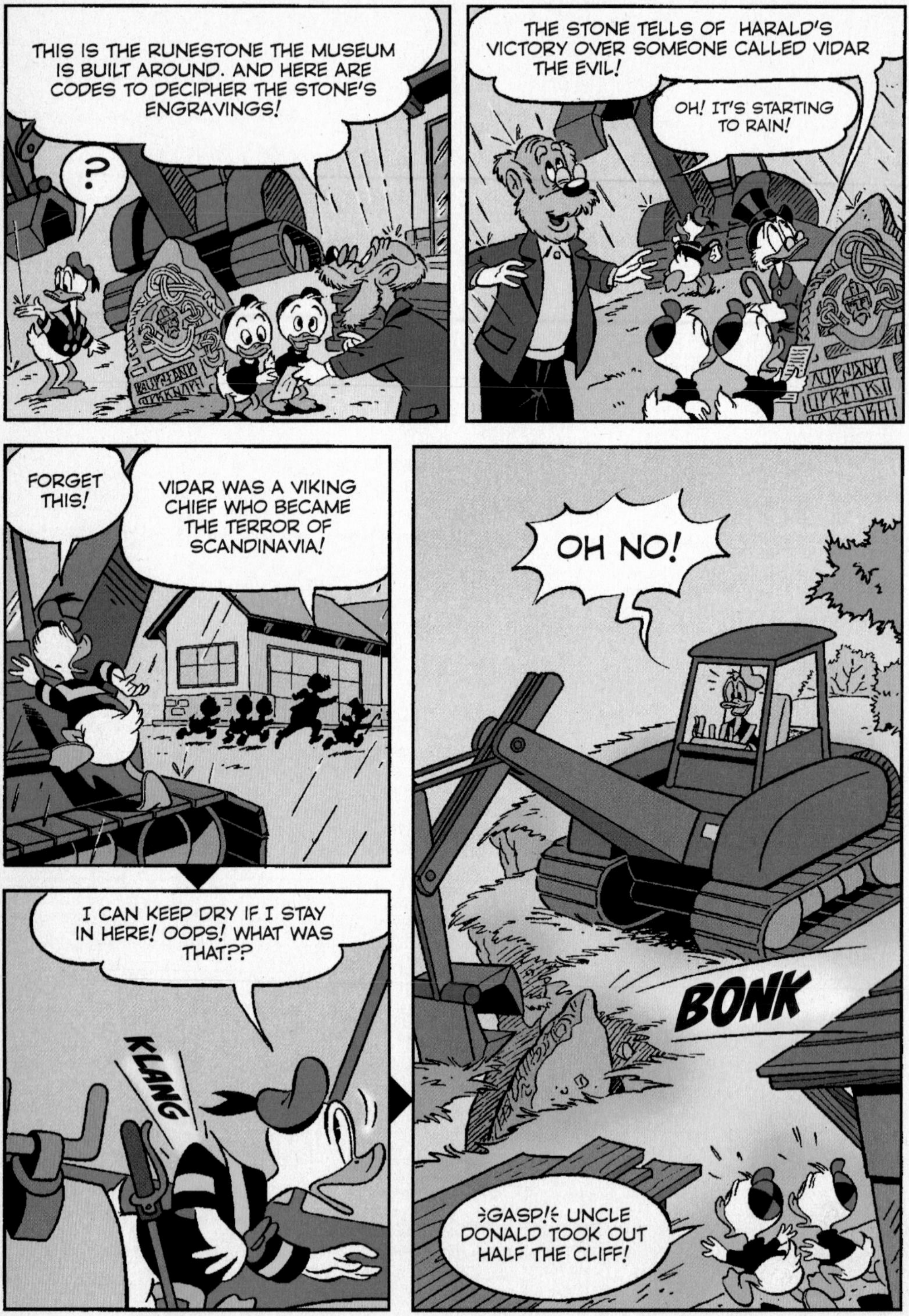
THIS IS THE RUNESTONE THE MUSEUM IS BUILT AROUND. AND HERE ARE CODES TO DECIPHER THE STONE'S ENGRAVINGS!
?
THE STONE TELLS OF HARALD'S VICTORY OVER SOMEONE CALLED VIDAR THE EVIL!
OH! IT'S STARTING TO RAIN!
FORGET THIS!
VIDAR WAS A VIKING CHIEF WHO BECAME THE TERROR OF SCANDINAVIA!
I CAN KEEP DRY IF I STAY IN HERE! OOPS! WHAT WAS THAT??
KLANG
OH NO!
BONK
GASP! UNCLE DONALD TOOK OUT HALF THE CLIFF!

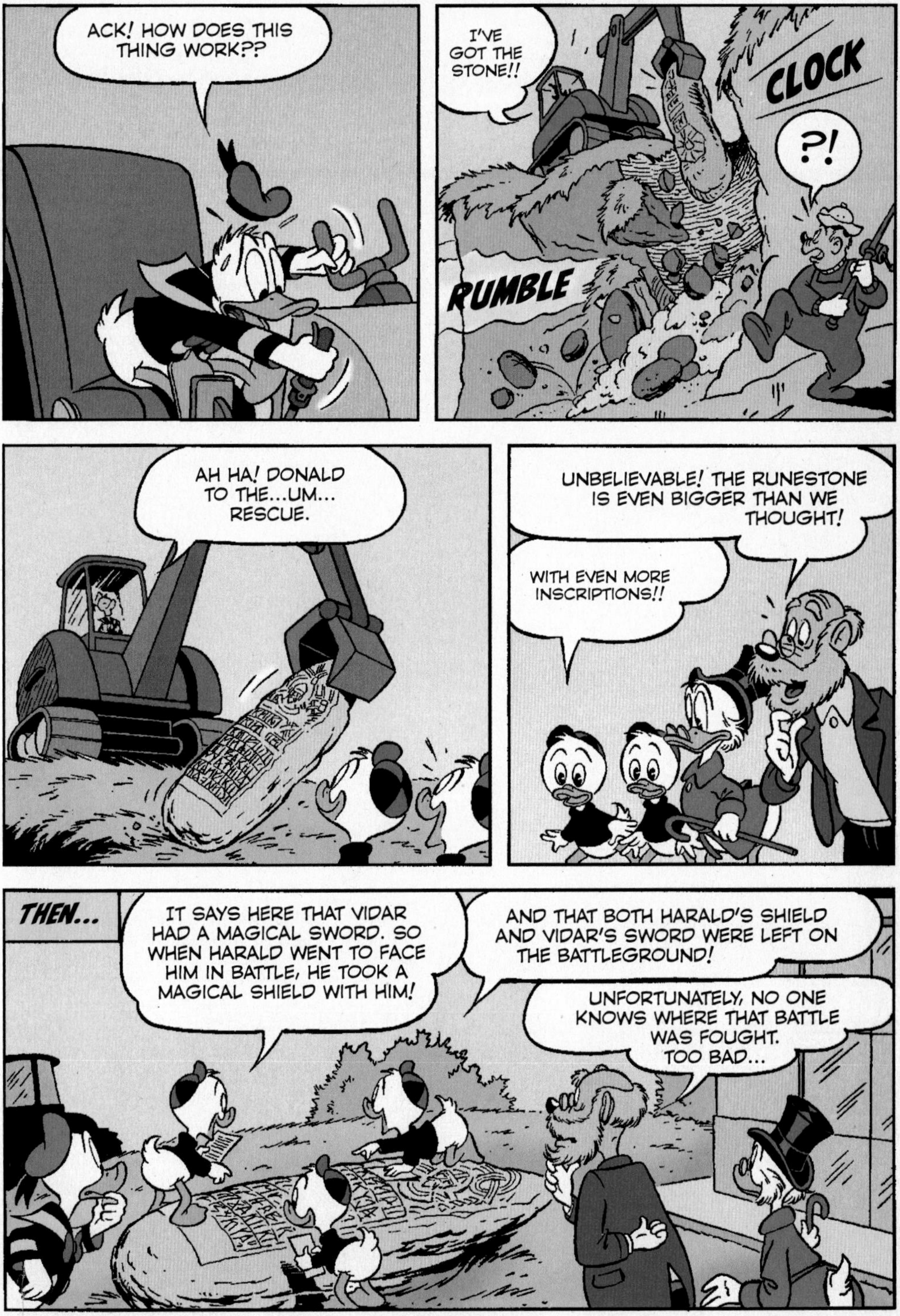
ACK! HOW DOES THIS THING WORK??
I'VE GOT THE STONE!!
CLOCK
?!
RUMBLE
AH HA! DONALD TO THE...UM... RESCUE.
UNBELIEVABLE! THE RUNESTONE IS EVEN BIGGER THAN WE THOUGHT!
WITH EVEN MORE INSCRIPTIONS!!
THEN...
IT SAYS HERE THAT VIDAR HAD A MAGICAL SWORD. SO WHEN HARALD WENT TO FACE HIM IN BATTLE, HE TOOK A MAGICAL SHIELD WITH HIM!
AND THAT BOTH HARALD'S SHIELD AND VIDAR'S SWORD WERE LEFT ON THE BATTLEGROUND!
UNFORTUNATELY, NO ONE KNOWS WHERE THAT BATTLE WAS FOUGHT. TOO BAD...

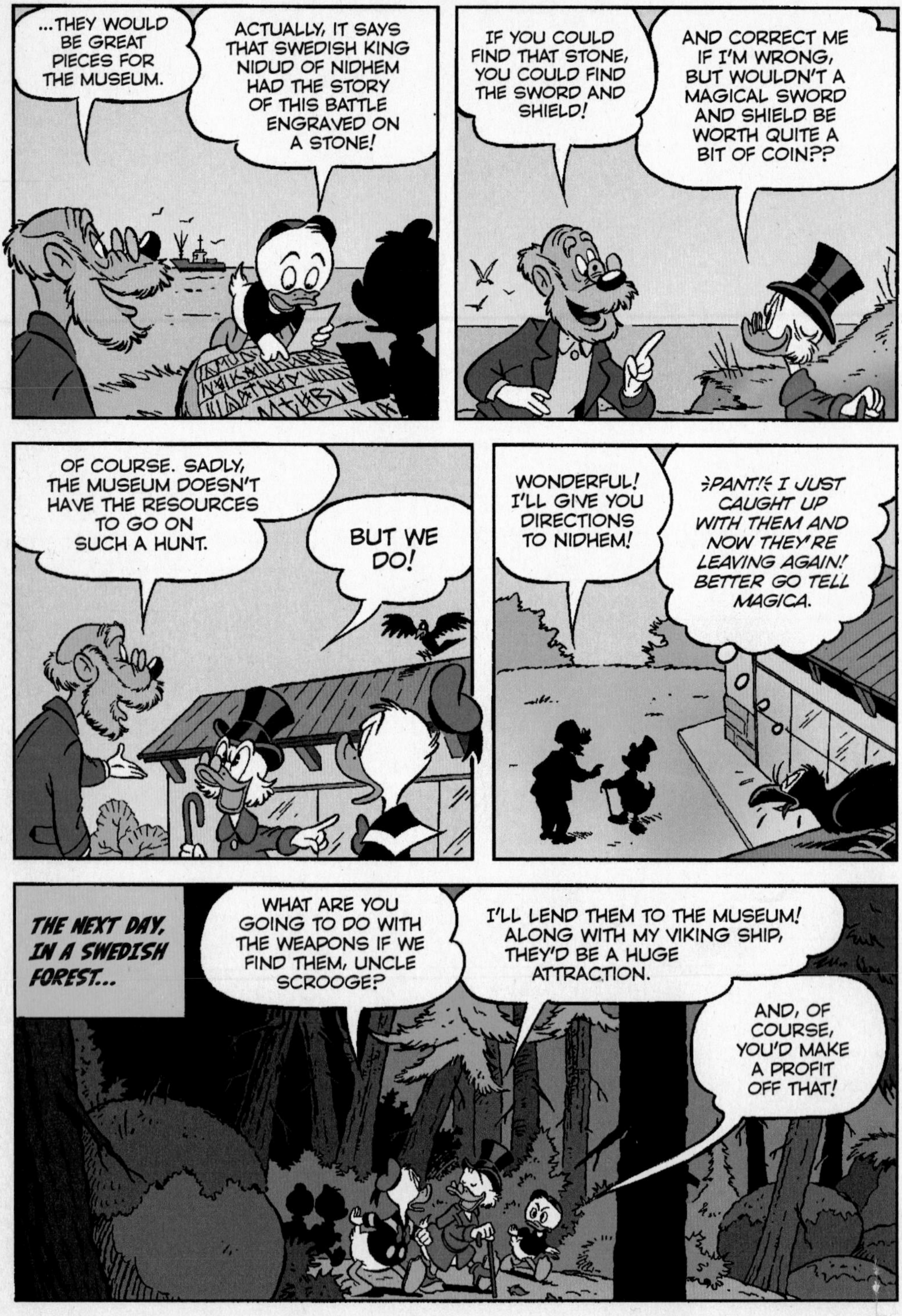
...THEY WOULD BE GREAT PIECES FOR THE MUSEUM.
ACTUALLY, IT SAYS THAT SWEDISH KING NIDUD OF NIDHEM HAD THE STORY OF THIS BATTLE ENGRAVED ON A STONE!
IF YOU COULD FIND THAT STONE, YOU COULD FIND THE SWORD AND SHIELD!
AND CORRECT ME IF I'M WRONG, BUT WOULDN'T A MAGICAL SWORD AND SHIELD BE WORTH QUITE A BIT OF COIN??
OF COURSE. SADLY, THE MUSEUM DOESN'T HAVE THE RESOURCES TO GO ON SUCH A HUNT.
BUT WE DO!
WONDERFUL! I'LL GIVE YOU DIRECTIONS TO NIDHEM!
PANT! I JUST CAUGHT UP WITH THEM AND NOW THEY'RE LEAVING AGAIN! BETTER GO TELL MAGICA.
THE NEXT DAY, IN A SWEDISH FOREST...
WHAT ARE YOU GOING TO DO WITH THE WEAPONS IF WE FIND THEM, UNCLE SCROOGE?
I'LL LEND THEM TO THE MUSEUM! ALONG WITH MY VIKING SHIP, THEY'D BE A HUGE ATTRACTION.
AND, OF COURSE, YOU'D MAKE A PROFIT OFF THAT!

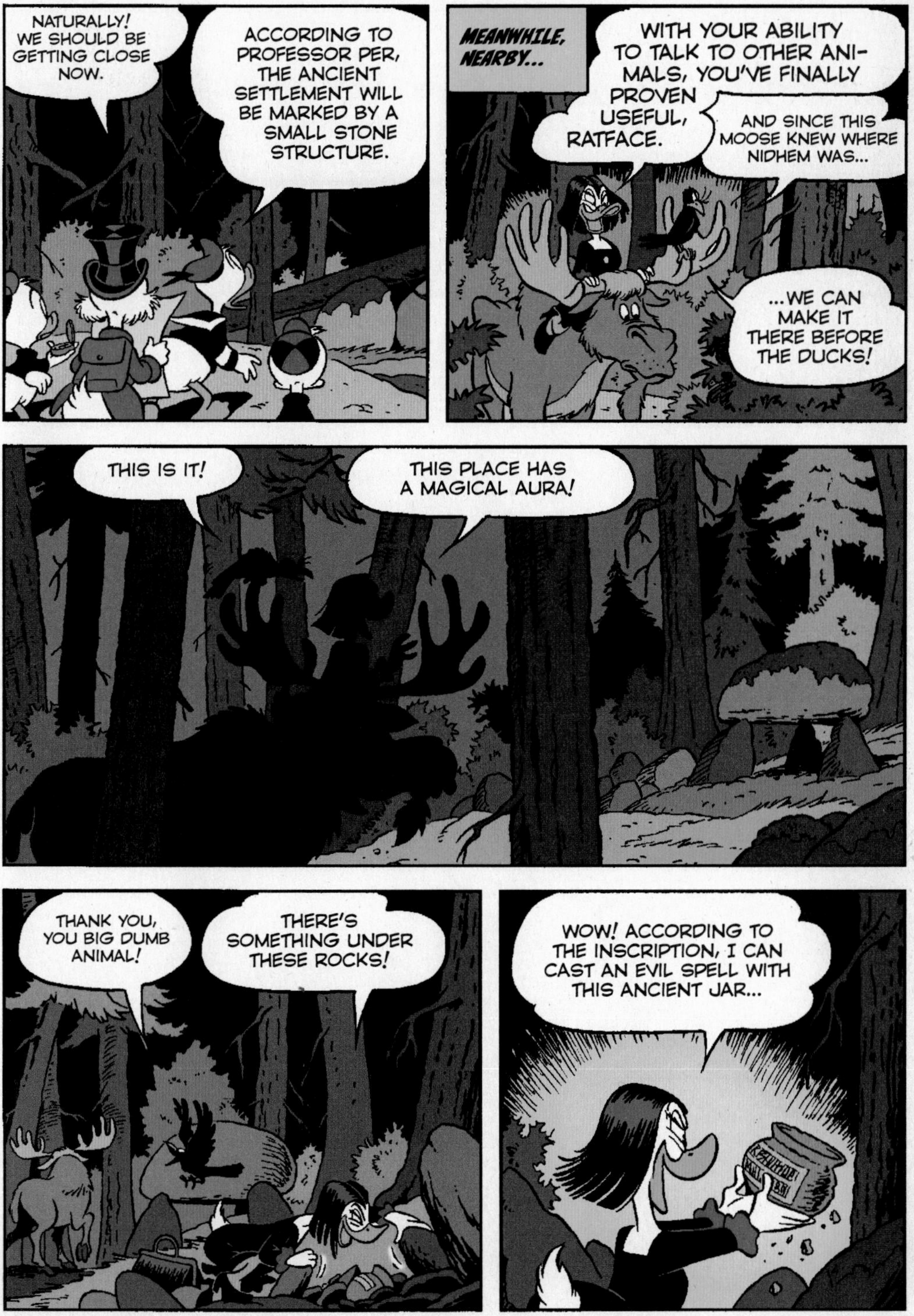
NATURALLY! WE SHOULD BE GETTING CLOSE NOW.
ACCORDING TO PROFESSOR PER, THE ANCIENT SETTLEMENT WILL BE MARKED BY A SMALL STONE STRUCTURE.
MEANWHILE, NEARBY...
WITH YOUR ABILITY TO TALK TO OTHER ANI-MALS, YOU'VE FINALLY PROVEN USEFUL, RATFACE.
AND SINCE THIS MOOSE KNEW WHERE NIDHEM WAS...
...WE CAN MAKE IT THERE BEFORE THE DUCKS!
THIS IS IT!
THIS PLACE HAS A MAGICAL AURA!
THANK YOU, YOU BIG DUMB ANIMAL!
THERE'S SOMETHING UNDER THESE ROCKS!
WOW! ACCORDING TO THE INSCRIPTION, I CAN CAST AN EVIL SPELL WITH THIS ANCIENT JAR...

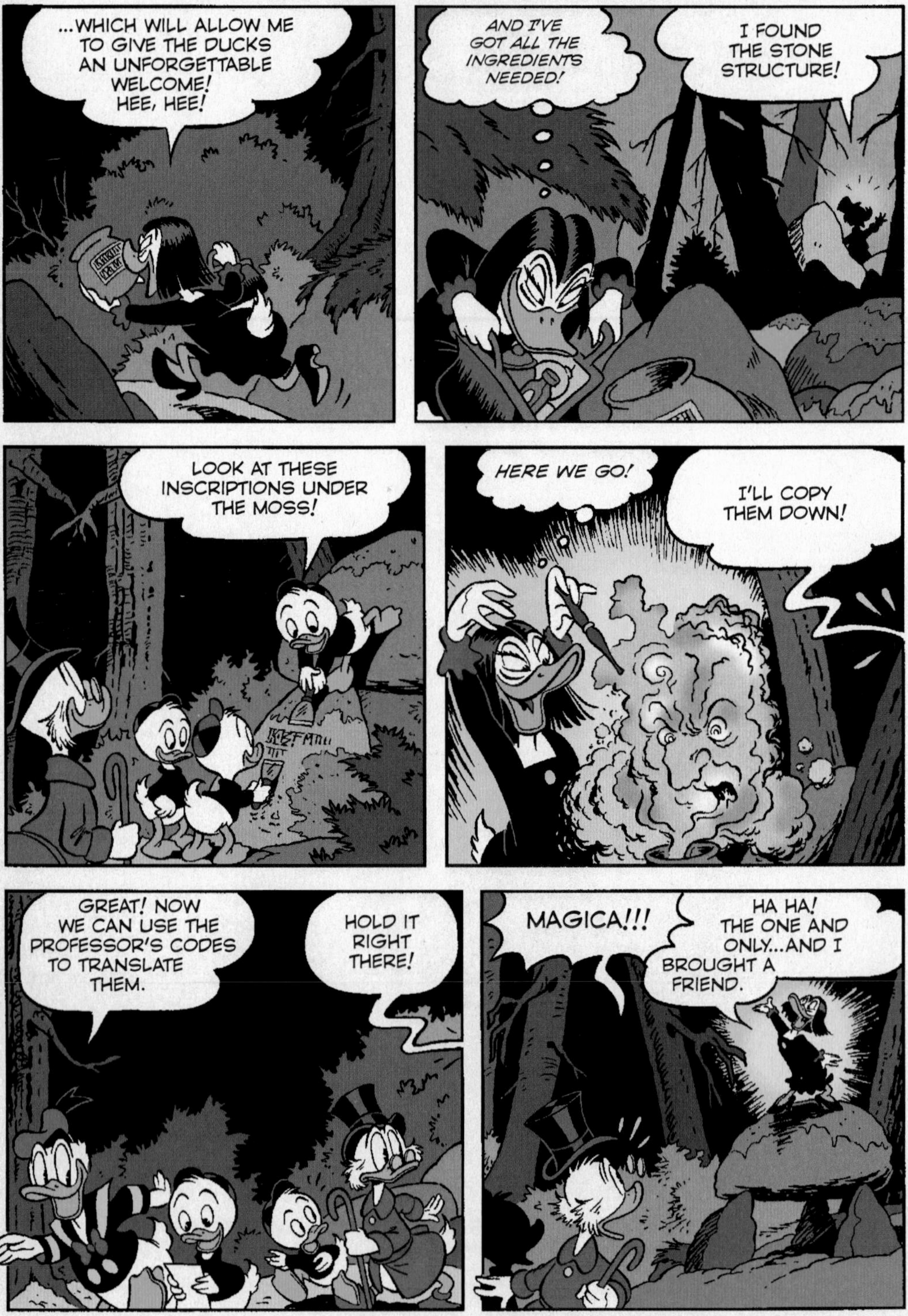
...WHICH WILL ALLOW ME TO GIVE THE DUCKS AN UNFORGETTABLE WELCOME! HEE, HEE!
AND I'VE GOT ALL THE INGREDIENTS NEEDED!
I FOUND THE STONE STRUCTURE!
LOOK AT THESE INSCRIPTIONS UNDER THE MOSS!
HERE WE GO!
I'LL COPY THEM DOWN!
GREAT! NOW WE CAN USE THE PROFESSOR'S CODES TO TRANSLATE THEM.
HOLD IT RIGHT THERE!
MAGICA!!!
HA HA! THE ONE AND ONLY...AND I BROUGHT A FRIEND.

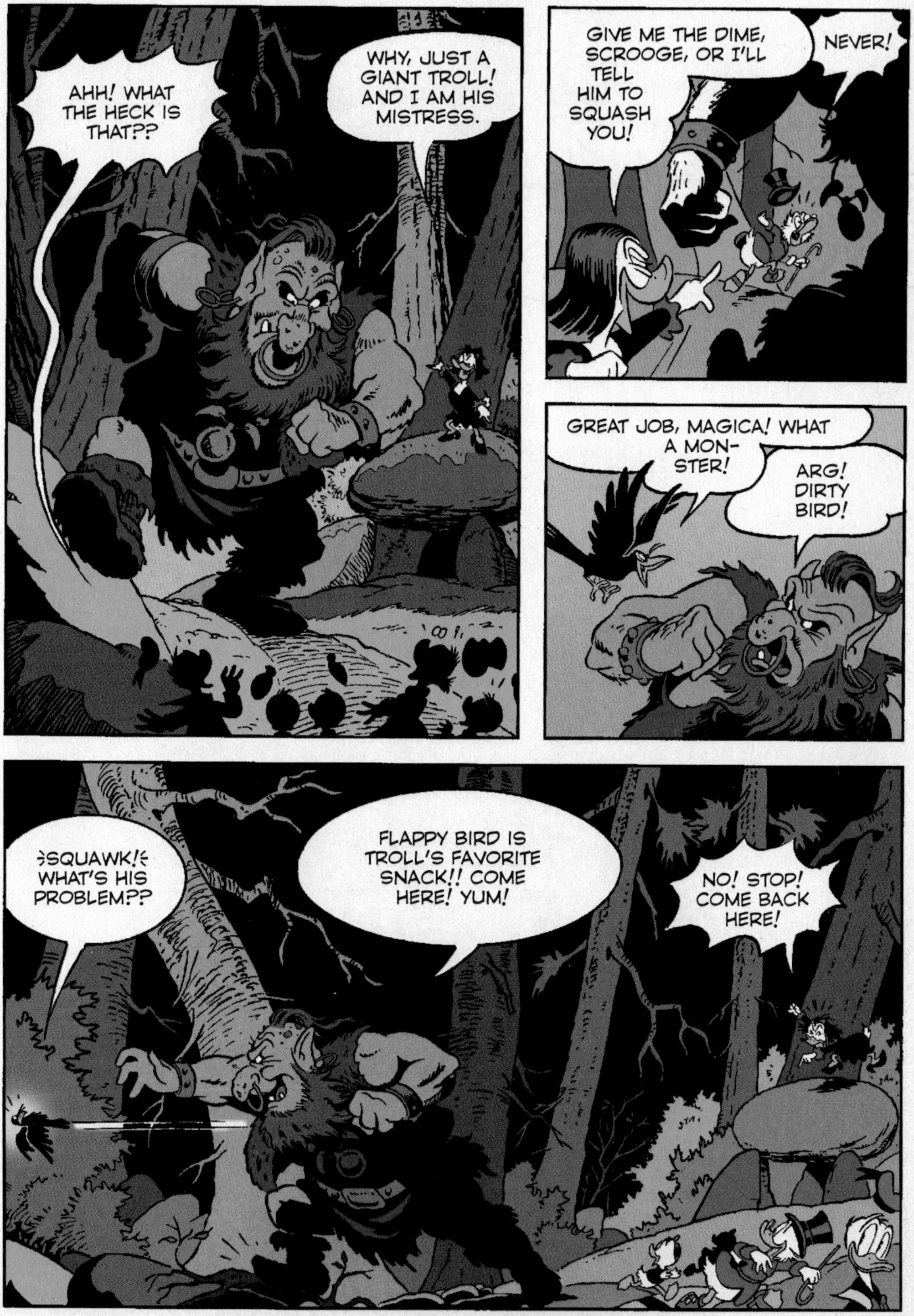

AHH! WHAT THE HECK IS THAT??
WHY, JUST A GIANT TROLL! AND I AM HIS MISTRESS.
GIVE ME THE DIME, SCROOGE, OR I'LL TELL HIM TO SQUASH YOU!
NEVER!
GREAT JOB, MAGICA! WHAT A MON-STER!
ARG! DIRTY BIRD!
SQUAWK! WHAT'S HIS PROBLEM??
FLAPPY BIRD IS TROLL'S FAVORITE SNACK!! COME HERE! YUM!
NO! STOP! COME BACK HERE!

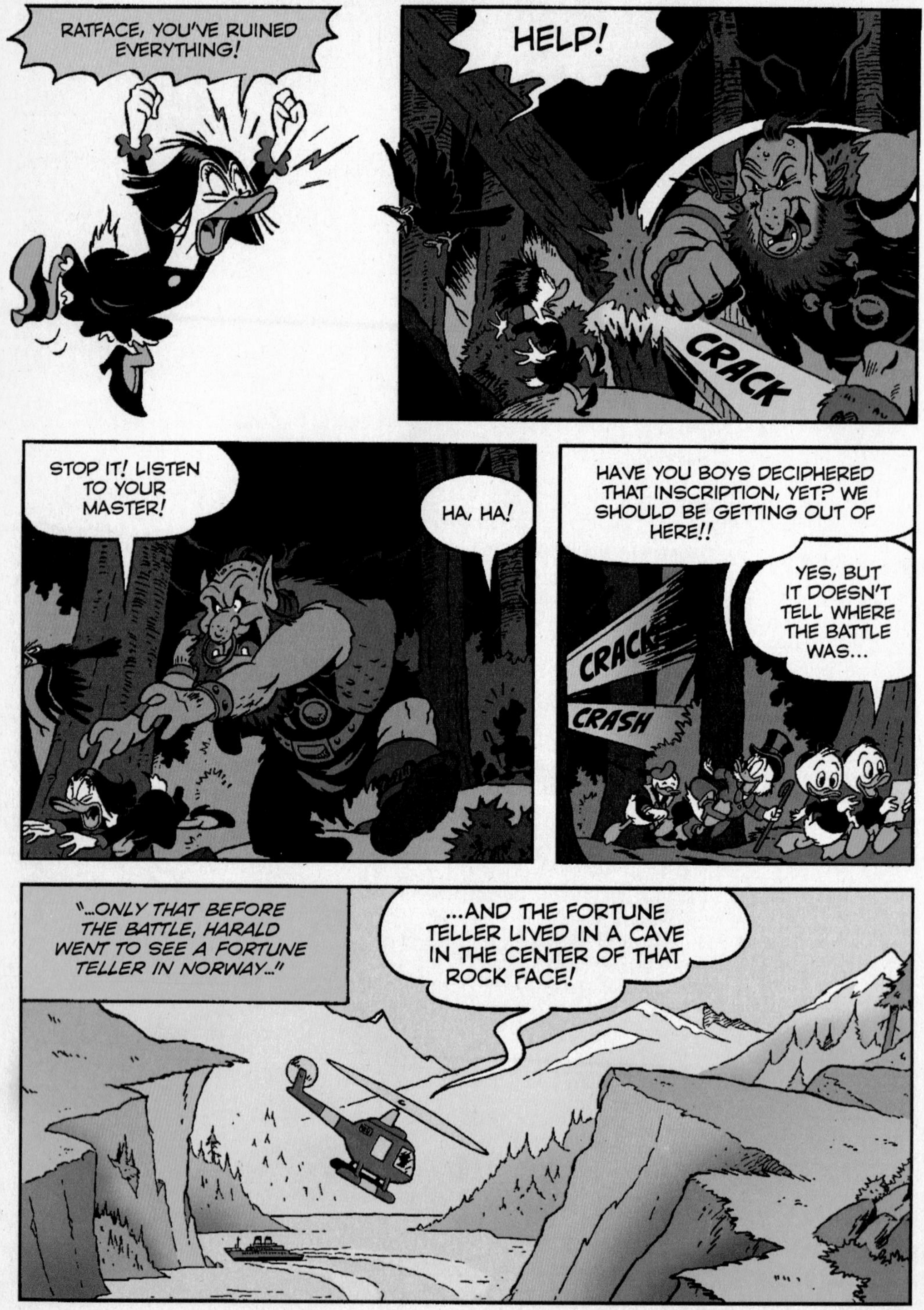
RATFACE, YOU'VE RUINED EVERYTHING!
HELP!
CRACK
STOP IT! LISTEN TO YOUR MASTER!
HA, HA!
HAVE YOU BOYS DECIPHERED THAT INSCRIPTION, YET? WE SHOULD BE GETTING OUT OF HERE!!
YES, BUT IT DOESN'T TELL WHERE THE BATTLE WAS...
CRACK
CRASH
"...ONLY THAT BEFORE THE BATTLE, HARALD WENT TO SEE A FORTUNE TELLER IN NORWAY..."
...AND THE FORTUNE TELLER LIVED IN A CAVE IN THE CENTER OF THAT ROCK FACE!

THE FORTUNE TELLER ADVISED HARALD WHERE THE MOST FAVORABLE PLACE TO HAVE THE FIGHT WOULD BE!

IF HARALD REALLY CAME HERE, MAYBE THERE'S A CLUE AS TO WHERE THE BATTLE TOOK PLACE.

IN ORDER TO REACH THE ENTRANCE OF THE CAVE, WE'LL HAVE TO LOWER OURSELVES FROM THE TOP!

CLICK

CLICK

IT'S A LITTLE SCARY!

DON'T WORRY! YOU'LL BE ATTACHED TO THE HELI-COPTER.

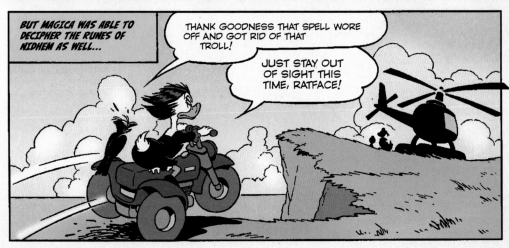

BUT MAGICA WAS ABLE TO DECIPHER THE RUNES OF NIDHEM AS WELL...

THANK GOODNESS THAT SPELL WORE OFF AND GOT RID OF THAT TROLL!

JUST STAY OUT OF SIGHT THIS TIME, RATFACE!

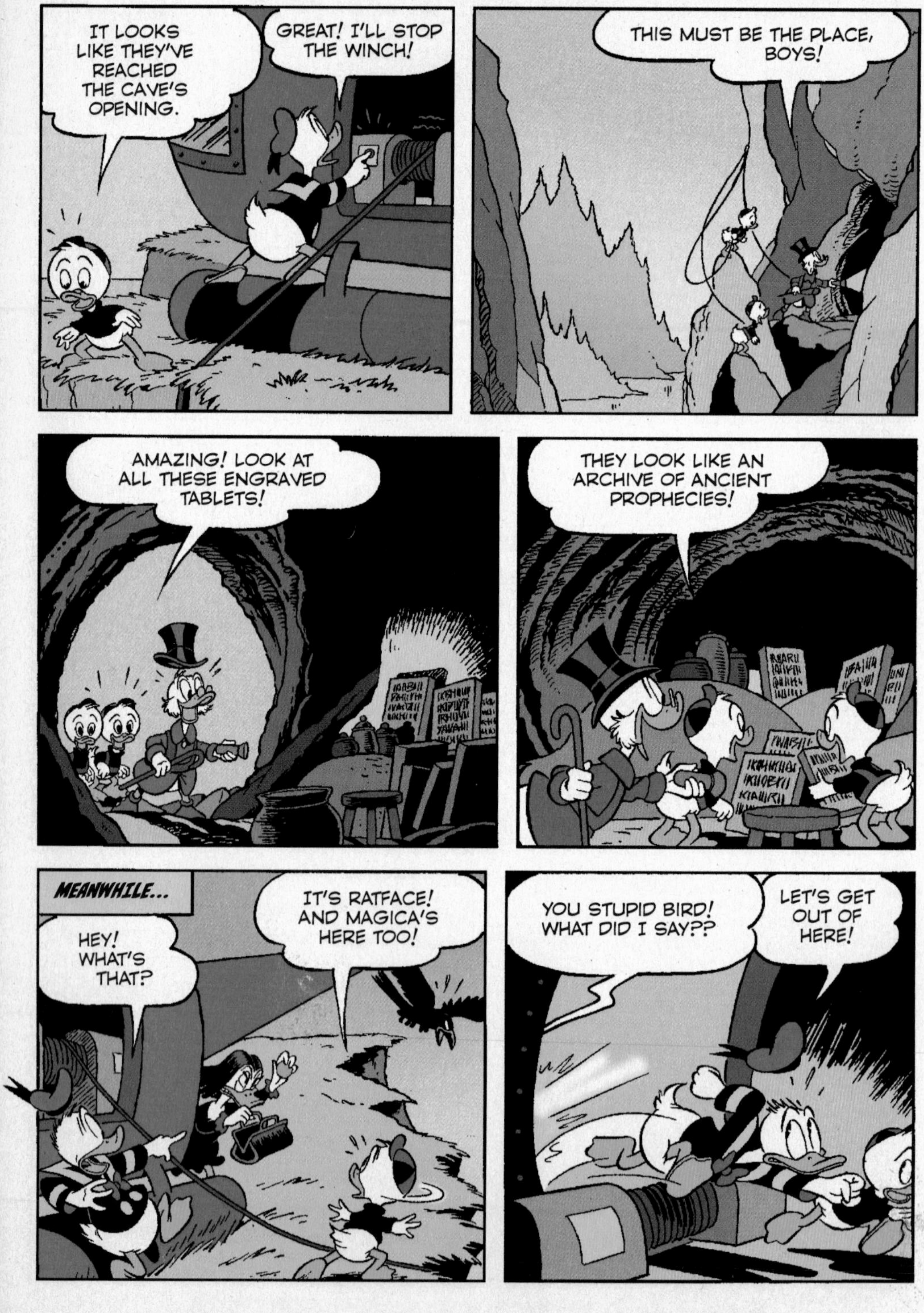
IT LOOKS LIKE THEY'VE REACHED THE CAVE'S OPENING.
GREAT! I'LL STOP THE WINCH!
THIS MUST BE THE PLACE, BOYS!
AMAZING! LOOK AT ALL THESE ENGRAVED TABLETS!
THEY LOOK LIKE AN ARCHIVE OF ANCIENT PROPHECIES!
MEANWHILE...
HEY! WHAT'S THAT?
IT'S RATFACE! AND MAGICA'S HERE TOO!
YOU STUPID BIRD! WHAT DID I SAY??
LET'S GET OUT OF HERE!

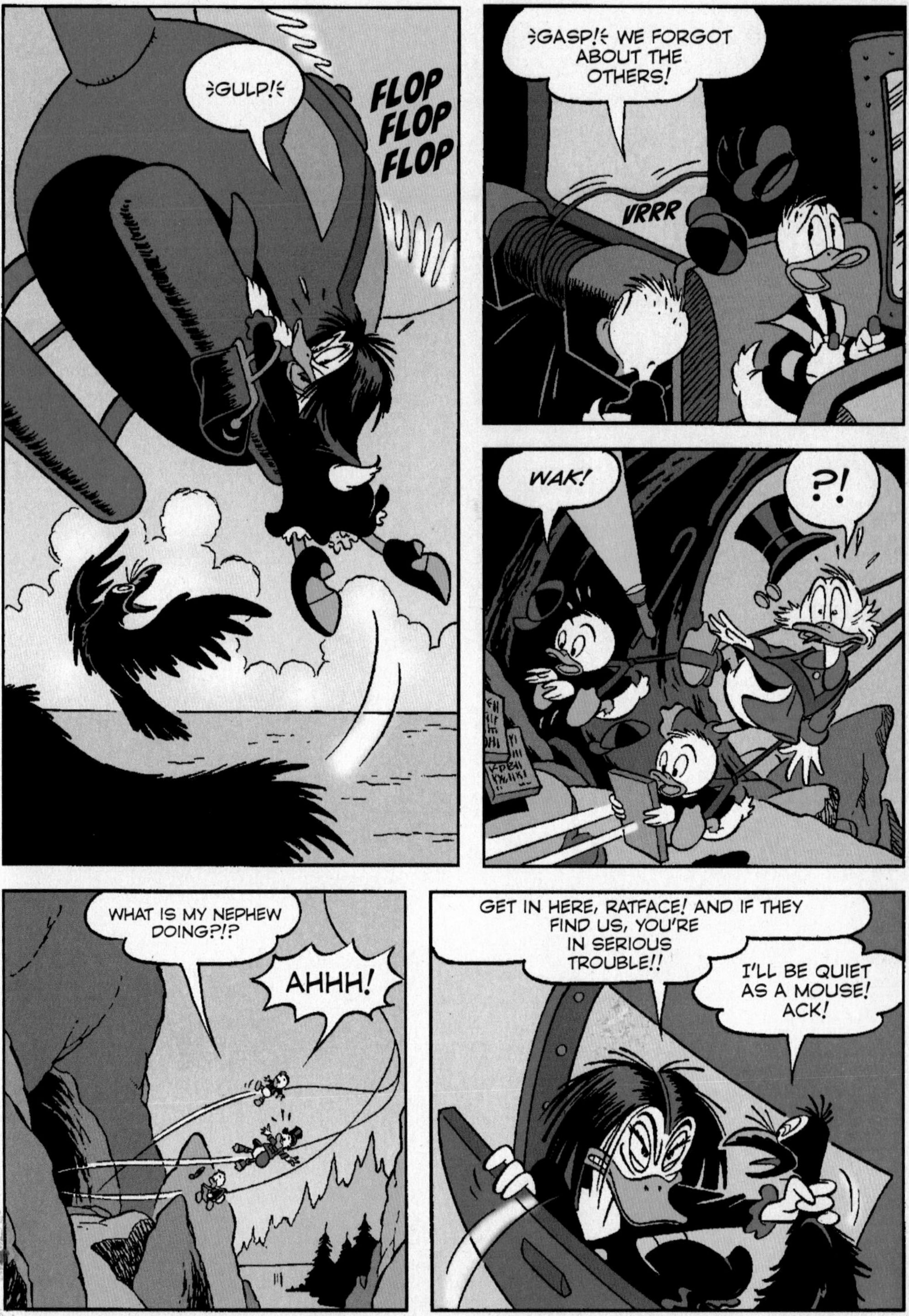
GULP!
FLOP
FLOP
FLOP
GASP! WE FORGOT ABOUT THE OTHERS!
VRRR
WAK!
?!
WHAT IS MY NEPHEW DOING?!?
AHHH!
GET IN HERE, RATFACE! AND IF THEY FIND US, YOU'RE IN SERIOUS TROUBLE!!
I'LL BE QUIET AS A MOUSE! ACK!

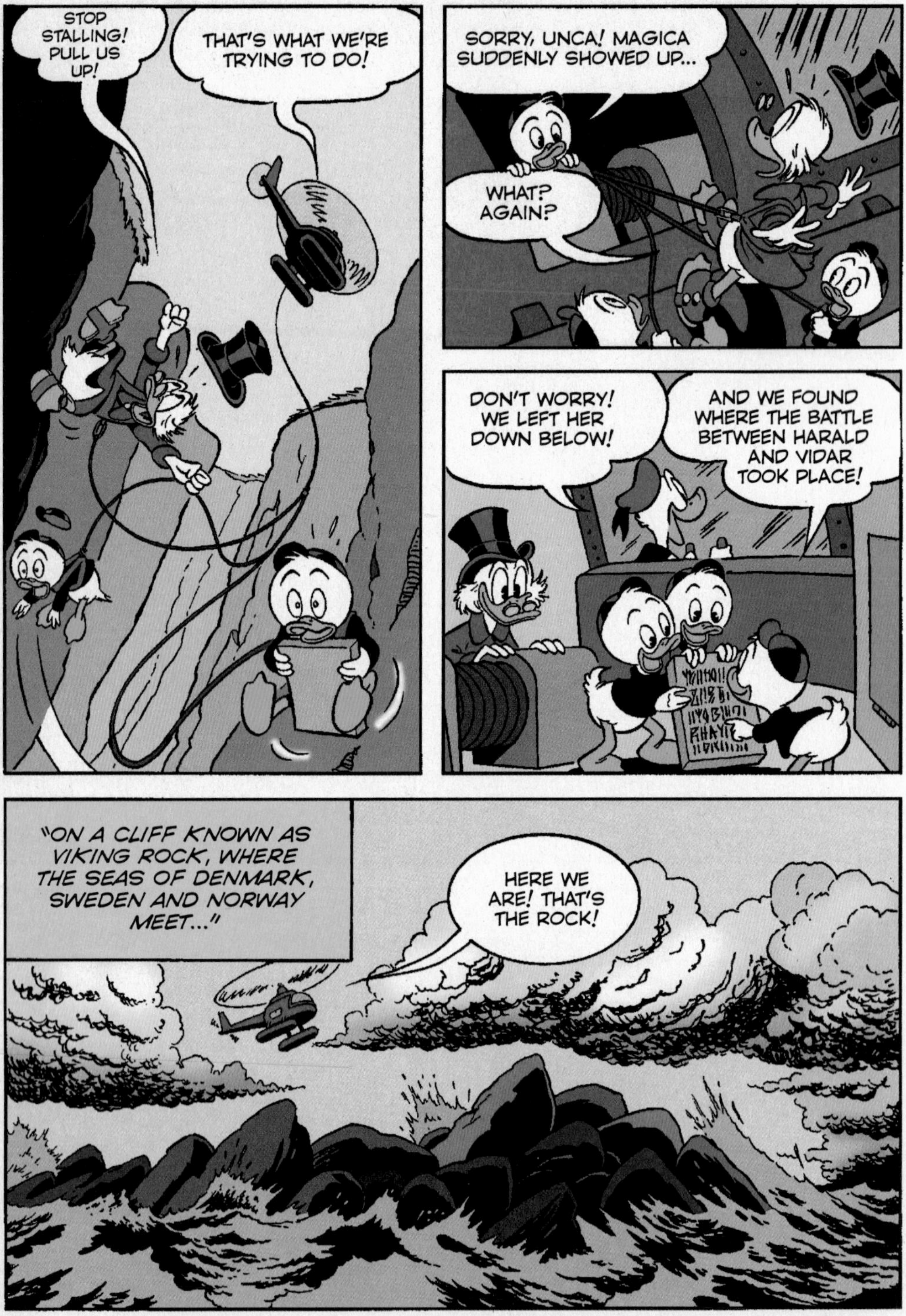

STOP STALLING! PULL US UP!
THAT'S WHAT WE'RE TRYING TO DO!
SORRY, UNCA! MAGICA SUDDENLY SHOWED UP...
WHAT? AGAIN?
DON'T WORRY! WE LEFT HER DOWN BELOW!
AND WE FOUND WHERE THE BATTLE BETWEEN HARALD AND VIDAR TOOK PLACE!
"ON A CLIFF KNOWN AS VIKING ROCK, WHERE THE SEAS OF DENMARK, SWEDEN AND NORWAY MEET..."
HERE WE ARE! THAT'S THE ROCK!

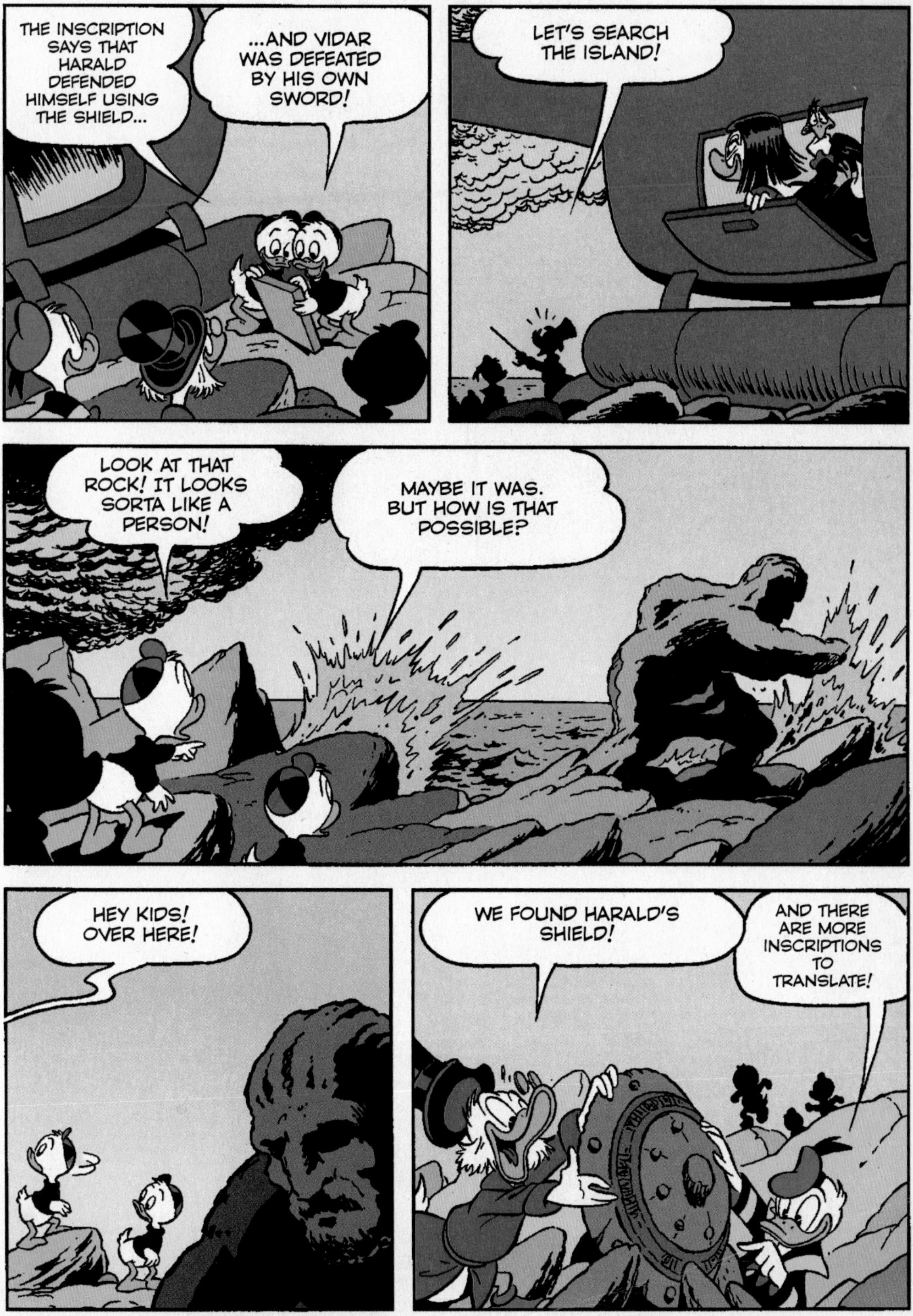
THE INSCRIPTION SAYS THAT HARALD DEFENDED HIMSELF USING THE SHIELD...
...AND VIDAR WAS DEFEATED BY HIS OWN SWORD!
LET'S SEARCH THE ISLAND!
LOOK AT THAT ROCK! IT LOOKS SORTA LIKE A PERSON!
MAYBE IT WAS. BUT HOW IS THAT POSSIBLE?
HEY KIDS! OVER HERE!
WE FOUND HARALD'S SHIELD!
AND THERE ARE MORE INSCRIPTIONS TO TRANSLATE!

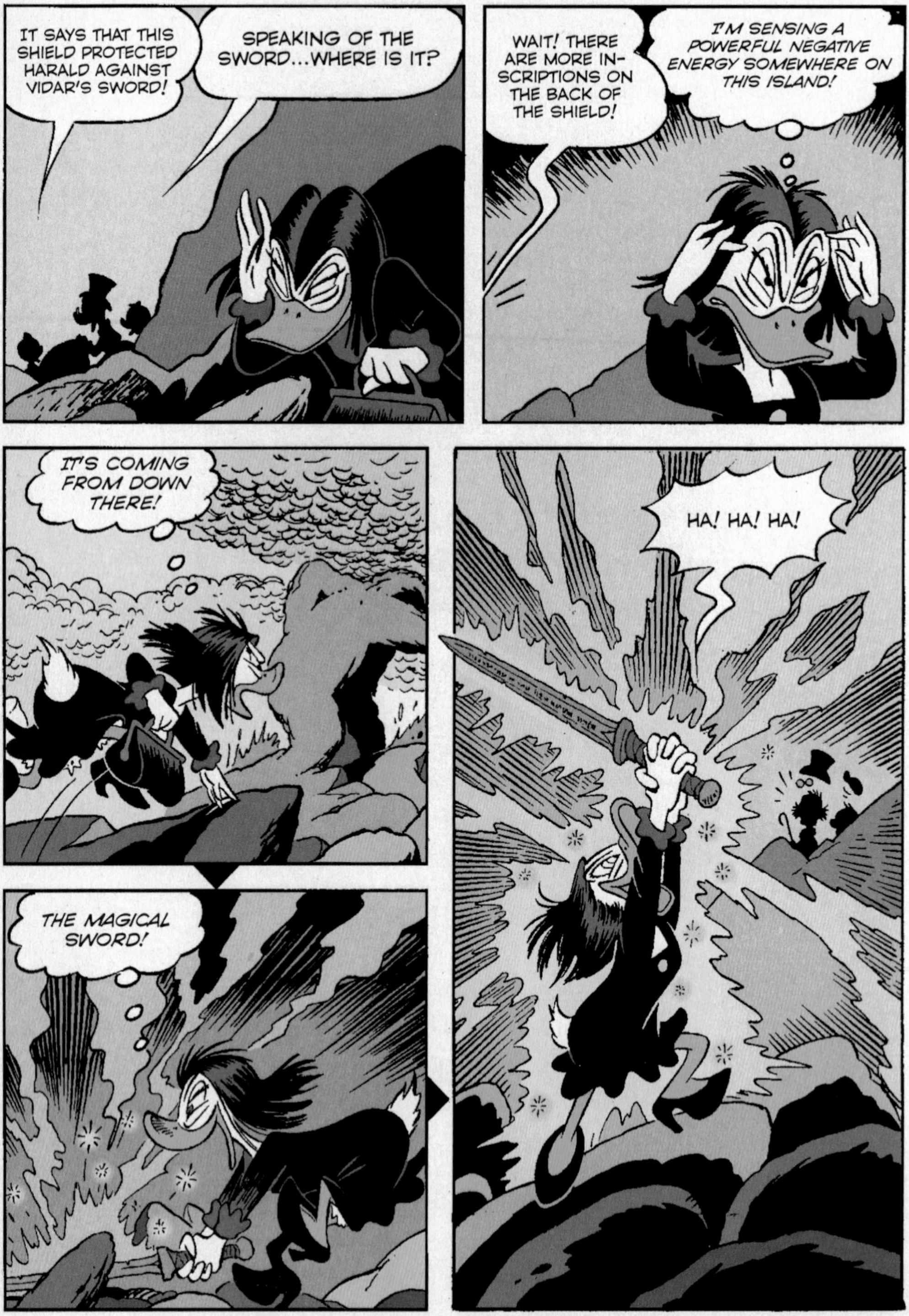
IT SAYS THAT THIS SHIELD PROTECTED HARALD AGAINST VIDAR'S SWORD!
SPEAKING OF THE SWORD...WHERE IS IT?
WAIT! THERE ARE MORE IN-SCRIPTIONS ON THE BACK OF THE SHIELD!
I'M SENSING A POWERFUL NEGATIVE ENERGY SOMEWHERE ON THIS ISLAND!
IT'S COMING FROM DOWN THERE!
HA! HA! HA!
THE MAGICAL SWORD!

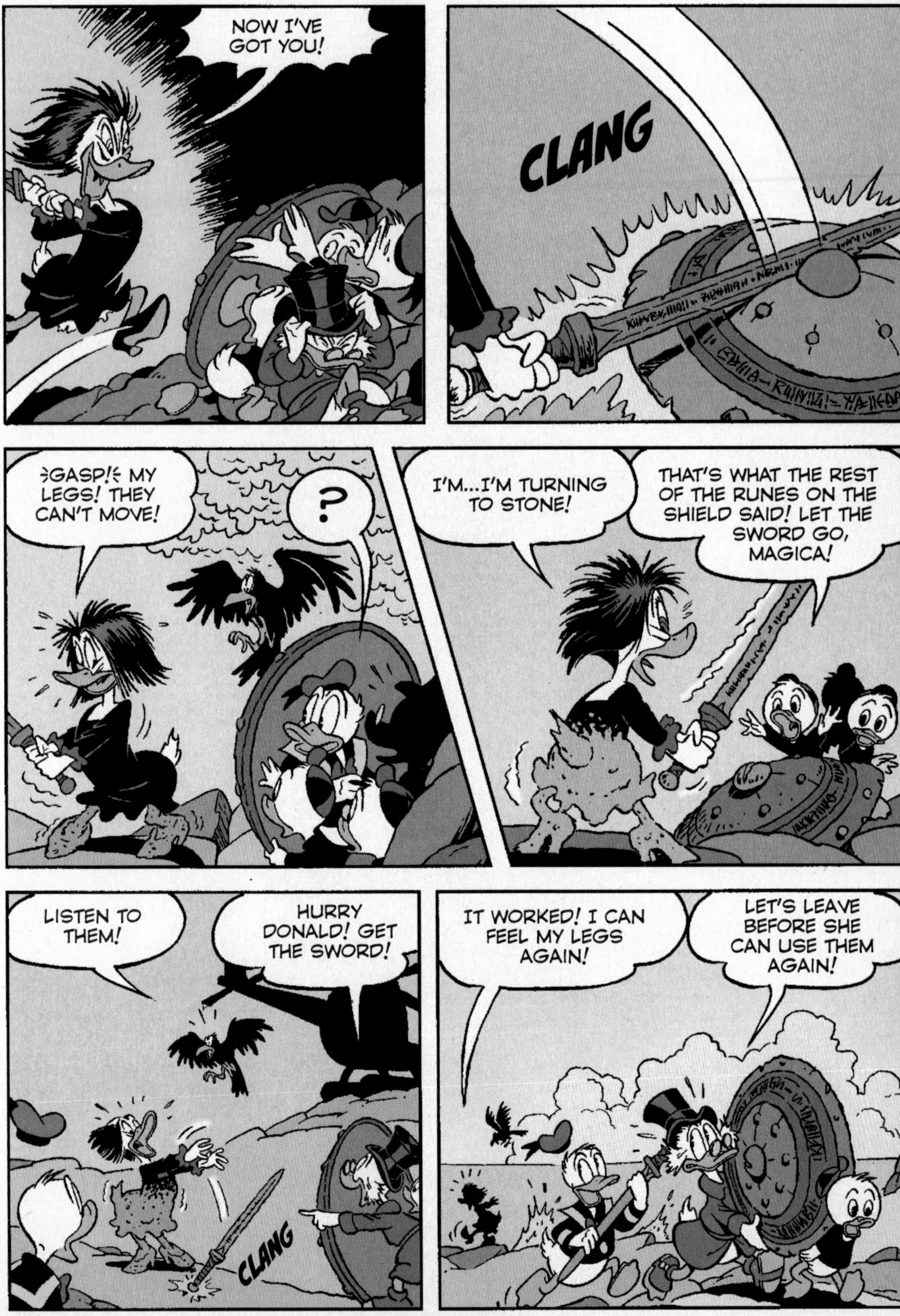
NOW I'VE GOT YOU!
CLANG
⋟GASP!⋞ MY LEGS! THEY CAN'T MOVE!
?
I'M...I'M TURNING TO STONE!
THAT'S WHAT THE REST OF THE RUNES ON THE SHIELD SAID! LET THE SWORD GO, MAGICA!
LISTEN TO THEM!
HURRY DONALD! GET THE SWORD!
CLANG
IT WORKED! I CAN FEEL MY LEGS AGAIN!
LET'S LEAVE BEFORE SHE CAN USE THEM AGAIN!

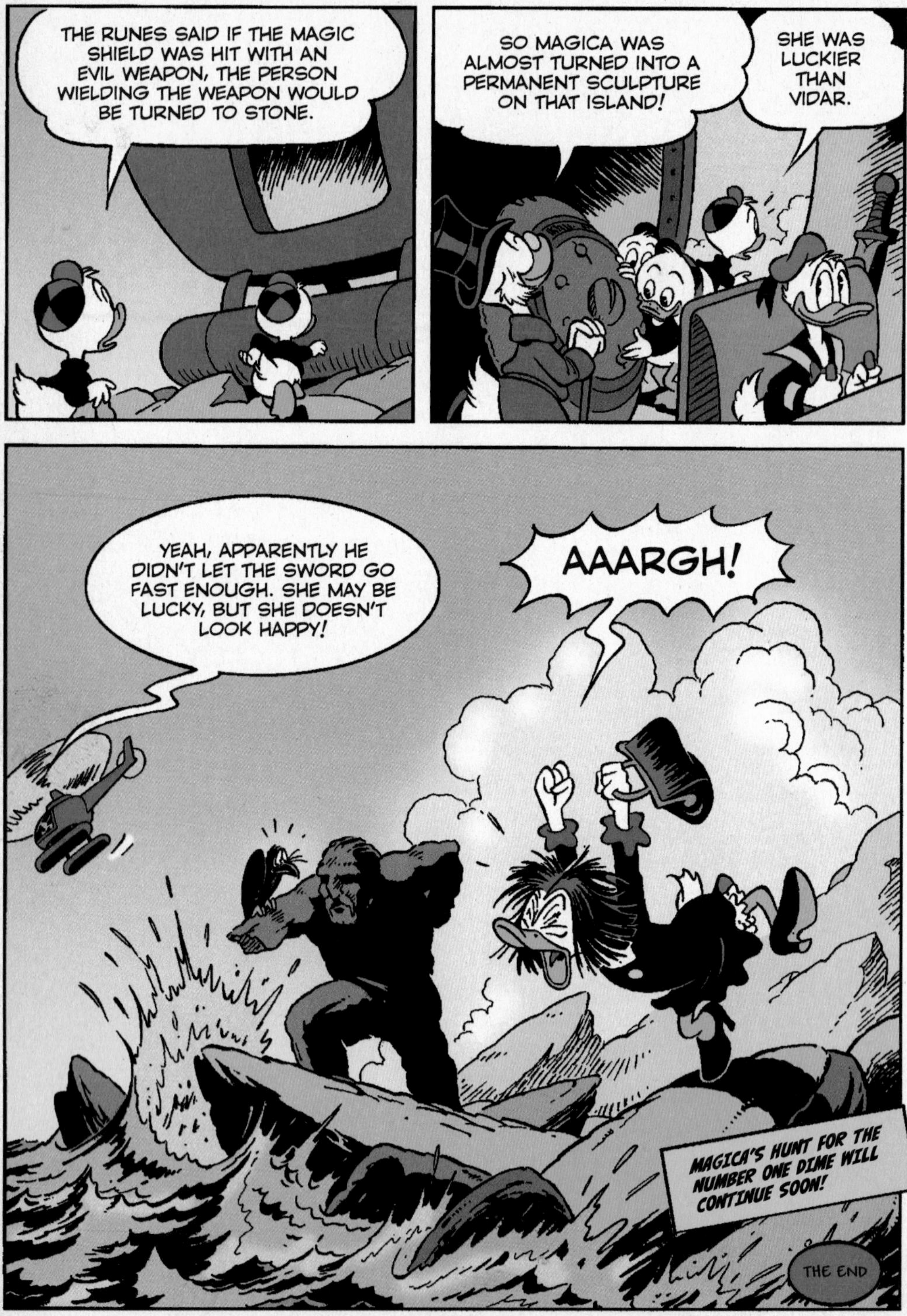
THE RUNES SAID IF THE MAGIC SHIELD WAS HIT WITH AN EVIL WEAPON, THE PERSON WIELDING THE WEAPON WOULD BE TURNED TO STONE.
SO MAGICA WAS ALMOST TURNED INTO A PERMANENT SCULPTURE ON THAT ISLAND!
SHE WAS LUCKIER THAN VIDAR.
YEAH, APPARENTLY HE DIDN'T LET THE SWORD GO FAST ENOUGH. SHE MAY BE LUCKY, BUT SHE DOESN'T LOOK HAPPY!
AAARGH!
MAGICA'S HUNT FOR THE NUMBER ONE DIME WILL CONTINUE SOON!
THE END

THE HUNT FOR THE OLD NUMBER ONE

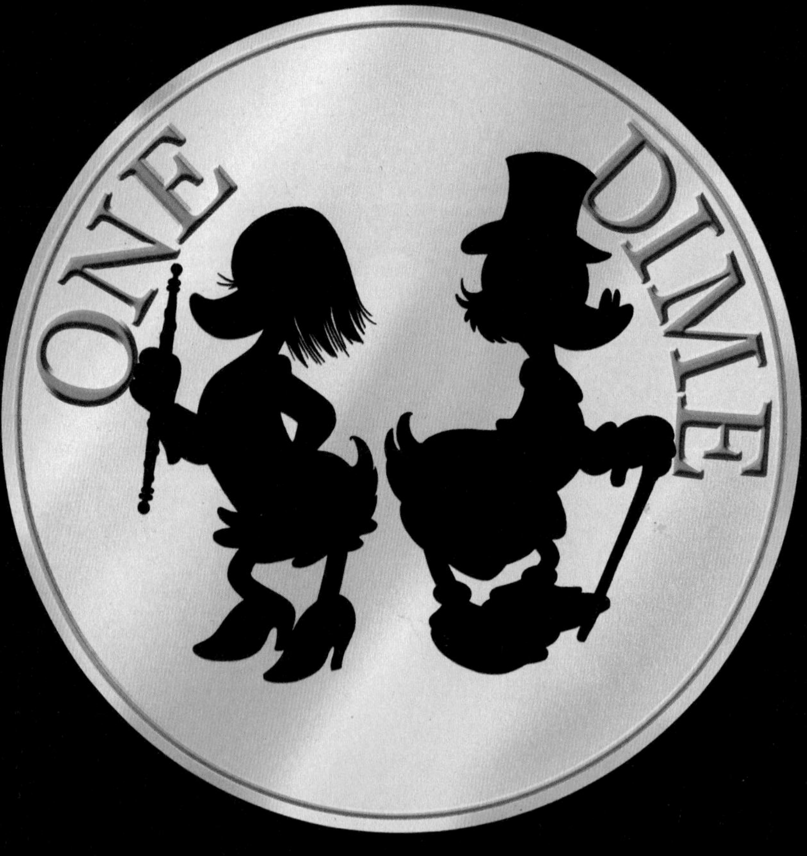
ONE
DIME

CHAPTER FIVE

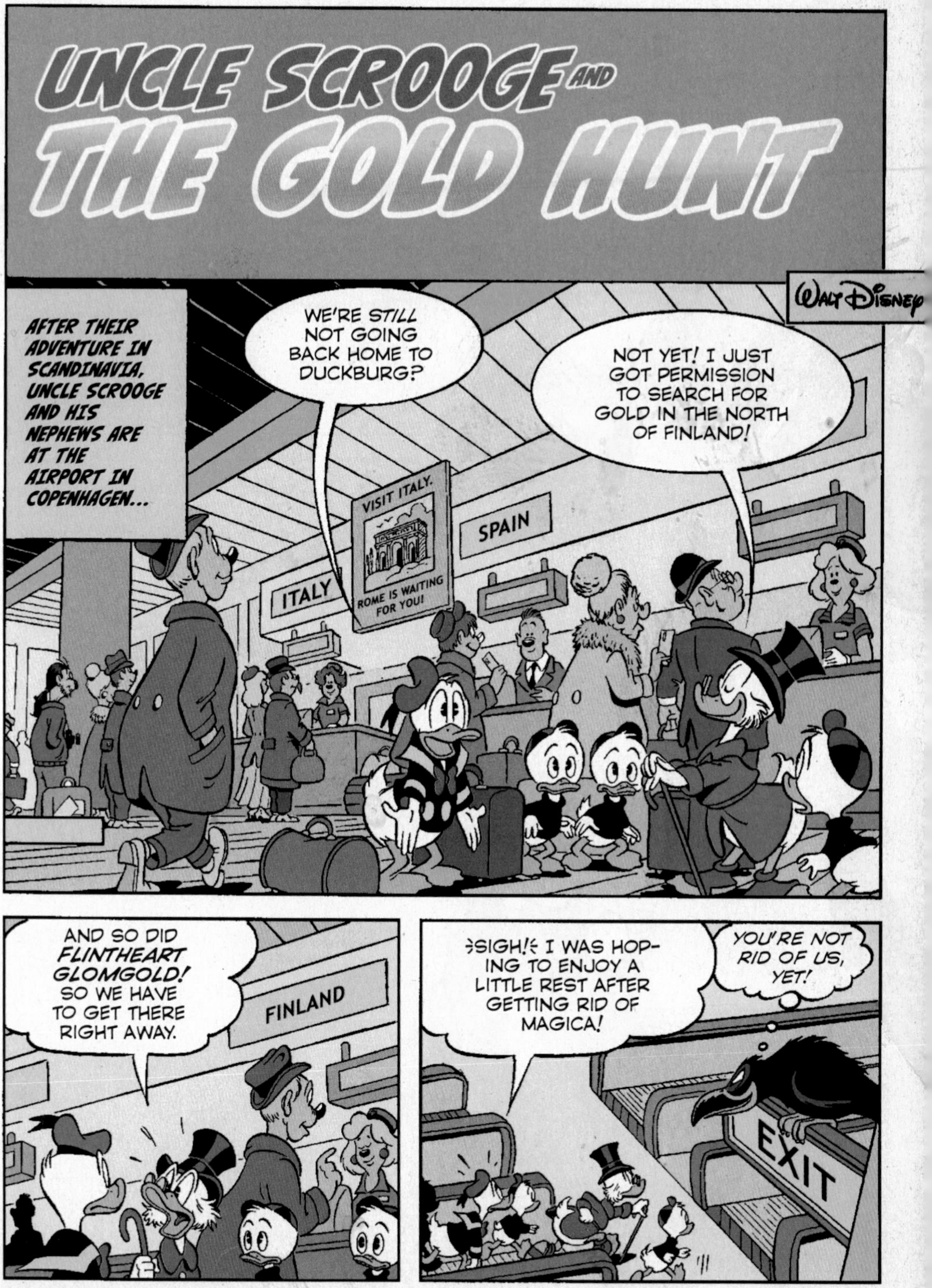
UNCLE SCROOGE AND THE GOLD HUNT
WALT DISNEY
AFTER THEIR ADVENTURE IN SCANDINAVIA, UNCLE SCROOGE AND HIS NEPHEWS ARE AT THE AIRPORT IN COPENHAGEN...
WE'RE STILL NOT GOING BACK HOME TO DUCKBURG?
NOT YET! I JUST GOT PERMISSION TO SEARCH FOR GOLD IN THE NORTH OF FINLAND!
VISIT ITALY. ROME IS WAITING FOR YOU!
SPAIN
ITALY
AND SO DID FLINTHEART GLOMGOLD! SO WE HAVE TO GET THERE RIGHT AWAY.
FINLAND
SIGH! I WAS HOPING TO ENJOY A LITTLE REST AFTER GETTING RID OF MAGICA!
YOU'RE NOT RID OF US, YET!
EXIT

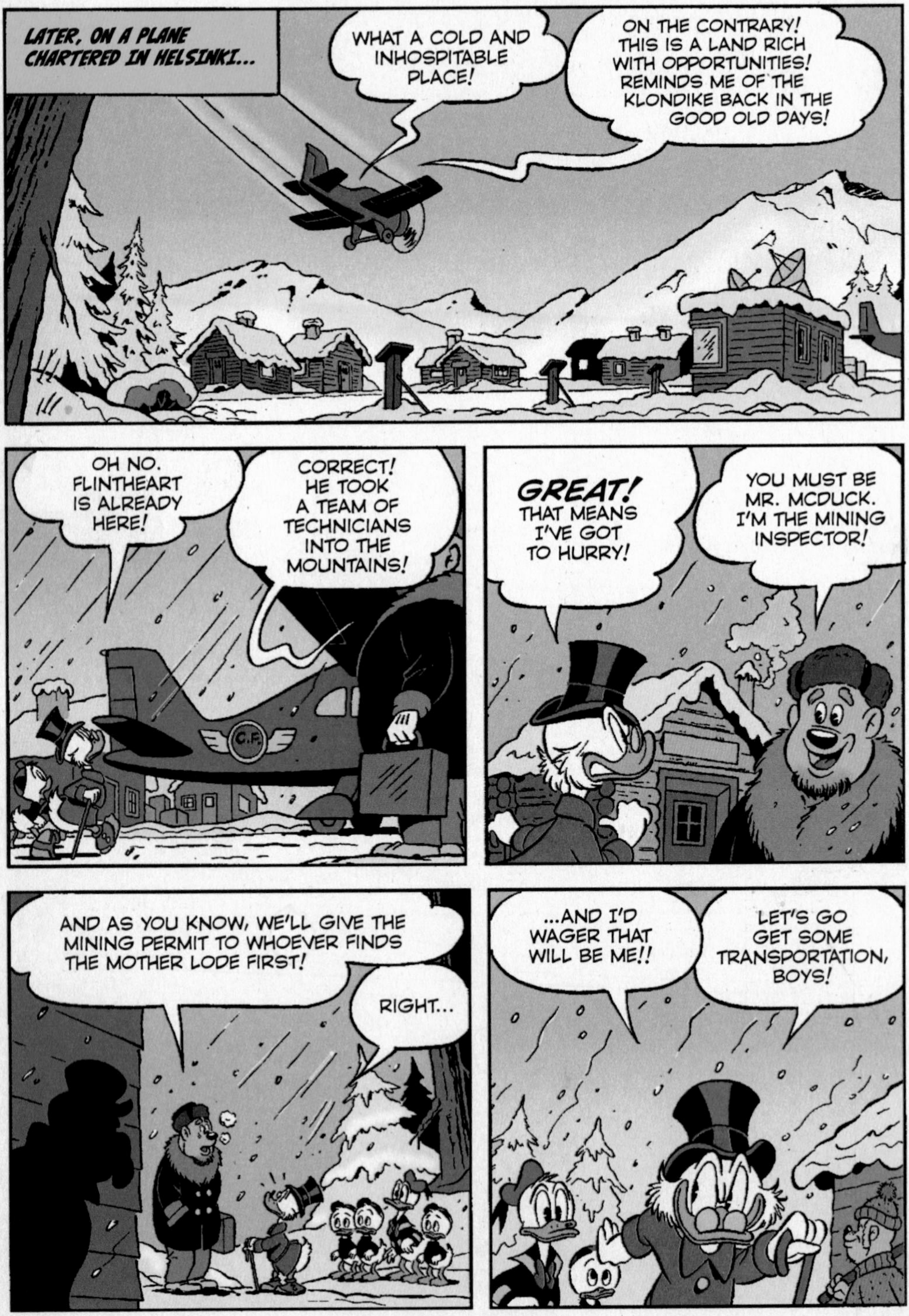
LATER, ON A PLANE CHARTERED IN HELSINKI...
WHAT A COLD AND INHOSPITABLE PLACE!
ON THE CONTRARY! THIS IS A LAND RICH WITH OPPORTUNITIES! REMINDS ME OF THE KLONDIKE BACK IN THE GOOD OLD DAYS!
OH NO. FLINTHEART IS ALREADY HERE!
CORRECT! HE TOOK A TEAM OF TECHNICIANS INTO THE MOUNTAINS!
C.F.
GREAT! THAT MEANS I'VE GOT TO HURRY!
YOU MUST BE MR. MCDUCK. I'M THE MINING INSPECTOR!
AND AS YOU KNOW, WE'LL GIVE THE MINING PERMIT TO WHOEVER FINDS THE MOTHER LODE FIRST!
RIGHT...
...AND I'D WAGER THAT WILL BE ME!!
LET'S GO GET SOME TRANSPORTATION, BOYS!

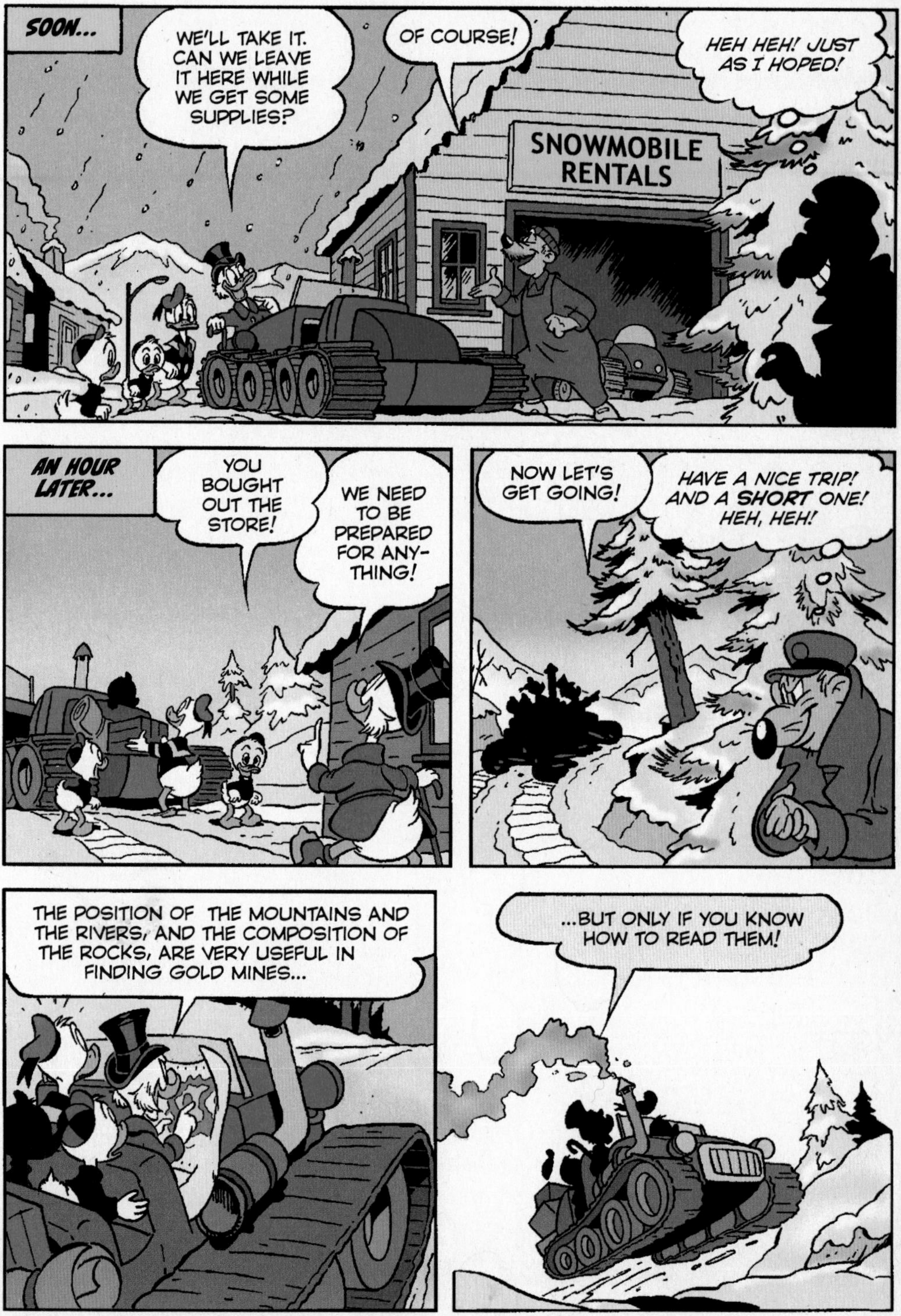
SOON...
WE'LL TAKE IT. CAN WE LEAVE IT HERE WHILE WE GET SOME SUPPLIES?
OF COURSE!
HEH HEH! JUST AS I HOPED!
SNOWMOBILE RENTALS
AN HOUR LATER...
YOU BOUGHT OUT THE STORE!
WE NEED TO BE PREPARED FOR ANY-THING!
NOW LET'S GET GOING!
HAVE A NICE TRIP! AND A SHORT ONE! HEH, HEH!
THE POSITION OF THE MOUNTAINS AND THE RIVERS, AND THE COMPOSITION OF THE ROCKS, ARE VERY USEFUL IN FINDING GOLD MINES...
...BUT ONLY IF YOU KNOW HOW TO READ THEM!

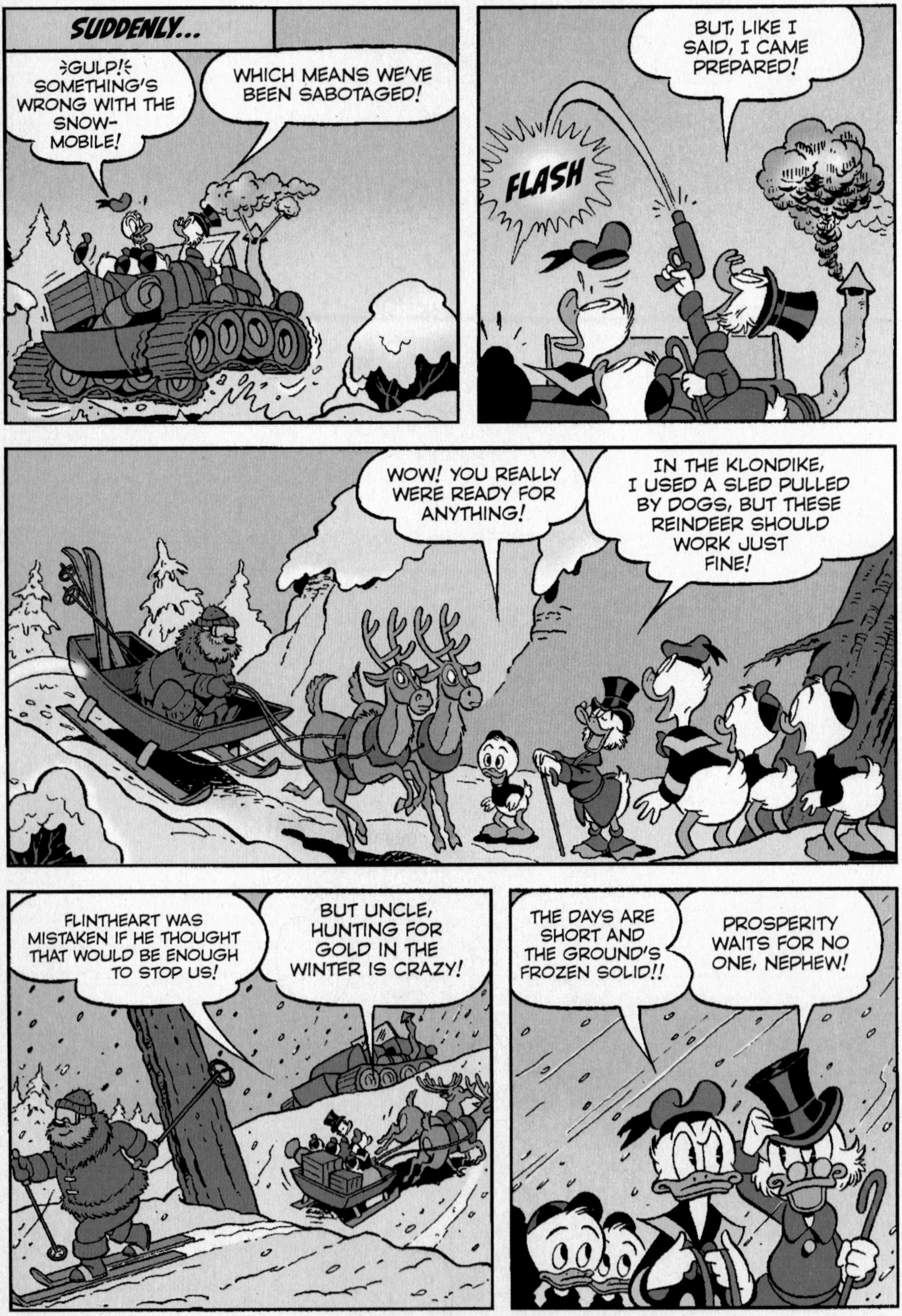
SUDDENLY...
-GULP!- SOMETHING'S WRONG WITH THE SNOW-MOBILE!
WHICH MEANS WE'VE BEEN SABOTAGED!
BUT, LIKE I SAID, I CAME PREPARED!
FLASH
WOW! YOU REALLY WERE READY FOR ANYTHING!
IN THE KLONDIKE, I USED A SLED PULLED BY DOGS, BUT THESE REINDEER SHOULD WORK JUST FINE!
FLINTHEART WAS MISTAKEN IF HE THOUGHT THAT WOULD BE ENOUGH TO STOP US!
BUT UNCLE, HUNTING FOR GOLD IN THE WINTER IS CRAZY!
THE DAYS ARE SHORT AND THE GROUND'S FROZEN SOLID!!
PROSPERITY WAITS FOR NO ONE, NEPHEW!

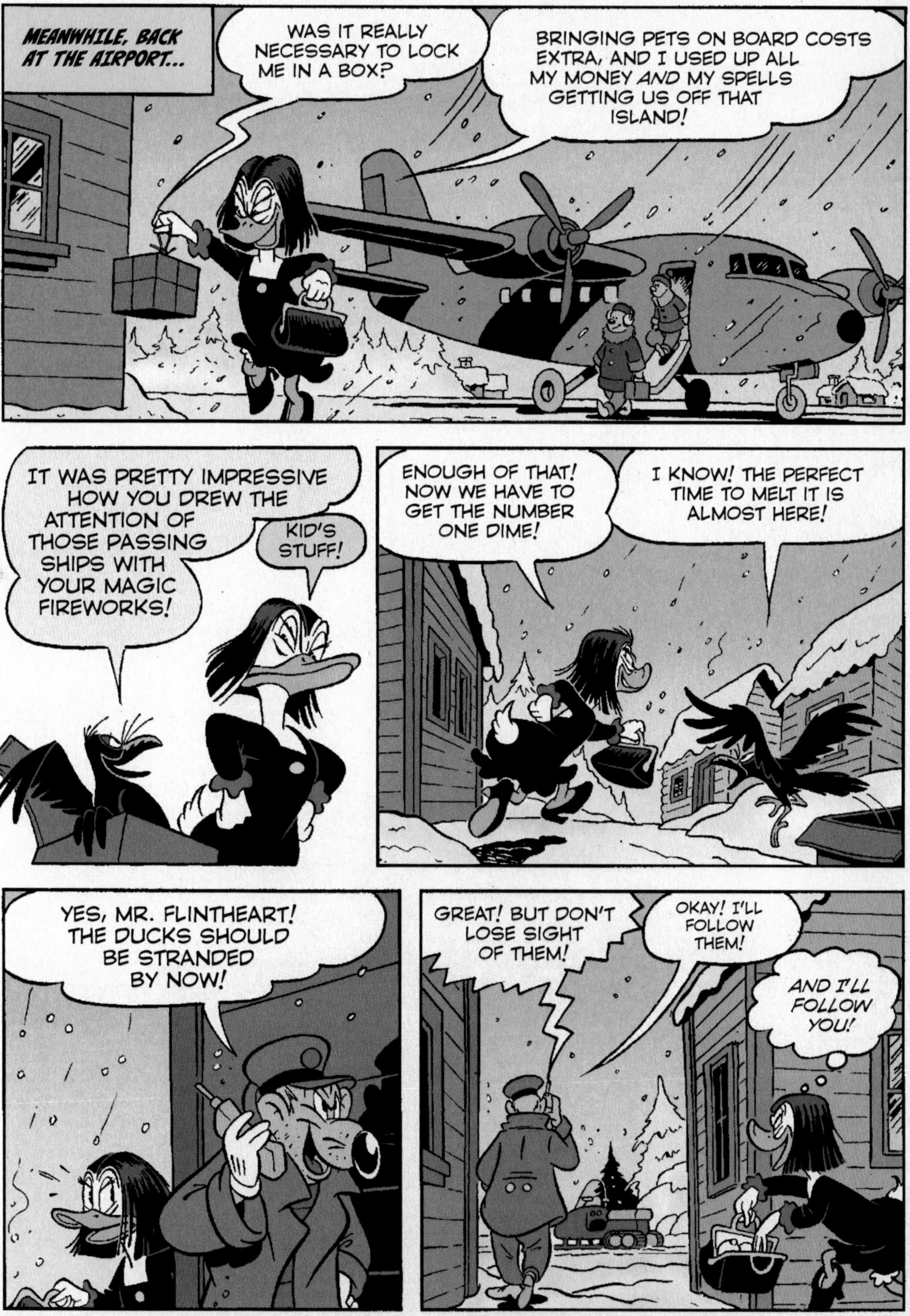
MEANWHILE, BACK AT THE AIRPORT...
WAS IT REALLY NECESSARY TO LOCK ME IN A BOX?
BRINGING PETS ON BOARD COSTS EXTRA, AND I USED UP ALL MY MONEY AND MY SPELLS GETTING US OFF THAT ISLAND!
IT WAS PRETTY IMPRESSIVE HOW YOU DREW THE ATTENTION OF THOSE PASSING SHIPS WITH YOUR MAGIC FIREWORKS!
KID'S STUFF!
ENOUGH OF THAT! NOW WE HAVE TO GET THE NUMBER ONE DIME!
I KNOW! THE PERFECT TIME TO MELT IT IS ALMOST HERE!
YES, MR. FLINTHEART! THE DUCKS SHOULD BE STRANDED BY NOW!
GREAT! BUT DON'T LOSE SIGHT OF THEM!
OKAY! I'LL FOLLOW THEM!
AND I'LL FOLLOW YOU!

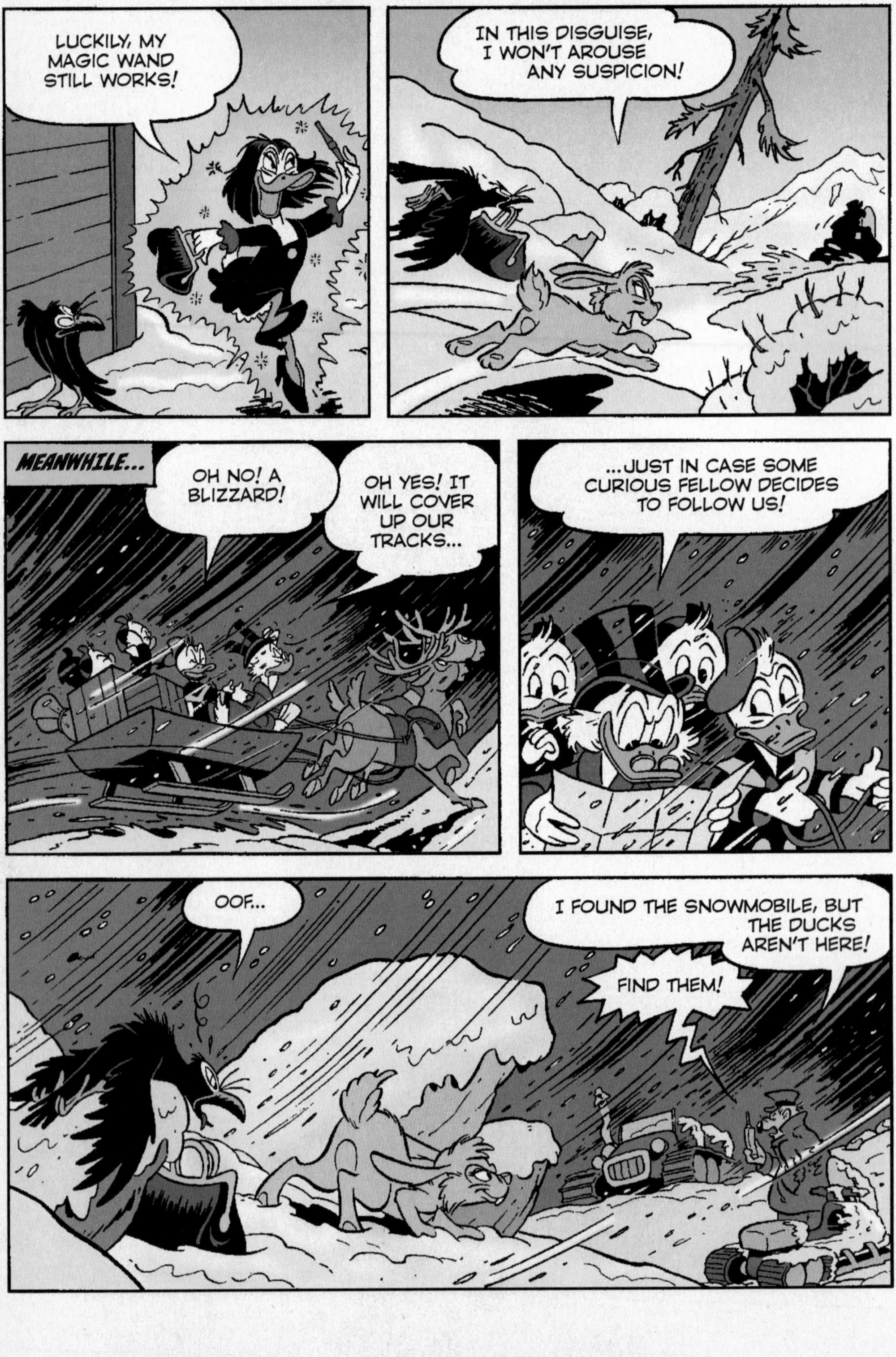
LUCKILY, MY MAGIC WAND STILL WORKS!
IN THIS DISGUISE, I WON'T AROUSE ANY SUSPICION!
MEANWHILE...
OH NO! A BLIZZARD!
OH YES! IT WILL COVER UP OUR TRACKS...
...JUST IN CASE SOME CURIOUS FELLOW DECIDES TO FOLLOW US!
OOF...
I FOUND THE SNOWMOBILE, BUT THE DUCKS AREN'T HERE!
FIND THEM!

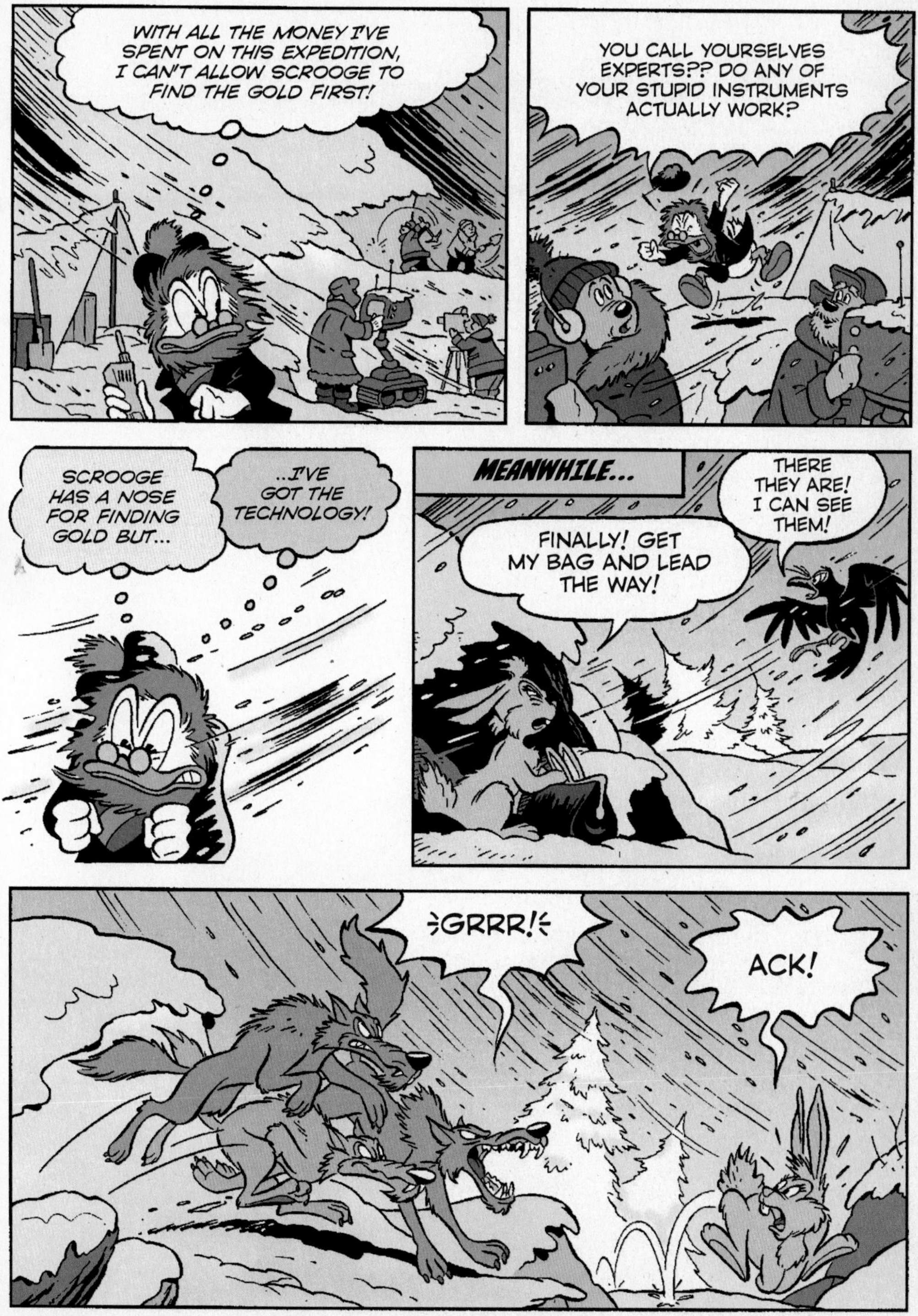
WITH ALL THE MONEY I'VE SPENT ON THIS EXPEDITION, I CAN'T ALLOW SCROOGE TO FIND THE GOLD FIRST!
YOU CALL YOURSELVES EXPERTS?? DO ANY OF YOUR STUPID INSTRUMENTS ACTUALLY WORK?
SCROOGE HAS A NOSE FOR FINDING GOLD BUT...
...I'VE GOT THE TECHNOLOGY!
MEANWHILE...
THERE THEY ARE! I CAN SEE THEM!
FINALLY! GET MY BAG AND LEAD THE WAY!
GRRR!
ACK!

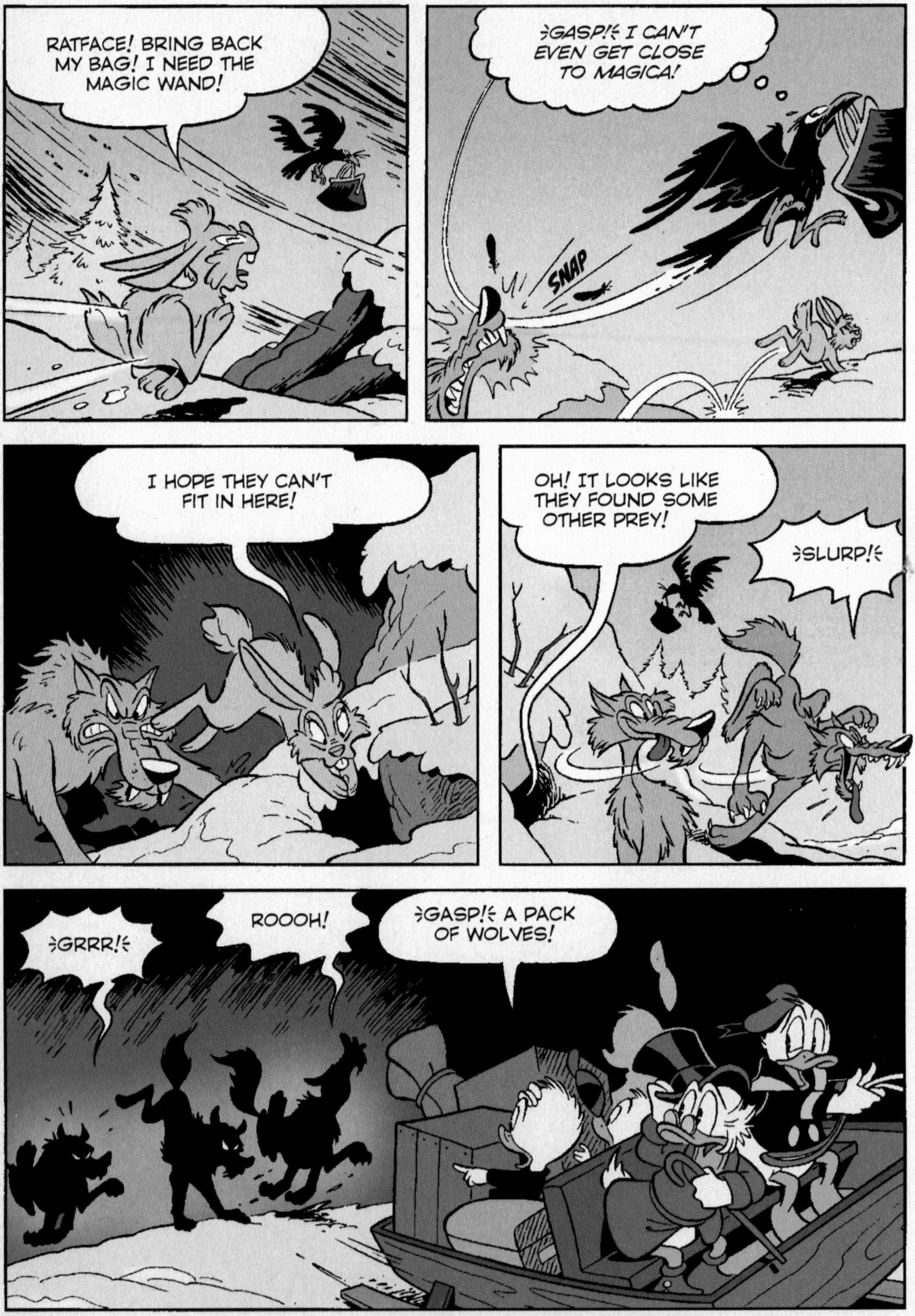
RATFACE! BRING BACK MY BAG! I NEED THE MAGIC WAND!
GASP! I CAN'T EVEN GET CLOSE TO MAGICA!
SNAP
I HOPE THEY CAN'T FIT IN HERE!
OH! IT LOOKS LIKE THEY FOUND SOME OTHER PREY!
SLURP!
GRRR!
ROOOH!
GASP! A PACK OF WOLVES!

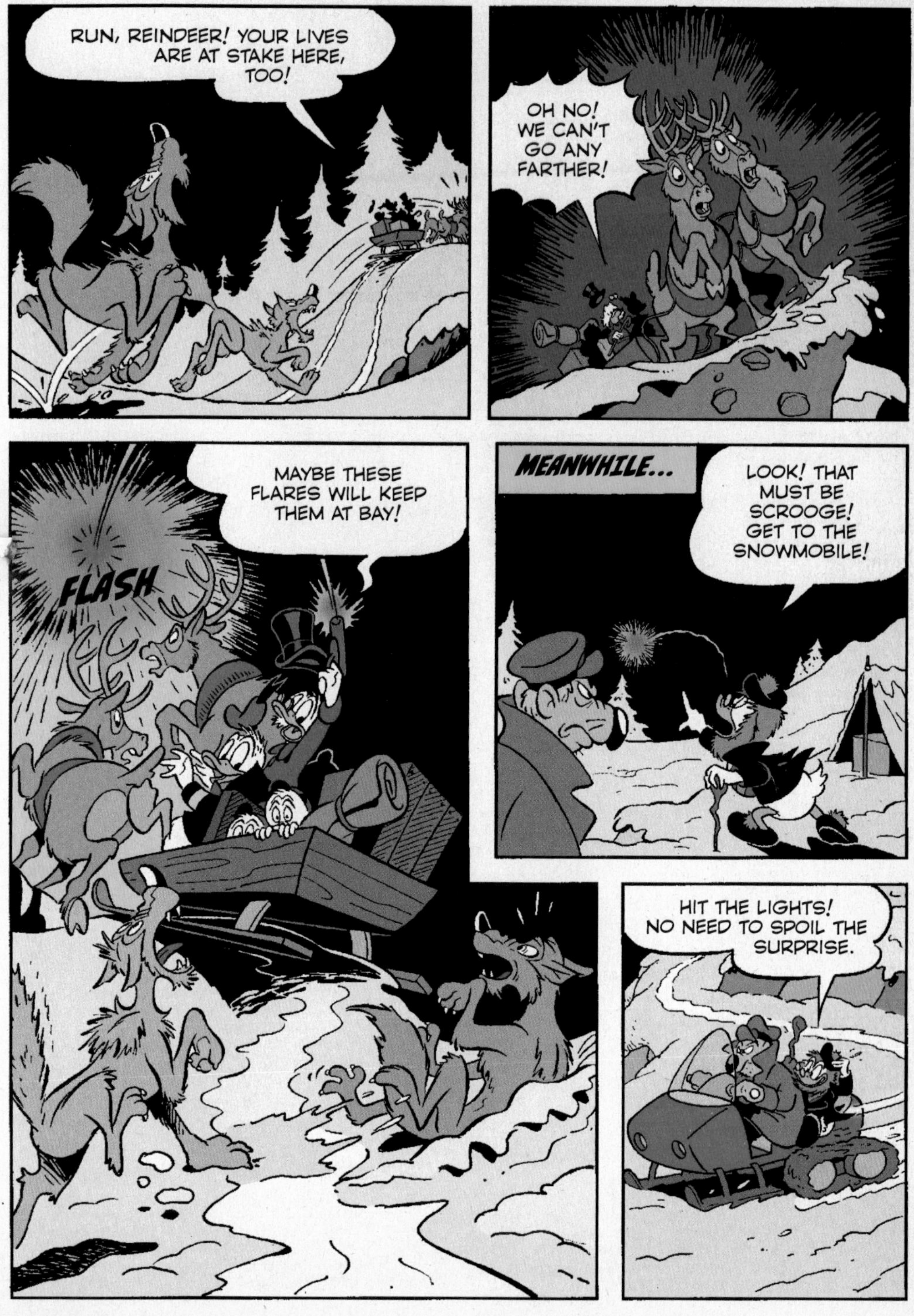
RUN, REINDEER! YOUR LIVES ARE AT STAKE HERE, TOO!
OH NO! WE CAN'T GO ANY FARTHER!
MAYBE THESE FLARES WILL KEEP THEM AT BAY!
FLASH
MEANWHILE...
LOOK! THAT MUST BE SCROOGE! GET TO THE SNOWMOBILE!
HIT THE LIGHTS! NO NEED TO SPOIL THE SURPRISE.

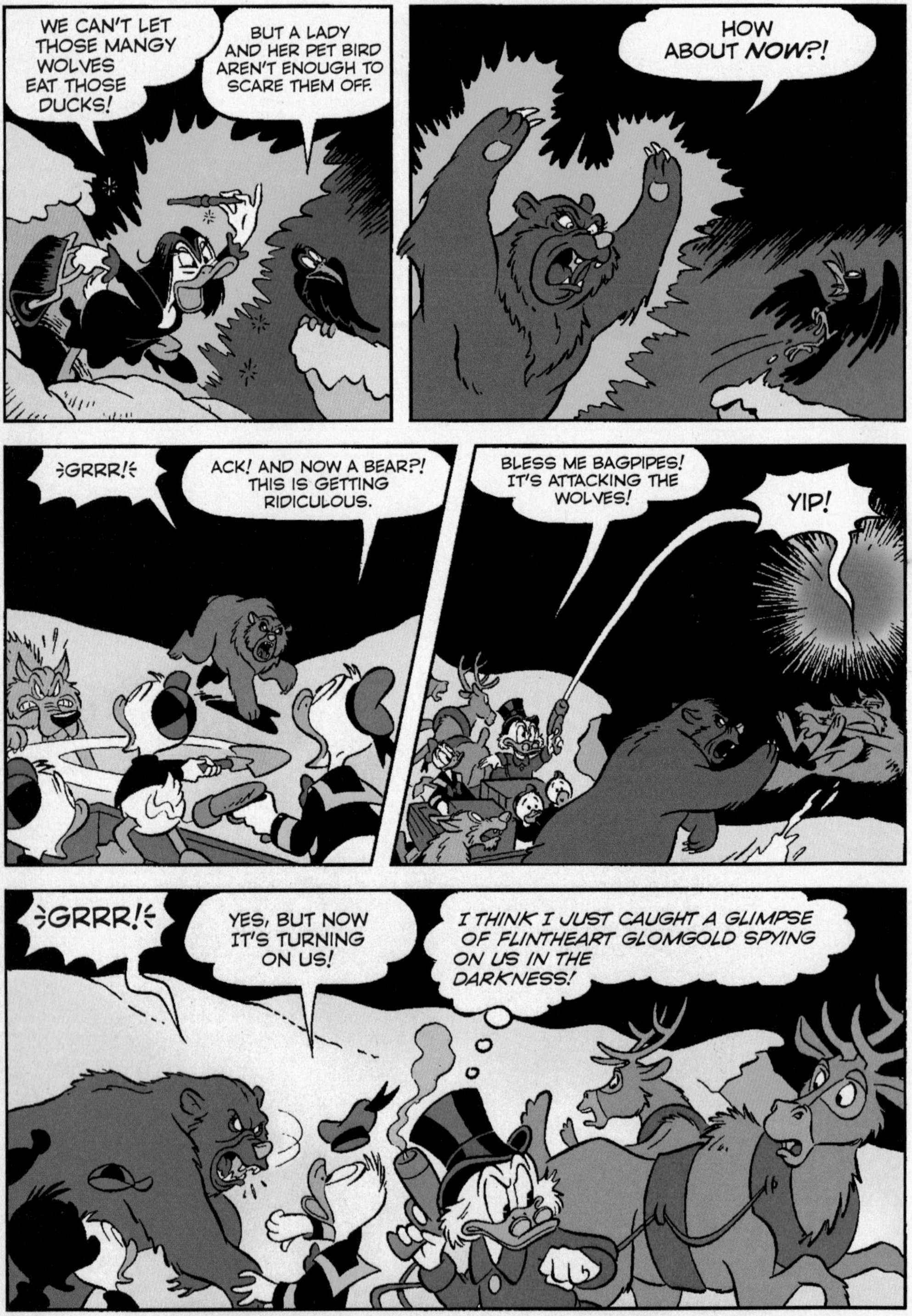
WE CAN'T LET THOSE MANGY WOLVES EAT THOSE DUCKS!
BUT A LADY AND HER PET BIRD AREN'T ENOUGH TO SCARE THEM OFF.
HOW ABOUT NOW?!
GRRR!
ACK! AND NOW A BEAR?! THIS IS GETTING RIDICULOUS.
BLESS ME BAGPIPES! IT'S ATTACKING THE WOLVES!
YIP!
GRRR!
YES, BUT NOW IT'S TURNING ON US!
I THINK I JUST CAUGHT A GLIMPSE OF FLINTHEART GLOMGOLD SPYING ON US IN THE DARKNESS!

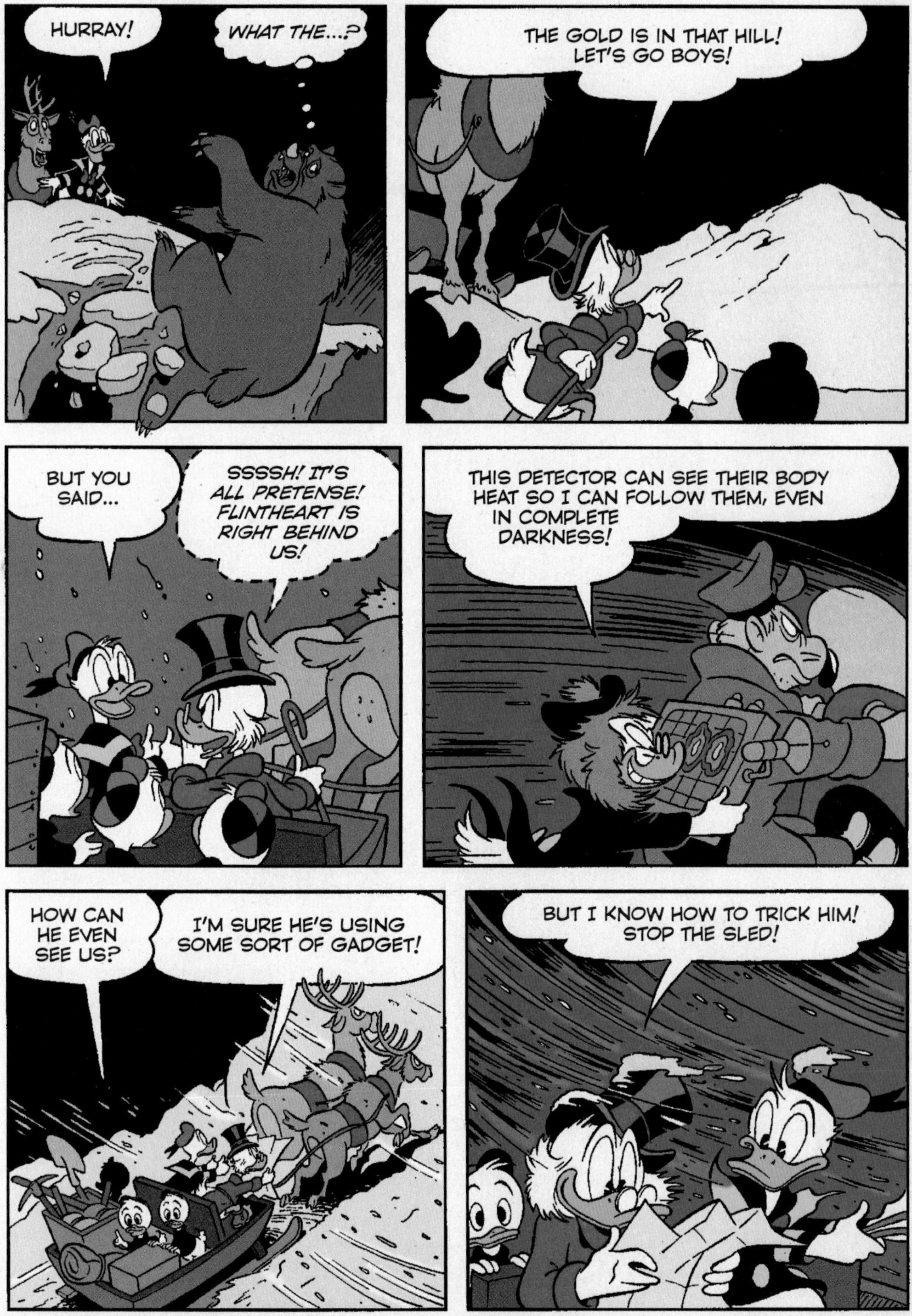
HURRAY!
WHAT THE...?
THE GOLD IS IN THAT HILL! LET'S GO BOYS!
BUT YOU SAID...
SSSSH! IT'S ALL PRETENSE! FLINTHEART IS RIGHT BEHIND US!
THIS DETECTOR CAN SEE THEIR BODY HEAT SO I CAN FOLLOW THEM, EVEN IN COMPLETE DARKNESS!
HOW CAN HE EVEN SEE US?
I'M SURE HE'S USING SOME SORT OF GADGET!
BUT I KNOW HOW TO TRICK HIM! STOP THE SLED!

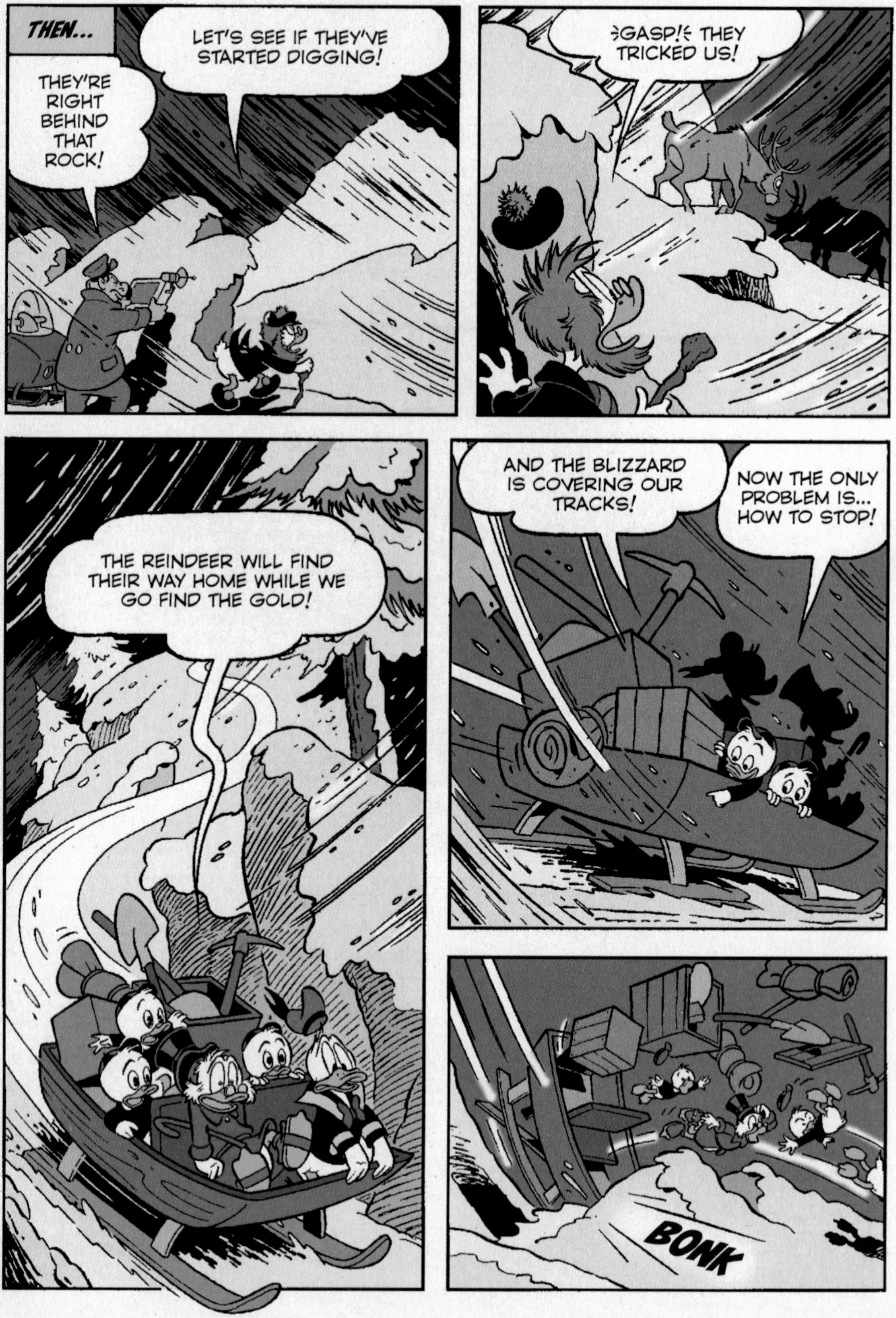
THEN...
LET'S SEE IF THEY'VE STARTED DIGGING!
THEY'RE RIGHT BEHIND THAT ROCK!
GASP! THEY TRICKED US!
THE REINDEER WILL FIND THEIR WAY HOME WHILE WE GO FIND THE GOLD!
AND THE BLIZZARD IS COVERING OUR TRACKS!
NOW THE ONLY PROBLEM IS... HOW TO STOP!
BONK

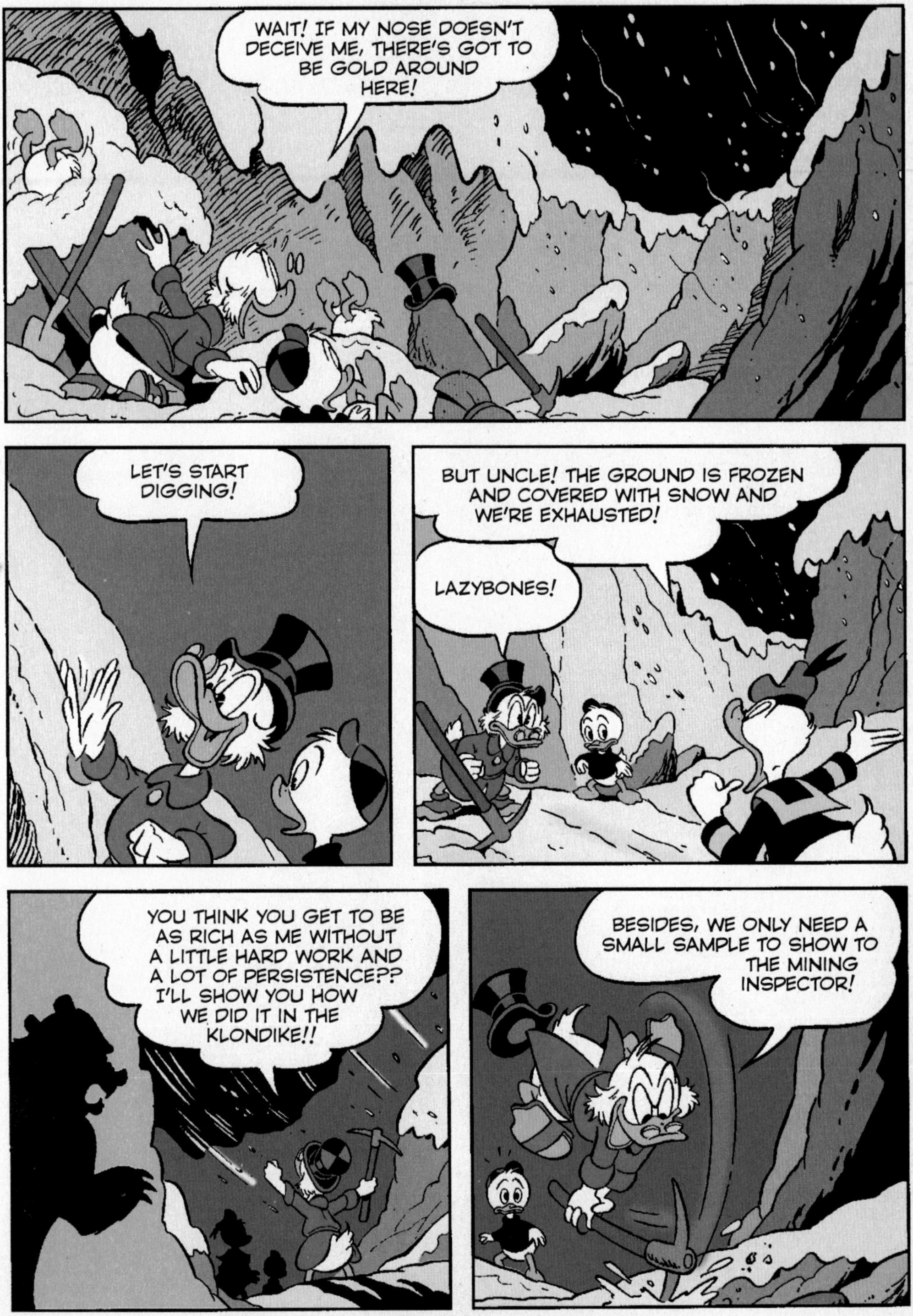
WAIT! IF MY NOSE DOESN'T DECEIVE ME, THERE'S GOT TO BE GOLD AROUND HERE!
LET'S START DIGGING!
BUT UNCLE! THE GROUND IS FROZEN AND COVERED WITH SNOW AND WE'RE EXHAUSTED!
LAZYBONES!
YOU THINK YOU GET TO BE AS RICH AS ME WITHOUT A LITTLE HARD WORK AND A LOT OF PERSISTENCE?? I'LL SHOW YOU HOW WE DID IT IN THE KLONDIKE!!
BESIDES, WE ONLY NEED A SMALL SAMPLE TO SHOW TO THE MINING INSPECTOR!

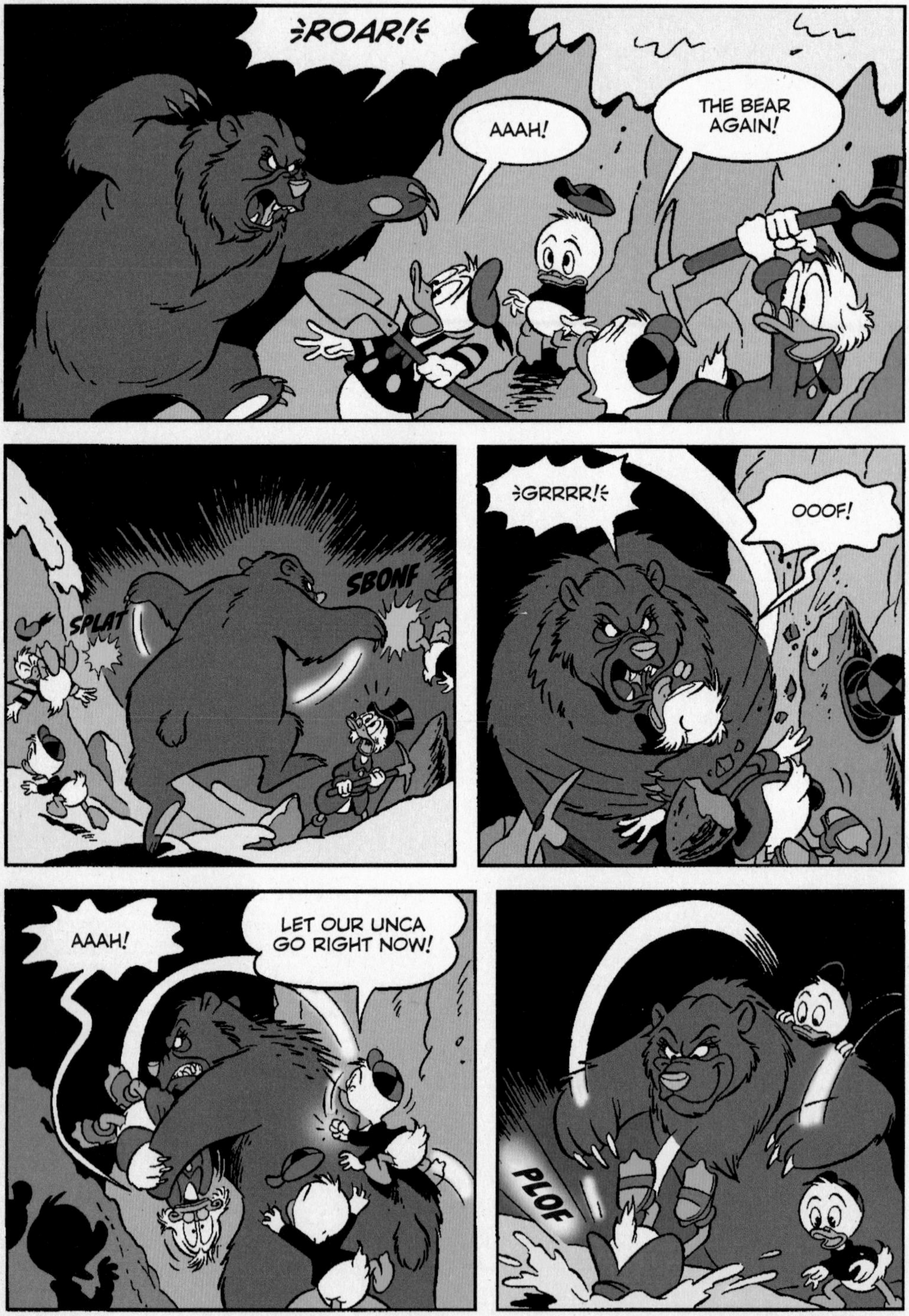
ROAR!
AAAH!
THE BEAR AGAIN!
SPLAT
SBONF
GRRRR!
OOOF!
AAAH!
LET OUR UNCA GO RIGHT NOW!
PLOF

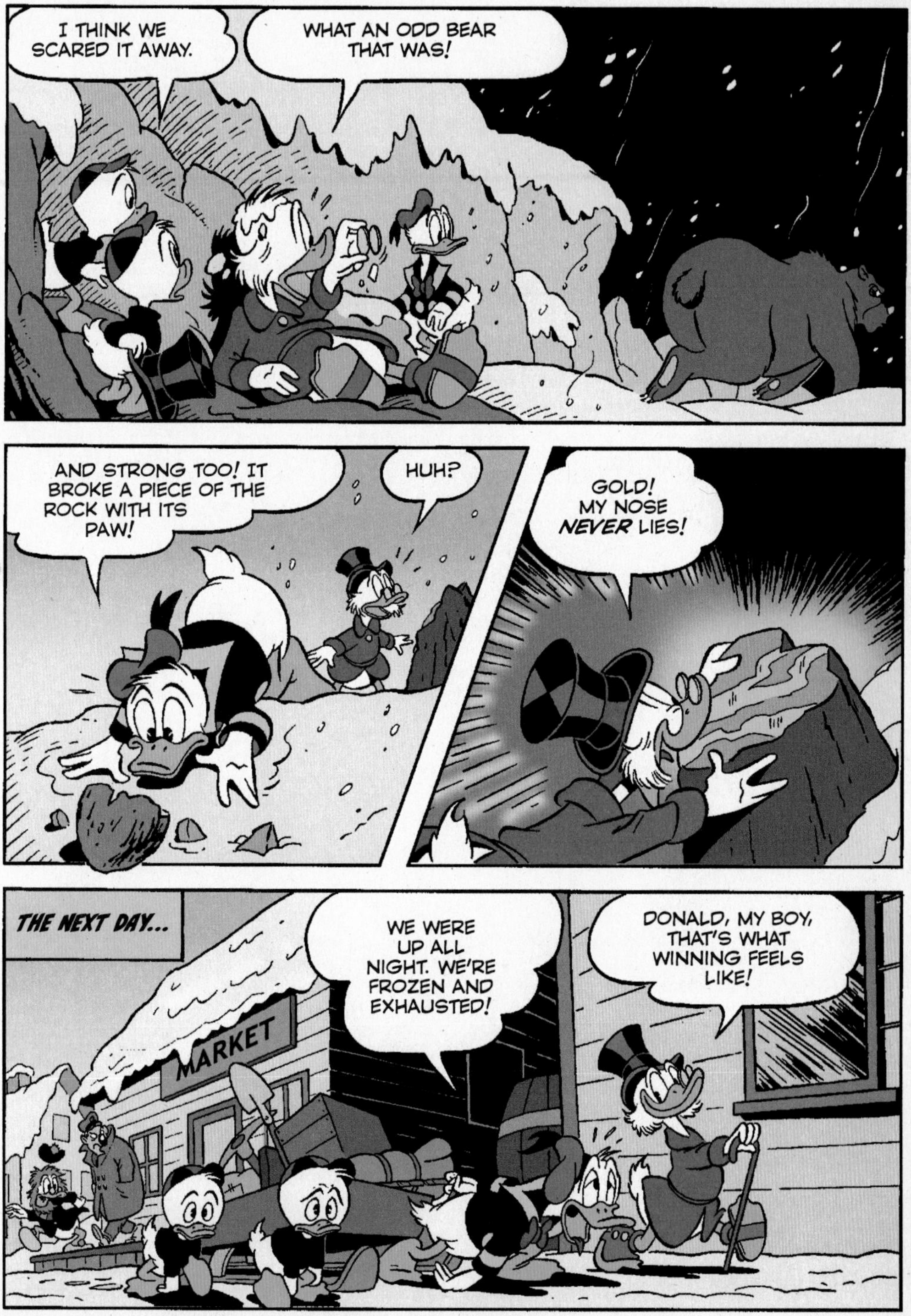
I THINK WE SCARED IT AWAY.
WHAT AN ODD BEAR THAT WAS!
AND STRONG TOO! IT BROKE A PIECE OF THE ROCK WITH ITS PAW!
HUH?
GOLD! MY NOSE NEVER LIES!
THE NEXT DAY...
MARKET
WE WERE UP ALL NIGHT. WE'RE FROZEN AND EXHAUSTED!
DONALD, MY BOY, THAT'S WHAT WINNING FEELS LIKE!

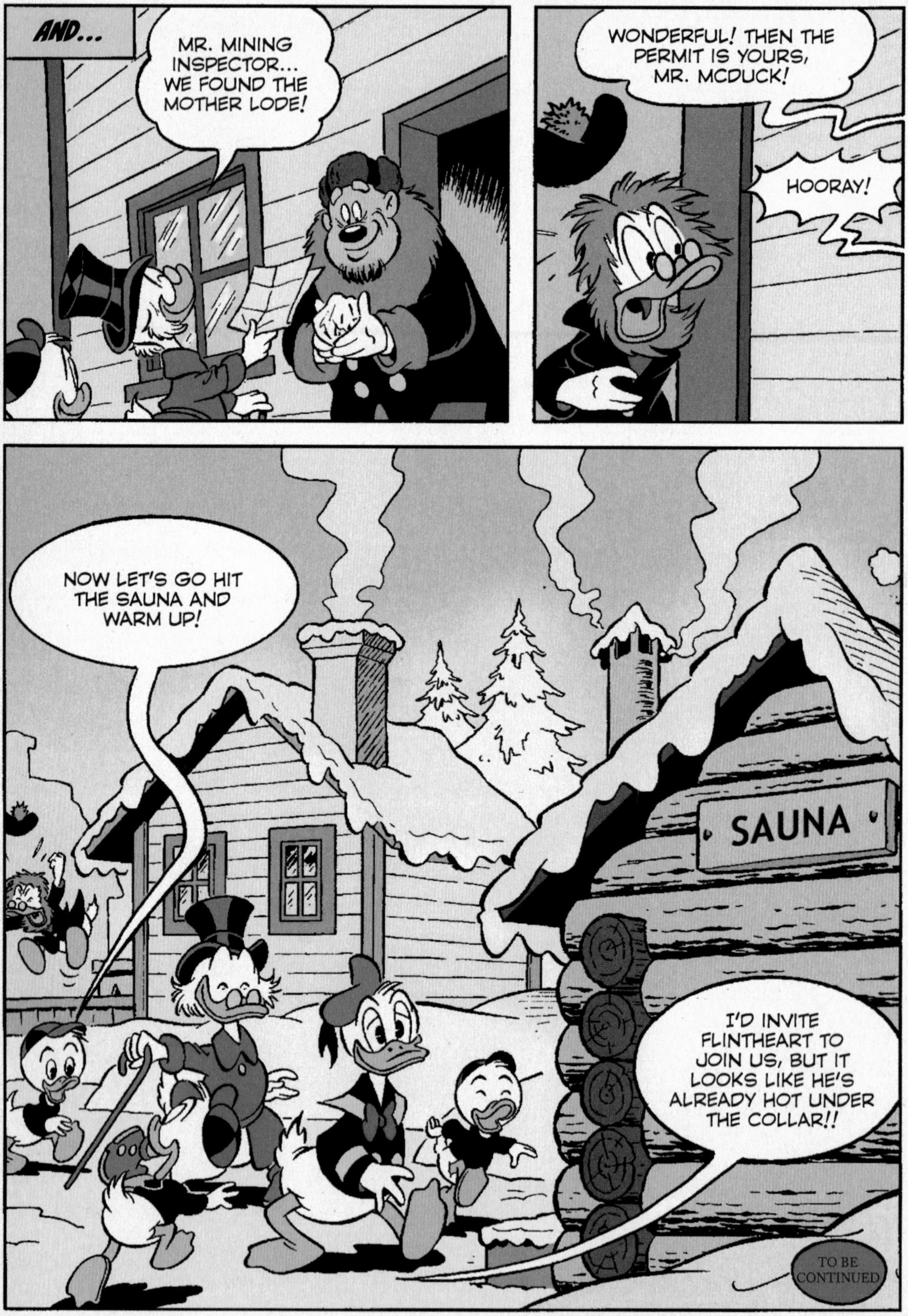
AND...
MR. MINING INSPECTOR... WE FOUND THE MOTHER LODE!
WONDERFUL! THEN THE PERMIT IS YOURS, MR. MCDUCK!
HOORAY!
NOW LET'S GO HIT THE SAUNA AND WARM UP!
SAUNA
I'D INVITE FLINTHEART TO JOIN US, BUT IT LOOKS LIKE HE'S ALREADY HOT UNDER THE COLLAR!!
TO BE CONTINUED

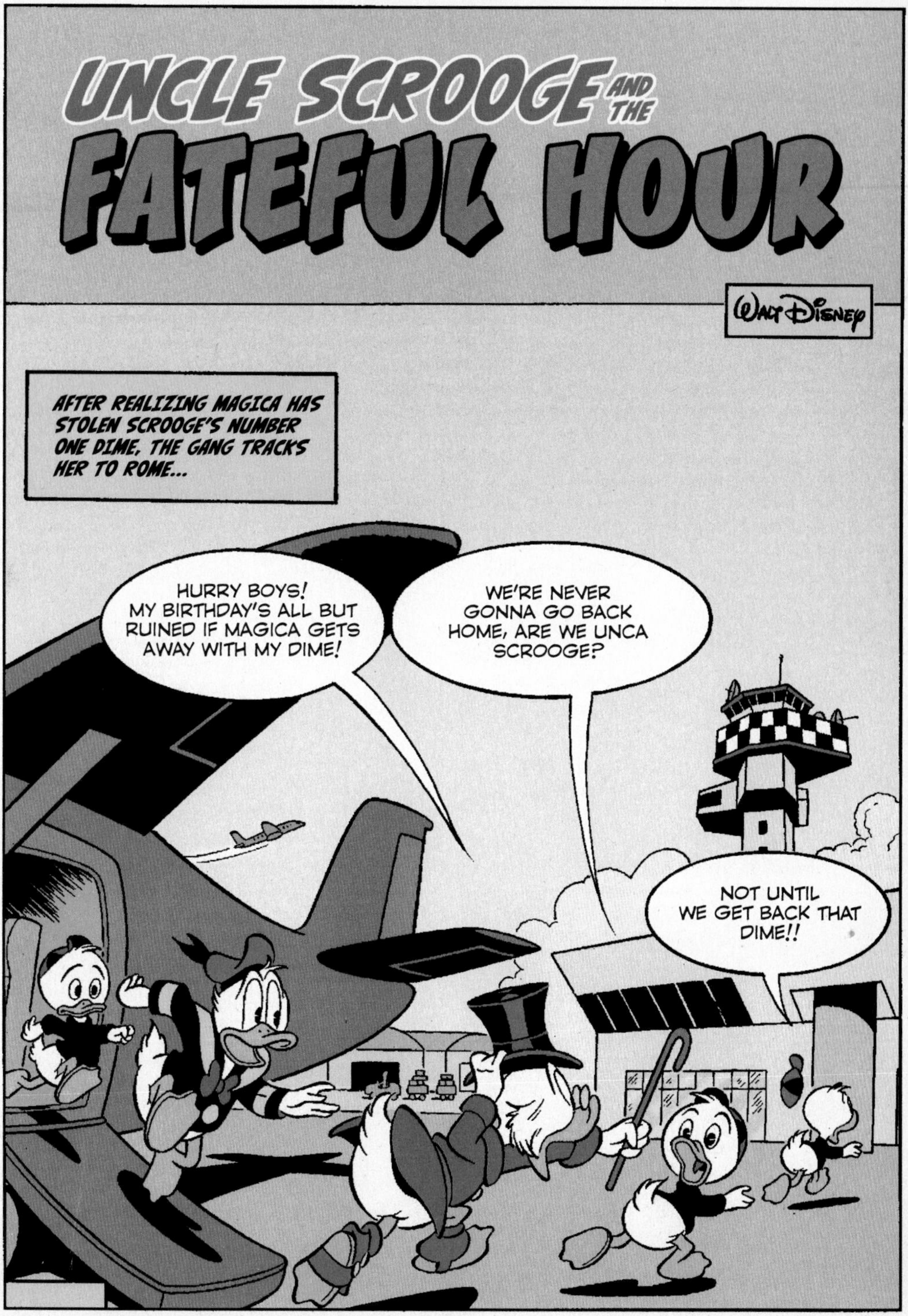
UNCLE SCROOGE AND THE
FATEFUL HOUR
WALT DISNEY
AFTER REALIZING MAGICA HAS STOLEN SCROOGE'S NUMBER ONE DIME, THE GANG TRACKS HER TO ROME...
HURRY BOYS! MY BIRTHDAY'S ALL BUT RUINED IF MAGICA GETS AWAY WITH MY DIME!
WE'RE NEVER GONNA GO BACK HOME, ARE WE UNCA SCROOGE?
NOT UNTIL WE GET BACK THAT DIME!!

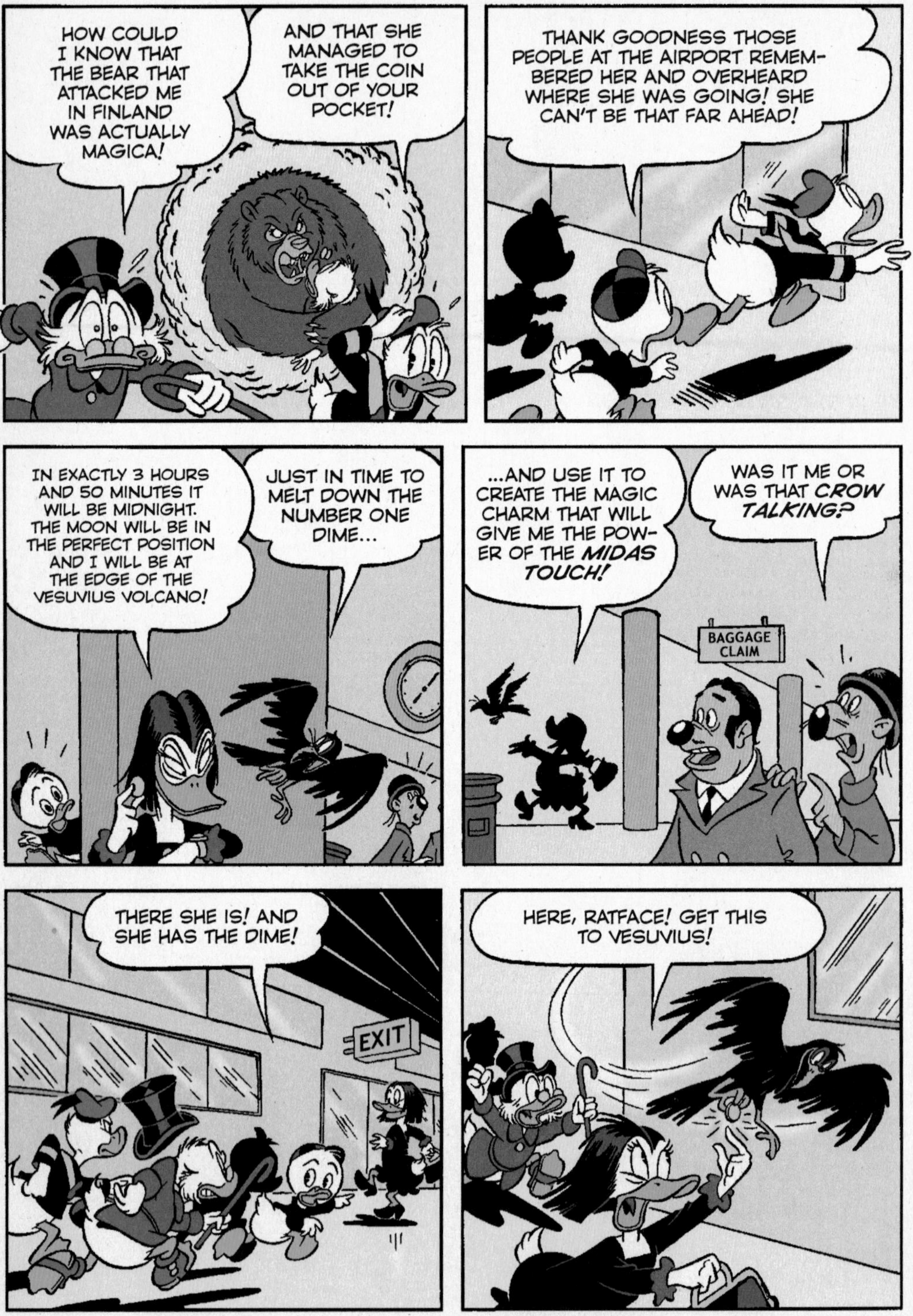

HOW COULD I KNOW THAT THE BEAR THAT ATTACKED ME IN FINLAND WAS ACTUALLY MAGICA!
AND THAT SHE MANAGED TO TAKE THE COIN OUT OF YOUR POCKET!
THANK GOODNESS THOSE PEOPLE AT THE AIRPORT REMEMBERED HER AND OVERHEARD WHERE SHE WAS GOING! SHE CAN'T BE THAT FAR AHEAD!
IN EXACTLY 3 HOURS AND 50 MINUTES IT WILL BE MIDNIGHT. THE MOON WILL BE IN THE PERFECT POSITION AND I WILL BE AT THE EDGE OF THE VESUVIUS VOLCANO!
JUST IN TIME TO MELT DOWN THE NUMBER ONE DIME...
...AND USE IT TO CREATE THE MAGIC CHARM THAT WILL GIVE ME THE POWER OF THE *MIDAS TOUCH!*
BAGGAGE CLAIM
WAS IT ME OR WAS THAT *CROW TALKING?*
THERE SHE IS! AND SHE HAS THE DIME!
EXIT
HERE, RATFACE! GET THIS TO VESUVIUS!

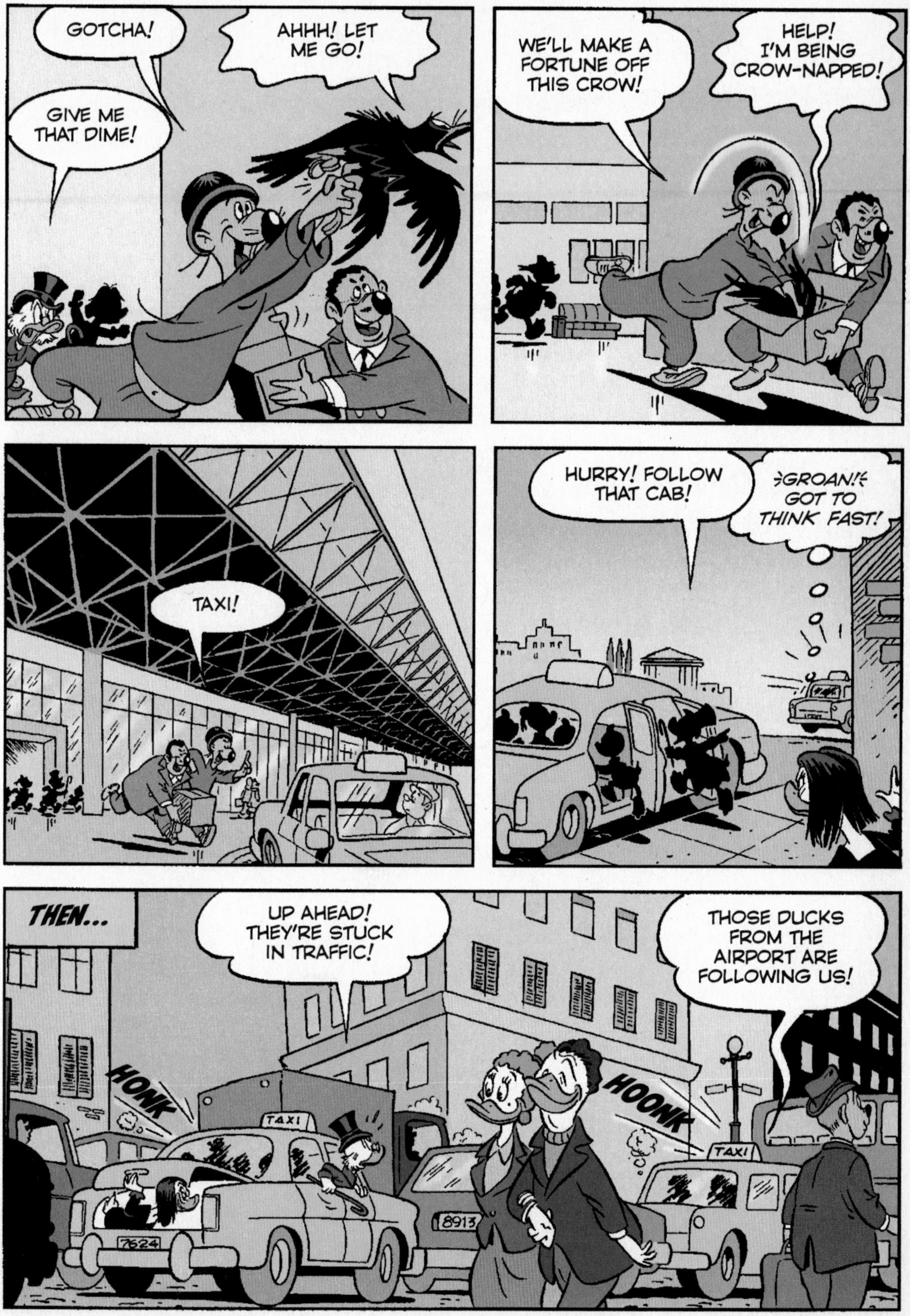
GOTCHA!
AHHH! LET ME GO!
GIVE ME THAT DIME!
WE'LL MAKE A FORTUNE OFF THIS CROW!
HELP! I'M BEING CROW-NAPPED!
TAXI!
HURRY! FOLLOW THAT CAB!
GROAN! GOT TO THINK FAST!
THEN...
UP AHEAD! THEY'RE STUCK IN TRAFFIC!
THOSE DUCKS FROM THE AIRPORT ARE FOLLOWING US!
HONK
HOONK
TAXI
7624
8913
TAXI

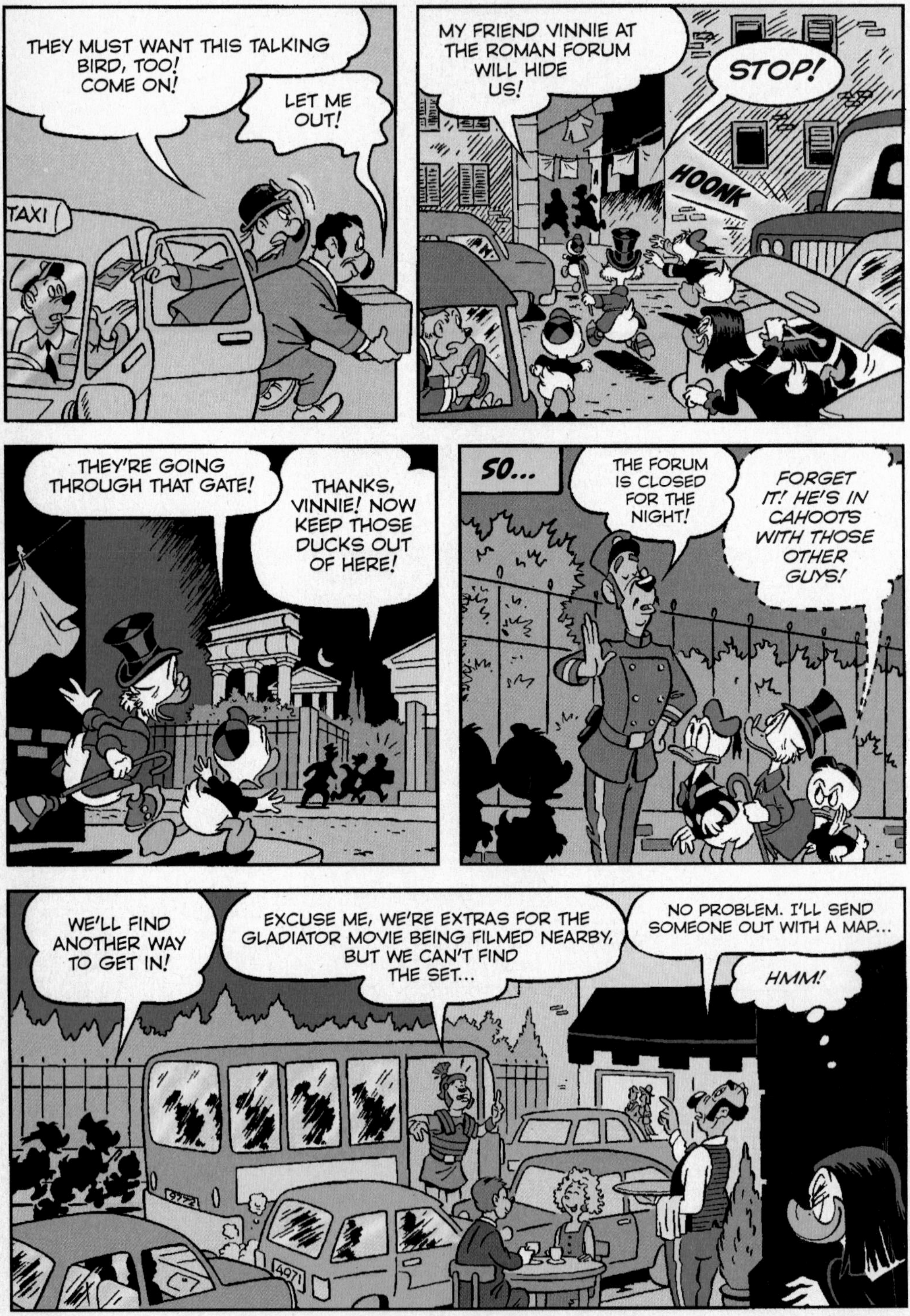
THEY MUST WANT THIS TALKING BIRD, TOO! COME ON!
LET ME OUT!
TAXI
MY FRIEND VINNIE AT THE ROMAN FORUM WILL HIDE US!
STOP!
HOONK
THEY'RE GOING THROUGH THAT GATE!
THANKS, VINNIE! NOW KEEP THOSE DUCKS OUT OF HERE!
SO...
THE FORUM IS CLOSED FOR THE NIGHT!
FORGET IT! HE'S IN CAHOOTS WITH THOSE OTHER GUYS!
WE'LL FIND ANOTHER WAY TO GET IN!
EXCUSE ME, WE'RE EXTRAS FOR THE GLADIATOR MOVIE BEING FILMED NEARBY, BUT WE CAN'T FIND THE SET...
NO PROBLEM. I'LL SEND SOMEONE OUT WITH A MAP...
HMM!

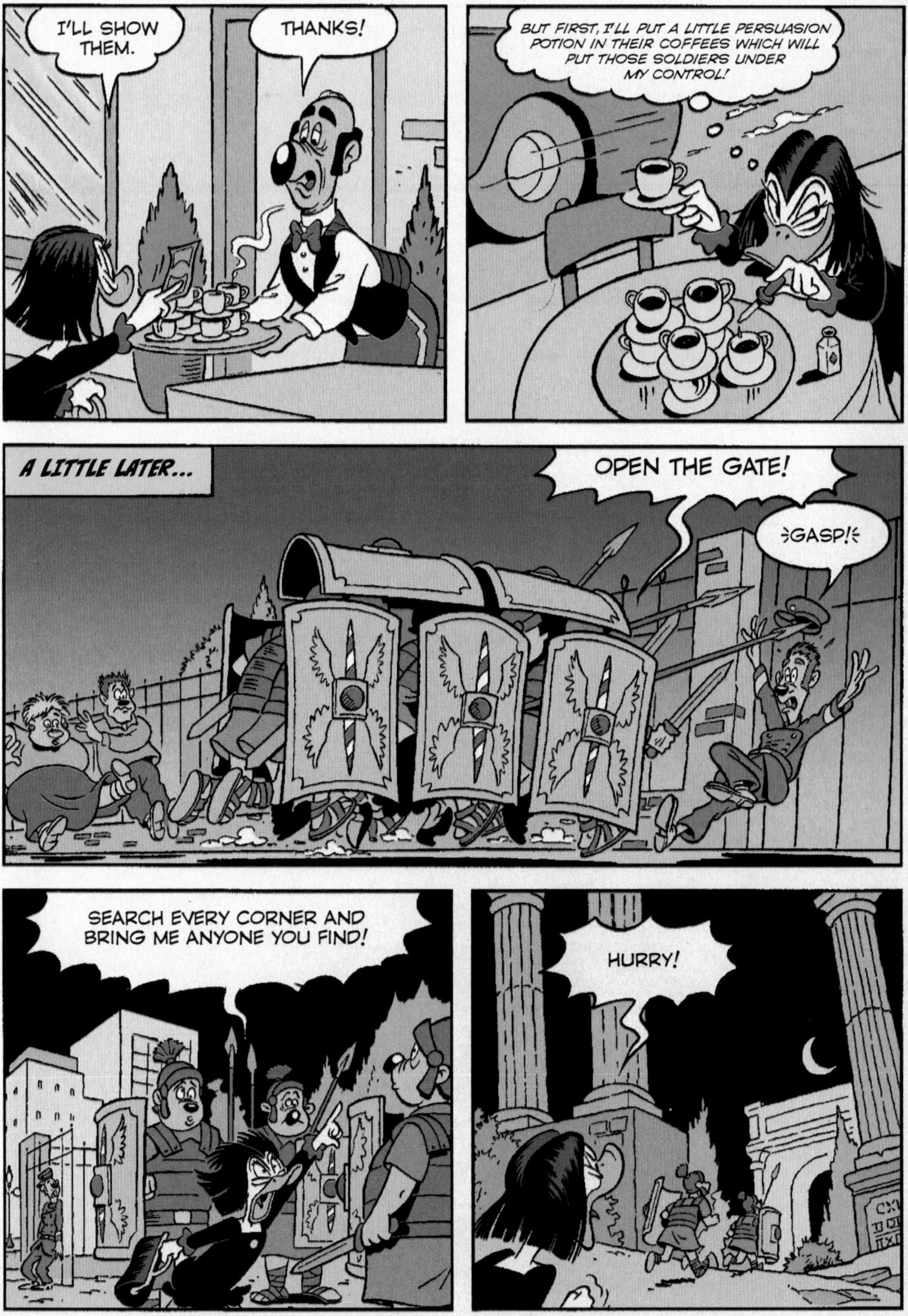
I'LL SHOW THEM.
THANKS!
BUT FIRST, I'LL PUT A LITTLE PERSUASION POTION IN THEIR COFFEES WHICH WILL PUT THOSE SOLDIERS UNDER MY CONTROL!
A LITTLE LATER...
OPEN THE GATE!
GASP!
SEARCH EVERY CORNER AND BRING ME ANYONE YOU FIND!
HURRY!

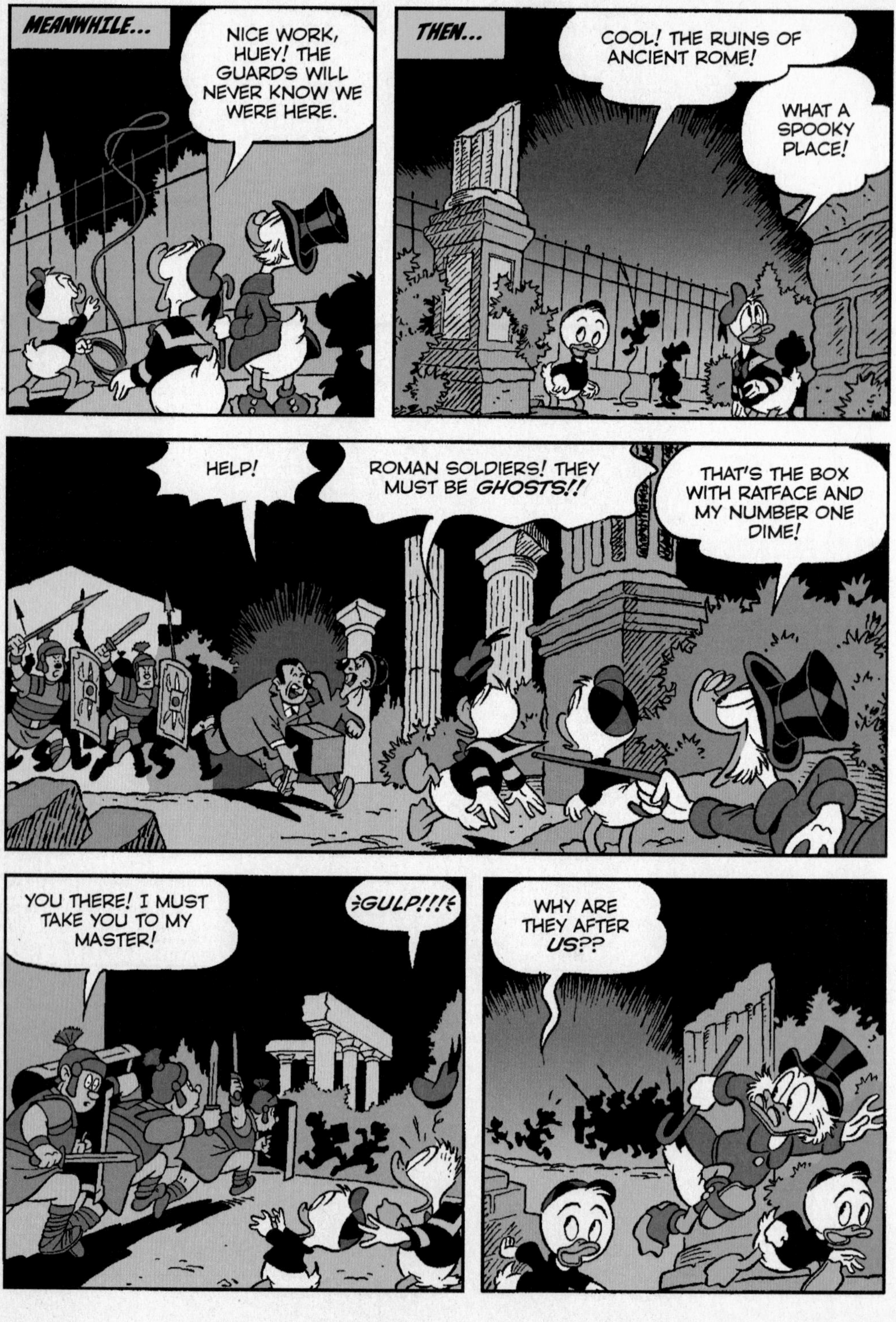
MEANWHILE...
NICE WORK, HUEY! THE GUARDS WILL NEVER KNOW WE WERE HERE.
THEN...
COOL! THE RUINS OF ANCIENT ROME!
WHAT A SPOOKY PLACE!
HELP!
ROMAN SOLDIERS! THEY MUST BE GHOSTS!!
THAT'S THE BOX WITH RATFACE AND MY NUMBER ONE DIME!
YOU THERE! I MUST TAKE YOU TO MY MASTER!
GULP!!!
WHY ARE THEY AFTER US??

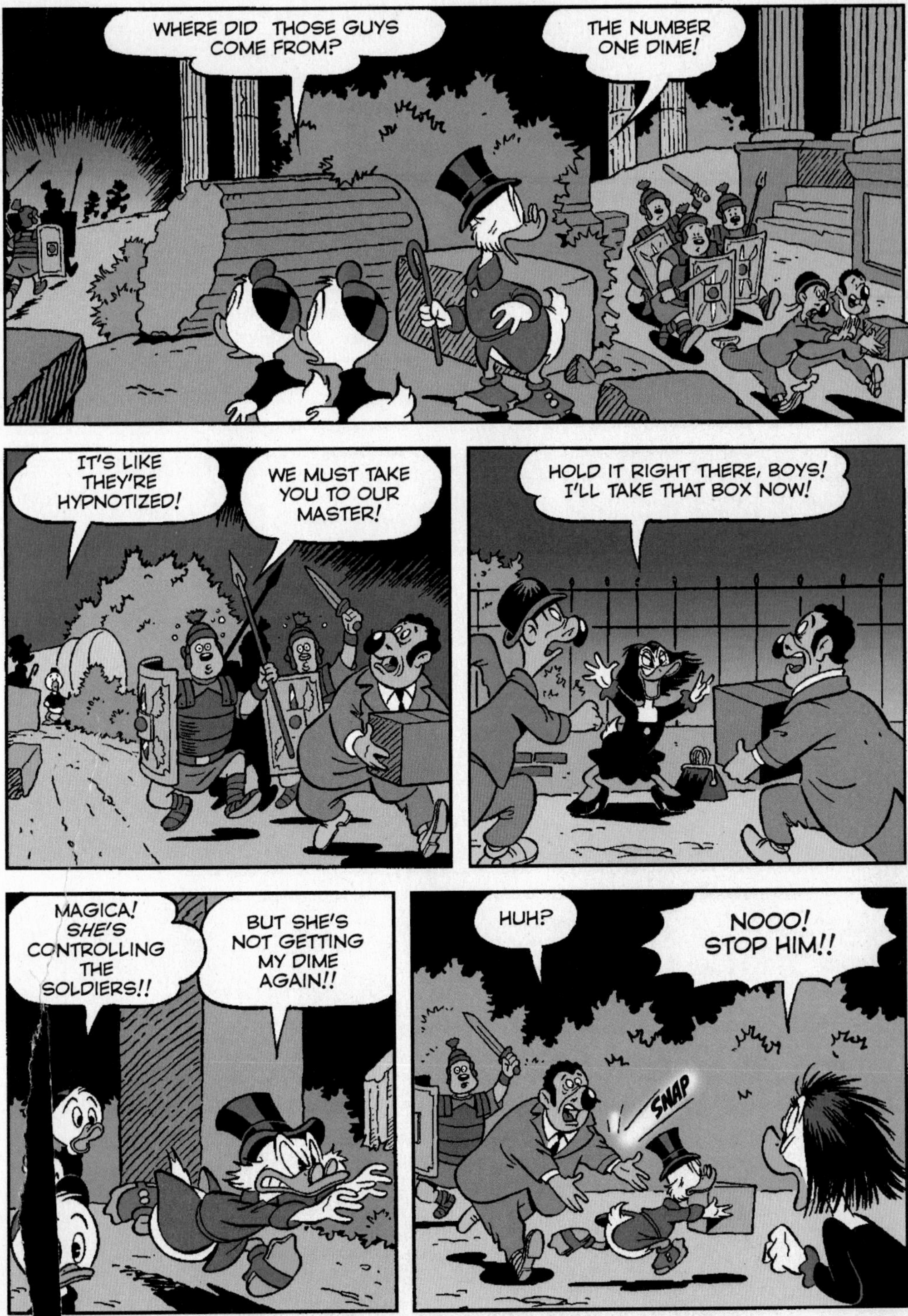
WHERE DID THOSE GUYS COME FROM?
THE NUMBER ONE DIME!
IT'S LIKE THEY'RE HYPNOTIZED!
WE MUST TAKE YOU TO OUR MASTER!
HOLD IT RIGHT THERE, BOYS! I'LL TAKE THAT BOX NOW!
MAGICA! SHE'S CONTROLLING THE SOLDIERS!!
BUT SHE'S NOT GETTING MY DIME AGAIN!!
HUH?
NOOO! STOP HIM!!
SNAP

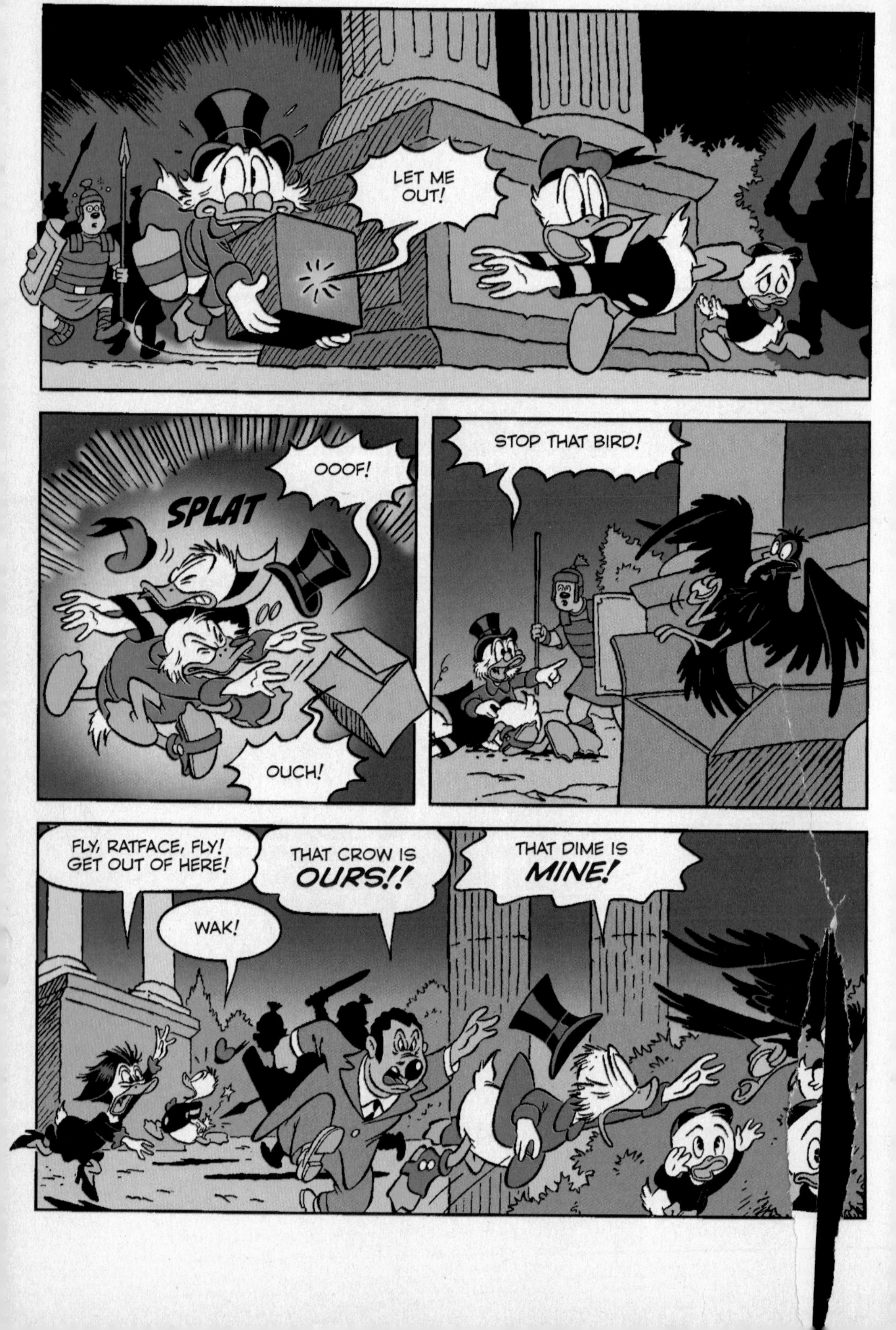
LET ME OUT!
OOOF!
SPLAT
OUCH!
STOP THAT BIRD!
FLY, RATFACE, FLY! GET OUT OF HERE!
WAK!
THAT CROW IS OURS!!
THAT DIME IS MINE!

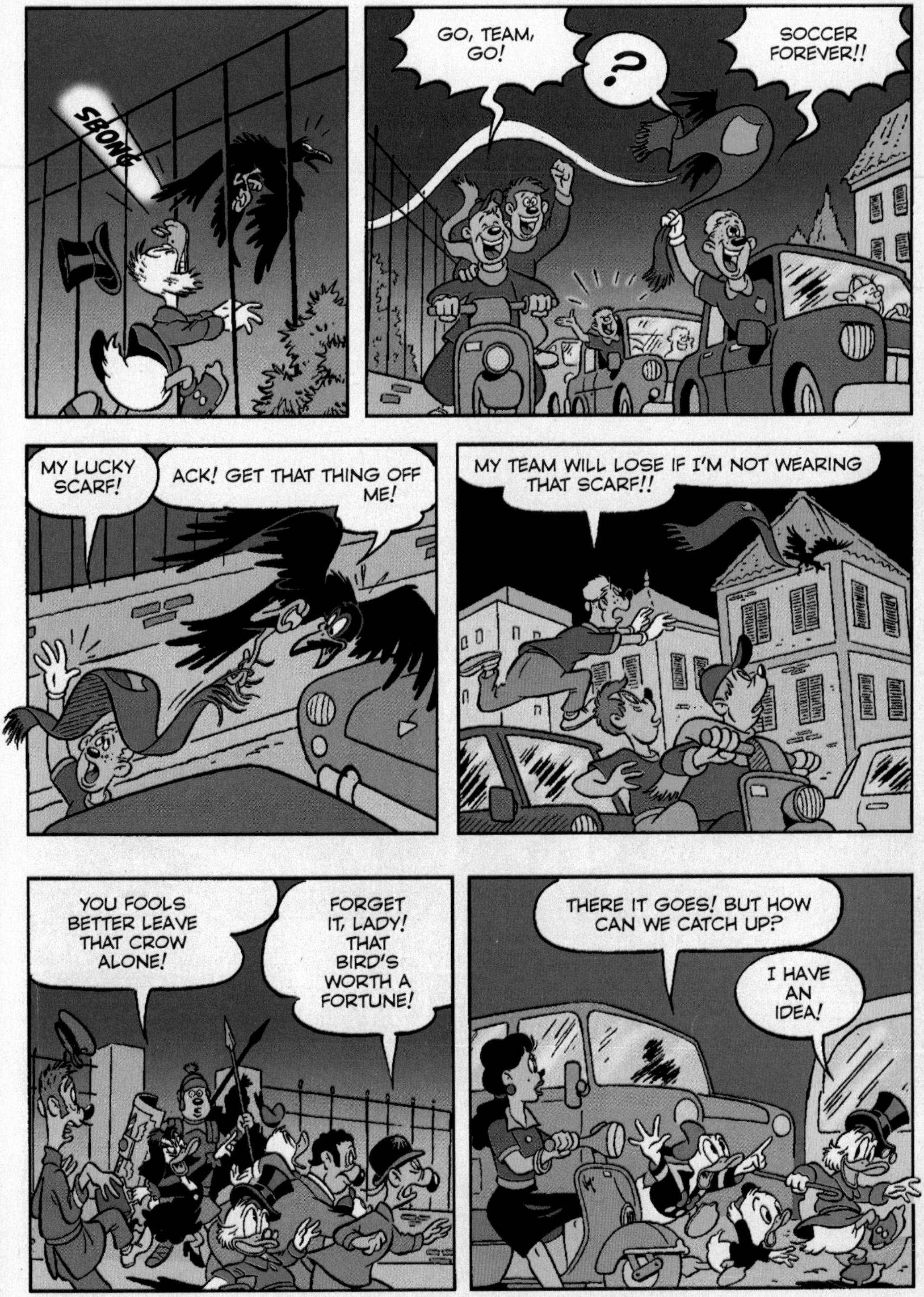
SBONG
GO, TEAM, GO!
?
SOCCER FOREVER!!
MY LUCKY SCARF!
ACK! GET THAT THING OFF ME!
MY TEAM WILL LOSE IF I'M NOT WEARING THAT SCARF!!
YOU FOOLS BETTER LEAVE THAT CROW ALONE!
FORGET IT, LADY! THAT BIRD'S WORTH A FORTUNE!
THERE IT GOES! BUT HOW CAN WE CATCH UP?
I HAVE AN IDEA!

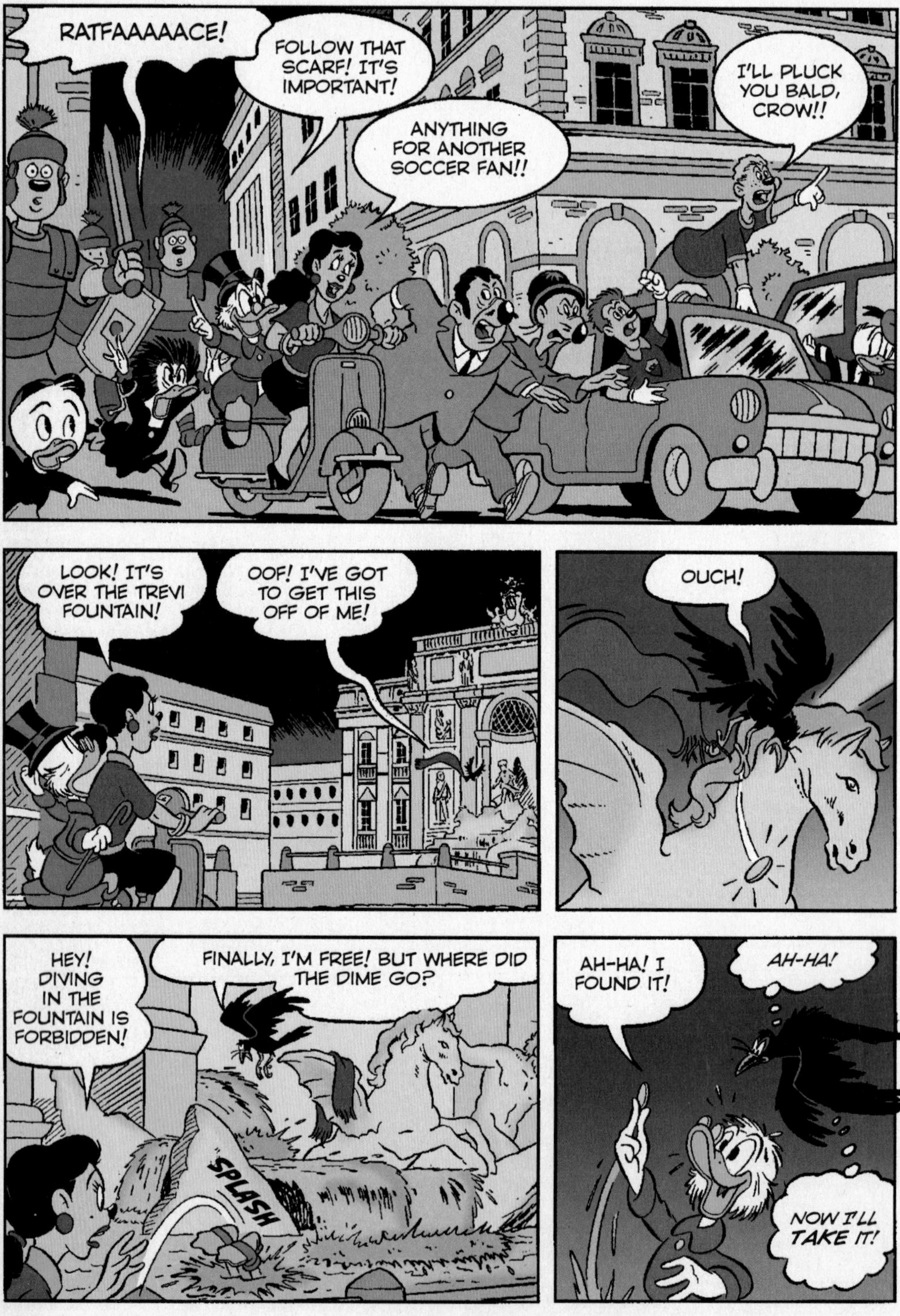
RATFAAAAACE!
FOLLOW THAT SCARF! IT'S IMPORTANT!
ANYTHING FOR ANOTHER SOCCER FAN!!
I'LL PLUCK YOU BALD, CROW!!
LOOK! IT'S OVER THE TREVI FOUNTAIN!
OOF! I'VE GOT TO GET THIS OFF OF ME!
OUCH!
HEY! DIVING IN THE FOUNTAIN IS FORBIDDEN!
FINALLY, I'M FREE! BUT WHERE DID THE DIME GO?
SPLASH
AH-HA! I FOUND IT!
AH-HA!
NOW I'LL TAKE IT!

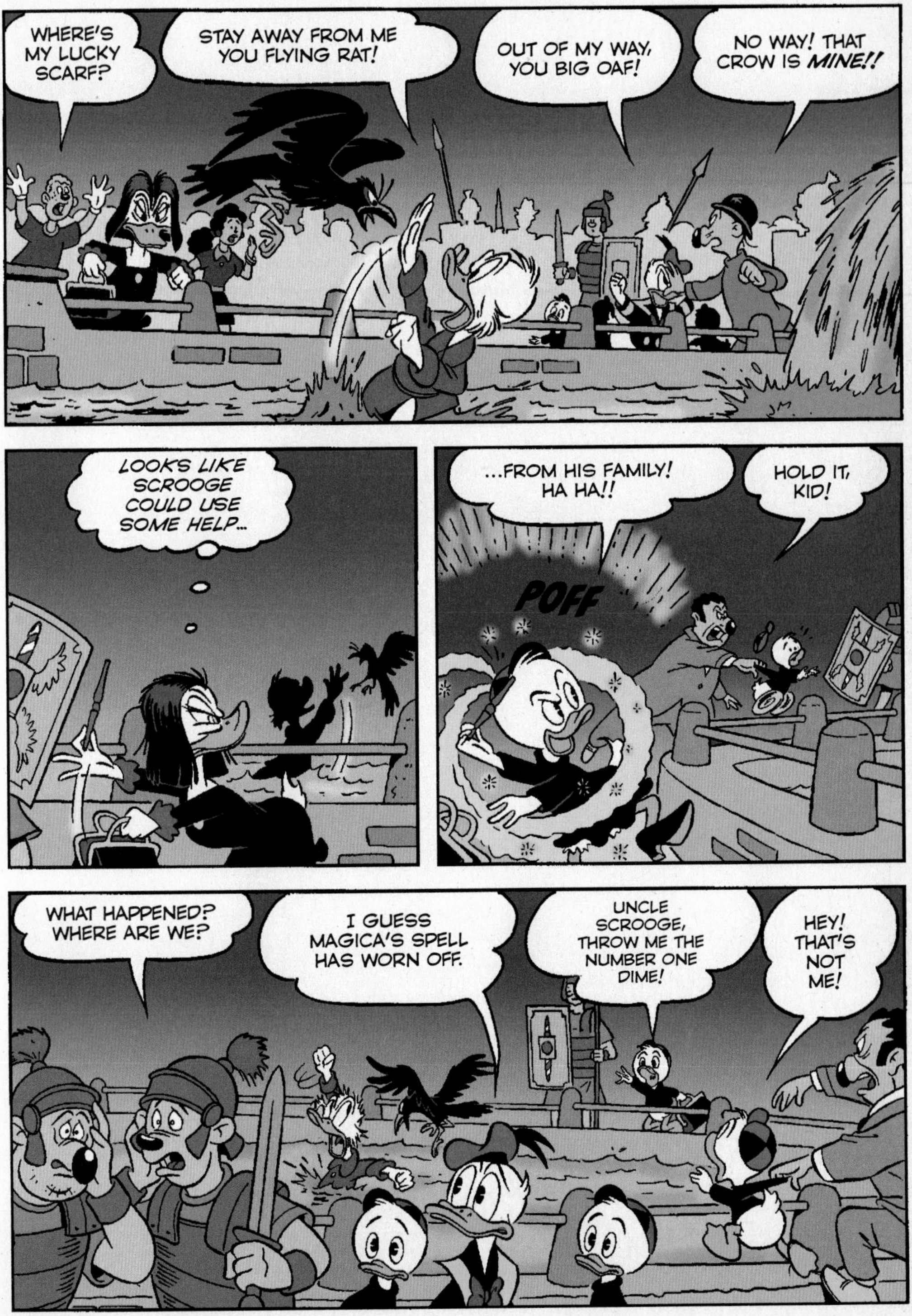
WHERE'S MY LUCKY SCARF?
STAY AWAY FROM ME YOU FLYING RAT!
OUT OF MY WAY, YOU BIG OAF!
NO WAY! THAT CROW IS *MINE!!*
LOOKS LIKE SCROOGE COULD USE SOME HELP...
...FROM HIS FAMILY! HA HA!!
POFF
HOLD IT, KID!
WHAT HAPPENED? WHERE ARE WE?
I GUESS MAGICA'S SPELL HAS WORN OFF.
UNCLE SCROOGE, THROW ME THE NUMBER ONE DIME!
HEY! THAT'S NOT ME!

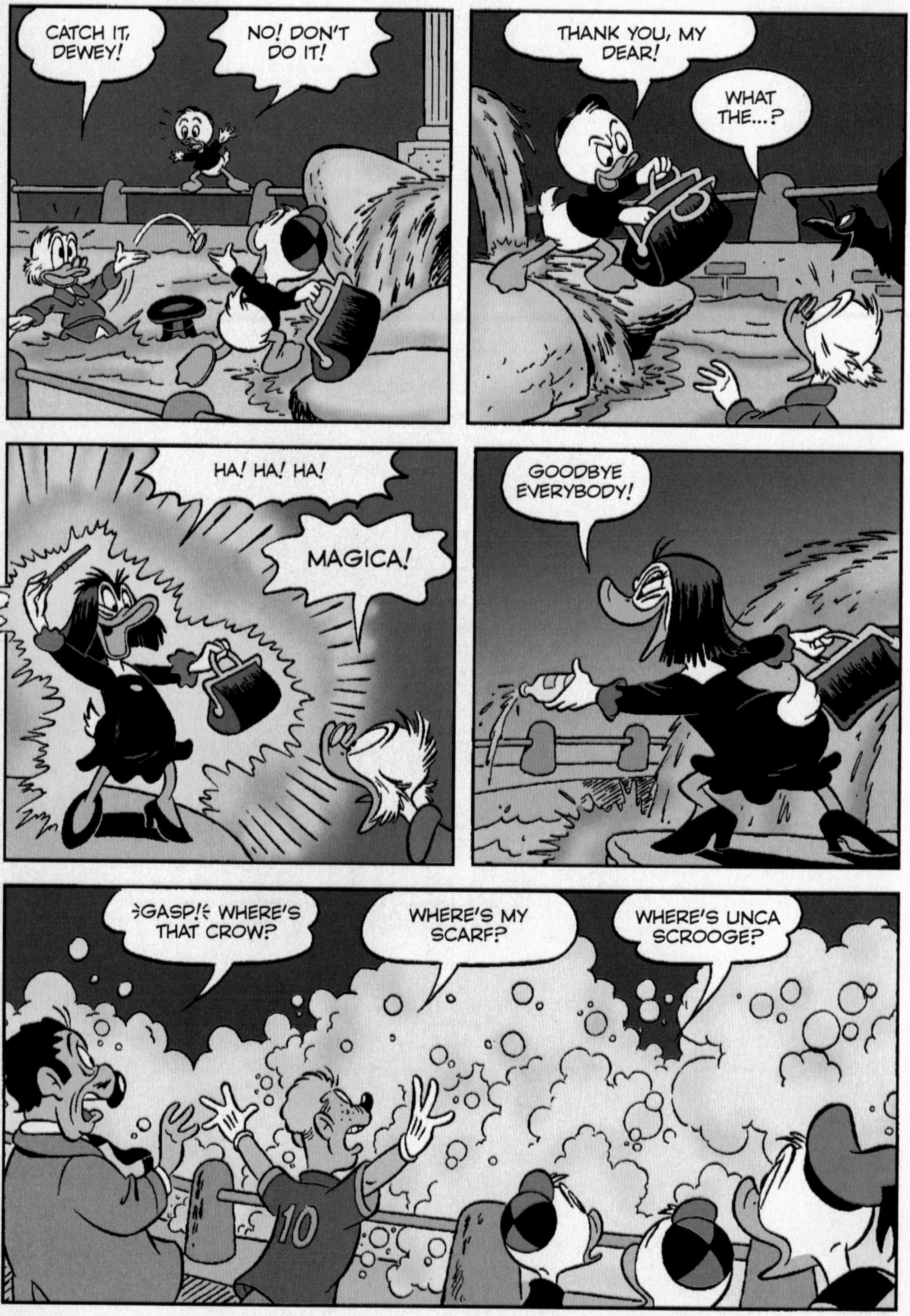
CATCH IT, DEWEY!
NO! DON'T DO IT!
THANK YOU, MY DEAR!
WHAT THE...?
HA! HA! HA!
MAGICA!
GOODBYE EVERYBODY!
GASP! WHERE'S THAT CROW?
WHERE'S MY SCARF?
WHERE'S UNCA SCROOGE?

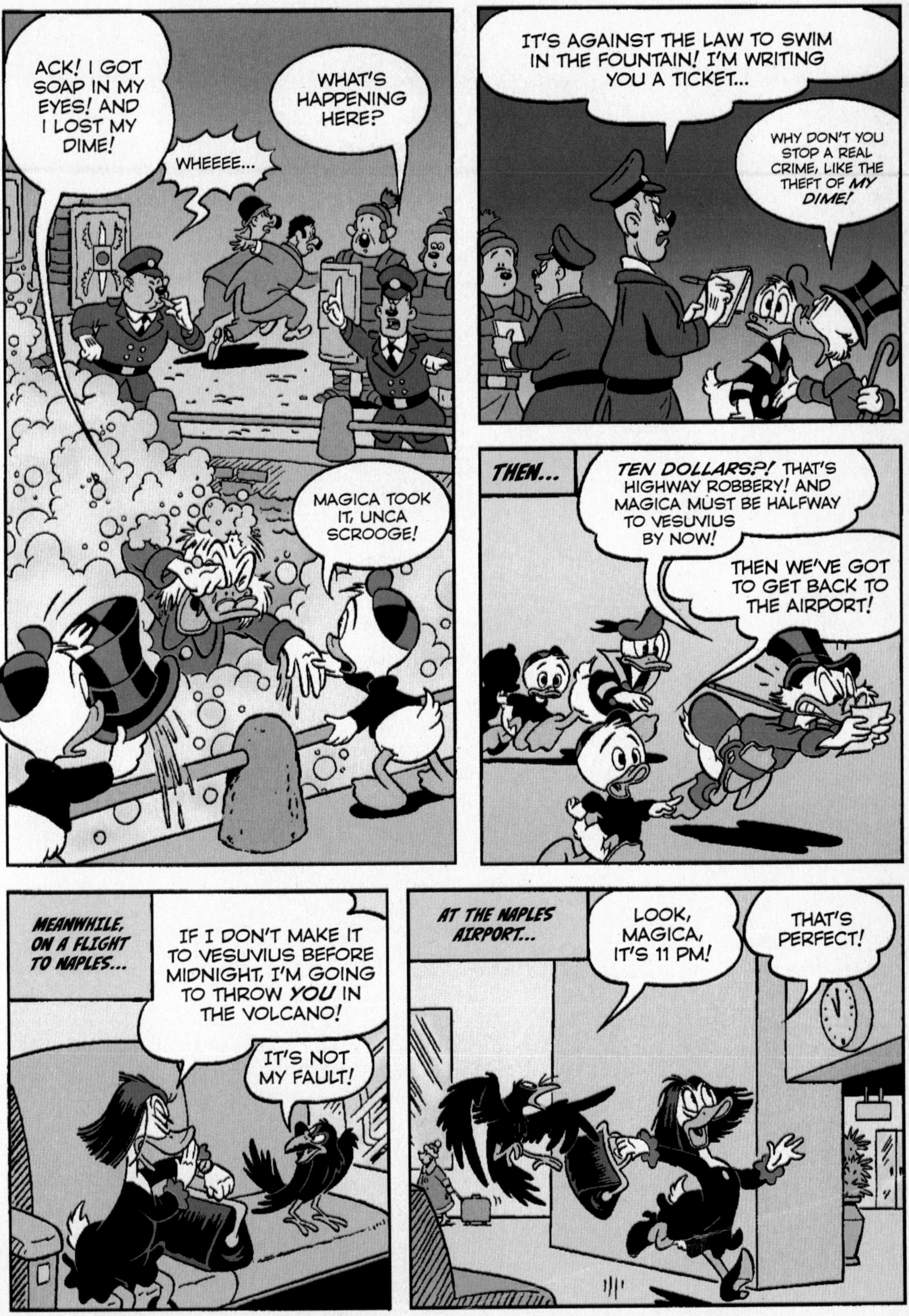
ACK! I GOT SOAP IN MY EYES! AND I LOST MY DIME!
WHEEEE...
WHAT'S HAPPENING HERE?
MAGICA TOOK IT, UNCA SCROOGE!
IT'S AGAINST THE LAW TO SWIM IN THE FOUNTAIN! I'M WRITING YOU A TICKET...
WHY DON'T YOU STOP A REAL CRIME, LIKE THE THEFT OF MY DIME!
THEN...
TEN DOLLARS?! THAT'S HIGHWAY ROBBERY! AND MAGICA MUST BE HALFWAY TO VESUVIUS BY NOW!
THEN WE'VE GOT TO GET BACK TO THE AIRPORT!
MEANWHILE, ON A FLIGHT TO NAPLES...
IF I DON'T MAKE IT TO VESUVIUS BEFORE MIDNIGHT, I'M GOING TO THROW YOU IN THE VOLCANO!
IT'S NOT MY FAULT!
AT THE NAPLES AIRPORT...
LOOK, MAGICA, IT'S 11 PM!
THAT'S PERFECT!

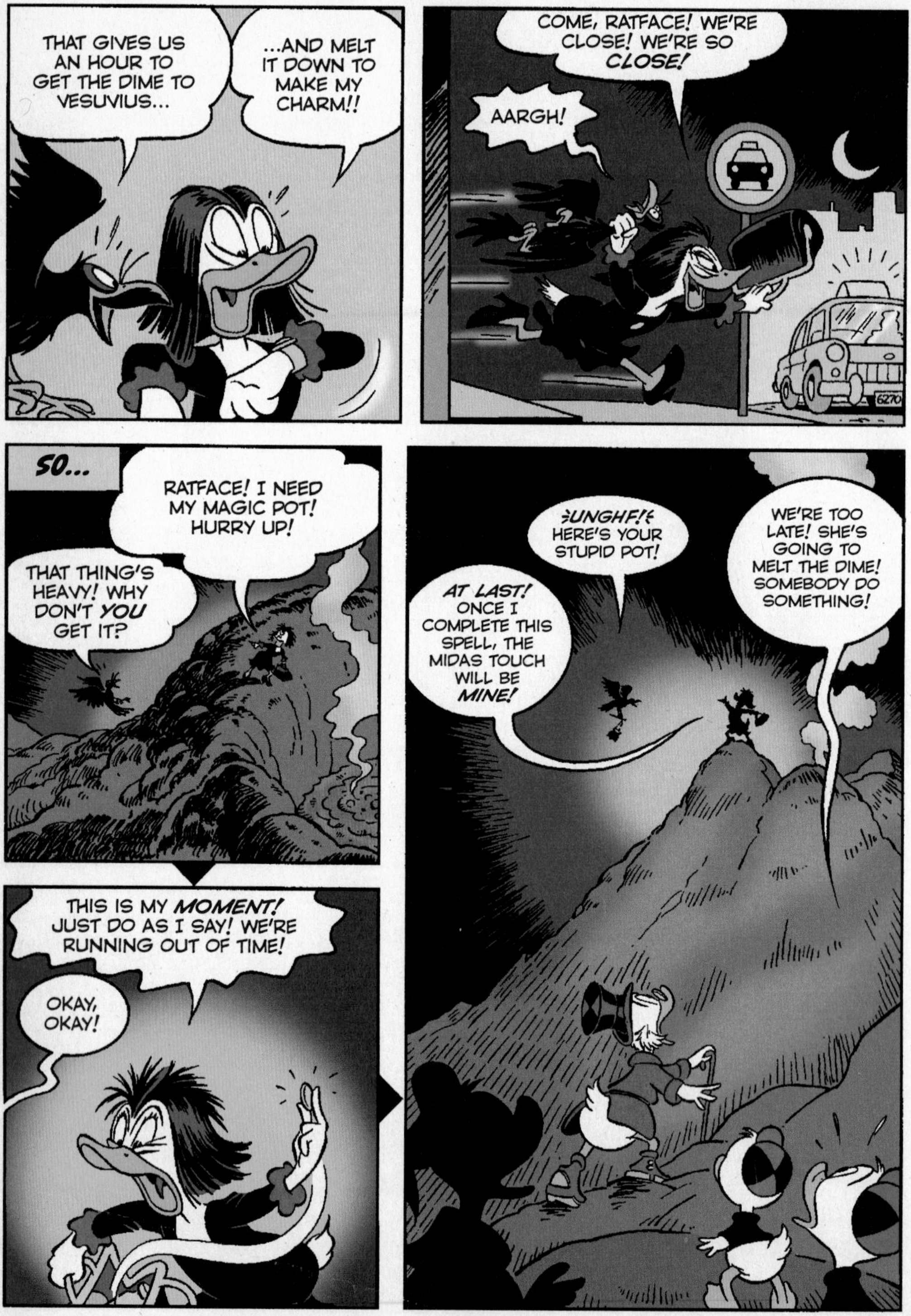
THAT GIVES US AN HOUR TO GET THE DIME TO VESUVIUS...
...AND MELT IT DOWN TO MAKE MY CHARM!!
COME, RATFACE! WE'RE CLOSE! WE'RE SO CLOSE!
AARGH!
SO...
RATFACE! I NEED MY MAGIC POT! HURRY UP!
THAT THING'S HEAVY! WHY DON'T YOU GET IT?
THIS IS MY MOMENT! JUST DO AS I SAY! WE'RE RUNNING OUT OF TIME!
OKAY, OKAY!
UNGHF! HERE'S YOUR STUPID POT!
AT LAST! ONCE I COMPLETE THIS SPELL, THE MIDAS TOUCH WILL BE MINE!
WE'RE TOO LATE! SHE'S GOING TO MELT THE DIME! SOMEBODY DO SOMETHING!

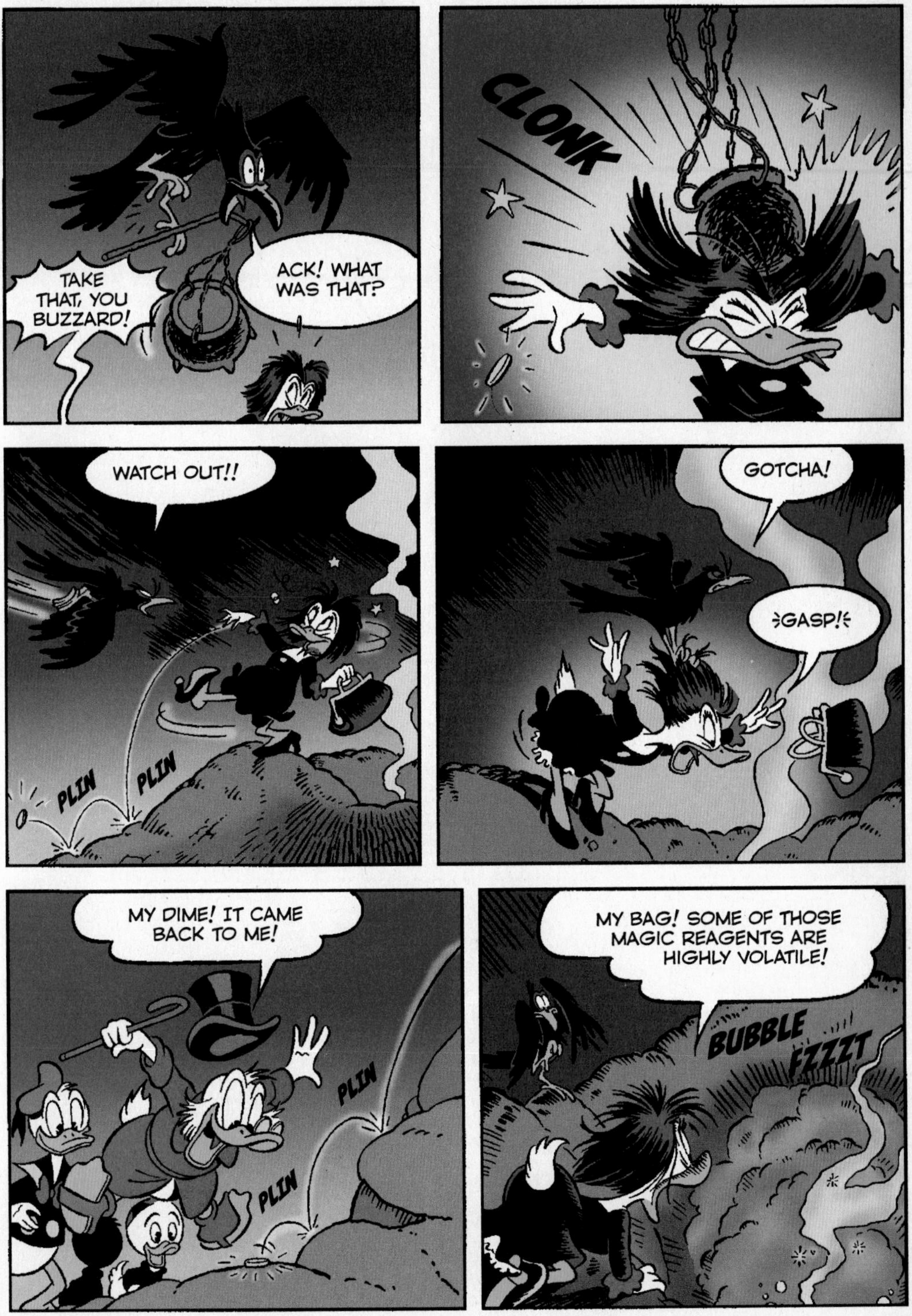
ACK! WHAT WAS THAT?
TAKE THAT, YOU BUZZARD!
CLONK
WATCH OUT!!
PLIN
PLIN
GOTCHA!
GASP!
MY DIME! IT CAME BACK TO ME!
PLIN
PLIN
MY BAG! SOME OF THOSE MAGIC REAGENTS ARE HIGHLY VOLATILE!
BUBBLE
FZZZT

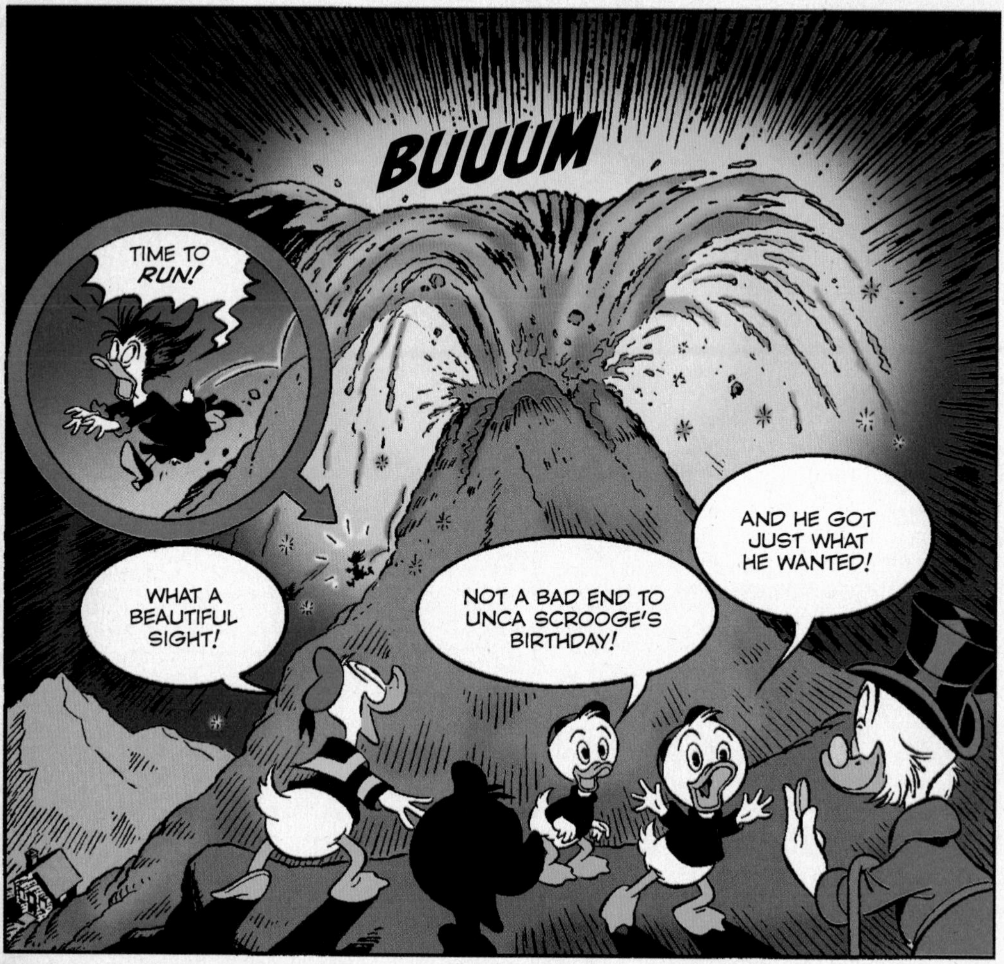
BUUUM
TIME TO RUN!
WHAT A BEAUTIFUL SIGHT!
NOT A BAD END TO UNCA SCROOGE'S BIRTHDAY!
AND HE GOT JUST WHAT HE WANTED!

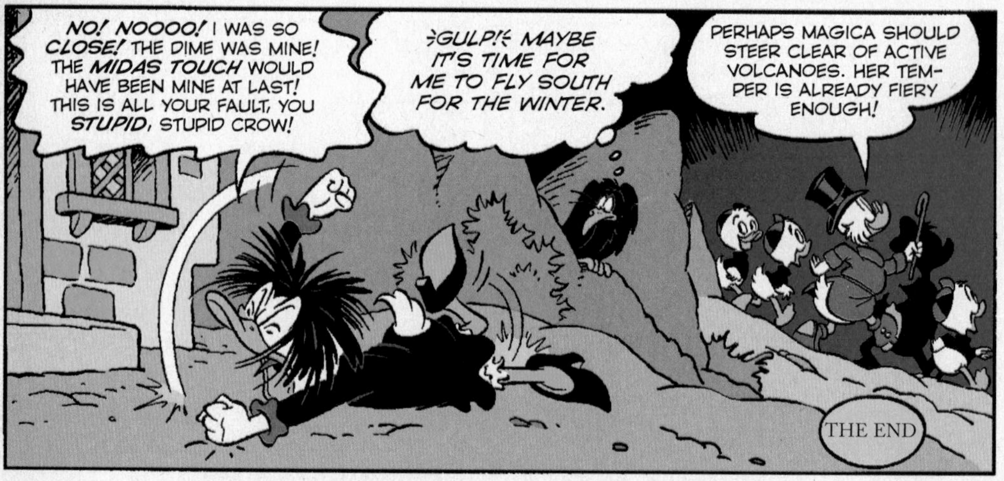
NO! NOOOO! I WAS SO CLOSE! THE DIME WAS MINE! THE MIDAS TOUCH WOULD HAVE BEEN MINE AT LAST! THIS IS ALL YOUR FAULT, YOU STUPID, STUPID CROW!
GULP! MAYBE IT'S TIME FOR ME TO FLY SOUTH FOR THE WINTER.
PERHAPS MAGICA SHOULD STEER CLEAR OF ACTIVE VOLCANOES. HER TEMPER IS ALREADY FIERY ENOUGH!
THE END

COVER GALLERY

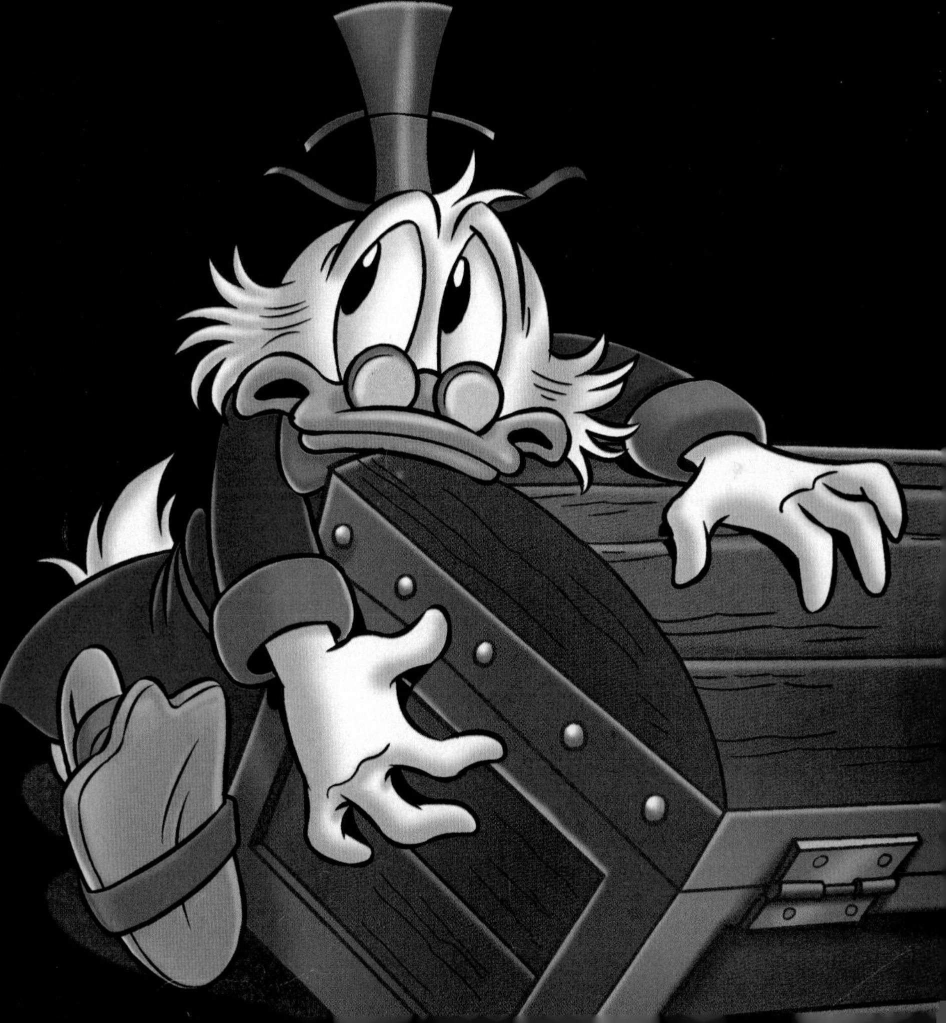

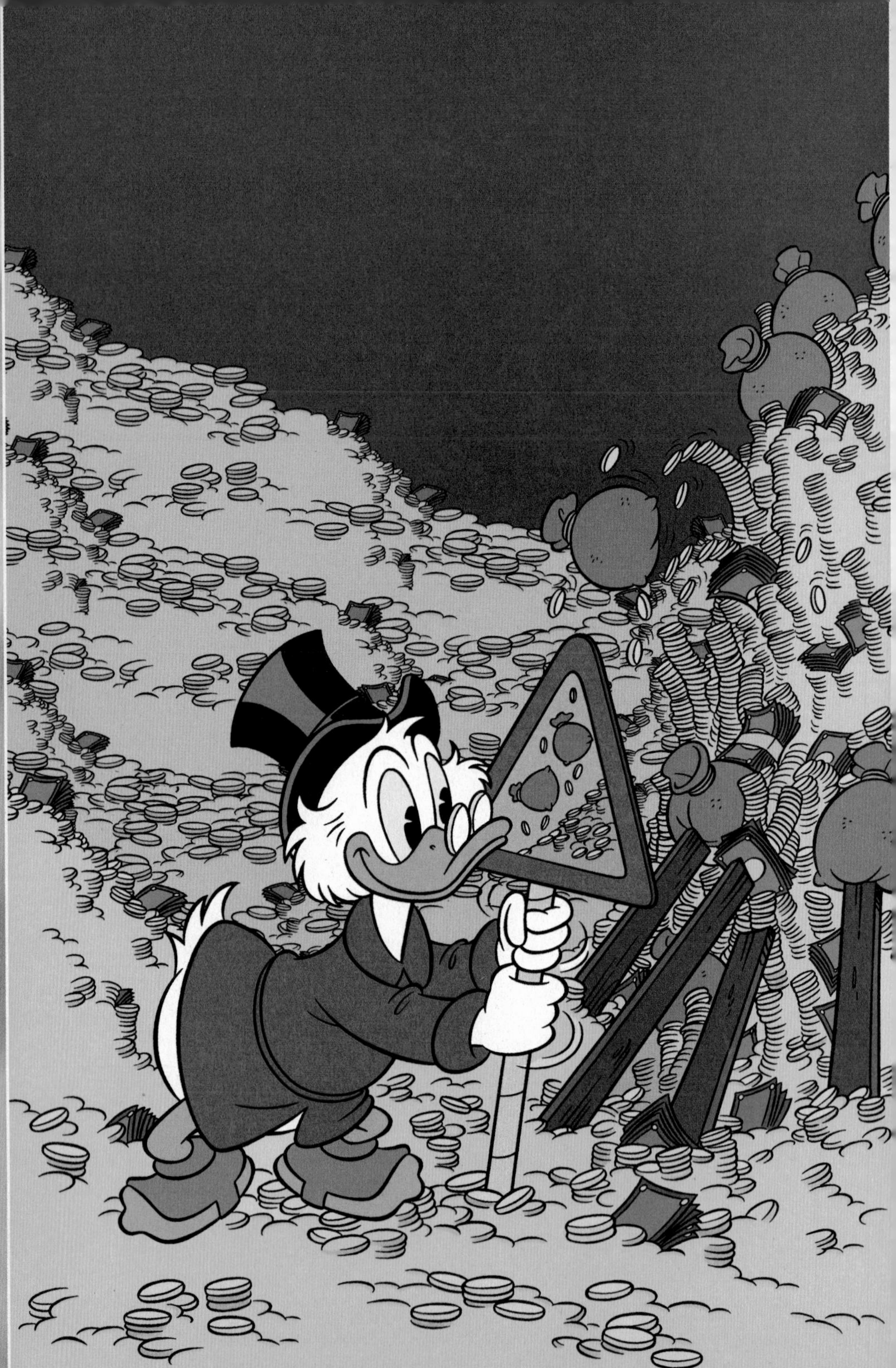

COVER 384A: TINO SANTANACH

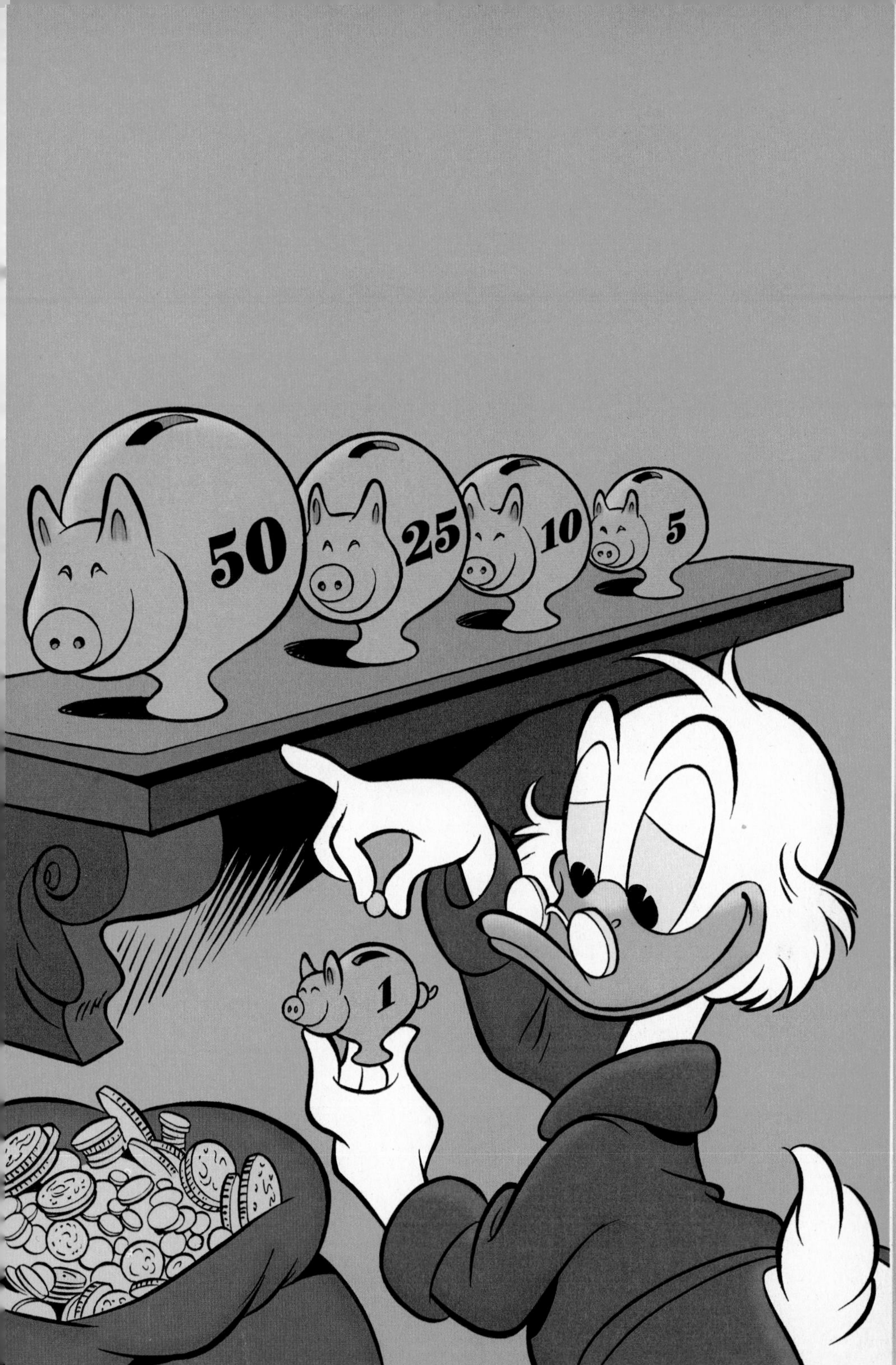
50
25
10
5
1

COVER 384B: DANIEL BRANCA

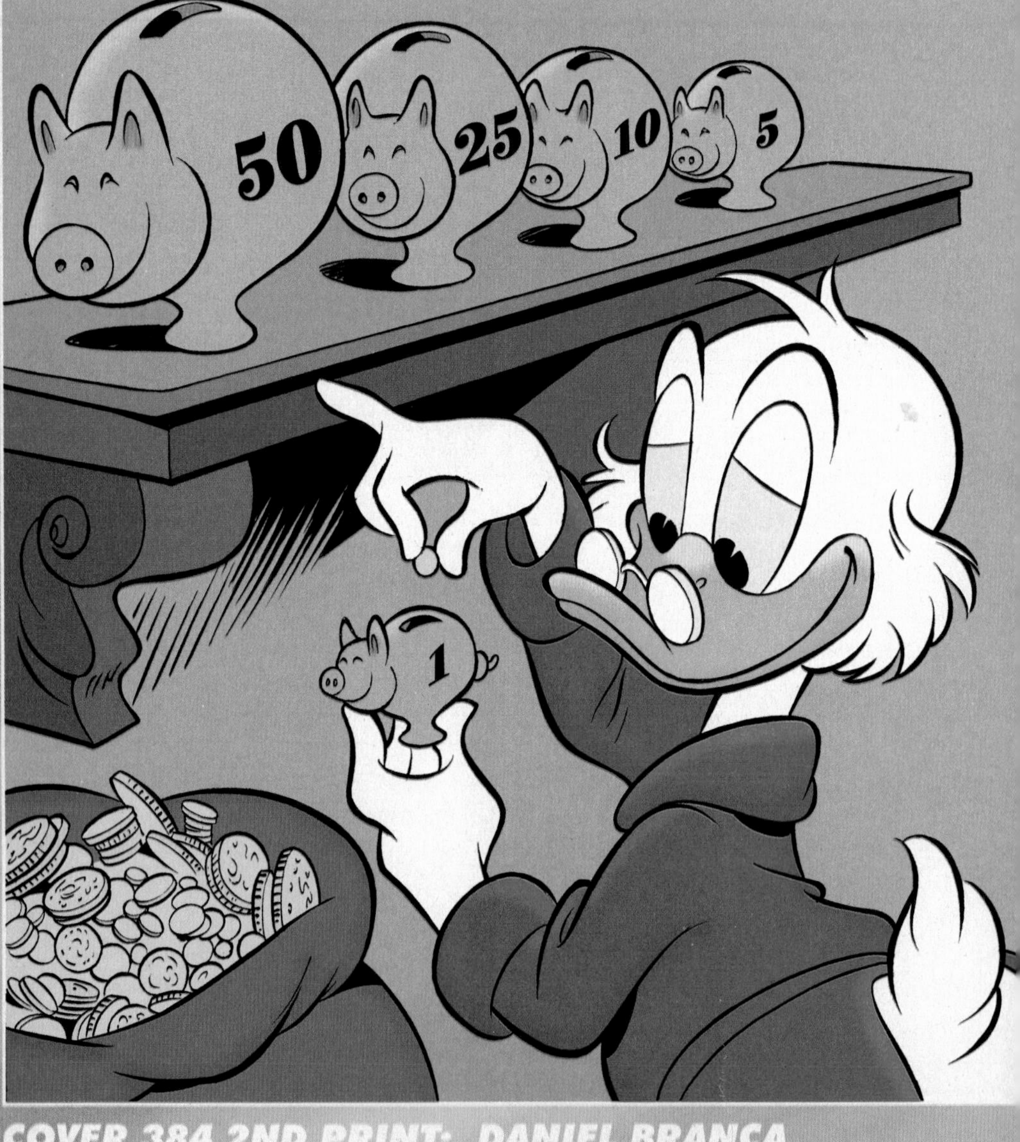
50
25
10
5
1

COVER 384 2ND PRINT: DANIEL BRANCA

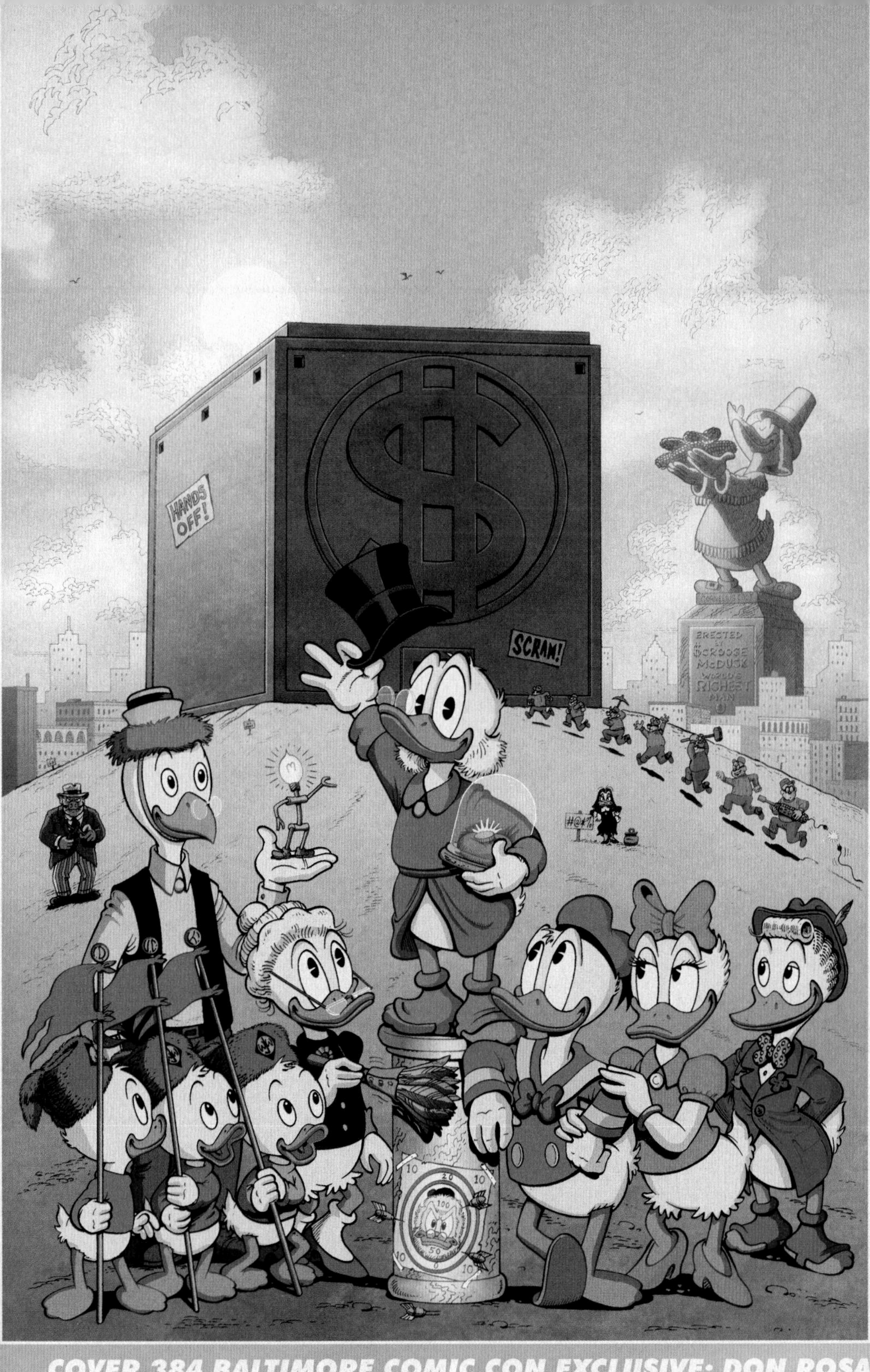
HANDS OFF!
SCRAM!
ERECTED BY $CROOGE McDUCK WORLD'S RICHEST MAN

COVER 384 BALTIMORE COMIC CON EXCLUSIVE: DON ROSA
COLORS / ANDREW DALHOUSE

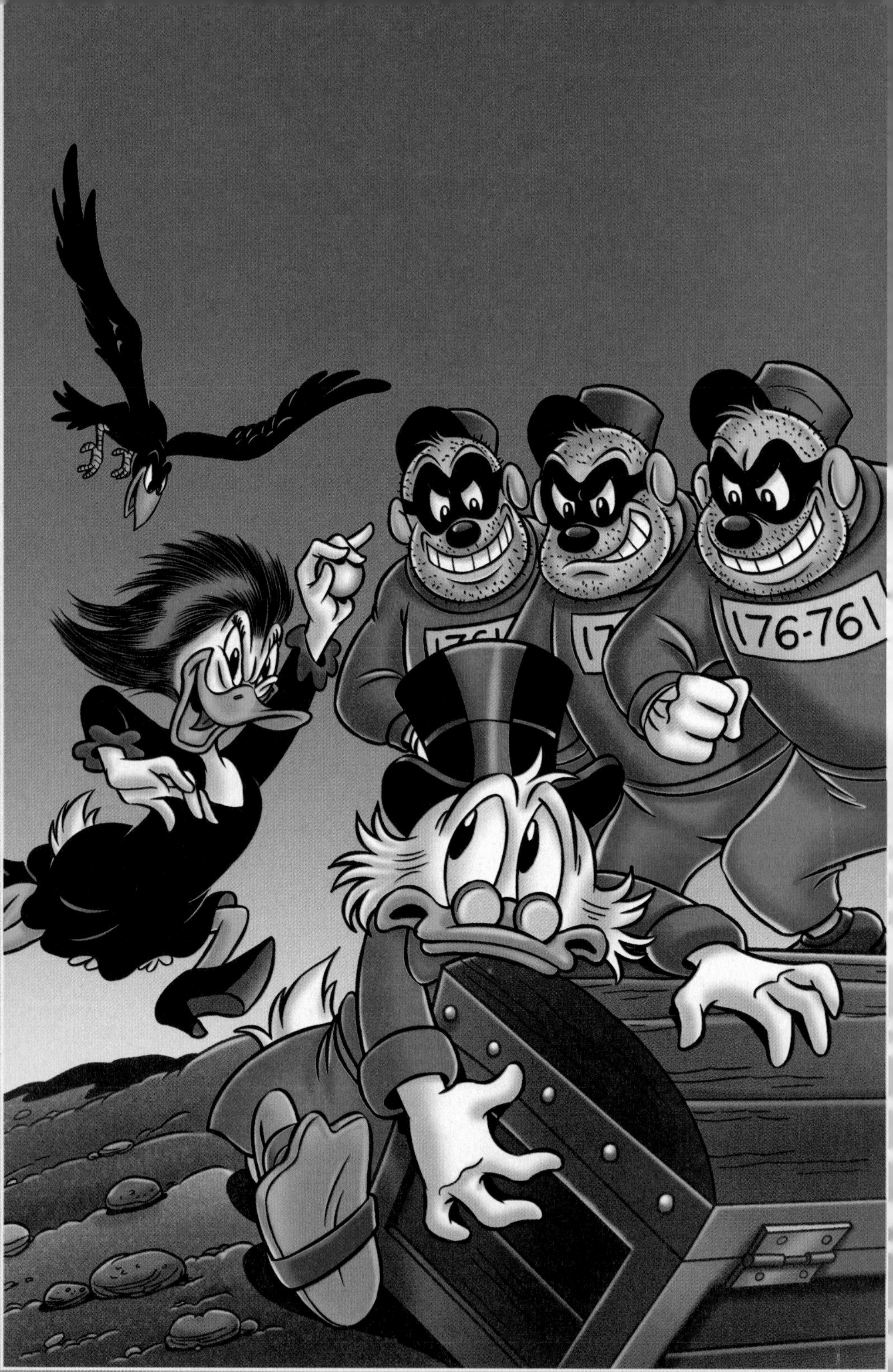
176-761
176-761
176-761

COVER 385A: MAGIC EYE STUDIOS

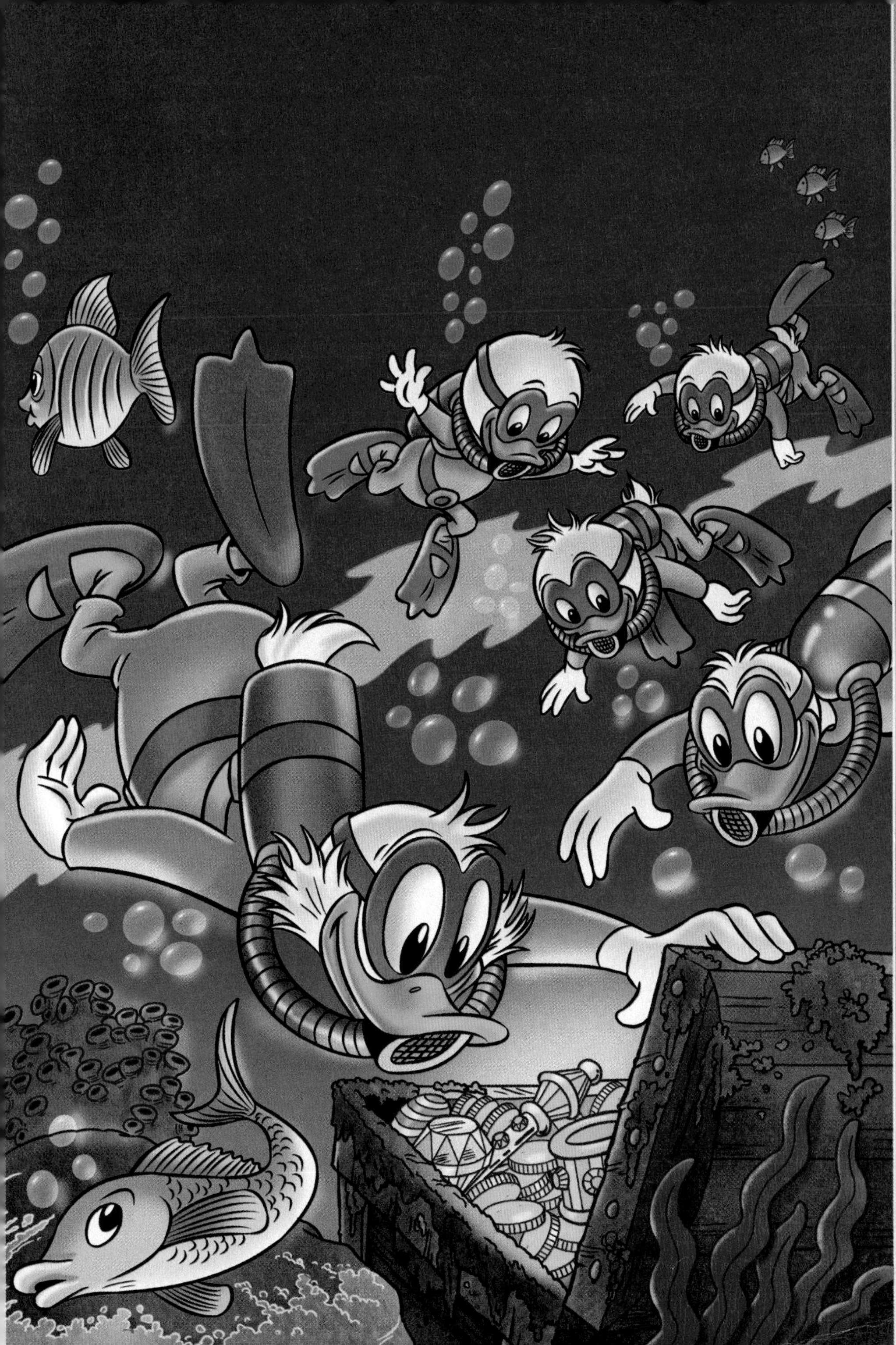

COVER 385B: MAGIC EYE STUDIOS

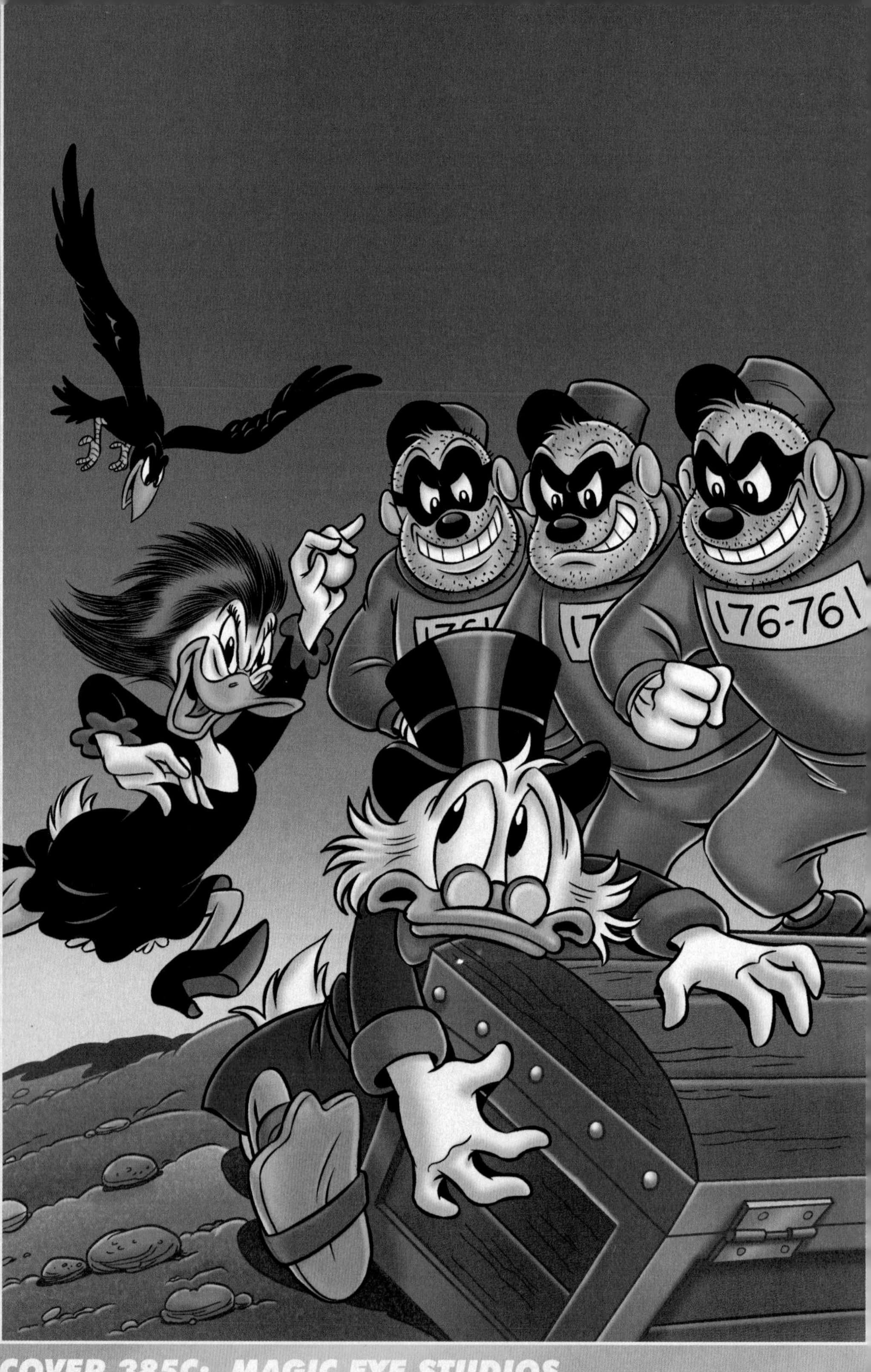
176-761

COVER 385C: MAGIC EYE STUDIOS

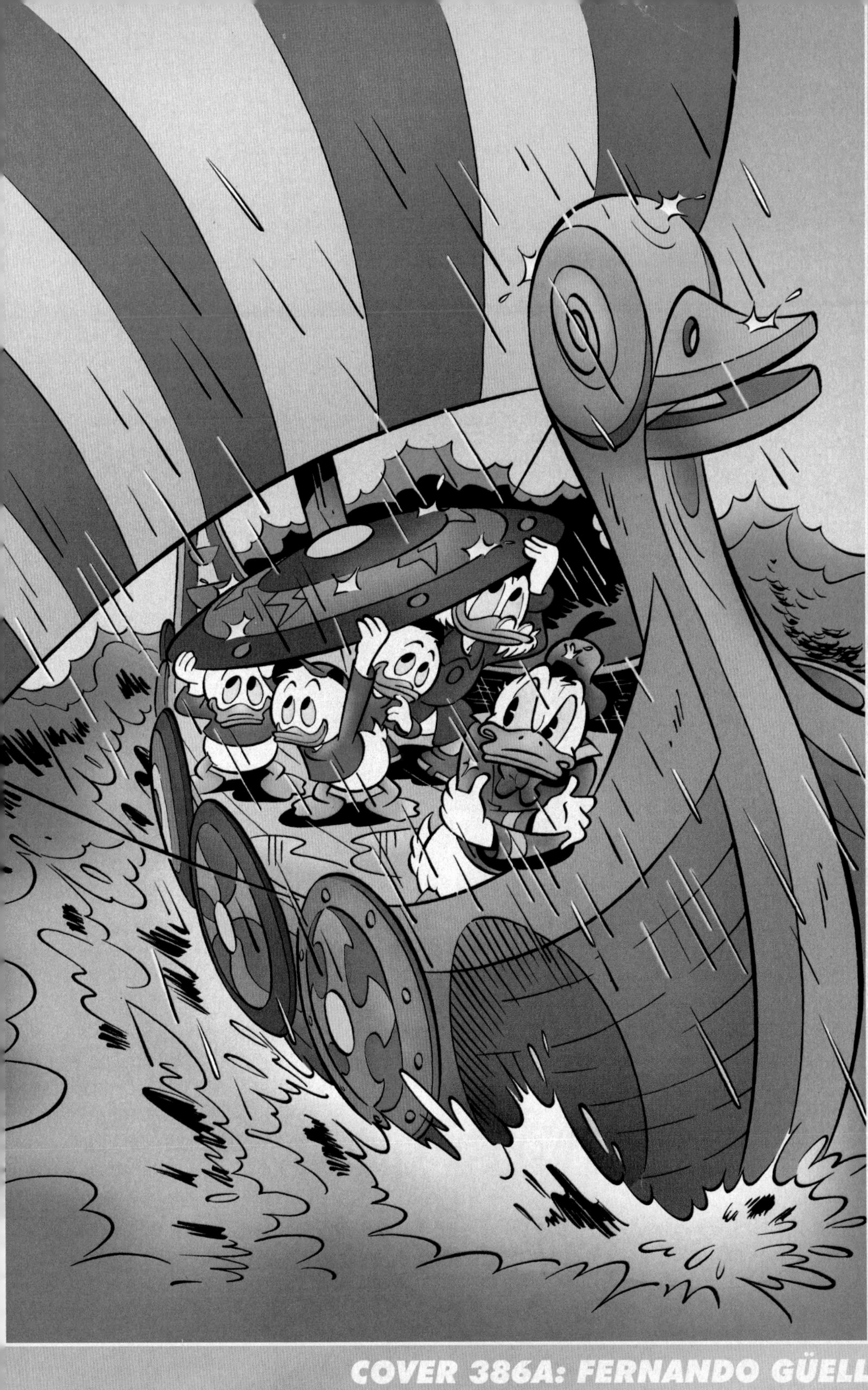

COVER 386A: FERNANDO GÜELL

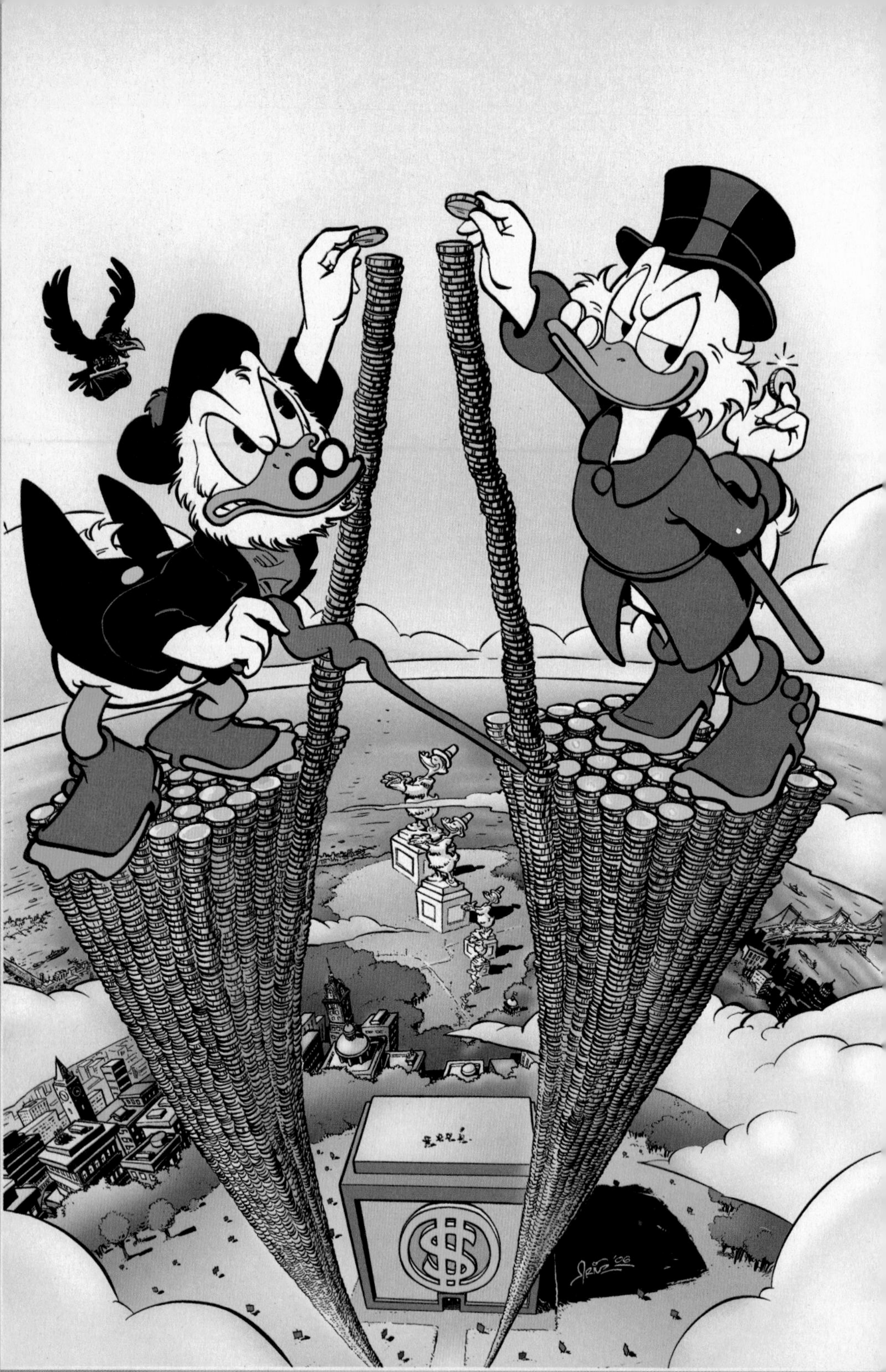

COVER 386B: ARILD MIDTHUN

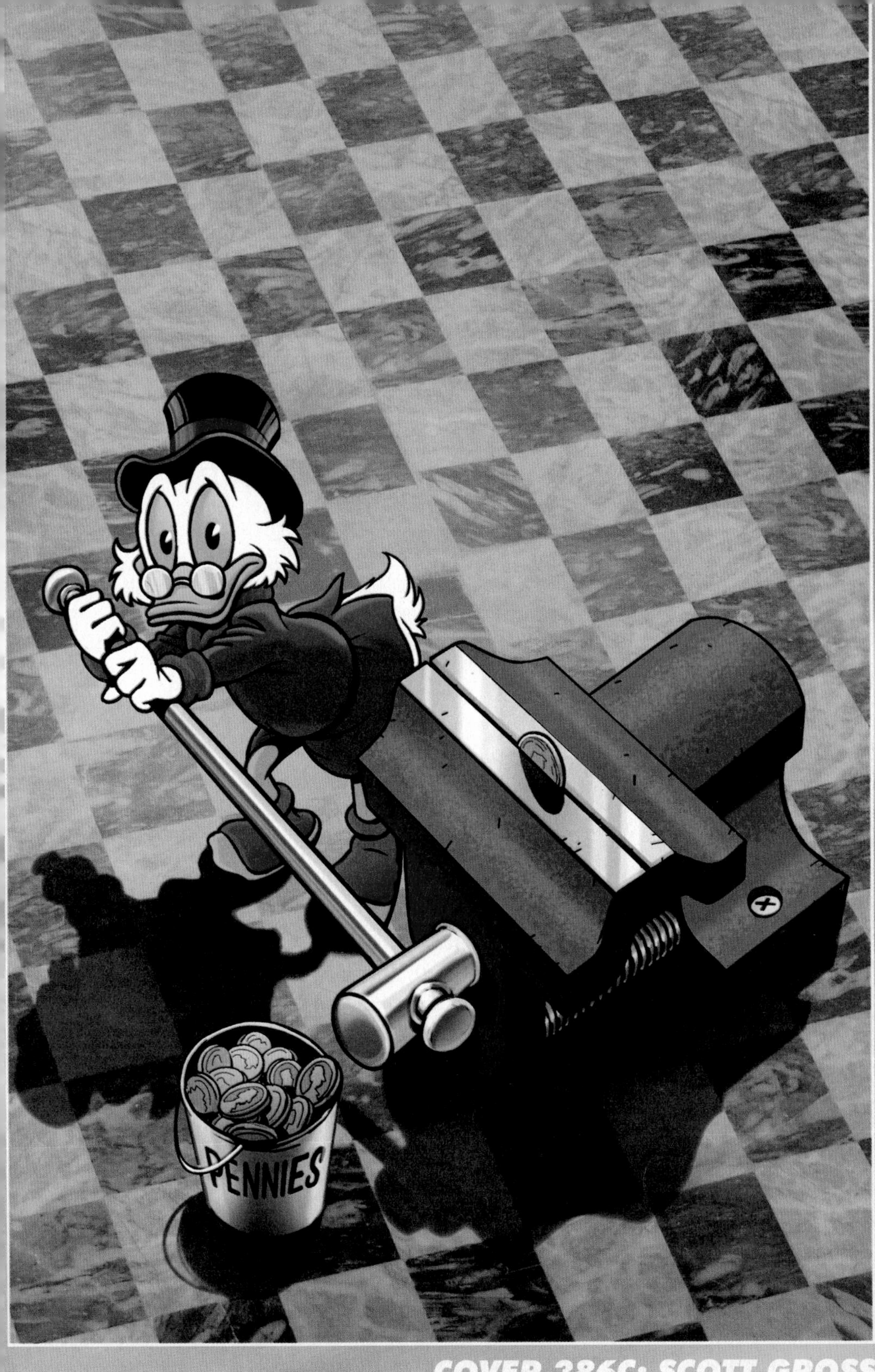
PENNIES

COVER 386C: SCOTT GROSS

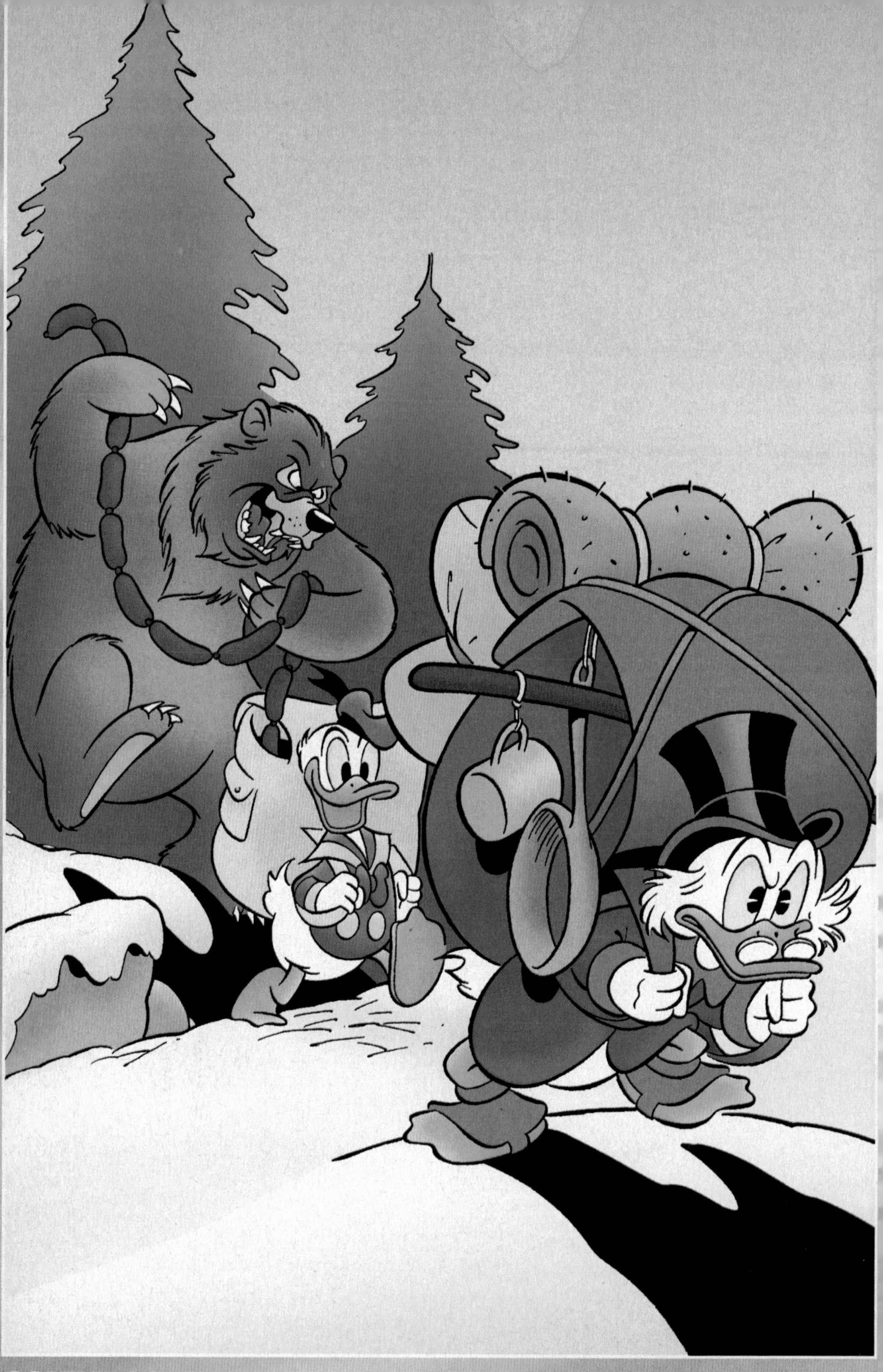

COVER 387A: WANDA GATTINO

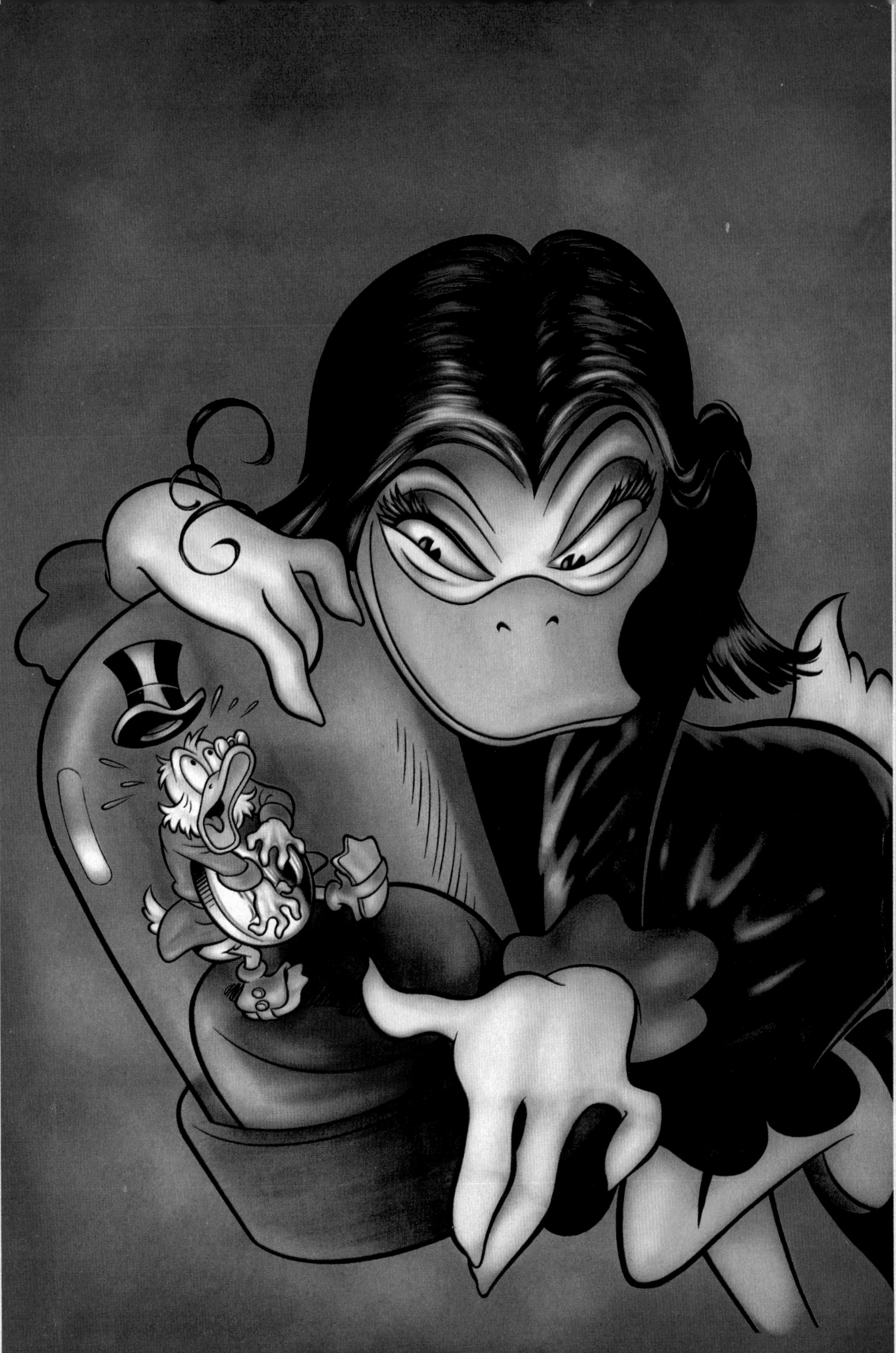

COVER 387B: CARLOS MOTA

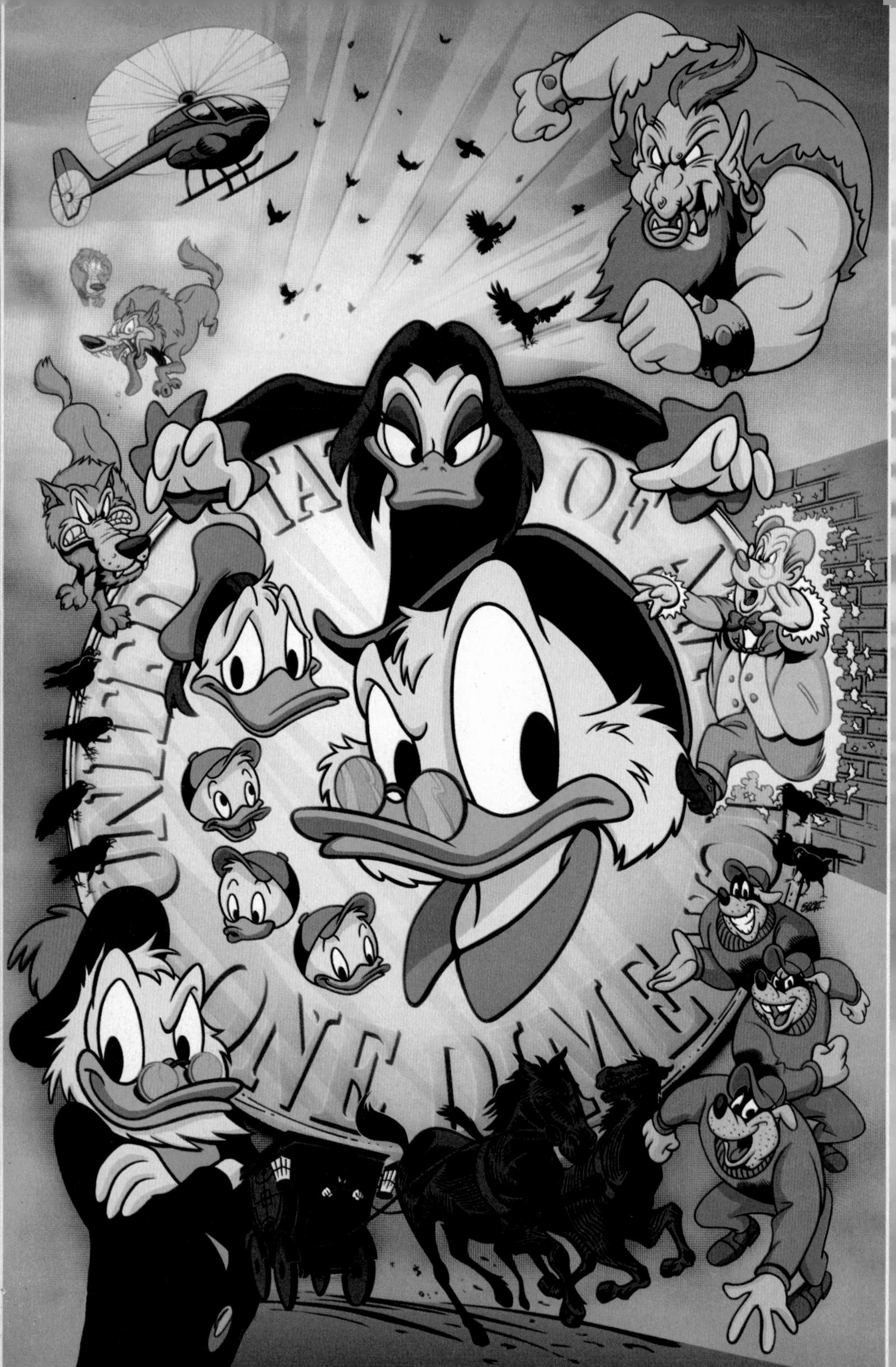

COVER 387C: SCOTT GROSS
COLORS / ANDREW DALHOUSE

GRAPHIC NOVELS AVAILABLE NOW!

BOOM KIDS!

Disney · PIXAR
TOY STORY

TOY STORY: MYSTERIOUS STRANGER
Andy has a new addition to his room—a circuit-laden egg. Is this new gizmo a friend or foe?

TOY STORY: THE RETURN OF BUZZ LIGHTYEAR
When Andy is given a surprise gift, no one is more surprised than the toys in his room... it's a second Buzz Lightyear! The stage is set for a Star Command showdown!

TOY STORY
BUZZ LIGHTYEAR
RETURNS

TOY STORY: MYSTERIOUS STRANGER
SC $9.99 ISBN 9781934506912
HC $24.99 ISBN 9781608865239

TOY STORY: THE RETURN OF BUZZ LIGHTYEAR
SC $9.99 ISBN 9781608865574
HC $24.99 ISBN 9781608865581

Disney · PIXAR
THE INCREDIBLES
FAMILY MATTERS

THE INCREDIBLES: FAMILY MATTERS
This action-packed trade collects all four issues THE INCREDIBLES: FAMILY MATTERS. Acclaimed scribe Mark Waid has written the perfect INCREDIBLES story! What happens when Mr. Incredible's super-abilities start to wane...and how long can he keep his powerlessness a secret from his wife and kids?

THE INCREDIBLES: CITY OF INCREDIBLES
Baby Jack-Jack, everyone's favorite super-powered toddler, battles...a nasty cold! Hopefully the rest of the Parr family can stay healthy, because the henchmen of super villains are rapidly starting to exhibit superpowers!

Disney · PIXAR
THE INCREDIBLES
CITY OF INCREDIBLES

THE INCREDIBLES: FAMILY MATTERS
SC $9.99 ISBN 9781934506837
HC $24.99 ISBN 9781608865253

THE INCREDIBLES: CITY OF INCREDIBLES
SC $9.99 ISBN 9781608865031
HC $24.99 ISBN 9781608865291

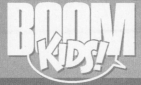

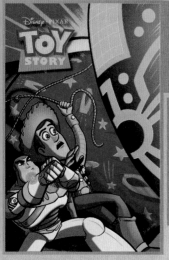

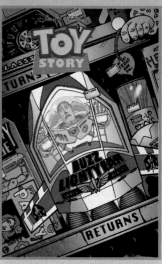

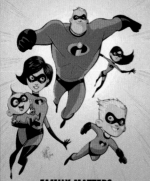

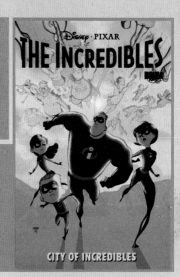

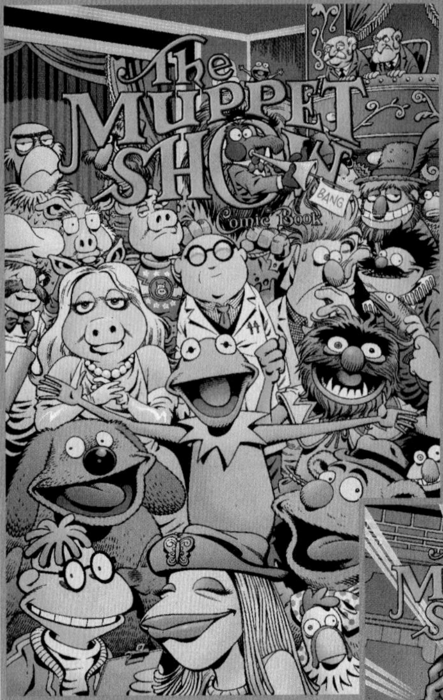
The MUPPET SHOW
Comic Book
BANG

MEET THE MUPPETS
This hilarious trade collects the first four issues of THE MUPPET SHOW, written and drawn by the incomparable Roger Langridge! Packed full of madcap skits and gags, The Muppet Show trade is certain to please old and new fans alike!

THE TREASURE OF PEG-LEG WILSON
Scooter discovers old documents which reveal that a cache of treasure is hidden somewhere within the theater...and when Rizzo the Rat overhears this, the news spreads like wildfire! Can Kermit keep everyone from tearing the theater apart?

ON THE ROAD
With the theatre destroyed after the search for the treasure of Peg-Leg Wilson, the Muppets take their act on the road... but with two very familiar hecklers in every town, will the show be a hit, or will our Muppet minstrels be run out of town in tar and feathers? Also: Fozzie and Rizzo have plans for a big budget PIGS IN SPACE motion picture, but is Hollywood prepared?

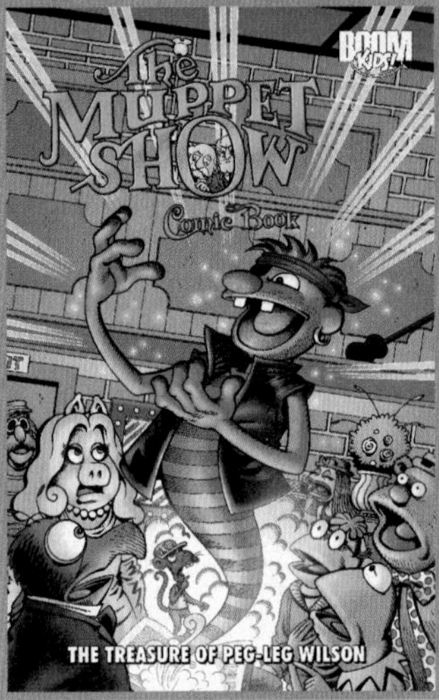
BOOM! KIDS!
The MUPPET SHOW
Comic Book
THE TREASURE OF PEG-LEG WILSON

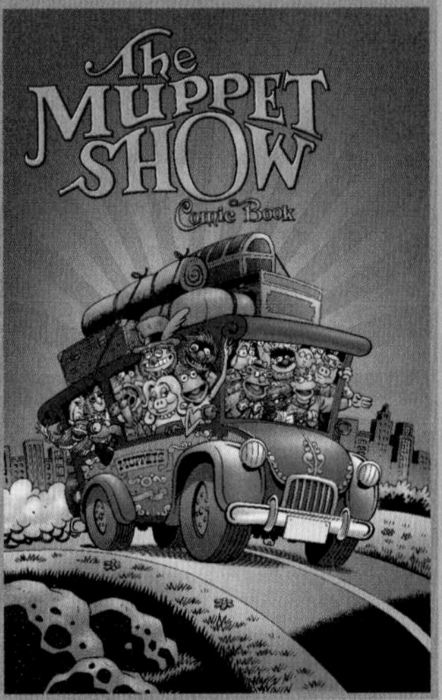
The MUPPET SHOW
Comic Book

THE MUPPET SHOW COMIC BOOK: MEET THE MUPPETS
SC $9.99 ISBN 9781934506851
HC $24.99 ISBN 9781608865277

THE MUPPET SHOW COMIC BOOK: THE TREASURE OF PEG-LEG WILSON
SC $9.99 ISBN 9781608865048
HC $24.99 ISBN 9781608865307

THE MUPPET SHOW COMIC BOOK: ON THE ROAD
SC $9.99 ISBN 9781608865161
HC $24.99 ISBN 9781608865369

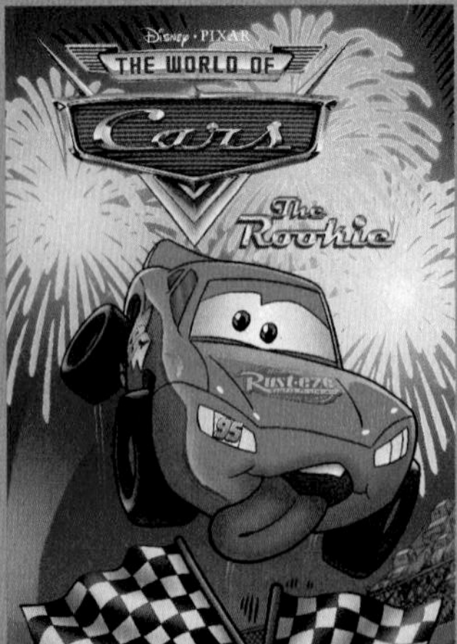
Disney • PIXAR
THE WORLD OF
Cars
The Rookie

CARS: THE ROOKIE
See how Lightning McQueen became a Piston Cup sensation in this pulse-pounding collection! CARS: THE ROOKIE reveals McQueen's scrappy origins as a local short track racer who dreams of the big time...and recklessly plows his way through the competition to get there! Along the way, he meets Mack, who help McQueen catch his lucky break.

CARS: RADIATOR SPRINGS
From writer Alan J. Porter, this collection of CARS stories is perfect for the whole family! After his return to Radiator Springs, LIGHTNING MCQUEEN is hanging out with his friends at Flo's V8 Café when he realizes that everyone knows his story...but he doesn't know anyone else's! McQueen wants to know how his friends ended up in Radiator Springs...and more importantly why they decided to stay!

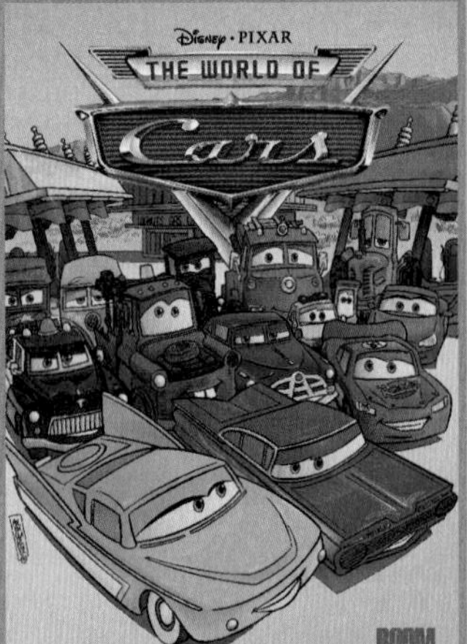
Disney • PIXAR
THE WORLD OF
Cars
BOOM KIDS
Radiator Springs

CARS: THE ROOKIE
SC $9.99 ISBN 9781934506844
HC $24.99 ISBN 9781608865222

CARS: RADIATOR SPRINGS
SC $9.99 ISBN 9781608865024
HC $24.99 ISBN 9781608865284

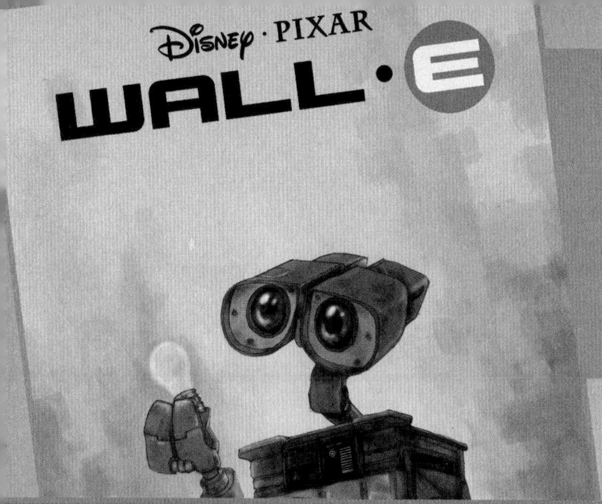
Disney · PIXAR
WALL·E

WALL-E: RECHARGE

Wall-E is not yet the hardworking robot we know and love. Instead, he lets the few remaining other robots take care of most of the trash compacting while he collects interesting junk. But when the other robots start breaking down, Wall-E must learn to adjust his priorities... or else Earth is doomed!

WALL E: RECHARGE
SC $9.99 ISBN 9781608865123
HC $24.99 ISBN 9781608865543

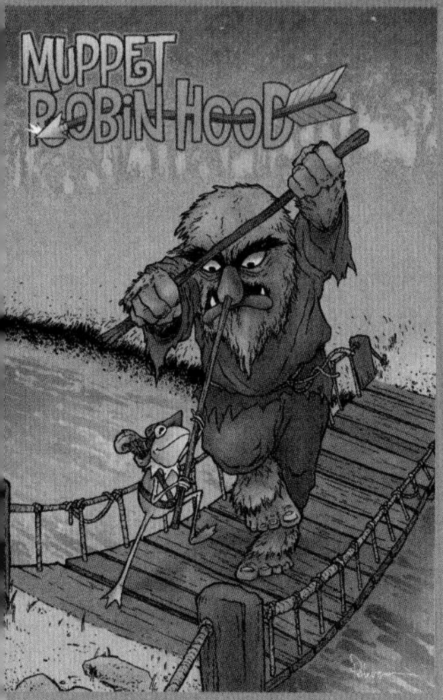
MUPPET ROBIN HOOD

MUPPET ROBIN HOOD

The Muppets tell the Robin Hood legend for laughs, and it's the reader who will be merry! Robin Hood (Kermit the Frog) joins with the Merry Men, Sherwood Forest's infamous gang of misfit outlaws, to take on the stuffy Sheriff of Muppetham (Sam the Eagle)!

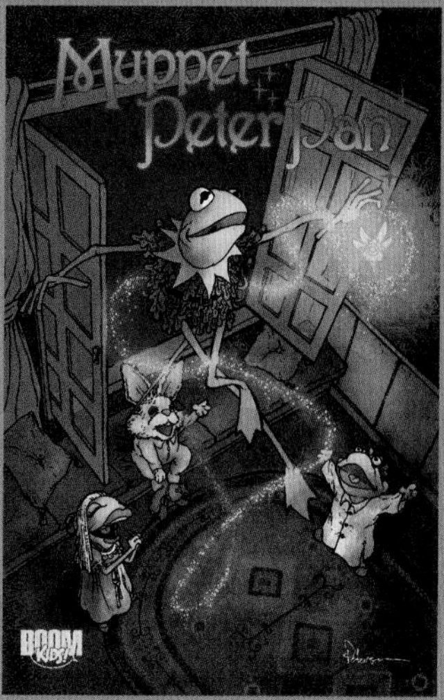
Muppet Peter Pan
BOOM KIDS!

MUPPET PETER PAN

When Peter Pan (Kermit) whisks Wendy (Janice) and her brothers to the magical realm of Neveswamp, the adventure begins! With Captain Hook (Gonzo) out for revenge for the loss of his hand, Wendy and her brothers may find themselves in a situation where even the magic of Piggytink (Miss Piggy) can't save them!

MUPPET ROBIN HOOD
SC $9.99 ISBN 9781934506790
HC $24.99 ISBN 9781608865260

MUPPET PETER PAN
SC $9.99 ISBN 9781608865079
HC $24.99 ISBN 9781608865314

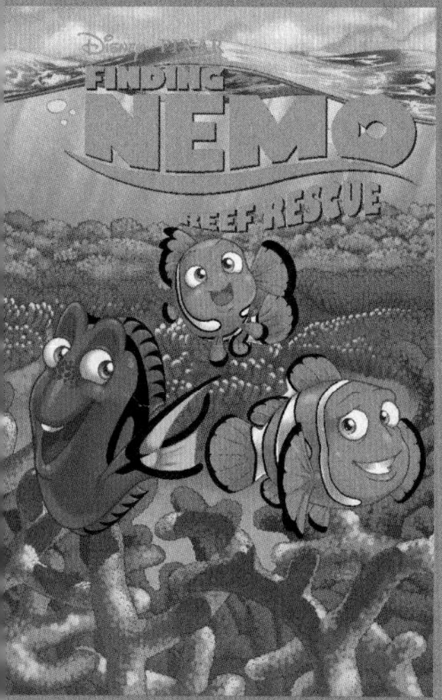
FINDING NEMO
REEF RESCUE

FINDING NEMO: REEF RESCUE

Nemo, Dory and Marlin have become local heroes, and are recruited to embark on an all-new adventure in this exciting collection! Their reef is mysteriously dying and no one knows why!

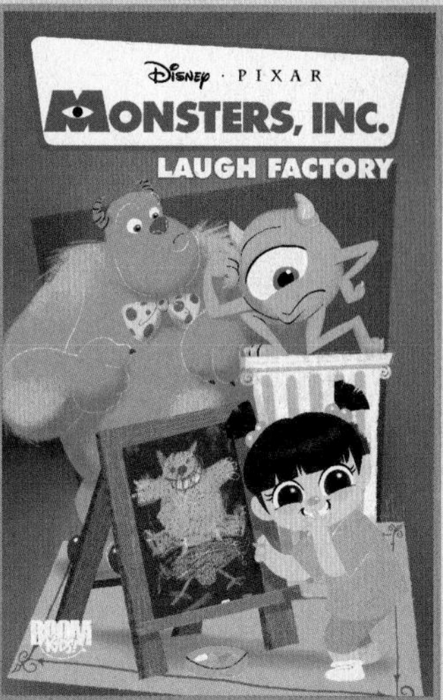
Disney · PIXAR
MONSTERS, INC.
LAUGH FACTORY
BOOM KIDS!

MONSTERS, INC.: LAUGH FACTORY

Someone is stealing comedy props from the other employees, making it difficult for them to harvest the laughter they need to power Monstropolis... and all evidence points to Sulley's best friend Mike Wazowski!

FINDING NEMO: REEF RESCUE
SC $9.99 ISBN 9781934506882
HC $24.99 ISBN 9781608865246

MONSTERS, INC.: LAUGH FACTORY
SC $9.99 ISBN 9781608865086
HC $24.99 ISBN 9781608865338

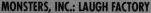

DISNEY'S HERO SQUAD: ULTRAHEROES

It's the year 2734 and the only one standing in the way of earth's utter destruction is...Mickey Mouse?! Join the four-colored fun as Mickey Mouse, Goofy, Donald Duck take to the skies to save the world.

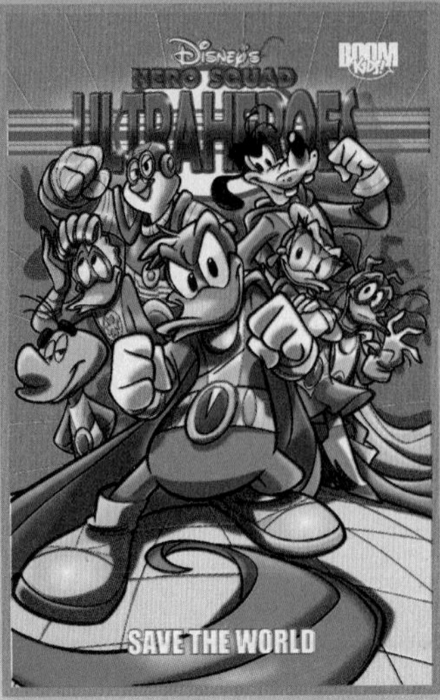
Disney's
HERO SQUAD
ULTRAHEROES
BOOM KIDS!
SAVE THE WORLD

DISNEY'S HERO SQUAD: ULTRAHEROES
SC $9.99 ISBN 9781608865437
HC $24.99 ISBN 9781608865529

WIZARDS OF MICKEY: MOUSE MAGIC

Your favorite Disney characters star in this magical fantasy epic! Student of the great wizard Grandalf, Mickey Mouse hails from the humble village of Mice-land. Allying himself with Donald Duck (who has a pet dragon named Fafnir) and team mate Goofy, Mickey quests to find a magical crown that will give him mastery over all spells!

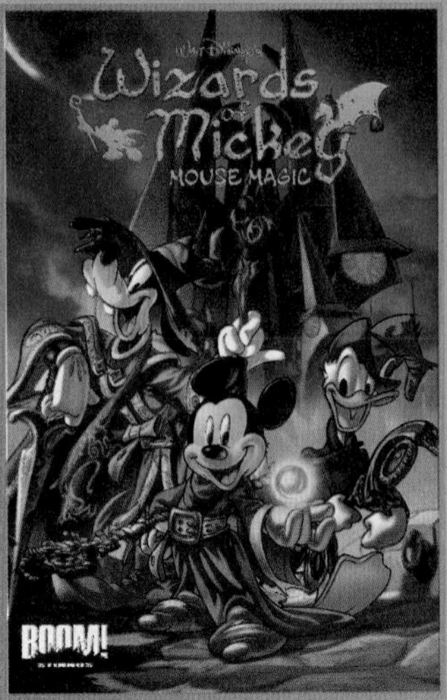
Wizards of Mickey
MOUSE MAGIC
BOOM!

WIZARDS OF MICKEY: MOUSE MAGIC
SC $9.99 ISBN 9781608865413
HC $24.99 ISBN 9781608865505

DONALD DUCK AND FRIENDS: DOUBLE DUCK

Donald Duck as a secret agent? Villainous fiends beware as the world of super sleuthing and espionage will never be the same! This is Donald Duck like you've never seen him!

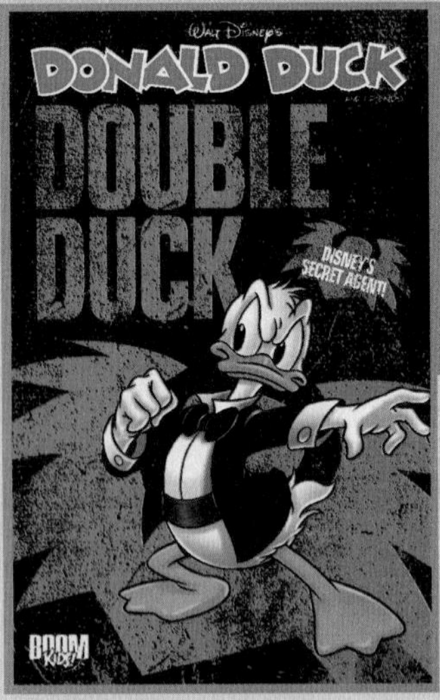
Walt Disney's
DONALD DUCK
DOUBLE DUCK
DISNEY'S SECRET AGENT!
BOOM KIDS!

DONALD DUCK AND FRIENDS: DOUBLE DUCK
SC $9.99 ISBN 9781608865451
HC $24.99 ISBN 9781608865512

UNCLE SCROOGE: THE HUNT FOR OLD NUMBER ONE

Join Donald Duck's favorite penny pinching Uncle Scrooge as he, along with Donald himself and Huey, Dewey and Louie embark on a globe spanning trek to recover treasure and save Scrooge's "number one dime" from the treacherous grasp of Magica De Spell.

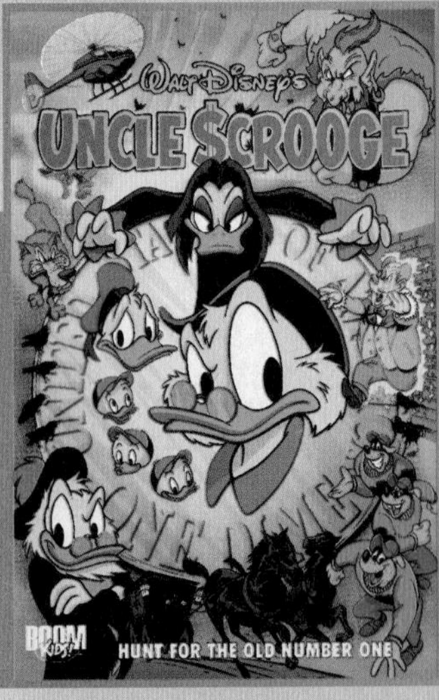
Walt Disney's
UNCLE $CROOGE
BOOM KIDS!
HUNT FOR THE OLD NUMBER ONE

UNCLE SCROOGE: THE HUNT FOR THE OLD NUMBER ONE
SC $9.99 ISBN 9781608865536
HC $24.99 ISBN 9781608865536

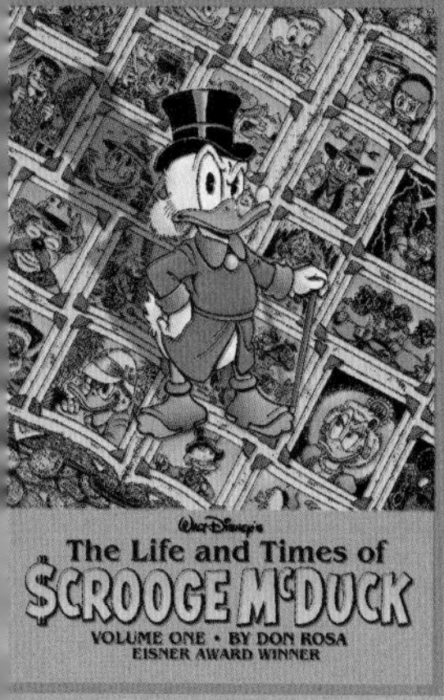
Walt Disney's
The Life and Times of
$CROOGE McDUCK
VOLUME ONE • BY DON ROSA
EISNER AWARD WINNER

THE LIFE AND TIMES OF SCROOGE MCDUCK VOL. 1

BOOM Kids! proudly collects the first half of THE LIFE AND TIMES OF SCROOGE MCDUCK in a gorgeous hardcover collection — featuring smyth sewn binding, a gold-on-gold foil-stamped case wrap, and a bookmark ribbon! These stories, written and drawn by legendary cartoonist Don Rosa, chronicle Scrooge McDuck's fascinating life. See how Scrooge earned his 'Number One Dime' and began to build his fortune!

THE LIFE & TIMES OF SCROOGE MCDUCK VOLUME 1 HC
HC $24.99 ISBN 9781608865383

THE LIFE AND TIMES OF SCROOGE MCDUCK VOL. 2

BOOM! Kids proudly presents volume two of THE LIFE AND TIMES OF SCROOGE MCDUCK in a gorgeous hardcover collection in a beautiful, deluxe package featuring smyth sewn binding and a foil-stamped case wrap! These stories, written and drawn by legendary cartoonist Don Rosa, chronicle Scrooge McDuck's fascinating life.

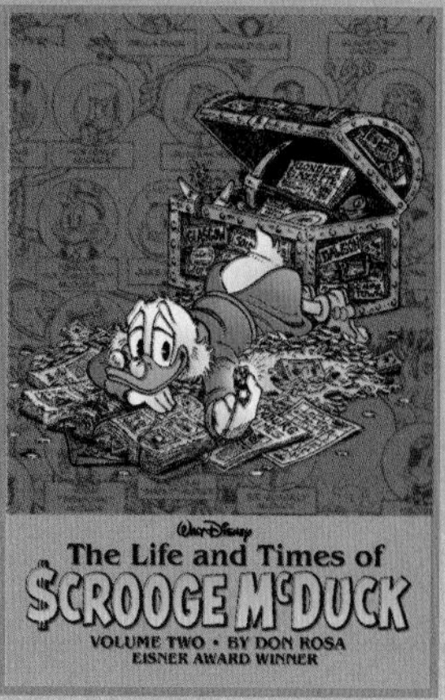
Walt Disney
The Life and Times of
$CROOGE McDUCK
VOLUME TWO • BY DON ROSA
EISNER AWARD WINNER

THE LIFE & TIMES OF SCROOGE MCDUCK VOLUME 2 HC
HC $24.99 ISBN 9781608865420

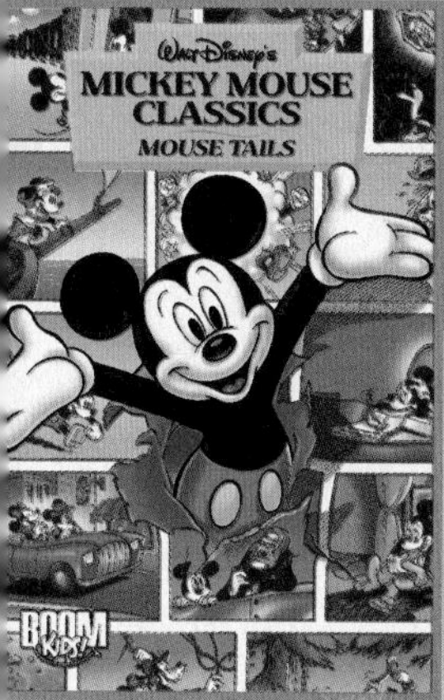
Walt Disney's
MICKEY MOUSE CLASSICS
MOUSE TAILS
BOOM Kids!

MICKEY MOUSE CLASSICS VOL. 1

See Mickey Mouse as he was meant to be seen! Solving mysteries, fighting off pirates, and just generally saving the day! These classic stories comprise a "Greatest Hits" series for the mouse, including a story produced by seminal Disney creator Carl Barks!

MICKEY MOUSE CLASSICS: MOUSE MAYHEM
HC $24.99 ISBN 9781608865444

DONALD DUCK CLASSICS: QUACK UP

Whether it's finding gold, journeying in the Klondike, or fighting ghosts Donald will always have help with Huey, Dewey, Louie, his much more prepared nephews, by his side! Carl Barks brought Donald to prominence, and it's only fair to start off the series with some of his most influential stories!

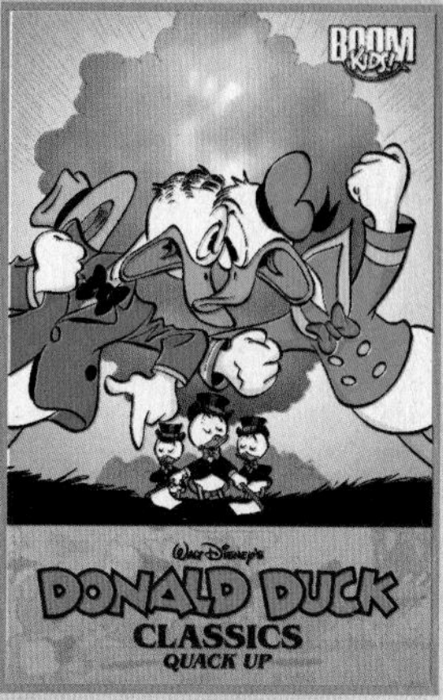
BOOM Kids!
Walt Disney's
DONALD DUCK
CLASSICS
QUACK UP

DONALD DUCK CLASSICS: QUACK UP HC
HC $24.99 ISBN 9781608865406

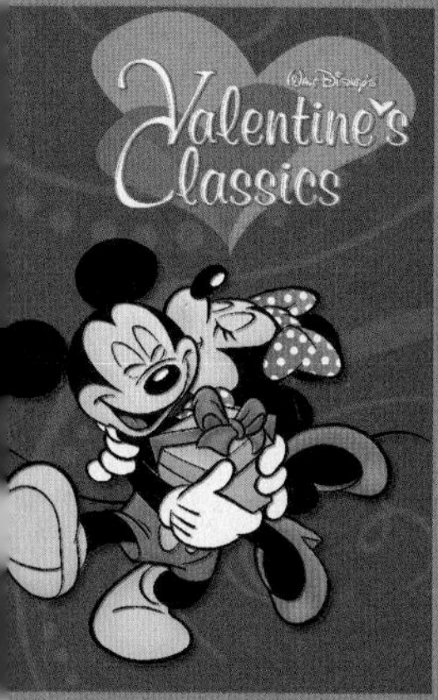
Walt Disney's
Valentine's
Classics

WALT DISNEY'S VALENTINE'S CLASSICS

Love is in the air for Mickey Mouse, Donald Duck and the rest of the gang. But will Cupid's arrows cause happiness or heartache? Find out in this collection of classic stories featuring all your most beloved characters from the magical world of Walt Disney! Featuring work by Carl Barks , Floyd Gottfredson, Daan Jippes, Romano Scarpa and Al Taliaferro.

WALT DISNEY'S VALENTINES CLASSICS VOL 1 HC
HC $24.99 ISBN 9781608865499

WALT DISNEY'S CHRISTMAS CLASSICS

BOOM! Kids has raided the Disney publishing archives and searched every nook and cranny to find the best and the greatest stories from Disney's vast comic book publishing history for this "best of" compilation.

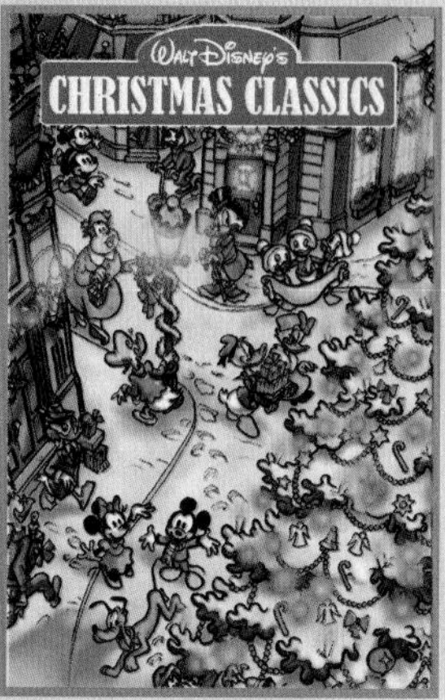
Walt Disney's
CHRISTMAS CLASSICS

WALT DISNEY'S CHRISTMAS CLASSICS VOL 1 HC
HC $24.99 ISBN 9781608865482

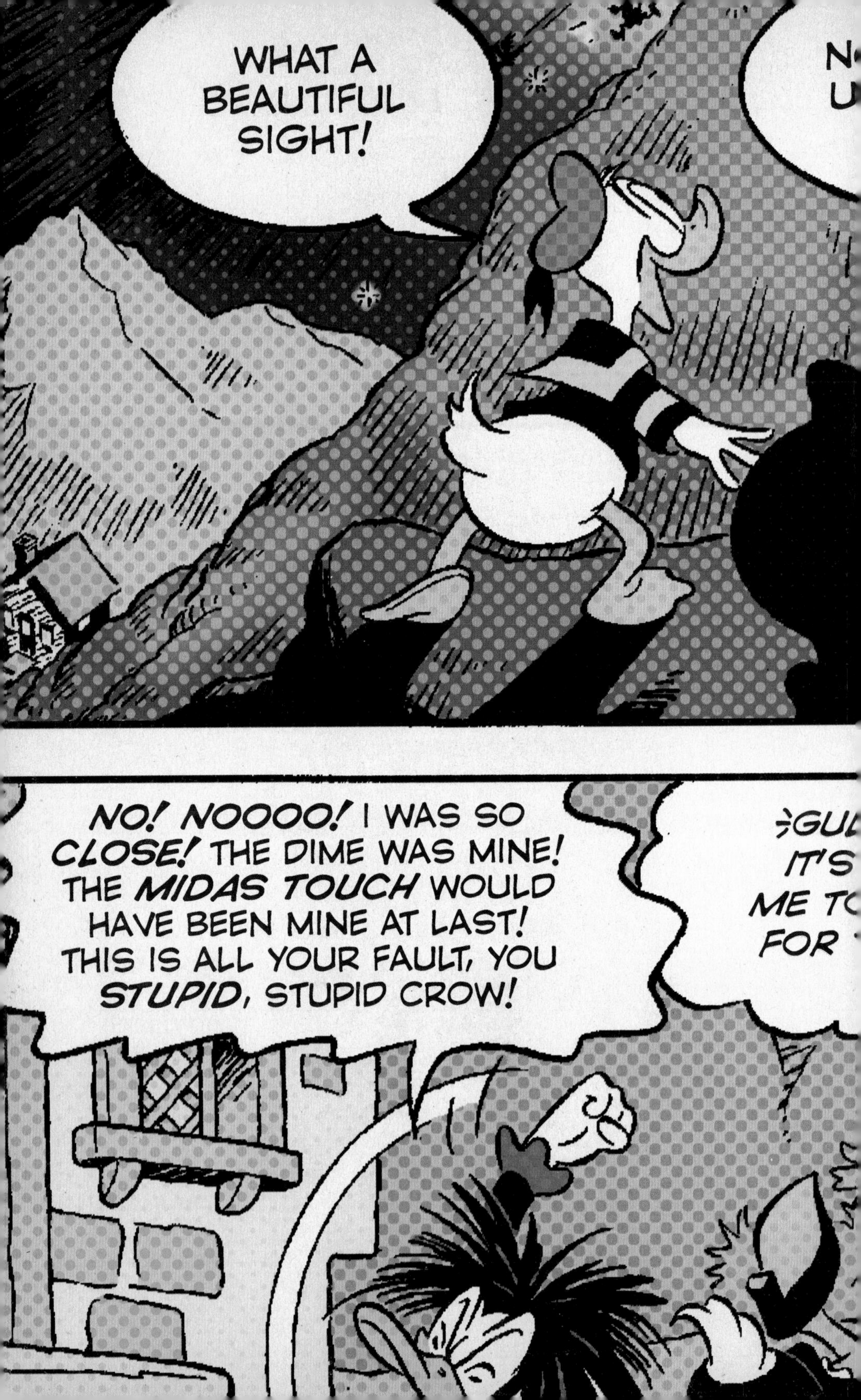
WHAT A BEAUTIFUL SIGHT!
NO! NOOOO! I WAS SO CLOSE! THE DIME WAS MINE! THE MIDAS TOUCH WOULD HAVE BEEN MINE AT LAST! THIS IS ALL YOUR FAULT, YOU STUPID, STUPID CROW!